Praise for *Family Trust*

"*Family Trust* reads like a brilliant mashup of *The Nest* and *Crazy Rich Asians* (with a soupçon of *Arrested Development* for good measure). It's dark and funny and entertaining and thoughtful all at once. The best kind of family drama. I loved every page."

—Cristina Alger, author of *The Banker's Wife*

"A globe-trotting, whirlwind, tragi-comic family saga that wrings tears from absurdity and laughter from loss. A joy to read from start to finish."

—Andrew Sean Greer, author of *Less*, winner of the
2018 Pulitzer Prize for Fiction

"Wang speaks with authority, insight, and irony about the ethnic and socioeconomic realities at business school, in Silicon Valley, in mixed-race relationships and marriages. A strong debut."

—*Kirkus Reviews*

"All hail Kathy Wang! Not only does *Family Trust* deftly weave together a rich family drama, biting corporate satire, and deeply felt immigrant story, Wang tackles the big questions: Does my life have meaning? Who will remember me when I'm gone? What's the ROI on a Harvard MBA? A sharp, spirited, and wholly original take on the American Dream."

—Jillian Medoff, bestselling author of *This Could Hurt*

"A wicked and witty send-up of Asian-American Silicon Valley elite, a delightful debut that Jane Austen would have approved of."

—Micah Perks, author of *What Becomes Us*

"Astute... [Wang] brings levity and candor to the tricky terrain of family dynamics, aging, and excess [and] expertly considers the values of high-tech high society."

—*Publishers Weekly* (starred review)

"Funny and compelling."

"A family's past and present, as well as their hopes for the future, are thrown into blistering focus after a cancer diagnosis threatens the Huang patriarch. *Family Trust* offers an exquisite rendering of the way relationships evolve and are nurtured over a lifetime, and of the circumstances that either draw individuals closer or drive them apart."

FAMILY
TRUST

KATHY WANG grew up in Northern
California and holds degrees from UC
Berkeley and Harvard Business School.
She lives in the San Francisco Bay Area
with her husband and two children.

FAMILY TRUST

KATHY WANG

HEAD
of
ZEUS

First published in the US in 2018 by HarperCollins
First published in the UK in 2018 by Head of Zeus Ltd

9 7 5 3 1 2 4 6 8

A CIP catalogue record for this book is available from the British Library.

ISBN (HB): 9781789543414
ISBN (XTPB): 9781789543407
ISBN (E): 9781789543421

Printed and bound in Great Britain by
CPI Group (UK) Ltd, Croydon, CR0 4YY

Head of Zeus Ltd
5–8 Hardwick St
First Floor East
London EC1R 4RG
WWW.HEADOFZEUS.COM

FOR MY MOTHER

FAMILY TRUST

CHAPTER 1

STANLEY

Stanley Huang sat, naked but for the thin cotton dressing gown crumpled against the sterile white paper in the hospital room, and listened to the young doctor describe how he would die.

It had begun six months earlier, the first time he grew concerned about his weight. He'd arrived home to San Jose via shared shuttle bus—the concluding act to his latest vacation, a two-week pleasure cruise through the Mediterranean—and strode straight for the master bathroom upstairs. Followed closely by his wife, Mary Zhu, as she harped on about shoes worn inside the house—a gross violation of the clean room–like conditions she worked so hard to achieve before each trip.

"I don't understand why you can't just do this one thing I ask," she complained. "Just kick your sneakers off by the door; you don't even have to put them away! You always want everything to be spotless, but you have no idea how hard it is to keep a home clean."

Stanley ignored her, as he could. It was his house, not hers.

He took the stairs two at a time. He was eager to visit his bathroom. The amenities of the lower-tier cabin they'd inhabited for the past two weeks had included a small porthole with a view of the ocean and daily replenished cologne-scented toiletries, but no bathroom scale. Stanley had made a habit of weighing himself each morning after his first urine for the past twelve years, ever since his divorce from his first wife, Linda Liang.

The screen blinked. 145. A four-pound loss.

There was a brief wave of pleasure before the undertow arrived; 145 couldn't possibly be correct given the events of the past two weeks, where he had willingly and pleasurably gorged at every meal on the *Hidden Star*, alternating between the butter garlic shrimp and poached flounder mains each evening. Normally Stanley ate with a moderate interest in health, taking care to consume meat sparingly and forcing himself to order at least one steamed vegetable plate when dining out. The one exception was on holiday, especially an all-inclusive already funded eight months in advance, on a vessel specifically selected for its bounty of complimentary food options and relative absence of hidden fees and surcharges. The Star Grill—the onboard steakhouse—featured a chocolate fondue, which he ordered unique combinations of each night. Dark with almond slivers. Milk with toffee chunks. Add a splash of Amaretto.

Stanley came off the scale, waited for it to reset, and stepped back on. The number still read 145. A year earlier it'd been 170. His weight loss since then had been gradual, pleasing—the result of increased exercise and improved diet, he had thought. Some mornings he skipped the routine with the machine altogether, stringing together days of abstinence until he once again strode on, jubilantly expectant, on each occasion happily gratified by the result. Another two pounds lost. Three! Controlling one's weight was easy, he crowed to Mary, who struggled with her figure and who, given his aggressive hinting, had ceased eating dinner most days altogether. All you needed was self-discipline. Eat enough vegetables, and you could indulge in anything else you wanted.

But that afternoon, back from the cruise and awash with jet lag and joint pain and the telltale facial bloat of twelve days of gastronomic bacchanalia over international waters, Stanley was worried. The loss simply didn't make sense. Never before had he been so light; were he to continue dropping at the same rate, he'd soon be the same size as his early days in high school, at the number-five-ranked Boys' Institute in Taipei. He decided he needed to schedule a medical appointment, a chore he usually enjoyed. Stanley was seventy-four and took a considerable interest in the medical miseries of his peers; doctors' visits accomplished the dual tasks of both occupying his day and providing reassurance that his health continued to be in top form.

What followed next, a full week later—the earliest Kaiser Permanente could secure an open slot with his general physician—wasn't the quick dismissal Stanley expected. Instead, there came a series of drawn-out diagnoses. First the rather vague gallbladder disease, which the specialists were only able to initially elaborate on in terms of statistics: 50 percent an inflammation, 40 percent a problem with bile flow, 10 percent cancer. After that last horrifying word was set loose, left to hang stinking in the air, the theory then moved on to diabetes, a condition that would have ordinarily terrified Stanley but which, compared to cancer, seemed eminently reasonable, a diagnosis that managed to be lethal only when one was too poor or too stupid to follow basic medical and dietary guidelines. Then diabetes was set aside for a peptic ulcer, which had seemed positively benign in comparison with everything else. And that had been the end of it, until today.

"Pancreatic cancer," the doctor said, "is something we can't rule out at this point."

His name was Neil Patel, a baby-faced Indian man whom Stanley had met once before, back when the presumed issue was still his gallbladder. The CT scan showed something that looked to be a mass near the head of the pancreas, Dr. Patel said, though they couldn't be certain. Additional tests were needed, likely a biopsy. The doctor was quick to add that this wasn't a diagnosis but merely a possibility—one of many potential outcomes, and thus no impetus for a panic.

"Please don't obsess," he said. "At this point it isn't necessary or helpful. There's always the chance it could be nothing serious." Yet his face betrayed the true nature of his sentiments, the youthful features marred by somberness. The harsh, bright sterility of the room amplified the grim atmosphere. Stanley closed his eyes, though the fluorescent light still rained through.

After he provided initial guidance for what was to follow, Dr. Patel left the room. "I'll be back in a few minutes," he said. "Please think of any questions you might have."

As the door closed, Mary reached for Stanley's shoulder. "Should we call your family?"

"Fred only," Stanley said. He patted his lap as he searched for his phone and wallet, before realizing he wasn't wearing pants. They must be in Mary's bag, he thought, but didn't want to make eye contact. He wanted her gone from the room; he wished he were completely alone and had never entered this place. His stomach rumbled. Somewhere inside, nestled deep within secretive cavities, small portions of his body were actively betraying him.

"Fred!" Mary cried. Fred was her least favorite of Stanley's children. "Don't you mean Kate? Daughters are always better in these situations, aren't they?"

When Stanley was silent, she charged on. "Besides, if you're worried about having to tell people, Kate will handle that for you. She'll call Fred, and the rest of them." *Them* to no doubt include Stanley's ex-wife, Linda, a source of both mild dislike and eternal fascination. Though Mary liked to ask Stanley about Linda on occasion, he had never once answered any of her questions to her satisfaction.

"Fred," Stanley said. "Call him now."

CHAPTER 2

FRED

At Saks Fifth Avenue in Palo Alto, the premier department store of the increasingly upscale Peninsula Shopping Center, designer handbags were the biggest movers. While for multiple seasons fashion magazines and pundits had proclaimed the death of "the It bag," in the Bay Area—the land of athleisure and yoga pants, where there existed precious few avenues for distinguishing apparel—the designer bag still reigned supreme. In response, the merchandising powers at Saks had dedicated nearly half of the first floor to the celebration and consumption of said accessory, and it was here that Fred Huang sat, slouched over on a leather padded bench, waiting for his girlfriend to sell a $62,000 watch.

Erika Varga stood a short distance away, in the relatively diminutive space of the fine jewelry department, gently flirting with the older man facing her. All around them the lights were dimmer than in the rest of the store, to accentuate the glints of precious stones while softening the sags and jowls they adorned. The soft gray cardigan and black pencil skirt Erika wore were too warm given the weather—come the end of her shift, Fred knew she'd remove the sweater as soon as she walked outside, to better enjoy the balmy heat and sun-soaked palm trees that dotted the open-air shopping center. Though the formal skirt and high heels would still give her away. In this part of Palo Alto, especially in late summer, only retail workers dressed in black and patent leather.

"It's because you have *taste*," Fred could hear Erika say, her laugh ringing softly.

The watch wasn't tasteful. Even from a distance Fred could see the flash from the diamonds circling the elephantine dial, much too ostentatious a look for Silicon Valley. As Erika moved to close the sale, she took care not to alienate the customer's age-appropriate wife, nearby examining an Elizabeth Locke bracelet. Each time Erika mewed a coquettish reply to the man, Fred could see her simultaneously cast a conspiratorial glance at his partner: *These men really are just grown-up boys, aren't they?*

The wife, resplendently casual in an embroidered field jacket and a gold curb chain wound around her neck, smiled pleasantly without bothering to meet Erika's gaze. She appeared to possess ample experience when it came to her husband and the techniques of luxury shop girls; she continued to stoically finger the diamond-encrusted toggle while her other half belched a series of chortles and quips. After a particularly jolting guffaw, she checked her watch and released a sigh of resigned endurance.

"I'm about to make your day," the man announced. "You've sold me! What do you think about that!" His voice echoed out from the small space, an announcement to all nearby that a Very High Value transaction was about to go down. Typical nouveau blowhard, Fred thought. He made sure to appear as if he hadn't heard anything, in case the man looked over.

"You've made a wonderful selection," Erika replied. "You'll have this piece forever."

She excused herself and parted the curtains toward the back room, adjusting her walk to lend a provocative sway to her ass. A minute later she reappeared, with a half bottle of champagne and two glasses on a silver tray. "Just a little celebration."

The sound of the cork as it popped drew all available eyeballs within a certain radius. When they looked over, they saw Erika—the second button of her cardigan now undone, with the lace camisole underneath peeking through—pouring for the customer and his wife. The man was insisting something; Erika reached smoothly underneath the podium and brought out a third glass, which the customer proceeded to fill. *"Salut!"* he cheered. For a brief, unhinged moment, Fred imagined he had said *slut*. He shook his head, and the vision departed.

This was always when he found Erika most attractive: when she was selling. The first time Fred had been made aware of the importance of selling was when he was at Harvard Business School. He'd been thirty and in a relationship with Charlene Choi, a fellow MBA and spoiled Korean princess who in four years would become his wife and in seven his ex. The student body in those days had still been obsessed with high finance—the heady days of the first tech bubble were safely behind, while the second was still in its early stages of percolation—and in class the professors had all impressed upon them the importance of salesmanship, the massive gift and rare talent it was to be able to convince agents in a free market to willingly part with resources. It wasn't enough to possess an expertise in the emerging markets or the quant ability of a Russian Asperger's: finance was at its heart a rough universe, a *trader's* world, where a good percentage of the top bosses had grown up poor and hustling. You had to be able to sell, to be a real player.

In the beginning, everyone took the lesson seriously. The Sales Club had a flurry of enrollments, and the lone salesperson in Fred's section, a former GE aeronautics rep, had enjoyed alpha status for nearly a week, at one point speaking for five minutes uninterrupted—an eternity in the classroom—on a case study on Jack Welch. But over the following months, attitudes reverted back to the status quo. The optional early-morning negotiations seminar lost its luster in the face of the raging hangover triggered by the late-night cavortings at the Priscilla Ball—the annual cross-dressing party—the night before, and plus, there were so many other variables that seemed to play a defining role in success. One's parents, for example, and selection of partner. Many assumed that Harvard, with its 70/30 male-to-female ratio, was full of sexual opportunists, and while this wasn't necessarily *untrue*, the excavation went in both directions. For every penniless fortune huntress brandishing an engagement ultimatum, there was a corresponding Adonis attached to a Sternman or Mortimer with lavish stables and a horseface; there were nearly as many famous last names in Fred's class among the women as among the men.

Given his relationship with Charlene, Fred's only attempt at striving had been strictly platonic: a close friendship with Jack Hu, the lone male scion of a billionaire family in Hong Kong. They shared a circle because they were both Asian men, a minority whose numbers at Harvard were carefully and deliberately contained each year by the administration. The fact that Jack was slightly dull, both in mind and wit, was vastly outweighed by his vast wealth, and for two delectable years Fred had imagined himself as part of this gilded orbit, one where bodyguards trailed at a discreet distance and residences were maintained at the Mandarin Oriental downtown, instead of on campus.

Of course, Fred didn't have Jack all to himself. Billionaires were in high demand within the HBS student population, and Fred soon found himself in competition for Jack's favor with a bevy of assorted suitors, a group that included not only the other Asian men but also the predatory women, all of whom seemed to regard Jack's stutter and predilection for playing *Civilization* for hours as simply adorable. And the Asians weren't the only problem! There were also the South Americans, Europeans, Jews, Eastern Europeans, Africans, African Americans, and regular vanilla-white Americans—each bloc eager to make the acquaintance of fascinating personalities whose families' real estate holdings were rumored to include entire acres in Knightsbridge and downtown Sydney. All hungry, though luckily— given the numerous plum targets available—less inclined to devote the focused energy to drawing Jack out of his initial shyness than Fred was. Jack finally venturing to ask, after months of mild conviviality, over steaming bowls of beef pho in Harvard Square, if Fred had ever disappointed his parents. "My dad, he's angry I missed my cousin's wedding in Cap Ferrat."

Or while sharing a thin-crust pizza at Pinocchio's—pepperoni with extra mushrooms, since it was Jack's favorite—"Have you ever had the feeling that one of your professors was trying to network with you?"

Or at the Indian buffet in Central Square, both hovering over the chicken tikka masala: "I have to fly to Singapore next week. There's drama with the board over succession planning."

"Oh?" Fred would casually reply each time, taking care never to look up from his food. He had learned that enthusiasm frightened the rich and powerful, as they recalled parental exhortations to never trust the less fortunate, who were unpredictable in their poverty. He pampered Jack in their interactions, but not obviously; feted him, but not ostentatiously. And over time Jack felt comfortable in their camaraderie, and they became friends.

After graduation, they vowed to keep in touch, but Fred was always bad at that sort of relationship maintenance, like remembering to attend others' birthday parties so that when the time came, they in exchange would grace his own. So it was only five years later, at the reunion, that he understood how much reassurance his friendship with Jack had provided, like a long-stowed savings bond one could recall at will. Jack was already married by then, and they'd shared a few minutes of superficial banter before he was spotted and quickly pulled away, his patrician wife tossing back a sympathetic smile as they receded. It was then that Fred knew he had lost it, had abandoned out of sheer carelessness his brief, tenuous connection to the very top of the 1 percent.

Until that morning.

From: Jack888@babamail.com
To: Fred@Lion-Capital.com
Subject: Founders' Retreat

Fred,

It's been a while . . . how long since we last talked?

On my end I'm good, still managing the family business. It's been satisfying to see it grow, though I wish I didn't have to live in Hong Kong. The air is shit. Sherry still gets on me for playing video games, she says I should have more serious pursuits now that I'm past forty and have three kids. Are you on *Dota*?

You may not have heard, but Reagan Kwon (remember him? a year above us) and I have done a few deals together since school, and I've been unofficially advising him on Thailand's economic development fund since the beginning of the year. Your name came up as a

possible partner on the US side. Thoughts? It's a few billion right now,
but growing.
Reagan and I will both be at the Founders' Retreat this year in Bali.
Hope we can catch up there!

Jack

Jack, back from the beyond. A *few billion* (US dollars, Fred hoped).

And Reagan Kwon.

Reagan Kwon, like Jack, was part of Asia's economic royalty, though considerably more colorful. Unlike Jack's parents, who were notoriously private, the elder Kwons were the sort of wealthy couple who loved to see their names on buildings and charity invitations, and they actively encouraged their cosseted only son to make a similar mark for himself. Reagan had started out at Harvard a social star, flying his entire section of ninety to Vegas on a chartered 747 for his birthday. No one was exactly certain where the Kwon money originated, though there was gossip of precious metals and mining and the old shah of Iran. There was even a kidnapped family member or two in the lineage, as well as rumors of lopped-off pinky toes; whispers of the entire ordeal having been orchestrated by an ex-mistress, a stunning former Miss Hong Kong frozen out by the family after what she still insisted was a perfectly innocent pregnancy scare.

Reagan had barely interacted with Fred during school, though of course he knew Jack. While Reagan was more popular, Jack's family had the greater fortune; that equation meant it was the former who doggedly pursued the friendship expected by both families. Reagan invited Jack to all his parties and once went as far as to ship a Japanese blow-up doll to Jack's apartment at the Mandarin in a misguided attempt at a practical joke. The box had been labeled as a grand-father clock, and Jack, assuming it was an antique sent by his parents, enlisted the help of an assistant concierge to unpack the deceptively heavy carton. He'd been so humiliated once the oversize figure had been revealed, and at such a loss to explain its origin, that he could only think to call Fred, who had hurried over. Jack was paranoid about being photographed or captured on security cameras with the offend-ing object, so after some struggle Fred brought down the doll himself using the service elevator and heaved it into the trash bin headfirst, pausing briefly to admire the lifelike limbs and chest. Noting that even for an occasion such as this, Reagan had purchased the very best.

Fred knew peripherally that since graduation Reagan had calmed somewhat and that in the past few years he and Jack had partici-pated together in multiple investments, mostly Asian copycats of US start-ups. People like Reagan and Jack (or at least their family office advisors) generally didn't bother with less than 20 percent annualized returns, preferably with tacit government backing. Whatever it was they were proposing, it meant serious money.

The rattle of heels. Erika had excused herself from her customer and was striding toward him, shoes pounding in even rhythm. "Do you see?" she asked. She lowered her voice. "Right in front of you."

Fred peered over her shoulder. The wife's untouched champagne sat on top of the glass Cartier display, water pooling around its base. It appeared to have been abandoned in her quest for comfortable seating—she was now sunk into a fat chair in the far corner, the Eliz-abeth Locke bracelet still wrapped around her hands. Fred noticed the security guard's eyes pass over. One couldn't be too careful these days, no matter how moneyed or white the patron.

"The glass?"

Erika made a grimace. "Disgusting," she hissed. Fred knew she'd have to clean everything when her customers left, rinsing the crystal in the crude sink in the back and wiping down the counters. She bore a violent animosity toward such tasks, insisting they were beneath her job description.

"Don't worry about it. Shouldn't you be getting back to your customer? You made a big sale, right? Congratulations."

She shrugged. "We're almost done. Here." She cut over a business card from her palm. Erika asked all her customers for them, looking up the names after work. She kept only the prime specimens, the companies and titles she thought Fred might be impressed by. "This one's nothing compared to you. He works in *mortgages*. I should tell him what you do."

Fred suppressed a groan. "Please don't bring up my job with your customers."

"But so many of them are in your industry," she complained. "It's ridiculous, this resistance you have. And also don't you see now, how the wives behave? It makes me so angry that they think they're better than me, when . . . well, we're kind of engaged, aren't we? We basically live together; all my things are at your place. And the men, I'm quite certain a lot of them would be very interested to know I actually understand something of their work! You know my style, I always do better when I'm chatting as a friend, not as *staff*. How do you think I sold this watch? Michael will be thrilled we finally got rid of it. It's been sitting in the display for almost a year!"

"I know you're an excellent salesperson. That's why you don't need to mention anything about me or Lion Capital."

"But Amanda talks about her husband all the time, and he's just a regular *broker* at TD Ameritrade. Amanda says he's proud that she talks about him. He even jokes that she should give out his card to customers!"

"Good for Amanda's husband. Not for me."

"This is so stupid." Erika's mouth twisted with displeasure. "I'm just *proud* of you!" And she abruptly swiveled, gliding back.

This was his fault, Fred understood. He had created this problem. From the beginning of their relationship Erika had been so eager for him to be a certain type of man (the finance god, the technologist, the power broker) that over time he'd developed a bad habit of aggrandizing his work, relaxing all the anxieties his ex-wife had worked so hard to instill. Fred Huang, the Venture Capital God! He knew that how he'd represented his particular vantage point in the overwrought matrix that made up Silicon Valley's power structure hadn't been—if one wanted to be brutally fair—particularly accurate. But it had all been so easy, as Erika lacked even a rudimentary understanding of the caste system that ruled his world. Didn't he rate a little fun, after what he'd been through with Charlene? Didn't his ego deserve some time in the sun?

Charlene, a fellow HBS alum, had known implicitly where Fred's job lay in his industry's pecking order: near its swampy bottom. Lion Capital, the investment arm of its larger parent company—Lion Electronics, the technology behemoth headquartered in Taiwan—awarded its employees none of the traditional perks of venture capital, such as carried interest or management fees, where the real fortunes were made. Lion was *corporate* venture capital, which meant it invested cash from its parent's balance sheet and, as it generally went for the industry, paid modestly. While a senior partner at a traditional venture firm like Tata Packer could be expected to take home anywhere between $2 and $4 million per annum, Fred—the second-highest-ranked investment professional at Lion—garnered a mere fraction: $325,000, a pittance in Silicon Valley! Nowhere close to what was needed to buy a house in Hillsborough or responsibly stay any longer than a few days at Post Ranch Inn or Amangiri.

While with his ex this fact had lain between them, Charlene's sighs as she leafed through *Architectural Digest* a tacit reminder of his ongoing parity with the average corporate chump, with Erika it had been entirely deprived of oxygen from the start. She never saw his pay stubs and didn't have a loose network of hundreds of classmates as well as a particularly haughty cousin who worked in private equity. The only proof of status Erika had ever required was his title (managing director) and industry (venture capital), and her hearty approval had gushed with full force. Urging him, as she had with each delighted smile, to brag with reckless bravado:

- Why wouldn't I be able to find the wrapping paper at Target? I did a $250 million IPO last quarter, didn't I?
- Griffin Keeles and I flew on a private plane; it was no big deal.
- Teslas are a dime a dozen. I could buy one whenever I want. Could afford to get you one too!

Exquisite Erika, who was at her most appealing when captivated by his swagger; the loose hazelnut curls and light filtered through green eyes, a thrilling contrast to the plain blacks and dark browns of the Asians he'd mostly dated before. Her youth set off by the classic luxury of her wardrobe, the result of careful utilization of employee sales and double-discount days. Her elegant posture and doe-like features and spectacular breasts; more than adequate compensation for the occasional crudity.

For outside the learned confines of the retail environment, Erika could be unpolished, even crude. She was the only woman Fred knew who regularly flipped the bird at reckless drivers, and given even the most minor of lapses, she regularly barked at service staff. At times, Fred almost liked the crassness. Charlene had possessed perfect manners, relentlessly honed during the course of a childhood spent in a twelve-bedroom turreted monstrosity in Bergen County, while the lone other white woman he'd seriously dated before Erika—Tiffany Cantor, a college volleyball player turned ad sales rep at Google—had been uniformly sweet to the point of near sickening. Gushing *"thank you so much"* nonstop at restaurants, impressed beyond belief that the food they ordered and would be paying for was actually being delivered to their table. And if the establishment happened to be ethnic, always layering on an extra "And everything tasted *wonderful.*"

Once, when Fred was in a bad mood, he'd informed Tiffany that most of the cheap restaurants they patronized didn't care what she thought of the food, and he could certainly vouch that the Chinese ones didn't. As if the Cantonese chefs and Hispanic line cooks had been waiting their entire lives for a pretty Caucasian girl from Huntington Beach to cast her approval over their cuisine! Tiffany had blushed a deep crimson. This was just how she'd learned to behave, she explained, to establish incontrovertibly that she was a nice person before the other party invariably docked her for being attractive and thin and blond. "You wouldn't be able to understand," she added, before quickly raising her hands to her mouth in horror. Because a truth had accidentally materialized that until then had always lain between them unspoken: that she as a young white woman was desirable in America, and Fred as an Asian man was not.

Fred of course was already aware of this stereotype, had discussed it ad nauseam with other friends over the years—first with indignation, then with rage, and then with the mild acceptance that turned to pride when he walked into bars and restaurants with Tiffany. He was proud of his outward refutation of it—he was six two, lean but built, and conventionally successful; he had no difficulties attracting women. So he'd been surprised to feel the warmth of inarticulate anger and shame return so quickly in the midst of what had at the time been his greatest romantic triumph to date; he rapidly shifted topics, and they'd proceeded as if it were just a throwaway comment, already left by the wayside. When they arrived back at the apartment, Tiffany went after him with a focused determination that seemed to prove she'd understood the unexpected candor of her statements; the fact that she went down on him—a service she had rendered only once prior in the three months they had dated—solidified his theory.

None of this was a problem with Erika. Erika didn't like most ethnic restaurants, and in *particular* the cheap authentic ones, an admission that in native Bay Area circles was viewed with the same muted horror as Holocaust denial or the use of trans fats. She'd been twenty-seven when she emigrated from Hungary, and her impression of dating culture in the United States was constructed around entirely different ideals: red roses and lobster entrées and warmed desserts à la mode. She had little excitement for popular peer-reviewed eateries with $7 tapas and yuzu sangria—to her these were just cheap outings, designed to land her in bed with the least amount of spent resources.

Unlike past girlfriends, Erika never offered to pay for meals or activities, which Fred thought he'd mind more than he did. Each time he treated, she was graciously thankful though not gratuitously so, which he found he preferred to the usual tedious routine of wallet fumbling. The check lingering awkwardly on the table at the end of the night, his date reaching into her bag after a precisely timed delay; the halfhearted attempt to offer a credit card before it was tucked away. The woman sheepishly thanking him after it was all over with a small undertone of resentment, as if Fred were personally responsible for making her violate some bullshit tenet of female equality she didn't really believe in the first place.

Erika simply sat, watched him pay, and said thank you. She wasn't complicated about these things, she said. American women complicated too much.

In the parking lot, as they walked toward his car, Erika once again brought up her father's upcoming birthday. "Are you going to send him a present?" she asked. "And maybe something small for my mother?" When he was quiet, she hounded on. "Because there's only so much time left, to ship economy. Of course if you still want to buy something next week you can, but then you'll have to use FedEx, pay for overnight. It's a waste of money, no? Better to spend on the actual gift."

They entered the BMW—a decade-old 3 Series Fred was determined to drive until he had enough in his house fund to justify an auxiliary splurge on a Big Swinging Dick vehicle—and instead of answering he turned up the volume on NPR. Even before they'd met, Fred had never liked the sound of György and Anna Varga, two supposed Budapest intellectuals who, despite regularly espousing the superior merits of Socialism, made it clear they fully expected to spend their retirement in spacious comfort in sunny California. The elder Vargas regarded their two adult children as the primary means of attaining said goal, and they had practically shoved Nora— Erika's older sister—into the arms of a distant American friend of a friend thirty years her senior who had been visiting Budapest on a hall pass. The fact that Nora had subsequently become impregnated by Dominik—who then divorced his wife and moved Nora to Northern California, only to freak out and repeat the entire scenario anew three years later—had been disappointing only in that Nora had merely managed to wrest a studio apartment in Fremont for herself and baby Zoltan out of the deal.

When György and Anna booked their first visit to the Bay Area, Nora and Erika had obsessed for weeks prior to their arrival, going as far as to rent a black Cadillac Escalade to transport them in lavish comfort. Eager to impress, Fred had invited the group to Seasons, a Michelin two star serving upscale French-Californian in Los Gatos, where he'd ordered the tasting menu with full wine pairings for the table. When the bill arrived, Fred had fully expected to pay—had already estimated in his mind the exact hit in terms of tax and tip—but it still galled to not even have György make an attempt for the leather folder, especially as he and Anna had been the only two to opt for the caviar and black truffle supplements.

"Hello?" Erika poked him between the ribs. "Did you hear what I said?"

The light outside was undergoing the rapid shift from warm to cool as they approached San Francisco; there was a chill in the car, and goose bumps rose along his arm. Fred raised the window to buy a few seconds of time.

"Your father," he said finally, "is an idiot."

Erika sighed, as if she'd anticipated this. "I told you already, you misunderstood what he meant about the Jews. It's *cool* in Hungary to be Jewish. The most successful Hungarians are all Jewish."

"And the Chinese—excuse me, I mean, *Orientals*—are all criminals."

"He didn't say that. He just isn't used to them. Fred, please."

When their group had first entered Seasons, Fred had assumed György's gaping to be directed at the opulent yet modern decor—the broad redwood beams and pressed gold leaf ceiling, the wine cellar made entirely of glass and visible from the dining room—and felt proud of his choice. The restaurant was a reflection on him, after all: proof to Erika's parents that he had the culture and resources to look after their daughter in a splendid fashion. Until then, he'd made a deliberate point of ignoring certain particulars regarding their interactions, such as a habit of communicating with him as if he were an exotic animal of unknown provenance, enunciating at a louder decibel; classifying their confusion over certain adjectives as his language deficiency, not theirs. It was only after overhearing Erika's gently worded explanations during the sea bream appetizer course that Fred realized György assumed they'd been taken to some sort of lower-class establishment. That György had expected the best restaurants in California to be filled with Caucasian faces, not yellow and brown.

"In Hungary, you have to understand that most of the Chinese, they are not so rich. And there are barely any Indians. He was just confused, Fred. He didn't know."

"Uh-huh. And just how *confused* is György over you dating someone Chinese?"

"He understands . . ." Erika hesitated. "He understands that in America things are different."

"In America? What if you were back in Budapest?"

"In Hungary, of course it would never happen."

"That's an insane statement to make." He jammed angrily at the nearest button on the dashboard, which unfortunately turned the air-conditioning on full blast. "Don't you understand how racist that makes you sound?"

Erika remained calm. To her *racist* wasn't such a bad word, unless used in conjunction with *uneducated*, which she found far more insulting. "It is the truth," she said. "How can someone be so angry over the truth?"

"Because it's ignorant. And based on the worst stereotypes I've had to battle against my entire life, that Asian men are less desirable than every other race, because we're passive, and small, and not worthy of female attention."

"But I don't have those thoughts," she protested. "It's just that I never knew any Chinese before I moved here. And I'm sorry, but it is true, that in Budapest they do crime. Though they mostly keep it between themselves," she added charitably. "In Hungary, if you bring a gift to someone's house, the first thing they will check for when they are alone is whether it was made in China. Because then they know whether you paid a lot or a little."

"Oh really? So everything made in China is cheap? So your father wouldn't like it if I bought him an iPhone?" That had been the ongoing hint for Christmas the year before, with Erika laying the groundwork in September and campaigning through mid-December. Fred had shipped György and Anna the joint present of an iPad mini and a $100 iTunes gift card instead. Collectively the two had cost less than one smartphone, and that wasn't even including the continuing overhead of a data plan.

"Well no," Erika said. "Everyone knows the iPhone is very top."

"How can you say all that then, about Made in China being cheap, when your whole family worships Apple products? Which are *made in China*? Don't you see how stupid, how uneducated, it makes you seem?"

"Let's not say such things." Erika placed a soft hand on his shoulder, ignoring the salvo, unusual for her. "Besides, the only thing that matters is you and me. And you are mine. My successful venture capitalist, for whom I am so grateful."

THAT EVENING FRED LAY IN BED, BLINKING THE SLOW ACKNOWL-edgment of late-night wakefulness. Insomnia had been descending often lately, a worrisome development as he thought it possibly a symptom of low testosterone. Was he having a midlife crisis? He considered a rededication to one of his interests, before realizing he no longer had any. He used to be passionate about so many things— photography, basketball, traveling. Now the ardor was gone. The disturbing thought flickered that perhaps this was the natural course of life events, that at some point vigor and vitality were supposed to be replaced by marriage and children.

"Erika," he whispered. He cleared his throat, first softly, and then louder. "Erika." He nudged her with his foot, enough to shift her leg. She lay still, prettily snoring.

Fuck it—he was going to watch porn. Fred tiptoed to the laptop on his desk. Dare he bring it back to bed? No, she might wake, and then he'd be in for it; Erika was surprisingly puritanical about such matters. He decided to stay in the chair.

When he opened the browser, he discovered that Erika had started a Twitter account. Why hadn't she told him? Though Fred himself didn't use Twitter, had never bothered to even register a username. The stars of his industry tweeted habitually, racking up audiences ranging from hundreds of thousands to tens of millions; he knew whatever paltry following he'd manage to attract would only serve as a humiliating comparison.

He examined the page. A quick scroll revealed Erika was largely sharing articles with mentions of Lion Capital, and reposting general Silicon Valley news: "Tech IPOs Predicted to Surge in 2016," one announced. "The Bubble That Wasn't a Bubble!" Innocuous enough, until he unearthed several alarming interactions between Erika and what looked to be complete strangers.

"Untrue," she'd tweeted, at some random pundit who had commented that a certain managing partner at Sequoia dressed too casually for industry standards. "My VC fiancé wears jeans everyday. He is too busy to be bothered with fussy dress. He thinks big picture, only."

Fred moaned and slammed shut the lid, as waves of secondhand embarrassment gathered and pooled. How many more of his thoughts were out there, being parroted into written evidence? Privately claiming to a girlfriend—over a second bottle of Opus One at Bistro Jeanty—that one was a so-called rainmaker in Silicon Valley was very different from having the same convictions bullhorned for the general public. What else had she been writing? And more important, *where*? The whole incident reminded him of when he'd told his mother he was the most popular freshman at Claremont High, only to overhear her boasting of it verbatim on the phone to friends with children the year above him at the same school weeks later. "My Fred is so well liked," she'd crowed. "So many birthday invitations! And he goes to all the dances!"

When he woke again it was late morning. Erika was already awake and out of bed preparing breakfast, the routine she always reverted to when she knew she'd annoyed him. The unnerving sensation he'd felt late in the night still lurked, and he was struck by an acute desire to reread Jack's email. As soon as he reconfirmed its existence, Fred thought, he'd feel better. *Reagan Kwon. A few billion.* He repeated it like a mantra. Beneath the blanket, there began the early rumblings of an erection. As he reached for his phone, to bring himself to climax, the screen lit with a call from his father.

CHAPTER 3

LINDA

M a? Are you listening? Dad has *cancer*."

Linda Liang sat with her eyes closed, noisily breathing to drown out the dramatics of her only daughter. She was on one of her favorite pieces of furniture, a shimmered lavender chaise purchased a decade earlier during the Gump's after-Christmas sale for 80 percent off (already on clearance, she had finagled an extra 10 percent due to a small chip on one of the back legs). The chair had been worth it; it was still in excellent condition. She massaged her temples and swung up her feet, kicking her shearling slippers onto the floor.

"Are you there?"

Asking obvious questions was one of Kate's annoying habits. Linda didn't feel like answering just yet, and let the silence hang. What was one supposed to say, when one's now-ex–husband of thirty-four years

was struck with such a diagnosis? A man whose sole medical emergency until that point had been a minor knee operation, a half-hour
outpatient surgery where upon discharge he had grown increasingly
unbearable, barking orders to be fetched another glass of water, the
TV remote, the latest *Barron's*—each issue of which he'd halfheart-
edly peruse for mere minutes before setting it aside for yet another
demand? A month-long ordeal cut short only when Linda happened
across newspaper classifieds he'd saved, advertisements for escort services in places like Oakland and Berkeley, the top contenders ostentatiously circled in garish red marker? Divorce meant no longer being
obligated to feel the pit in her stomach upon hearing such news of
cancer, of looking over to the other side of the bed at night and crying
out in fear for the other person. Linda allowed herself a brief naked pause to let any tender sentiments bloom and wash through, but
found herself devoid. A blessed relief.

"What kind of cancer?"

"I'm not sure," Kate said, in the reverential tones she assumed
when speaking about anything medically related. "Something serious." In a small voice: "Do you think he might die?"

"Oh, please don't cry," Linda said softly. When confronted with
her children's emotions, she always lapsed back into Mandarin and
the protections of its language barrier. "You don't know what kind
of can—ah, illness, it is, do you? Did your dad tell you any details?"

"No." Kate let out a theatrical sniff. "I haven't even spoken to him.
He isn't picking up his phone. I don't know if he tried to reach me and
I somehow missed the call, but Fred's the one who actually told me
the news."

"Oh? How did he take it?" Linda knew that as with most grown
men, there existed within her son a small, desperate flame that cast
about for some heroic light he could shine on his father. Given that it
was Stanley, however, he might have to settle for martyrdom. "What
did Fred say?"

"He was worried, of course. Though, honestly, he was so weird about it. He barely knew any details, and then he started going on about how he was going to be so busy at work the next few months. As if *work* were the important thing now!"

"If Fred didn't know, it's probably fine. He would have heard otherwise. Your father, he's always been so healthy. And there are so many minor sorts of cancer these days. Half my friends probably have had some kind. Especially the men; prostate is very popular. You just go to the bathroom a lot, after you are cured."

"You think?" Kate's voice had cleared somewhat.

"Of course. There's nothing to worry about."

Even as she said it, Linda knew she was lying. Stanley was seventy-five now, a dangerous age, and the last time she'd seen him—nearly four months earlier, at Jackson Ho's own seventy-fifth birthday party, hosted by his wife and children at China Garden—even she had taken note of the weight loss. Stanley had been proud of it at the time, as he strutted back and forth between tables in a ridiculous fitted leather coat, making his greetings. His dementedly placid wife by his side, the flatterer who had no doubt advised on the fashion abomination. Ten years earlier Mary had been pushing dim sum carts at that very same restaurant while moonlighting as a massage therapist on the weekends, a category of employment that was a source of never-ending speculation for Linda, whose questions both Fred and Kate refused to indulge. Children always punished you for being petty, all while conveniently forgetting you had washed their stained sheets and underwear for the first eighteen years of their lives.

Stanley wouldn't be the first older man in their group felled by an indulgent diet and a habit of overexertion—both by-products, Linda thought, of a younger second wife. She had seen how Mary pushed the desserts at Jackson's banquet, ostentatiously refilling Stanley's bowl with serving upon serving of tapioca coconut pudding, joking that every day was his birthday in their household. Linda would have never done such a thing when they were married: it was demeaning, of course, but everyone also knew that such dishes contained spectacularly high amounts of sugar and sometimes lard, both toxins! Though who was to say that Mary hadn't been trying to kill Stanley, at some unconscious or perhaps even conscious level? Marriage with Stanley was difficult, Linda knew, and undoubtedly Mary had at some point entertained the thought of what it would be like to live alone but with her husband's resources. She certainly had little incentive to extol clean eating and exercise. Linda wondered how Mary had taken the news and whether she had yet begun to panic. Stanley likely didn't even have a will; he was loath to consider any topic related to his mortality.

"You talk to your dad's wife yet?"

"Mary? No, I didn't think to contact her. You think she knows anything?"

Linda felt a weight settle, the disappointment of her children's continued ignorance in presuming themselves the center of their father's universe. Mary cooked Stanley's meals, stuffed him full of the Costco cream puffs he adored; she slept with him, massaged his feet, made him feel like a man. What had Kate or Fred done lately to compete? "If you don't hear anything by the end of the week, you should call."

"All right. Maybe I'll talk to Fred tonight too, after I've put the kids to bed. I've got them alone for the rest of the day, so it's going to be a handful."

"Where's Denny?"

"He's at a meeting."

"What kind of meeting? This for his business?" With just the slightest emphasis on *business*, as if the word weren't quite adequate to capture the activities of Linda's son-in-law, who as far as she could observe had craftily engineered himself a situation where he spent the majority of his daylight hours unaccounted for, lazing about in a cozily furnished attic while his wife assumed the entirety of the household income.

Kate released a loud sigh. "Yes, for his business. He's meeting with a group of investors for his start-up and then eating dinner afterward."

"Investors? So they gave him money already?"

"The stage Denny's at with his company, there's a lot of emphasis on networking," Kate said, ignoring the question. "The right connection could make CircleShop."

"Okay, okay." Linda had tired of the conversation. It was already late afternoon, and she wanted to start her tasks for the evening. "Anything else you want to discuss?" she asked. Gently, so as to not arouse suspicion.

"Why?" Kate said, suspicious anyway. "Are you going somewhere?"

As if her leaving the house were an event, one that required advance clearance! Ever since they'd left home and begun their own adult journeys, Kate and Fred seemed to regard her existence as a sort of grandfather clock, to be set in the corner and forgotten but always there when they looked for it, chiming with daily regularity. The two generally viewed her reluctance to try new things or venture to foreign territories with snobbish pity: oh poor Ma, too frightened to expand her mind with crucial new skills such as sous vide cooking or hatha yoga stretches! In Linda's opinion, the failure of imagination went both ways. Neither Kate nor Fred had ever considered, for example, the reason behind her never having visited Vietnam being not an absence of adventure or daring but simply a complete lack of interest. She and Stanley had both immigrated to America from poor (at the time) Asian countries—why would she ever pay good money to visit another?

After the divorce, they became even more callous. Now Fred and Kate considered her to be something preserved, static . . . as if she were in a tomb! They'd grown accustomed to the idea of her alone, she knew, her eternal gratefulness for their sparse phone calls and opportunities to dispense free babysitting, her home exactly as they had last left it, its hospitality and contents welcome to them anytime. Of course there were the normal exhortations, that she should *get out there and date*—find a new partner, as if it were so easy (though it certainly had seemed that way for Stanley, hadn't it?). But these were just vague pleasantries, the sort tossed out by young girls to their unattractive friends. Were a boyfriend actually to materialize, Linda knew Kate and Fred would go into near shock, disguising their unease until they could return home and call each other, ripping the suitor to shreds.

"Ma? Did you hear me? I asked, why do you have to hang up now? What's going on with you today? You don't seem like you're fully there."

"It's nothing," Linda said, adjusting her voice back to its normal brusque tones. "It's just you're always saying how busy you are. I don't want to take up your time."

"Oh," Kate said. "I suppose you're right." From her background there cut in the faint noise of crying—little Ella, probably, while the other one banged on something that sounded like it was shattering. "I should go."

After she hung up, Linda realized they hadn't discussed Stanley again. Kate would call her soon with an update anyway; until then there was nothing more for her to consider.

––––––––––

The first time Linda saw Tigerlily, she'd been disgusted.

She'd been at Shirley Chang's house (show-off, who was always insisting that everyone "drop in" at her palatial estate in Atherton before setting off to their ultimate destination), and the women there were gathered around phones, comparing photos of grandchildren and favorite tai chi videos before they migrated to Golden Dynasty for lunch. It was Friday, which meant $20 lobster noodles, though even if it had been another day of the week Linda still would have come. Life alone in retirement meant filling up her calendar with events like these, outings that lasted more than an hour but no more than three or four, where she woke up the following morning and felt rested but thankful again to be alone. It'd been a particularly trying few weeks, filled with anxious calls from Kate and Fred following the additional revelations of Stanley's cancer diagnosis; she was eager to reenter the orderly world of her female peers, where the gossip was vicious and the ailments kept mild.

Even though she'd been to Shirley's house dozens of times— usually after she'd picked up a friend or two along the way, since half the women were terrified to drive on the freeway—Linda didn't really like her. She was loud and too braggy. Someone in Shirley's position shouldn't need to describe in intricate detail how she was able to sustain her plush lifestyle entirely off dividends, especially since everyone knew that Cindy Yi, who was there that day, had recently lost half her retirement savings in an ill-advised franchise scheme in Shenzhen. But since Shirley and Linda had attended the same high school in Taipei, the #1 Girls' School (so named as it was, without dispute, number one), and then the same college (Taiwan University, also number one), and now were both in the Bay Area, they were forever part of the same circle.

Shirley motioned to Linda and patted the marled champagne tweed on the love seat beside her. She'd undertaken a thorough redecoration of both herself and the house after her husband, Alfred, had passed, and each now reflected the Versailles-lite sensibilities of a provincial Chinese government official. The sofa featured long, oversize tassels of braided gold foil and silk, as did the matching pillow; next to them, carefully positioned on the floor, was a five-foot statue in mottled green porcelain of a rearing horse. Its sibling, an even more gargantuan monstrosity in bronze, towered over the pathway of sculpted bonsai in the garden.

"How are you?" Shirley asked. "Your health doing okay? Children good?"

"Yes, thank you."

"How about Stanley? He's sick, I hear?" Shirley wore an expectant look, like a fat cat about to be presented with an animal part.

Linda wasn't surprised Shirley knew about Stanley. Ever since his diagnosis had been confirmed he'd been on a tear, dialing up all their mutual friends to tell them the news. He was almost celebratory about it, as he reveled in the intense interest and sympathy the words *pancreatic cancer* instantly elicited. Typical delusional behavior, and now he'd gone and infected the children with his madness! Roping Kate and Fred into weekly lunches and dinners, for what he called "powwow" sessions, to discuss his illness. Only positive thoughts allowed, naturally, which the children were happy to indulge: Kate with her printed internet articles promoting miracle recoveries and alkaline diets, Fred and his research into medical trials and some "super cancer center" in Utah. Stanley encouraging of all of it, more more more, me me me!

He'd been bothering Linda too, of course. Three times so far! Pestering her about doing a group meal with what he was irritatingly calling "the family," each time making crude reference to his dwindling mortality. So far, Linda had resisted. What did Stanley's illness have to do with her having to endure a lunch with his bovine second wife? Just because he was suffering, so should she? Though that was precisely the sort of sentiment someone like Shirley would agree with. Shirley, who had always favored Stanley. The two of them puffing each other up with their elementary chatter, hollow blowfish with nothing inside.

"Stanley is okay." Linda noted with satisfaction Shirley's look of disappointment that she hadn't inquired into how she knew of Stanley's diagnosis. "We do not speak much."

"You like my earrings?" Shirley asked, pivoting. "You should buy a pair." She tucked a strand of dyed brown hair behind her ear, revealing a diamond solitaire surrounded by two halos of accent diamonds. "I can refer you to my jeweler. We used a Harry Winston design!"

"My ears are not pierced." Even if they were, Linda would never have considered the Vegas showgirl monstrosities currently on display, which covered nearly the entirety of the chubby lobe they adorned. Linda herself preferred simple jewelry that didn't draw unwelcome attention, though lately as her portfolio had climbed to uncharted heights she had indulged in a few Seaman Schepps brooches for variety. Not that she'd ever reveal her favorite designers to Shirley; she'd immediately go out and purchase the most ostentatious pieces, rendering the entire brand untouchable.

"Sit closer," Shirley urged. "Check out my game." She tilted her tablet so that its screen could be seen only by the two of them. "What do you think?"

Linda looked down. The blurred image of a man in his seventies wearing an argyle sweater was nestled in Shirley's lap.

Milton Y, 72 years, Sunnyvale, California.

"What is this?"

Shirley flashed a secretive smile. "It's my dating game," she whispered. "I use this to meet men."

"A game? What kind of game is it where you can meet men?"

"It's not actually a game! Linda, you really are so naive sometimes. It's a dating program called Tigerlily. It's like those personal ads newspapers used to have, but it's all on the internet now. Look." Shirley swiped, and another Asian septuagenarian appeared. "There are millions of single men on here. And a lot of Chinese! Of course there are other races—I've even seen a few blacks—but you can adjust for all that in your settings. Although you can't select for Taiwan as a separate group from China. I guess they don't want to be political."

She expertly maneuvered the program to display various levers for ethnicity, age, and location and then brought up another screen. "This is my profile. Sometimes my dates are surprised when they meet me after seeing my photo, but never as surprised as I am to see them, believe me. It's something you'll find out; everyone uses old pictures."

The one Shirley had selected was actually fairly recent, from their last reunion in Taiwan, though something was different about her face. It looked as if a child had scribbled a fat peach-colored crayon all around her forehead and eyes, giving her skin the puddled, waxy look of a melted candle. Below her avatar was written *Shirley C, 65 years, Hillsborough, California*. She had chosen a different town ostensibly to protect her privacy, though Linda noted Shirley had made sure to select for her fake address an equally prestigious location as her actual city.

"You can't blame me for reducing my age a little bit, ha. I can pretend I don't even get Social Security yet! Want a referral? We'll each get $20 in free credit. I need it. Who knew love and dating could be so expensive?"

Linda felt a shudder of revulsion. The word *dating* incited a puritanical embarrassment in her, the same feeling she got when someone her age referred to their boyfriend or girlfriend. These were descriptors she believed she and her cohorts should have long aged out of, on their way to more dignified pastures. Of course none of them had ever *really* dated, as Taiwan in the '50s and '60s had been an exponentially more conservative setting than the United States. Almost all the women she knew had married the first boyfriend they ever had, with a wide margin of results. Practically no one got a divorce—she was the only example in their group—which was why the suicide rates were so high, and Shirley was now showing her this disgusting program.

Ever since Alfred passed, Linda had noticed Shirley cropping up in her periphery with increasing frequency. For a while, each time her phone rang, there had been a decent chance it was Shirley, calling to invite her to some opera outing, mah jong night, or private shopping event. As if all of a sudden they had something in common, as if being alone were enough to link them together! Linda felt strongly that her choosing to be single set her apart from Shirley, who would have never opted to live alone had her husband not just up and expired, probably to rid himself of her incessant chatter. As a general rule Chinese women of their generation didn't believe in separation; they would suffer bankruptcy, shadow families, abuse (mental and even sometimes physical) and still consider a dissolution of their marital union outside the realm of possibility. So who but Linda knew the true difficulty of divorce after three decades of marriage, the endless suffering and self-humiliations endured to cross the finish line? There was a reason why no one else had done it; they hadn't the determination to push through the fear. And now Shirley felt she had the right to show her this . . . trash!

Next to her the offender sat unaware, grunting as her fingers flew past an array of the bald and graying. "Here's someone I went on a date with last week," she said. "But he was only interested in, you know, a nurse with a purse."

"I do not know how to use these sorts of things," Linda said, cutting her off cold. "I am too worried about scams and my reputation." To her these were fighting words, meant to wound, but Shirley simply shrugged and waddled to another seat.

Linda instantly regretted having spoken so quickly. It wouldn't have hurt to hear Shirley out. It'd been harder than she thought, to be on her own. The house was frightening at night—there had been three break-ins on her street that year alone, and each week she spent the evening before trash pickup day in a state of paranoid agitation as the sounds of cans rolling to the curb jolted her awake. Linda had detested Stanley so much by the end of their marriage that she'd

dedicated nearly every modicum of available energy toward the sin-
gular goal of his vacating the house—she hadn't given nearly as much
thought to what it would be like after, the yawning of weekends and
weeks glommed together, how early the days turned black once winter
began.

IT WASN'T UNTIL A WEEK LATER, ON A SUNDAY, THAT LINDA RE-
called Tigerlily. Kate was supposed to have shuttled Ethan and Ella
over in the morning—an event Linda had looked forward to all
week—but then huffily declined after Linda caveated that she could
take them for only two hours instead of the entire day. "My shoulders
are hurting," she explained on the phone.

"It takes us thirty minutes just to get everyone loaded in the car
to get over there," Kate said. "Not to mention the fact you won't drop
them back off at my house."

"I don't understand the car seats! They make me so nervous." She
hated those enormous contraptions, which the children had howled
at the sight of when they were younger; the octopus-like straps she
could never completely untangle, Kate's warnings about the risk of
severe injury or decapitation were the seats not used exactly right.
Who would possibly want to drive, under such frightful conditions?

"It's the law. I'm happy to walk you through the steps again. Didn't
I even write them down last time?"

"My back, it aches when I bend for the buckles. How about I put
pillows on the seats instead, make it higher for the kids to sit?"

"Let's just forget the whole thing," Kate said with a loud exhale.
"Okay?"

Linda had hung up abruptly and then called Fred, who hadn't
answered, twice to complain. She pondered, as she did occasionally,
what it would be like to have a third child. One of Shirley Chang's

few redeeming qualities was a son who at thirty-six was still unmarried and living in her guesthouse; now that Linda was alone and past a certain age, she had to admit there was a certain appeal in having a shut-in for a child, provided he or she wasn't your only one or engaged in active terrorism. A little companionship at dinner and the knowledge of another body in close proximity at night would be of comfort. There had been another burglary on the street behind hers that week, and the rumor was that thieves were targeting houses with shoes outside, as they were an indication that the inhabitants were Indian or Asian and had hidden stores of gold. In response, she'd gone to Home Depot and purchased an inexpensive doormat that read *wipe your paws* in swirling script. It was the kind of item Linda thought only a white family would have on display, the sort with a brave male presence on the premises, eager to confront intruders.

With her morning now free, Linda weighed her options. She had a standing invitation from Candy Gu to join in her weekly ballroom dancing class, but the thought of so many people her age in good cheer was too intimidating for her current mood. The one time she'd gone, nearly all the women had worn colorful full skirts and clattered about in flashing heels; she'd stood near the back in her usual loose blouse and slacks, feeling drab.

She decided to speed walk at the school track several blocks away. Neither Fred nor Kate had attended Oak Elementary—instead they'd gone to Auburn, a considerably lower-ranked institution where the classrooms had teemed with children and the teachers bore a uniform expression of grim determination. It had been due to their address at the time, a location for which Stanley was completely to blame (as if she'd ever choose to live in Campbell!). Linda recalled how busy the field at Auburn always was, continually crammed in the off-hours with young mothers pushing cheap strollers. The lower bleachers dotted with exhausted grandparents who prodded their charges to run ragged, while they sat stonily on the metal benches, dreaming of their home countries.

In contrast, the grounds at Oak were nearly empty. The denizens of Palo Alto had better things to do on their weekends, such as paid activities or partaking in brunch, a meal Linda had completed three times in her life and still failed to comprehend the merits of. The lone other soul present was a heavyset blonde in a tracksuit, someone she recognized from the neighborhood. The woman was circling the track at a lumbering pace while noisily talking on her headset, one of those rude Americans who unapologetically occupied shared space as if it was birthright. She was near Linda's age (the hair was really more a stringy taupe) and appeared retired, but Linda knew there was practically no chance of interaction. The woman likely didn't even think she spoke English, regarding her as just another sexless Asian dotting her periphery—someone who could be ignored at will, like a houseplant. She had a surprisingly deep voice, a booming alto, and Linda's own efficient gait meant that she circled twice for every oval the blonde completed. Each time they overlapped, her peace was jarringly disturbed:

"Wish you were here, babe. I'd be making us dinner. Yep, my famous Costco roasted chicken. I unpack it myself and everything." Cackle cackle. Cackle cackle.

"These days the kids are complaining that *I'm* the one who's loud. Can you believe this shit. . . . I'm out on the back deck, having fun with my friends, and they're texting me to be quiet. Texting! And it's barely eleven p.m. What ever happened to good old face-to-face—"

"You don't even know how old I am. Guess, just guess. Oh baby, *stop!*" Followed by an ear-splitting squeal.

In the evening, after she tired of playing Four Winds Supreme, her online mah jong game, and was perilously close to exhausting the $20 budget she allowed herself per day, it suddenly occurred to Linda that the blonde had been speaking to a man, a person she was romantically involved with. How stupid and unimaginative men were! A bottle of cheap hair dye, and from its results they were seemingly able to conjure up all sorts of romantic desires, even given a particularly base specimen like her neighbor. Each time Linda had overtaken her, she'd been hit with a rancid stench far worse than the Chinese herbs Fred and Kate used to complain about, and her pants had been saggy and stained. The woman's dishevelment extended to her home, which appeared to have never been altered from its original tract origins, and her front yard was nearly entirely populated with discarded furniture and a decaying camper and motorboat. She was the sort of resident whose continuing presence in the area was the result of pure stubbornness, fiercely holding on to her dilapidated lodgings while contemporaries cashed out and moved away, to havens like Colorado or Nevada, where they would no longer be besieged by minorities recklessly driving expensive foreign sedans.

For the longest time Linda had herself avoided driving a luxury automobile for this very reason, the desire not to be seen as a stereotype. Now, such self-consciousness struck her as foolish. Why shouldn't she have a nice car? She should go out and buy one soon, she thought. Life was short. And surely if this snaggletooth possessed the bravery to seek companionship, she might do the same? And she stared at the tablet in her hands and recalled the words of Shirley Chang.

Tigerlily was easy to install. Her information was instantly populated with the Facebook profile she never used, and the program immediately prompted whether she'd prefer the Mandarin keyboard as the default. When the list of available men in her area popped up, she quickly shut off the screen.

Throughout dinner she forced herself to ponder other topics— taxes and whether she was unhappy with either of her children. She ate methodically, watched a one-hour national news program, and wrote a polite email to her lawyer. It wasn't until she had washed the dishes, taken out a small bag of trash, and settled into bed with her teeth brushed that she allowed herself to reopen the application.

LINDA'S FIRST VIABLE TIGERLILY MATCH, A RETIRED MECHANICAL engineer named Norman Wu, asked her to dinner at Café Luca. Linda used to go to Luca when she'd worked at IBM and had fond memories of dining there with coworkers. In his messages Norman was polite and wrote elegantly—she had looked forward to the meal ever since the invitation. Would she order her normal Spaghetti Classico, even though it had red sauce and could be messy? She decided she would; she was a neat eater, and it was best not to make compromises so early in a relationship.

In person, Norman looked like his photos, albeit older. When she first saw him, Linda was struck by a grim fear that she too appeared that aged and scuttled to the bathroom to reassure herself. She pet her face in the mirror. She didn't *think* she looked that bad—she thought she might still even be able to pull off *handsome*—but there was nothing she could do about it, either way. She applied a fresh coat of lipstick.

After she reemerged, Norman solicitously guided her to her seat. Linda noted that his brown tweed blazer and coordinating slacks were a fitting match for her gray crepe Max Mara. "It's the best table in the restaurant," he said. "I always tip big, so they know to save it for me." The restaurant was nearly empty; aside from themselves, there was only one other group, a family of four with an upset baby. "It will fill up soon," Norman assured her. "I had to make reservations."

Over appetizers, they swapped details not covered by their Tigerlily profiles. While Norman had followed a high-achieving track similar to hers in Taiwan and had even gone to the same college, Linda was relieved to hear they were three years apart. The Bay Area Taiwanese community was small—she preferred any potential suitors not be exposed to gossip regarding her and Stanley. They discovered they'd shared the same statistics professor, and Linda's update that Dr. Chao was now deceased surprised Norman and lent their conversation an air of shared intimacy. He was impressed she had obtained a master's in chemistry at Stanford. He himself had earned a PhD in applied mathematics from UCLA. By the time their pasta arrived, they were chatting at a nice clip.

"How long have you been alone?" Norman asked. Linda liked that he didn't use the word *single*.

"Let me think. Over ten years. How quickly time passes."

"Your husband," Norman ventured delicately. "He is no longer . . . here?"

"Oh no, he lives in San Jose. We divorced."

He raised an eyebrow. "That is unusual. Most of the women I meet are widows."

Linda laughed. "Not me," she trilled. "It was my decision." She was having a good time, she realized.

"As for myself, I didn't have a choice. My wife passed away. Cancer." Norman looked down and speared into a piece of penne covered in clam sauce.

Linda quickly composed herself. "I'm so sorry," she murmured. "How long were you together?"

"Forty years. We married in 1975, right after I finished my PhD."

Linda resisted the forward math in her head. "My goodness," she said. "That's a very long time."

"My wife, she was like a perfect angel," Norman continued. "She knew everything. She cooked such mouthwatering Hunan food—my parents were from the Changsha region, and she always used just the right sort of rice noodles in the soup. Everything to do with the house was managed by her. We had two new roofs put on during our marriage, and I barely knew anything about either of them, because she always arranged for the work to be done when I was gone. She didn't want me to be disturbed, she said! And do you know, the month after she died, I discovered I had no money in my wallet? Why are so many Chinese restaurants still all cash? And when I went to the ATM, I couldn't understand how to use it! And then I figured out that Nancy had been putting twenties in my wallet, every week, all these years."

"Home repairs can be very difficult. I'm constantly managing them. Just last month I received a quote for $16,000 for new windows. Sixteen thousand dollars for glass! Can you believe it? And after they finished I had to spend the rest of the day cleaning; they left streaks everywhere."

"You sound just like my Nancy." Norman shook his head. "Although to be perfectly honest she wasn't the cleanest person; she could be very messy."

"I'm the exact opposite. I can't go to bed each night unless everything is back in its proper place." Linda wondered if she was sounding too boastful but decided to charge forward. "I was the oldest of six, so I always had to take care of everyone, make sure everything was clean, before I could start my homework."

"I would love to live somewhere neat. My mother kept a very clean household. Do you live in the same house as before your divorce?"

"Yes, for the last seventeen years in the same place. Palo Alto." Stanley's final and only compromise in their marriage, the house itself the stuff of horrors but built on the lot of her dreams. She'd begun the remodel the same year he married Mary.

"Palo Alto," Norman repeated. "What a nice city. We always thought of moving there, because of the good schools. And you mentioned something earlier about a triplex in Cupertino? So that must be an investment property then? Very good rents, I hear, near Apple."

The evening's flirtatious light took on a sinister glare; all at once Linda saw that Norman was the sort of widowed-slash-divorced man she had been encountering in ever greater frequency, a tribe whose solitary goal in dating was to secure a suitable replacement for the deceased or estranged as rapidly as possible. Michael Chan, who together with his wife, Faith, had been one of her and Stanley's most frequent mah jong partners, had put out feelers less than a week after Faith's funeral, when the donations to battle lymphoma in her name had still been rolling in. There was no other choice—he couldn't keep a household, couldn't cook, couldn't do anything, Michael despaired. He needed a wife!

One appeared on his arm a few scanty months later, a self-described hairstylist with an awful haircut, thirty years his junior. Recently from China, of course. Most of them were. Young, but given the ages of Linda and Stanley's classmates, not too young; faces of regional newscasters past their prime, an occasional failed marriage left behind on the mainland.

Not all of these recently unattached men ended up with younger consorts. There were some who sought an entirely different bracket: women their own age, or near it, who like them had arrived in the United States on educational visas decades earlier. Women similar to their first partners in career or schooling, who could read and understand an English-language newspaper. Women who'd already established families, raised adult children, heckled them to the Ivy League, and had no desire to repeat the process. Women who were rich. That last attribute was always the key qualifier, and Linda recognized the housing chatter currently being lobbed her way as the nefarious tentacles of a single man on the make for a wealthy partner. No doubt her would-be suitor was moving through a list of open questions in his mind right now, as he sought to accurately gauge her resources. Would she be able to assume the entirety of her own medical costs until the ultimate end and, if necessary, assist with her husband's? What level of health coverage could she afford? Was it basic—as in no frills, no private rooms, no specialist referrals, long wait times—or was it concierge medicine at Stanford Hospital? Had she selected, and already paid for, a funeral plot (as they could reach up to $40,000 and beyond, depending on the size and location)? Did she already possess her own paid-off housing and fully funded 401(k) (and thus not serve as competition against the man's own adult children for future inheritance proceeds)? What was the state of her investments? What percentage of them were in a Roth IRA? Had she already started taking distributions?

Linda personally knew of several examples from her own social circles who had made such matches; Stanley himself had been the recipient of attentions from a certain older woman years back, a fellow Taiwan University graduate who possessed the double whammy of both childlessness and substantial real estate holdings in the Bay Area. Linda had heard through her friend Yvonne Ho that the woman had invited Stanley on several overnight outings, their relationship proceeding to the point where they had planned a riverboat cruise on the Danube. Ultimately, however, Stanley hadn't been able to commit. He had given the excuse to Kate and Fred—the latter of whom had been particularly disappointed, given the woman's ownership of several prime lots in Woodside—that she was simply too old to keep up with him. Privately to Linda, however, during a quiet lull at the wedding of a mutual friend's daughter, Stanley had admitted that he couldn't cope with her money. "I already had one wife more capable than me," he commented. Stanley was always magnanimous in private, especially back then, in the throes of a burgeoning social life with widows of distant acquaintances and thirtysomething Cantonese shop girls with poor English.

Linda never let herself forget that the freedom she enjoyed had come only after carrying a man on her back for thirty years. Maintaining her steadily increasing salary at IBM until retirement, while she doggedly combed through the library's Value Line archives at night. Making copies of the investment reports for each of her target companies, painstakingly analyzing the numbers. Taking great care to hide from Stanley any knowledge of the accounts, for she'd known he'd surely usurp the funds for some hideously flawed scheme.

It wasn't until the day she asked for a divorce—carrying in her hands the binder from Charles Schwab to soften the blow—that she came clean on all she had done for him, on top of raising his children, preparing his healthy and fine-tasting Chinese food, and keeping a spotless home. What a 17 percent annualized return looked like, when sustained for more than two decades.

It occurred to Linda that perhaps it was no longer her right to demand from life an alternative; that if she were to continue meeting men from Tigerlily they'd all turn out to be identical anyway, the same man wearing a different face. Mercilessly hunting for the financially capable woman to fold his laundry and iron his shirts, the nurse with a purse to smooth his path toward life's inevitable end, never daring to cross the finish line first herself. That maybe over the years she had worked herself into a groove so deep that no matter how much she tried to deviate from it, she'd always eventually find herself tumbling right back in, rolling down its curve with natural momentum.

AFTER THE INITIAL TEN MATCHES, EACH MEMBER OF TIGERLILY was limited to one new profile a day unless they paid for additional currency, called Petals. Most users never forked over a cent—they simply signed on and checked their results before moving on to the next free option. Linda only knew of Tigerlily, however, and at this point in her life she almost always opted to spend for convenience. The indulgence in overt luxuries such as handbags had lost its luster as she grew older and more paranoid about events like home invasions; she'd spent so long being frugal that she now found it difficult to enjoy the release of money on physical goods. Before long she'd spent $200 on Tigerlily. Then $500, an amount that unlocked additional privileges: suddenly there were increased messaging capabilities, and a whole slew of privacy filters had been removed, which meant she could see how often a prospective candidate had viewed her profile. Once Linda hit $5,000, a fat packet arrived at the house, welcoming her to Tigerlily Deluxe. The materials inside detailed an entirely new tranche of services at her disposal.

That was when online dating became truly, very interesting.

CHAPTER 4

KATE

I n all her years growing up in various houses in progressively improv-
ing school districts of the Bay Area, Kate had never once seen her
mother unnerved. Not during the 1989 Loma Prieta earthquake, when
as a kid she'd tripped and bashed her skull against the sharp corner of
a cabinet, only to emerge after the shaking stopped, blood stream-
ing from her forehead; not when Stanley—in a moment of deliberate
rage—managed to kill one of the family pets; not even when Fred and
then Kate herself failed to gain admission into Stanford, which had at
the time been her mother's most ardent dream. Linda was a consistently
cool operator who considered emotions nearly meaningless—to her
there was no point in wasting time talking when there was action to
be taken. So when Kate picked up the phone her senior year at UCLA
and heard a known yet unfamiliar voice on the other end, so rattled,

so shaky, on the edge of *pleading*—it had been like a bright red-alarm flare shot into the sky.

"I cannot sleep," Linda blurted, and then paused. "I can never sleep now."

Kate looked at the wall clock. Eleven p.m., an hour that for her mother constituted the middle of the night. "Ma, what's wrong? Are you okay?"

"My friends, they don't understand. . . . I've made a mess of my life."

"What's going on?" Kate panicked. "What can I do? What's happened?" And waited for Linda to give her action points, as she had her entire life, but instead her mother lapsed into silence.

"I want you to live your life," Linda eventually said. "Don't bother with mine. This is for me to handle." She hung up. Kate called back immediately, letting the house phone ring, until finally Stanley came on the line.

"Don't worry about Ma," he said, sounding sleepy. "She'll feel better in the morning. Okay?"

But then two days later the phone rang again, this time past midnight. "I have nothing to live for," Linda confessed. "I should just die."

And then again the next day, at 2:00 a.m.

Her mother always ended each conversation with "I want you to live your life," insistent that there was nothing to be done. She refused to acknowledge Kate's suggestions to see a counselor, confide in a friend, or spend the weekend with her in Southern California. It was an impossible situation, her silences indicated, one with no viable solution. Yet the calls only ceased—instantaneously, altogether— when Kate announced she was returning home.

Linda never asked what made Kate change her mind about moving to Cincinnati to take a job with Procter & Gamble after graduation; never inquired into the frantic last-minute recruiting that had been necessary, after which she'd hastily signed the first decent offer to come her way. Kate understood this to be her mother's coping mechanism for having practically forced the move, cashing in twenty years of karmic chips of, until then, never demonstrating any weakness or violent emotion. What it must have already cost Linda's pride to share, even in the broadest of descriptions, her despair over Stanley's cheating, the bleakness of her marriage, the fright of finding herself in such a situation! And so Kate felt an important and simple mission had been placed before her: Finish school. Return home. Save mother.

By the time she graduated and was back in the house, however, Kate found her parents had already moved on to another phase of marriage, one vastly different from the psychological torture chamber vaguely alluded to in Linda's calls. Far from being at war, Stanley and Linda instead appeared to be quite amiable, as if miming the parts of an American sitcom; Linda querying which toppings everyone wanted for pizza night, while Stanley watched television at a considerate volume and voluntarily cleared the dishes after dinner. On the weekends, Stanley took measurements of Fred's old bedroom, plotting what exercise machines would make best use of the space; Linda scoured the Home Depot circulars, hunting for deals.

While there existed in the household a not-unwelcome surface placidity, it was evident to Kate that lurking underneath were disturbing elements of a scale and nature that mirrored the superficial cheer, and the first fault lines began to show a few months later. Arriving home early from work one afternoon, Kate parked the car in the garage, only to find the entrance locked from the inside. She had to use the bathroom, and her pounding grew more insistent until finally, Linda opened the door. Through the crack Kate glimpsed messy hair and a thin satin bathrobe—a violent divergence from the image she usually had of her mother, who left her bedroom fully dressed in a Brooks Brothers twinset every morning at seven. A man's voice, one foreign to her, sounded lightly in the background.

"Come back later," Linda hissed, and Kate fled to the restroom facilities of a nearby Barnes & Noble. She returned home well after dinner to find Stanley in the living room, watching TV, while Linda cut fruit in the kitchen. No mention was made of her earlier arrival, and Kate put it out of her mind. The experience jarred so greatly from her impression of Linda—who'd only ever displayed the most prudish of attitudes toward sex, leaving the room whenever a graphic scene came on TV—that it was easy and convenient to justify it as a fluke.

A few weeks later, however, Stanley asked her to dinner alone, a rare father/daughter outing. As they left the house, Kate saw Linda watching from the window with clenched teeth; at the meal itself, at Lemon Fish, her father extolled to her the virtues of his latest diet, which incorporated copious amounts of ginseng. "I just have to tell you, I feel such *vitality*," he said. "My body is feeling its *vitality*."

The final straw came two months later, when while hunting through the storage area in the laundry room for her old Helen Gurley Brown paperbacks, Kate unearthed a red Gump's shopping bag. Inside, she found a delicates drying rack, the satin robe her mother had worn, and a bottle of female lubricant. That night, she crept to the front yard after Linda and Stanley had shut the doors of their respective bedrooms and called her brother for reinforcement.

"Let them deal with it," Fred said. He'd already moved to New York by then and was working in banking at Morgan Stanley. "I don't even want to imagine Mom and Dad having sex with each other, much less other people."

"You think I do? I'm the one living here! It's happening literally yards away from where I sleep. Coitus parentis."

"So you think it's some kind of open-marriage thing?"

"I'm not sure. I think Mom's might have been a onetime deal." Kate had carefully observed Linda after the initial incident, and since then she had returned home early several times unannounced. Each instance she'd found Linda sitting in the garden, fully clothed in her normal sweater and slacks, reading the *Wall Street Journal*. "All I know is that things here are messed up."

"Ummm." Kate could hear Fred typing; he was still in the office, even though he was three hours ahead. "So then how certain are you about this? Because I still can't fully comprehend that our parents are hooking up with random people. I've never even seen the two of them kiss! Remember when they got trapped into doing that dance with all the other parents at Uncle Phillip's wedding? I didn't think it was possible to stand so far apart and still be partnered."

"There's definitely something going on. With Dad, I think if I just snooped around, I'd find proof pretty easily. With Mom, I'm not so sure. You know how secretive she is."

"Then how do you know she's doing anything at all?"

Kate squeezed her eyes shut—the memory of glossy material tied haphazardly; Linda's hair in disarray. "I just know, okay?"

"Fine. Jesus."

"I don't know how much longer I can live like this."

"Whoa." Kate recognized in her brother's voice the tendrils of panic, concern that their parents' problems might somehow overflow into his territory, disturbing his carefully crafted distance. "I'll think about how I can help, all right?"

"Swear? Because I really need some assistance."

"I swear. Don't do anything crazy in the meantime."

HALF A YEAR LATER, THE PROBLEM ESSENTIALLY SOLVED ITSELF, when she was kicked out of the house. Kate's presence, her parents hinted, was getting in the way of their marriage, depriving them of the privacy necessary to complete its repair. They had enjoyed their time with her; now, she was encouraged to depart as quickly as possible. Likely out of guilt over the hasty expulsion, Linda offered to assist with the down payment on a condo in a nearby development.

But by this time X Corp had gone public, and even a low-level analyst like Kate, thanks to a relatively early employee number in the low thousands, was flush with cash. After a brief search she hurriedly bought a town house near Peninsula Shopping Center; it was the immense gains on this property that, five years later, combined with some vested stock, she was able to trade toward her current home.

She'd debated between two properties at the time, and in the end opted to pay thousands more for the teardown on the superior lot. "You made the right decision, value wise," her real estate agent, a sharp-nosed pro named Eileen Jacobs, told her. "A new house on that land is going to be worth a bundle, somewhere down the line. But it could be a while, and I don't know how you're going to stand living in there in the meantime."

But Kate found that she actually enjoyed fixer-upper living: the squabbles with contractors, the organization of permits, the endless remodeling debates. Over the years she painstakingly updated the property as tranches of X Corp equity were refilled and became available, and she performed many of the smaller repairs herself over long, reclusive weekends alone. She gave the house a name, Francie, after the heroine in *A Tree Grows in Brooklyn*, and baked cakes for the neighbors as a preemptive apology for the construction noise. Linda had insisted such gestures were unnecessary, arguing that given her unmarried status they could be interpreted as sinister: the spinster down the block targeting the husbands of distracted working moms. For once, however, Kate had known she was right. The residents on her street were predominantly white and enjoyed traditions like Christmas lights in December and American flags in July—a stark contrast to their neighborhood growing up, where the decor remained unchanged year-round and going door to door with baked goods would have been viewed with naked suspicion at best, an introductory volley to a heavy-fisted follow-up for a school fund-raiser. In Los Altos, Kate's neighbors gushed over her Irish cream pound cake and inquired into how Francie was doing, as if the home were a real-life baby. Over the holidays, wonderfully twee hand-lettered Christmas greetings were dropped off in her mailbox, addressed to Kate and Francie Huang.

On one of her visits Linda picked up a card. She read the dedication out loud. "Who is Francie?" she asked.

"It's the house, Ma. I gave it a name. It's a little joke we have in the neighborhood, because I spend so much time working on the place that it's almost like my baby. Get it?"

Linda's mouth was set in a line. "A house is not a baby."

"Of course not. But it's important, isn't it? You always said a family *and* a house were necessary. I'm just doing the second part now. You must understand; why else are you making such a big deal about keeping the Palo Alto place in the divorce?"

"The point is to have them at the same time," Linda answered. "Didn't I teach you this much?"

———————

In the evening, after the kids had gone to sleep—or at least been installed in their respective rooms, alternately muttering to themselves and wailing at the injustice of bedtime—Kate walked through Francie, moving from space to space. She wore Ethan's and Ella's small backpacks on each arm for the exercise, which allowed her to easily pick up and deposit misplaced thermos bottles, books, and stray items of clothing. The routine was one of those crucial time-savers that were supposed to make life bearable for working moms with young children, a small item on a long list of suggestions Kate always found inane but still couldn't stop herself from reading online.

Linda had left the house an hour earlier, after covering dinner and the first half of the bedtime rush while Kate dropped off two books and multiple bags of produce at Stanley's. Her father had been insistent that she come in and watch as he performed a series of stretches, all while Mary hovered nearby, every few minutes aggressively offering up a variety of tasteless red bean pastries. It was the sort of imposition that would have driven Stanley crazy in earlier years—as a child, Kate had felt hot pinpricks of nervousness whenever someone took too long to check out at the grocery store or back up from their parking spot, as there would inevitably come a point when Stanley's annoyance abruptly spilled over to rage, and he would start barking that they needed to hurry up, hurry the fuck up, *who the fuck did they think they were?* But his illness had accelerated the relaxation of former standards that very strict adults tend to go through as they age, and now Stanley seemed to not care at all that she had mentioned she couldn't stay when he'd answered the door. Instead he'd sat cross-legged on the white shag carpet in the family room, slowly contorting into a position he called the "praying butterfly." As the delay extended, Kate had felt an increasing sense of panic, as she imagined Linda eyeing the wall clock in her kitchen. She'd been careful to obscure the exact nature of her outing, couching it as a series of quick errands, since she knew Linda viewed Stanley's requests as inane, a list of useless demands of which only the lowest-hanging fruit should be given consideration. When Kate finally returned home, however, her mother had immediately struck at the heart of her obfuscation. "And how's your father?" she asked, posing the question as if indulging a child an imaginary friend. "You just saw him, mmm?"

Kate hesitated for only a moment before deciding against lying, which rarely worked with Linda anyway. "He's fine. In a good mood, actually. He's been seeing a lot of friends, going out, watching movies."

"Oh? So he's doing very well now?"

"I wouldn't go that far. He's supposed to return soon to Kaiser for a few more tests, to see what kind of treatment they can pursue. I was dropping off some fruits and vegetables I picked up at the farmers' market; apparently his doctor said he should try to eat healthier."

"Why can't he go get his own food? Since he has so much time to have fun?"

"There were also a few books he wanted me to buy. You know how he loves reading."

"Huh." Linda snorted. She held a dim view of Stanley's literary prowess. "He doesn't *read*, just flips pages on the treadmill. He's not exercising now, is he? He should be resting!"

"So you *do* care. Why don't you have dinner with us? He asks about it literally every time I see him. It would really make him happy, improve his spirits."

"His spirits? Didn't you just say he's in such a good mood?"

"You know what I mean. And who knows how much time he has left?" Kate paused, waiting. "We should make the most of it, regardless of what happens."

"Hmm." Linda sniffed the air, as if a particularly strong odor had just passed. "And my time isn't valuable?"

IN THE KITCHEN NOW, KATE WENT TO THE FRIDGE TO TOSS OUT old food. She guiltily upended a large bowl of Thai chicken stir-fry, slamming down the garbage lid so as to avoid witnessing the waste. She had cooked it herself, in a rare hour of domestic experimentation, but neither Denny nor the children had liked it, and she'd only been able to stomach eating half before she gave up and shoved it toward the back with the cold beverages. She tried not to be irritated by the fact that she was always the one who ate the unwanted leftovers, busily calculating the days of meals remaining and their relative shelf lives, whereas Denny thought nothing of bringing home an extra chicken shawarma just because he happened to be driving by Dish n' Dash. Why not? What was the point of stressing over $43 of wasted wild-caught turbot, sacrificed so the family could indulge a craving for pizza? Life was short, and then you died. The ultimate argument.

As she riffled through the retrieved mail stack, Kate saw little of importance: the usual flyers and catalogs, many of which were inexplicably mailed in duplicate. She had long ceased shredding credit card applications, figuring anyone looking to steal her identity could find easier routes to do so, and chucked them intact in their envelopes. There was a long-overdue holiday card from her college roommate, an angry Missourian named Lizzy who now lived in Piedmont. Lizzy was a copywriter who worked from home while caring for her three young children and spent her days getting into fights on social media. Kate made a note to ask her over for brunch the following weekend—she'd time the invite with sufficient advance notice to still be polite but close enough that most likely Lizzy would turn it down, thus earning herself credit for having reached out without actually needing to endure another rage-filled soliloquy over the agony of raising twins. "I am not a spectacle!" Lizzy liked to declare. "Motherhood is not an event!"

Halfway through, Kate noticed she had already set aside two issues of *The Economist*, as well as a smattering of other titles. This was highly unusual. Even during his most slovenly periods, when the mail accumulated for weeks, her husband still did drive-by snipings. Denny firmly believed that reading was an integral part of his job as a start-up CEO, a practice routinely overlooked by the multitude of entrepreneurs he competed against on a daily basis, the twentysomething wunderkinds with bad skin and good PR who'd begun coding shortly after elementary school. He lamented there was something seriously wrong about a generation that assumed it could simply absorb necessary knowledge on demand, as if years of life experience and study could be distilled into an hour-long TED Talk or thread on Reddit.

Kate made her way to the attic, where she deposited the issues in their proper stacks. Normally the converted workspace had the atmosphere of a frat house in early morning: food and cables scattered about, a scent of human omnipresent in the air. It was only the previous year that Denny had started to allow the cleaners to tidy up during their visits—prior to that, conditions had been even worse, with Kate surreptitiously creeping up each week to clear out crusted dishes and dirty mugs. It was gross, but there'd also been a charming element to the task: a glimpse into a hidden sphere of her husband, his daily belongings accumulated in messy piles only he knew the system behind.

Now the long desk was almost entirely bare, aside from a warehouse-size box of sparkling water bottles. Kate tried to recall the last time she had come up. A month? Longer? She used to regularly ask Denny about how his work was progressing, though as the plans for CircleShop had advanced she found him increasingly pricklish on the topic. "It puts pressure on me when you nag," he complained. "I enter a shitty headspace."

She wandered over to the blank monitor screens. Next to them, Denny's agenda lay open. She thumbed through it, taking care not to wrinkle the paper. Apart from a few meetings, there was remarkably little for the past two and upcoming six months.

Where was all the work for CircleShop? Normally the dry-erase board was filled with the scribbled momentum of Denny's brainstorm sessions with his team of hired-gun programmers, and the counters were strewn with articles of interest, partner pitches, and sample term sheets. (Denny was in the middle of fund-raising, supposedly close to securing an angel round of hard commitments.) Kate looked around and noted with alarm that even the standing easel that acted as the scrum board was empty, entirely devoid of black permanent marker and the neon sticky notes that outlined tasks to be done, in progress, and finished. Had the concept imploded? Undergone a dramatic pivot? But it was a crucial period, and it was unlikely that Denny—who had plowed the past year of his life full-time into CircleShop's current business model—would suddenly give it all up before the platform had even launched. Just last weekend she had ventured a gentle inquiry into the work's progress as they prepared breakfast—she had been relieved to find him optimistic, even cheerful on the topic. "I feel like a crucial stage's been passed," he said. "I can breathe."

So then why were Denny's days empty?

What was her husband doing, up in the attic?

———————————

Sonny Agrawal was a genius.

That at least was the undisputed party line within X Corp, the technology behemoth where Kate had worked for more than a decade, an eternity in Silicon Valley. While it was true that X Labs—the so-called moonshot group Sonny headed, where projects such as the eradication of entire insect species were studied—was located not at headquarters but at one of X Corp's auxiliary buildings, where high-cost, low-revenue divisions were shuffled to by their parent after they'd lost their initial luster, it was a dire mistake to underestimate him, an error that had been made only by the least politically savvy over the years.

Sonny had already been decades into a lauded career as one of MIT's most renowned physics professors when Alexei Sokolov, then an impressionable undergraduate, had enrolled in his much-heralded and oversubscribed course on special relativity; eight years later, after Alexei had launched X and it was clear the start-up was well on its way to deca-unicorn valuations, he'd been insistent on bringing on board the professor he'd worshipped in college. Sonny's official title was EVP, executive vice president, but he was known throughout X Corp for possessing the highest status of all: FOS, or Friend of Sokolov. Each quarter he was threatened with public career flagellation before acquiescing to being hauled in front of a skeptical board of directors to explain an ever-widening gap between R&D and revenue—that he survived each time, seemingly without consequence, only further cemented his position.

Possibly it was the decades of ingrained experience with an explosively tempered parent that made Kate such an ideal employee for Sonny, or maybe it was one of those mysteries of personality combination, the fact that she required little stated praise or verbal recognition to remain motivated (for which she gave thanks to Linda Liang). Whatever the reason, at three years as a director in product management, Kate had enjoyed a tenure multiples of length longer than any of Sonny's other direct reports, the rest of whom had either quit or been fired during one of his more furious sulks. So far she'd outlasted the number-one-ranked mathematics graduate of Tsinghua, two of Sonny's first cousins, and a mouthy quantum computing engineer from NASA; the latest casualty, a postdoc specializing in the bewildering field of contemplation, had left of his own volition to return to male modeling.

Even with Sonny's idiosyncrasies, Kate didn't mind her job. It provided a degree of freedom convenient for the operation of a household containing two young children; most days, Sonny legitimately followed through on a stated disinterest in micromanagement and gave little care if Kate left early or arrived late. It was only during the rare periods when the Labs were close to launching a viable product—and thus subject to increased scrutiny from corporate overlords—that Kate put in the sort of hours she used to, earlier in her career, before kids. On those occasions Denny did the pickups from school, the feeding of dinner, and the bedtime routines, while Kate stayed late at the office harassing factories and browbeating engineers into submission.

TWO YEARS EARLIER, WHEN SONNY APPEARED AT WORK AFTER THE Christmas holiday on crutches—the aftermath of a minor skiing accident in Lake Tahoe—the entire office had held its breath. Sonny was the sort of academic-cum-executive who even in the rosiest periods of health found a task like brewing tea inexplicably frustrating; after his injury, such minute yet indispensable chores became nearly impossible. His residence, a renovated cottage in Menlo Park with a myriad of thresholds and a layout that bizarrely had all the bathrooms located on the second floor, had become a deathtrap; in response, he began to keep increasingly long hours at the office, where as the senior man on the totem pole any passing employee could be finagled into doing his bidding. This practice was quickly halted by human resources, however, after an employee complained of carpal tunnel brought on by the repetitive motion of pushing Sonny for hours back and forth in the office hammock; afterward his mood, generally pleasantly imperious before, descended into morose and biting.

"Why should I help mankind," he carped, "when man does not help me?" He refused to make any product decisions, ditching meetings and executive reviews; as Sonny was the crucial linchpin for nearly every engineering and research milestone, work slid to a halt.

X Corp eventually solved the problem by hiring a team of geriatric nurses, a pair of six five identical twin Samoans, to assist Sonny both in the office and at home. The nurses were issued temporary employee badges, and at least one was usually found within arm's length of their charge at all times, caddying various electronics or occasionally Sonny himself to his next destination. Once Sonny's leg healed, the Samoans moved on, but by then he'd become obsessed with the concept of a personal assistant to perform a variety of tasks, adapting to learned preferences over time. Sonny was convinced he should be able to arise each morning, call for hot chai, and have the kitchen kettle immediately switch itself on; if he accidentally left his X Corp pullover by the front door the night before, he wanted it transferred by drone to his bedside by 6:00 a.m., so as to not suffer the indignity of walking downstairs without a layer of fleece to combat the frigid morning air. It had taken the Samoans nearly a week of daily attempts to learn exactly how he liked breakfast; once they mastered eggs over easy, he bemoaned their failure to execute requested amendments.

"Sometimes a man wants something different!" he howled, having usurped a program review to launch into a monologue of his latest personal frustrations. "Did I not state *very clearly* the night before, that I would like oatmeal and slippers by the door in the morning? And yet what do I get instead? Eggs, again. On a blue plate, the first thing I see when I wake, those disgusting, quivering little yolks. Fucking eggs. Fucking *idiots*."

Everyone had looked nervously around for the Samoans, who were both thankfully out of earshot, examining dried mango snacks in the break room. "If I had a machine, a real AI operating off a universal platform like I've been saying we need to develop," Sonny continued, "I wouldn't need to say *anything*. It would already know from my latest digestive results to offer something high fiber and to gauge from temperature readings that my feet would feel cold in the morning, and everything would have been executed to perfection. A dream! But because we're stuck with humans, with all their revolting errors, what do I get? Runny eggs and *cold feet*. Do you know how that feels, when you are recovering from a knee injury? Like the devil himself is pushing tiny hot knives into your soles, and I will no longer tolerate. . . ."

The latter half of the rant eventually led to the genesis of Slippers, the code name for the machine learning project soon fast-tracked to the highest priority levels within X Labs. Sonny proposed Slippers as the central "eyes and ears" of the home, though his long-term vision had it everywhere: at the gym monitoring posture via smartwatch, at the office in the laptop as a minutes recorder and fact-checker, and in the air via drone, tracking children on their way to school while scanning for activity from known pedophiles nearby. A perfect virtual assistant to manage every irksome detail of a busy person's life, its multitude of functions enabled by the design of Slippers as a pure software platform, compatible with any hardware host meeting its specifications, rendering it universally ubiquitous.

"This will be the greatest achievement of our lives," Sonny had boomed at the kickoff, which featured a Hawaiian barbecue and Elvis impersonators wearing blue suede moccasins. The crowd had been restless that day; even in those earlier times, the employee base was jaded about the idea of their ill-functioning hoverboard and X-ray vision goggle prototypes ever hitting the market. "You will tell your grandchildren about how you worked on Slippers."

Nate Singleton, an associate product manager with the look of a valedictorian, who'd reported to Kate at the time, had rolled his eyes. "Million to one this thing dies a quick and painful death," he predicted. "Come next season, Agrawal will be all gung ho again about his floating country on the sea. And any evidence of this little project will have been removed from the premises."

SINGLETON HAD BEEN THE EARLY FORESHADOWING OF A CERTAIN breed of cynical millennial, a tiresome species soon to invade the halls of the Labs in force, but he hadn't been entirely wrong. Two years later, while the pair of wireless devices Kate held in her palm were a direct result of Slippers, they hadn't come from the Labs. As soon as Sonny's tinkerings had given indications of wider commercial applications, they'd immediately caught the attentions of Ken Bullis, the company's chief brand officer, a marketer who spent the majority of his time marketing himself both internally and externally as a "product guy." Bullis was notorious for trawling the halls of X Corp, seeking out products to glom on to; though he rarely succeeded in sucking his targets into his direct sphere of command, he had acquired a reputation for a certain instinct, a nose for those projects most arousing to executive management and investors. Once Bullis began to inquire into Slippers, the project had immediately piqued the interest of the greater leadership team, setting off a round of political jockeying.

The ultimate victor of the beauty contest was the consumer hardware group, led by its general manager, Ron Fujihara, who claimed his team had previously reviewed a similar idea and thus had *jus primae noctis* to the entire initiative. Once Slippers passed concept review, Fujihara—usually accompanied by Bullis, who had attached himself to the project like a barnacle—made a quarterly trek to the Labs to pet Sonny's ego and present the latest updates. Though isolated geographically, Sonny was still a Friend of Sokolov, and thus an enemy best avoided. That morning, Ron had presented Sonny with a set of wrapped engineering samples, neatly placed in a gift bag with a bottle of d'Yquem.

"For the mad genius," he said, with a little bow of his head. Just low enough to be polite, but not enough to be mistaken for deference. "Unprecedented quality of video and sound. Set it up in your place; check it out. The total immersive experience."

Sonny accepted the offering with a bitter smile. Then, after both Fujihara and Bullis were confirmed as having exited the building, he strolled over to Kate's desk, where he unceremoniously dumped the opened samples. "Look at this junk," he complained. "They're calling it a home AI. Why don't they just say what it really is: a glorified video camera that plays music? As if anyone would actually think to use these as real assistants, ask these dumb bots any actual questions. . . . And then Fujihara has the nerve to suggest I put it in my own *house*! So that he can spy, no doubt. Like I wouldn't be able to find a hidden 'God mode' in the software if I spent five minutes searching. . . . This is what they've reduced my ideas to. The dream of an omnipresent platform leveraging existing hardware to track changes in breathing, heart rate, blood pressure . . . all of it, vanished. Can you imagine how many more people would have been saved from heart attacks or strokes, had Slippers been allowed to flourish at the Labs? But instead Fujihara gives us a *pair of balls*."

Kate picked up the mandarin-size spheres and rotated them in her hand, enjoying the cool sensation. They reminded her of the medicine balls she used to play with as a kid in Chinatown. Turning them over, she noticed an area of smoother dimpling near the bottom. "What's this?"

"Hmm? Oh, the wide-array microphone. And right on top, to the left, you'll find the camera. They're using the same so-called proprietary lens as the one that's on that smartphone. The X Phone. All those marketing people, and we couldn't think of another name? Another one of Fujihara's, of course. He's just like the Japanese, so polite to your face, and then sneaky sneaky behind your back. You ought to know, you're Chinese. Just remember World War II whenever he tries to make nice with you. I told his team, the whole point of Slippers was that you don't *need* to use special hardware, it's the beauty of the platform, but do these people listen? First they blow $3 billion on those awful self-driving cars that got shut down anyway, and now they're trying to jam the extra parts from their failure of a phone into whatever slot they can. And they say *we're* the wasteful ones!"

———

At the top of the attic's staircase was a window that faced the side garden, with a small ledge protruding from its bottom. Due to the steep slope of the ceiling, the window was small, and only during certain afternoon hours did it let in enough sun to illuminate the space. The contractor had argued against it altogether, contending that its expense wasn't worth its relatively low utility, but Kate had insisted on it, as well as the ledge. She loved windows. When Denny first took over the attic, Kate placed a souvenir from their first trip to

Japan—a small lacquered wood vase from Kyoto—on the shelf, along with an expensive blood orange–scented candle, as a sign of goodwill. Welcome to your haven, she'd meant for them to say. I hope you do good work.

Denny had never mentioned the presence of either, both of which had been favorites of hers, but Kate had always considered it too petty an act to remove the items. Now, she found they served as ample camouflage for Slippers. The bottom of the vase was just large enough to completely obscure one of the black balls, while the bit that peeked out behind the candle appeared congruous with its shadow. Each of the spheres held a full charge and supposedly would only need to be returned to their base stations after a week.

Seven days, she thought, was plenty of time.

CHAPTER 5

FRED

When Fred first received the offer to join Lion Capital, he'd been ecstatic.

He had begun to believe that he might never recover from a crucial miscalculation made upon graduation from business school, of accepting a job at a large multinational conglomerate back in the Bay Area instead of returning to finance. Harvard had done this to him, he realized, by stuffing his head with case studies highlighting seemingly well-worn and accessible paths to the executive office; the featured C-suiters often appearing in person the day of their discussions, to tout the reliable benefits of meritocracy and pay forward their insights. The men (and they were all men, except for the rare human resources case) were uniformly impressive in their executive gravitas, though once they spoke, rarely actually impressive. These titans of industry were just like him, Fred thought, only older. And luckier. And so a conviction was born that he, too, could one day with enough persistence make it atop such venerated ivory towers—not because he, Fred Huang, was particularly special but merely because everyone else was so shitty.

It was only after Fred had been at the conglomerate for a full two years, and wound his way through a variety of positions, that he understood the extent of his folly. The rotational program he'd been hired into—in which new graduates were cycled through a series of four-month stints throughout the company for three years—had been pitched as a feeding tube to corporate leadership, a high-velocity shortcut to upper management. Only twenty of the nation's top MBA graduates were hired into the program each year; given enough time, they'd all eventually feast on the mighty carcass of executive perks.

The awful secret Fred and his cohorts soon discovered, however, was that even twenty was far too high a number when considered against the fact that each year, on average, only two members of senior leadership departed the company; there weren't enough strokes or intern pregnancy scares to healthily trim the existing management ranks to even a fraction of the desired numbers. And so a truth quickly emerged that even at the very top—as constituents of the so-called cream of the crop, selectively hired by one of the most celebrated names of American industry—most of them would need to be left behind.

At first, Fred hadn't accepted his fate. He was from Harvard Business School, after all, the only graduate his rotational year. The CEO had gone to HBS, as had the CEO before him, the chairman of the board, and the CFO. Surely that held some weight against, say, the two floozies from Kellogg, not to mention the smattering of associates who'd attended even worse institutions. He'd scored a perfect 800 on the GMAT and been one of the key analysts at Morgan Stanley when the conglomerate had hired the bank to spin off its appliance business. In terms of pure statistics, Fred was far above most of his peers, though he was careful to appear humble. In his mind, his superior qualifications stood out as clearly as a pair of perfect breasts in a swimsuit contest: encased in a flimsy outfit but best worn with a modest smile.

Over time, however, Fred came to understand that he wasn't so special. Not when measured against competition like Marsha Epler, one of the Kellogg floozies who, as it turned out, possessed an undergraduate degree in civil engineering. Female engineers were considered the rarest of breeds within the conglomerate and were accordingly tracked by human resources like coveted prey. So Fred shouldn't have been surprised by Marsha's selection over him for a choice expatriate rotation in Shanghai, despite his own spoken fluency and aggressive lobbying with the general manager, a fellow HBS alum. But Fred *was* surprised, and then even more so when Marsha returned from the assignment four months later with universal accolades, having exceeded her basic duties as acting deputy by opening a yoga studio in the Shanghai office. The initiative, called Sino Stretches!, was heavily publicized on the corporate intranet, with a dedicated article and photo: Marsha front and center as conqueress, looking ecstatically limber in a crescent lunge, a group of joyful Asians posed behind her.

"We can all learn so much from different cultures," her pull quote pronounced, "as we live in an increasingly global world."

The pleasant faces were later revealed to have been a sham—like any typical Chinese, the Shanghai team had waited until Marsha was safely settled back at headquarters in Mountain View before they unleashed their full ire, and the feedback on her rotation was brutal. Marsha was unbearably rude, the employees complained, and demonstrated little cultural sensitivity. She frequently lost her shit in meetings, berating partners in a manner that made it impossible for them to save face, and accepted an important customer's feigned attempt to pay the bill at a dinner where it had been entirely assumed

Marsha would be picking up the check. The rotation was widely considered a disaster; it was the worst recorded feedback in the history of the Asia region.

The next promotion round, Marsha was elevated to director while Fred received a lateral shuffle to the dying printer division.

A week later, at a Q&A panel for the MBA program with the conglomerate's executives, a top-ranked Indian Institute of Technology graduate raised his hand.

"Can the company definitively state it is not deliberately limiting Asian and Indian hires in order to meet certain diversity standards?" he asked. A little thrill went up Fred's spine. The head of human resources, a nervous woman named Joy with a drab face, paled.

"We are committed as a company to the concept—the concept of equality," she stammered.

"Right," Rajesh said. "But some are more equal than others." He squared his shoulders and gazed about the silent room, but Fred had been unable to meet his eyes. That night, however, he began to format his résumé.

THE WEEKEND BEFORE HIS FIRST DAY AT LION, CHARLENE AR-ranged a dinner at a well-reviewed Asian fusion restaurant in North Beach. Though the evening was technically for Fred, the attendance mostly reflected her friends; he himself didn't have many at that point, the by-product of an extended career depression. When they arrived, he was quickly paired off with another husband, a freckled redhead named Simon Barnes with a month-old haircut. Simon was married to Sonya Kim, a former BCG consultant who'd gone to Stanford with Charlene and now hosted a regional morning cooking show; due to her minor celebrity and status as the group's first young mother, Sonya was considered by Charlene to be both her closest confidante and most formidable frenemy.

"Sonya only dates white guys," Charlene commented once, with a touch of distaste. "But they don't need to have anything else special about them. Her boyfriend right after college was a DJ, and the dude right after that, the one she thought she'd actually get married to, was an *insurance agent.*"

As Fred sat, Simon clapped his back and asked what he knew of Lion.

"Not much," Fred confessed. "Just that they're big in technology manufacturing in Taiwan. I think my parents actually know more about the company than I do."

Simon snorted good-naturedly. "That Wang dude sounds like a character."

Wang as in Lion's chairman and founder, Leland Wang—the rags-to-riches icon who'd built up the tech behemoth from the initial $24,000 he'd managed to save from the toy factory at which he'd worked twelve-hour days for nearly a decade. The company's culture was peppered with lore regarding Leland and his frugality: how he preferred to fly economy (substantiated with a vintage photograph of Leland flashing the thumbs-up sign on China Airlines); how he still pilfered extra packets of soy sauce and plastic utensils at restaurants; his commitment to walking the factory floors once a week at a minimum, often disguised, to spot pockets of waste and abuse. That Wang continued to engage in such behavior as regifting to colleagues complimentary packets of Tsingtao Beer playing cards during the holidays, all while simultaneously accepting a seat on Sotheby's Asia Advisory Board—an honor granted to only the most prodigiously spendy of collectors—was spun as a matter of principle and dedication.

"He as cheap as they say?" Simon asked.

"I've never met him."

"Ah!" Simon nodded eagerly, as if Fred had stated that he and Leland were, in fact, the closest of friends. "And you're going to be doing corporate venture, is that right? Lion Capital? Hot space. Rumor is X Corp's doubling their own fund size."

Fred was surprised at Simon's knowledge of the finance world. He had never spoken with him about work, assuming from Charlene's commentary the man's employment in some low remuneration industry—the sort where job-related chatter would only serve to highlight the disparity between their positions, embarrassing them both.

"Where you at these days?" Fred asked.

"Work wise? Still Warburg. Nothing changes for me but my age."

Warburg *Pincus*? Charlene, normally meticulous about documenting the follies and achievements of friends and acquaintances, hadn't mentioned he worked in private equity. Fred eyed Simon's clothing, starting with the black North Face jacket. There was no company or school affiliation printed on the sleeve or chest, and it was so old the fleece was gathered in mottled balls. "I didn't know Warburg had an office in San Francisco."

"Oh, it's minuscule. Where they shove all the undesirables." Simon helped himself to another portion of steamed cod, spilling a bit of sauce on his unremarkable sneakers (Nike Air Pegasus). "This fish is good, huh? Now I see why Sonya always makes us order it. I usually never get to try it because she bogarts it all."

He must be in investor relations, Fred thought. Or the less prestigious operations side. "What do you work on?"

"Investments," Simon said. A few seconds passed. "Same boring shit. So Lion, huh? You must be excited."

"What sector at Warburg? Do you have a card?" Fred knew he was coming off as unbearably nosy, but he was overwhelmed by curiosity.

Simon continued to ladle fish. "Healthcare." When Fred didn't respond, he burped and set down his utensils. He dug into his pocket and brought out a wallet (old, beat-up Tumi), and passed over a card, from which the two words leaped into Fred's vision as if emblazoned in bright red capital letters. *Managing Director.* "I split between the New York office and here," Simon said, anticipating the next question.

Later that night, in bed with Charlene asleep next to him, Fred realized Simon had been assuming the role he himself had presumed to be playing, that of the More Successful and Magnanimous Party, and was bathed in chagrin. After everything he had been through in his career—the punishing hours of investment banking, the detailed strategizing to gain acceptance to HBS, the intricate plotting to escape the conglomerate—that it all should come to this, to serve as a receptacle for such piteous compassion! He concentrated on deleting all traces of the interaction, and by the next morning he had successfully swept it from memory. He would see Sonya Kim only twice more before his divorce; he never saw her husband again.

Yet it was Simon Barnes who now floated back into his consciousness—his ruddy face and that shocker of a business card—as Fred sat facing his boss and the senior managing director of Lion Capital, Griffin Keeles, and informed him of his invitation to the Founders' Retreat.

"The Founders' Retreat," Griffin repeated, in the Geordie accent Fred theorized was the reason his boss had originally been hired. It was Leland Wang's greatest regret that he'd achieved wealth too late in life for his progeny to attend Harrow or Cheltenham and thus possess that greatest of status markers, a European accent; though desperate measures had since been taken to rectify the situation, with multiple semesters at a Swiss finishing institute, it was rumored that the two Wang siblings were still unable to wield a knife and fork simultaneously.

Griffin reclined in his white Aeron; Leland believed in a moderate relaxation of the purse when it came to office furniture, since employees were expected to keep long and efficient hours. "I went once, as you may recall. Before the DataMinx IPO. It was in Maui that year."

"Right." As if Fred would ever forget. DataMinx had been his deal, his board seat, but Griffin had pulled rank when the miraculous request arrived that year, descending in Fred's email inbox like manna from heaven, inviting precisely one Lion representative into attendance at the vaunted retreat. Fred had spent the entire week Griffin was gone working from home in a furious sulk, still in shock over the shamelessness of the coup.

Now, he could read Griffin's expression perfectly. The twist of the dry thin lips as the Brit attempted to hide his surprise while his brain chugged through a series of calculations; the struggle to avoid what was ultimately the unavoidable question. "How did you get invited?"

It was a well-publicized fact that the Founders' Retreat—the week-long bacchanal held each year in a rotating tropical destination by the venture firm Motley Capital—was notoriously stingy with its invites. For weeks after Jack's email, Fred had agonized over this precise complication; there was no way he could compel an invitation with just a simple email to Motley, even one summoning all the political goodwill of Lion Capital. The only Lion employee who could conceivably pull that off was Leland himself, but Leland had a son—a buck-toothed imbecile he was actively grooming for future leadership—and Fred didn't want to risk planting *that* idea in his liver-spotted head.

Don Wilkes, the founder and chairman of the venerated Motley, was a fellow business school alum, though it would only be an exercise in embarrassment to attempt to use this tenuous connection. There were thousands of HBS grads in the Bay Area but only one Wilkes, who had managed to sell his online-gaming start-up, Mirror-Stream, to Intel for $7 billion at the peak of the first dot-com bubble; it was unlikely that dropping the HBS name would serve to land Fred even a coffee meeting, much less an invite to what was called the "Sun Valley of Tech," where corporate chieftains and officials from fiefdoms with high Gini coefficients talked shop and made merry. In the last stages of desperation Fred had emailed Jack, baldly stating his predicament; Jack had followed up less than a day later with the coveted invitation.

"An acquaintance asked me as his guest," Fred replied. "Jack Hu."

Griffin steepled his fingers. "This is a very unusual request. Would you be representing Lion, or were you thinking of attending in more of a . . . personal capacity?"

"Lion. It's a compelling networking opportunity, and as our parent company is based in Taiwan, it makes sense to attend the year the retreat is in Bali. Jack is also very connected in Asia." That way the trip could at least be expensed, though Fred would have to pay out of pocket for business class. Erika's best friend at Saks was getting married in two months; the night she told him the news, she'd surprised him in bed with a firm hold on his crotch and a superbly detailed narrative of all the ways she'd yearned to be fondled as a young schoolgirl in Budapest. In the delirium of the moment, he'd blurted out an invitation to Bali. The fact that Erika's colleague was a) engaged despite having met her boyfriend just five months prior, b) twenty-seven, and c) flying Lufthansa First to South Africa for her honeymoon, meant there was no way Erika was going to be seated in the back of the plane on the long haul to Hong Kong, sandwiched between elderly Chinese clipping their nails into the aisle—not if she was bartering her continuing silence on the marriage front for the next few quarters.

Griffin gave a weak cough. "Isn't it unusual for you to be attending on your own?"

Fred knew Griffin was angling to be invited along, a disastrous outcome. Were he to come he would no doubt immediately posture himself at events as the most senior representative from Lion, sucking all the oxygen out of Fred's personal orbit.

"Why? You went by yourself."

"Yes, but that was due to strict rules dictated by Motley. Whereas in this instance, it appears as if the invitation is a little more flexible, no? Somewhat more informal. It can be odd in these situations, to turn up solo. One person can give off a bit of a gate-crasher vibe."

"I'm not technically going alone, as I'll be attending with Jack, who procured the invite. It could be seen as an aggressive move to push him to secure another—I'm not sure it would portray Lion in the most desirable light—but I'm sure I could find a way to ask." He let Griffin eye him with an air of wary optimism before he dropped the bomb. "I just hope Jack doesn't mention anything about it to Leland, of course. Since they both keep a residence at 740 Park. But who knows? Maybe they don't even know each other."

FRED LEFT GRIFFIN'S OFFICE IN A GOOD MOOD. HE FETCHED HIS jacket and walked outside to the curb, to wait for Stanley. His father had insisted on picking him up for lunch, even though Fred repeatedly asked if he could get Stanley from the house instead.

"I'm still walking three miles every day," Stanley had said on the phone that morning. "I take the long route to the park from the house, speed walk over the freeway overpass, and then loop all the way around. When was the last time you exercised that much?"

At the restaurant, some faux-upscale American business pub Stanley selected that accepted his Entertainment 2-for-1 entrée coupon, Fred was better able to take measure of his father's condition. He was wearing his favorite sweatshirt, a dingy gray crewneck Fred remembered from high school. It looked looser than he recalled, but ever since he'd started seeing his father more often, it'd been harder to track gradual physical changes. "How are you feeling? How's your weight?"

"Oh. I'm okay." Stanley looked down at his arms and pushed up the sleeves of his sweatshirt. The ribbed edges barely grazed his skin. "Though you can see, I'm still too skinny."

"Did you start chemo yet?"

"I will. I'm waiting for Uncle Phillip to see me and give his *analysis*." Stanley pronounced the word with distinct reverence.

Uncle Phillip was actually not Stanley's uncle at all but his second cousin, a son of a distant relative who happened to live in the Bay Area; Stanley called him Uncle because it was what Fred and Kate knew him as. Phillip was the head of oncology at UCSF and a frequent speaker on the medical conference circuit; he commanded the eternal respect of his Asian elders because he had attended Johns Hopkins and lived in a huge mansion in Hillsborough. Fred wondered how many anxious phone calls from relatives of relatives and friends of parents he'd been summoned to deal with over the years.

"Did you get the book I asked you to order?"

The title had been some oversize tome on eating to beat cancer, a best seller that Fred had dismissed as utter crock as soon as he clicked the link in Stanley's email. "Not yet. I will soon."

"That's all right." Stanley picked at his fried chicken, separating the crisped batter from the meat underneath. "Kate already read it and highlighted the pages she thought I should pay attention to."

"That's great Kate has so much time." Fred fought a swell of irritation. He considered mentioning that he had been busy, engaged in important activities like getting invited to the Founders' Retreat, but Stanley wouldn't know what that was anyway, leading to an even more frustrating conversation. "And? What did you learn?"

"So much! I'm changing my diet. Trans fats, red meat, sugar— these are all poisons." Stanley pointed to the right side of his plate, at the pile of discarded chicken skin. "This is what was killing me. Palm oil."

"Right. Great. I'm glad to hear."

"I'm also peeing almost thirty times a day. Urine is a toxin that collects in your liver. The more you flush it out, the cleaner your body."

"Thirty times a day sounds extreme."

"I'm trying to go three times an hour. Mary agrees. She says it is one of the foundational elements of healing, along with meditation."

Jesus. A large knot had formed between his shoulders; Fred reached behind his neck and began to knead. "Mary is not a medical practitioner. Does she think she's a doctor because her sister performs laser facials? It's reckless for her to be giving you advice and even more irresponsible for you to be listening to it. Please, *please* review everything she suggests with your actual doctor, or at least Uncle Phillip. Or better yet, ignore it altogether."

"One of her friends had pancreatic cancer, much worse than mine," Stanley said. He'd deliberately ignored the dig at Mary, Fred noticed. "Mary's friend, she was huge, so, so fat. Then, she meditated five hours every day at the temple with the master, and now she is healed. And *thin*! Mary invited her to lunch just last week. She came all the way to my house, even though she lives in Millbrae. She just climbed Machu Picchu."

"Meditation, great." Fred tore the crust from his baguette and used the soft innards to sop up the last remnants of gravy on his plate. He felt Stanley's eyes on him.

"She also eats many vegetables. Not too much fruit. Fruit has a lot of sugar. As does bread."

"Mmm."

"We are going to see the temple master later. If I'm lucky, because I am already thin, I might heal even faster than Mary's friend. Because she was fat before, very unhealthy. Do you remember I asked to go to Wells Fargo after this? I told you, I have to go today."

"I remember," Fred lied. "We'll go."

The waitress arrived with the bill. She was college age, with a light sprinkling of acne; Fred had dismissed her as too basic as soon as they'd been seated. "Can I get you gentlemen anything else?"

Fred reached for the check. "No, we're fine." His eyes landed at her breasts, which were surprisingly good. The name tag read *Dana*.

She gestured with her chin toward the chicken skins. "You didn't like your meal? You want me to get something else for you to eat?"

"He's fine," Fred said. "He just wants to live forever."

"I do!" Stanley exclaimed. "My son is right! Though I wish he would eat more vegetables!"

"Your father is so cute," Dana said.

When the check was returned Fred saw she'd taken Stanley's entrée off the bill. "Comped by management" was the note beside it. Strangers were always charmed by Stanley's surface helplessness, a phenomenon that used to annoy Fred but which over time he had grown to accept, even approve of. He'd learned it was entirely possibly to carry deep resentment toward a person while at the same time experiencing genuine pleasure over their public adulation; it was even considered normal in some circles, especially if the person in question was family. Now that Fred himself was over forty he understood that it was best for a man to keep at least two faces: one for at home, through which he could vent his accumulated interior frustrations, and one for the public, which reflected none of them. Someone like Stanley—who had at one point demanded that an elderly relation who owed him money get down on her hands and knees to bow to him in apology—needed the faces more than most; even now, Fred could still clearly envision his great-aunt, her rough gray hair arranged in a low bun centered on her neck, as she knelt on the floor. Up until then she had been one of his favorite babysitters, a lenient woman who, each time he saw her, had pieces of wrapped moon cakes stashed for him in her pockets; after that day, he never saw her again.

INSIDE THE BANK, STANLEY MADE HIS WAY TO THE SAFETY DEPOSIT box line. "I want you to come with me," he said.

"Why?" Fred had planned on settling into one of the lobby's stuffed chairs to type out emails while Stanley completed whatever business he had. He'd already spotted a message from Griffin, and from the title alone (Industry Engagement: Roles and Responsibilities), he could already predict the content would be marvelously passive aggressive. "You need some help or something?"

"I want you to see my goodies. Find something for yourself."

"You just told me at lunch, you're not going anywhere."

Stanley blinked, unmoving. Fred sighed.

Inside the cramped beige cubicle, they stood over a rectangular metal tube. Stanley slid back the lid and revealed dozens of silk zip pouches in Chinatown patterns. He began to open them, scattering jewelry and the occasional ingot. "You can choose," he said, as gold and silver slid across his palms. "Anything you like. Maybe something you saw on me before? I can't wear anything now; the metals upset the balance of elements."

"I really don't know about this." The whole interaction was making Fred uncomfortable. The only jewelry he could recall on Stanley was a series of solid gold rings he'd switched off between on the middle finger of his right hand, but he hadn't seen his father wear one since the divorce. Fred's favorite as a child—the one with an onyx inlay—had left a clearly marked oval gash under his right eye for nearly a month when he was a teenager, after Stanley struck him for denting the Ford Windstar. He'd snuck the car out one evening when his parents were away at a wedding, to meet some friends for dinner; unaccustomed to the relatively large size of the minivan, he'd struck a pole backing out of his spot in front of California Pizza Kitchen. He'd thought he'd gotten away with it when a week went by and his parents still hadn't noticed; then one day he'd returned home from school and encountered Stanley waiting in the garage, his face mottled with rage.

"Please. I don't want these to sit here forever."

"All right, all right." Fred began to sift.

"Oh! Look at this one." When Stanley was excited, his accent became more pronounced. He slid a watch from a dark velvet sheath, a metallic blue face with a heavy bezel, attached to a chunky bracelet in stainless steel. "You know what this is? A Rolex! I bought it at a very good pawnshop in Las Vegas that I found with Mary. There are very excellent deals in that store, many treasures."

As a rule Fred didn't wear watches. In his world they were a marker of status, an arms race in which he occupied the relative space and standing of a minor island nation; only by opting out entirely did he feel there was any chance of saving face. There was always the strategy of donning a cheap model like Lloyd Blankfein—the chairman of Goldman Sachs who infamously wore a Swatch—but only the chairman of Goldman could get away with that since everyone already knew the size of his balls anyway.

Fred took the watch and compared it to the time on his phone. The second hand swept along, a sign of a genuine Rolex. He set it down gently.

"You like it, don't you?" Stanley asked. He gazed at the watch, his face impassive. Fred looked at him.

"Okay, I'll take it." He could always show it to Erika for an assessment, he thought, though he'd be annoyed if she made too much out of it being entry-level.

Stanley patted him on the shoulder. He looked at his phone. "Your mother is here."

Linda was already in the waiting area, drinking with distaste from a cup of complimentary coffee. She craned her neck until she saw Fred; she generally refused to meet Stanley unless at least one of the children were present.

"You should have joined us for lunch," Stanley said.

"I was busy." Linda viciously stirred at the brown liquid. "Did you get your will done yet?"

"*Ma,*" Fred protested. It was already late afternoon, and the bank's lobby was busy; he was certain that the people around them were eavesdropping on their conversation, judging him for his strange family.

"Not yet, not yet," Stanley was still smiling. "I'm having Fred pick pieces from the safe today. Kate will come next week. You should visit too."

Linda shook her head. "Stanley, listen to me. You need to do your will. Why won't you just take care of it now, especially with your health? You don't think at our age any one of us could go, anytime? I just updated my own last year. Living trust, to avoid probate. You should do the same."

"I will, I will."

"Remember our children. Our children are what will live on of us, of you. "

"Of course," Stanley demurred. "Should we look at the box now? You can have whatever you like."

"I don't want anything," Linda said shortly.

"Please?" he wheedled. "You don't have to take, just spend time."

"I don't think your wife would be very happy to know you are sharing the contents of your safety deposit box with me."

"Is that what you're worried about?" His face relaxed. "Mary is such an openhearted person. She would never mind if you took something. She is very generous."

Linda snorted. "Generous with what?" She paused. "Your money?"

"Linda. You are too suspicious. But I know it's only because you care about me." A strangled noise emerged from Linda's throat; Stanley either didn't hear or ignored it. "Mary is very frugal with herself, but with other people so kind, so giving," he continued. "She even used her own money to buy me Chinese herbs, because she wants so much for me to heal. Very expensive medicine too; I saw the prices! And she meditates for the cancer to go away, every morning and night."

Linda shook her head. "You two go. That way when your wife asks, you can say I never went anywhere near the safe."

Stanley sighed, defeated. He shuffled toward the back and waited in line for assistance. Since they had left the vault, he had to go through the entire sign-in process again. From behind, his pants looked even baggier, and Fred was reminded of how ill he was. He wondered if Stanley had done an internet search on pancreatic cancer as he had, at least a dozen times, and seen the sobering survival rates: fewer than 20 percent still standing after just one year, only 10 percent remaining after five. At the very least, Fred thought, Stanley should last until five—he'd always been very lucky. Fred saw Linda look in the same direction. She bit her lip, the same way she had when she visited Stanley in the hospital. The diagnosis had just been confirmed then; he'd been kept in the room for observation overnight, a concern over low blood pressure.

"Is he starting chemotherapy?" she asked.

"I think he's talking with Uncle Phillip first, for advice." Linda nodded. She found Phillip's qualifications comforting. "Why are you pressing him so hard on the will?"

She looked surprised. "I thought you would be interested. You're the one who asked me about it. If I had a copy."

Fred flushed. He had been browsing Woodside real estate listings, dreamily cobbling together the enormous down payments necessary in his head, when his mother happened to call. "I was emotional."

Linda remained tight-lipped. She didn't care for emotional responses.

The words came out in a rush. "I mean, he might have said something before. That me and Kate, we'd get something like $2 or $3 million. Each." An excellent sum, especially given that he'd always assumed Stanley to be a mediocre money manager. Fred had advised him years back to place the majority of his retirement savings into an age-targeted index fund, but he had no idea if Stanley had heeded the advice. Still, he must have made some smart choices, if there was $5 million in liquid assets . . . maybe closer to $6 or $7 million, if Stanley meant to leave Mary something. The old man had done well for himself after all, in the end—had proven his mettle, when it most mattered. If Fred did buy a house, it was going to be one he could live in for the rest of his life (meaning a fantastically prestigious address). He would teach his children about how their grandfather had worked to give them this home, the ultimate legacy.

He began to explain these lofty thoughts to Linda, but abruptly ceased when he saw her expression. He cleared his throat. "So . . . yeah. What do you think?"

She took a deep gulp of coffee. "I do not comment on your father's financial fitness. My information is not up-to-date. And of course, you are the one who was saying not to ask him any more about the will."

"I just don't want to stress him," Fred said quickly. He could feel his cheeks burning. "Of course," he then added, as he recalled what he was supposed to say in situations like these, "ideally he'd spend everything he has. Have fun, indulge himself. Buy a fancy car, go on vacation, enjoy some luxuries. That would be for the best."

Linda's eyes widened. "Oh? And who do you think gets to go on all the vacations with him? And drive the cars and keep all the nice things, after? Good to hear you have so many ideas for how Mary can enjoy your inheritance!"

"Well, it's his money, isn't it?"

"Most of it I earned for him, remember that! I was married to your father for thirty-four years. How long has he been married to Mary? Eight? Nine? You think that is enough to deserve half of everything?"

Half? That was news. Fred registered a quick bolt of alarm, before swallowing it. Stanley was at the front of the line now, looking back at them with a hopeful expression.

"He wants to spend time with you," Fred said. "You could just hang out. So what if Mary makes a fuss? He has all the power in that relationship, anyway. Remember how she wanted to move her sister in with them, and he wouldn't let her? And remember how when they got married, he went and got that PO box at the post office? So that all his bills and financial statements would go there and she couldn't snoop or find out anything."

Linda stood up. "This coffee is very bad," she announced. "The milk is old. I'm going to McDonald's for their senior cup. Only twenty-five cents."

"Don't you think Dad can handle Mary?" Suddenly Fred desperately wanted to hear his mother's confirmation. "He's not like those other old cowering Chinese men whose wives call all the shots. You know that underneath it all, he's a coldhearted bully. Remember how he was growing up? He can manage her."

The look Linda eventually gave him was a mixture of impatience and pity. "Your father's a fool," she said, and left.

CHAPTER 6

LINDA

WHAT IS CONCIERGE ROMANCE?

As an elite member of Tigerlily Deluxe, you now have privileged access to one of our most exclusive services: Concierge Romance. Concierge Romance works directly with you, the client, to understand your romantic goals and how they can best be achieved.

Tigerlily is one of the world's leading dating destinations, with more than twenty-five million members in over one hundred countries. For some clients, navigating this can be overwhelming and time-consuming. Here are some ways Concierge Romance can help!

INSIGHTS FROM EXPERTS. Often, those who are repeatedly "unlucky in love" are seeking a relationship ideal that may not be the best fit for their current life stage and situation. A complimentary consultation with one of our Concierge experts can provide valuable insight and direction.

EVER WONDERED HOW ATTRACTIVE YOU REALLY ARE? An accurate comprehension of one's physical allure has been scientifically proven to carry many benefits, including higher levels of satisfaction with one's choice of partner and increased sexual drive. However, family and friends may not always present a balanced view. At Concierge Services, we employ an expert panel to conduct our assessments, led by the former hiring manager of executive assistants at one of South Korea's top chaebols. We provide not only an objective ranking of one's attractiveness but also an action plan for improvements and neglected opportunities.

FINANCIAL PLANNING. Whether you're seeking increased monetary stability or a soul mate to share in the rewards of your success, having one's finances in order is an important step on the path to happiness and prosperity. Our team includes former investment professionals from some of the world's largest hedge funds and private equity firms, including TPG and Bridgewater Associates. At Tigerlily, we are uniquely qualified to help you plan for both your romantic and financial futures.

CURATION. Let our Concierge team present you with a curated list of matches, based on the results of our patented personality assessments and algorithms. Combined, our team has thousands of years of experience in the expert field of matchmaking.

YOUR IMAGINATION IS THE LIMIT! The above are only some of the ways in which Tigerlily's Concierge team can help guide you on your journey to romance. We're available 24/7, and no request is too small or difficult. Our joy is to bring you pleasure.

Linda made the call on impulse, after yet another failed match—this one with Andy Yu, a retired widower whose much-touted Ivy League education turned out to be an associate degree from community college and a few audited courses in asian studies at Columbia. On the phone, Linda declined most of the services the Concierge representative attempted to push (no way was she was giving out her Social Security number to a stranger), but she did submit to an in-person meeting the following week, at a local café. The consultant—or at least her name, Angela Lee—was Asian, which was a relief. Whenever Linda considered the divulgence of the personal details of her romantic life to a stranger, pangs of mortification began to creep and she was struck by an overwhelming desire to cancel; she knew the required disclosures would be nearly impossible, were the consultant Caucasian. White people operated by an entirely foreign set of standards. They thought love and happiness were an individual birthright, regardless of how unrealistic one's expectations might be. They believed that they all deserved secure retirements with luxury vacations and the best medical care, no matter how many financially stupid decisions they'd made earlier in their lives. And when they were Linda's age and got divorced and then remarried, they invited everyone over for Christmas and pretended it was one big happy family, referring to their new spouse's adult children and grandchildren as their very own, which was simply delusional.

The meeting with Angela Lee began with the usual icebreakers: Linda's past, what she did every day, what she felt hadn't worked in her marriage, what she was now looking to find. She dispensed with the questions easily, having perfected the answers long ago, for deployment with nosy friends and neighbors. Big family, lots of siblings, little attention from her parents growing up, which is why she chose to have only two children herself. Her idea of a perfect morning was gardening, a quick check of her investments, and a leisurely visit to the farmers' market, in that order. Her marriage had collapsed because her husband didn't have the intelligence to understand how dense he truly was; she now sought a partner who at least knew his own limitations, with a healthy enough ego that he would ask for assistance when necessary.

Angela typed her notes on a laptop, which she then tucked into an oversize Louis Vuitton tote. "Very good," she said.

"Are we done?" Linda asked. She rather liked the girl, whom she figured to be Malaysian or Indonesian-Chinese. She had a friendly, asexual vibe, like someone who often attended church. If there was extra time, Linda wanted to learn more details, like her age and college and marital status. She could then compare those statistics against Kate's.

"Almost. Linda—I meant to ask, have you ever considered a more remote relationship? With someone located farther from you?"

"You mean he would live far away?" That sounded suspect. Had she really already exhausted the entire supply of available Chinese men in the area? Who on earth was Shirley Chang gallivanting with all the time then? Koreans? "I don't understand how that would work."

"Well, we do live in a connected world. And hopefully any good prospect wouldn't stay distant forever." Angela leaned forward and smiled. "The idea is, by widening up your geographical preferences, we could find an even greater range of potential partners."

"Aren't there already enough nearby? I want someone with a similar background." Everyone knew that the best Chinese immigrants of their generation were settled in California, and mostly the Bay Area. There were some in Los Angeles, but then you ran the risk of ending up with some sleazy import/exporter. And Linda had no intention of being matched with some grocery store operator in, say, Reno.

"I completely understand, and we can definitely keep your matches limited to a twenty-five-mile radius. I just had the impression from our short conversation that you might find the traditional model of courtship, of going out for a series of dates in public . . . a little outdated. You appear to be a woman who hates to waste time."

Linda nodded. This was true.

"And I also thought that you might prefer a more private scenario, one where you could speak with a match several times before meeting in person. Some of our more discreet clients prefer this route."

"So . . . we talk on the phone?"

"Or your computer. Video chat. So you could see as well as hear each other."

"I don't like those. My daughter uses it, and the video is always fuzzy. Sometimes the picture is upside down and I can't turn it back over."

"My goodness, of course that would be frustrating. I do believe our app would be much easier to use. We specifically developed it with our senior clients in mind. Would you like me to help you through the install? We can do it now."

Linda hesitated. She'd heard variations of this exact promise before over the years, in regards to a myriad of technology-related matters. They always ended the same way, with Fred or Kate wringing his or her hands and drawing deep breaths, while Linda doggedly attempted to replicate the steps for connecting to the wireless network. She had secretly liked it when society's technological progress had outpaced her own mother's capabilities; she took satisfaction in the old woman's furious helplessness when confronted with fast-moving escalators and bleeping credit card machines. But Linda's mother had been a terrible parent, a cruel matriarch who pitted her children against one another in a never-ceasing campaign for control. Linda wasn't like that. Why, then, did her children treat her so much in the same way?

Across from her, the nice Asian girl with the face of a Mormon was handing back her phone. "Try it out," Angela said. "I've already populated it with the matches I identified for you. Tell me that isn't simple to use."

Linda made a tentative selection, and then another. Amazingly, the right screens appeared to be cropping forward, the correct results. She began to go faster, with confidence.

Until finally a photo of a man appeared, and she thought: *easy.*

———————

Out of all of Angela's selections, Linda's favorite was Winston Chu. Like her he was Chinese-American, having immigrated to the United States in the early '60s. They were each the oldest sibling of families that had produced far too many children, and both had endured decades of martyred suffering in their marriages before ultimately seeking divorce. When they spoke, it seemed as if they could start on any topic, immediately find common ground, and leap to the next.

To her surprise, Linda found she didn't miss the lack of in-person interaction. Wasn't video chat close enough to face-to-face—in fact, the very definition of it? She saw how Kate and Fred spoke with their partners, their eyes glued in the direction of their phones. At least she and Winston looked at each other when they talked, made eye contact as they relayed the details of their lives. It felt good to share all that she'd accomplished with someone who was actually interested, and Winston was gratifyingly impressed by each unfurled achievement— the triumphs that her own children considered so ordinary. That he was currently overseas, working on temporary assignment, only served to lend their relationship an air of safe convention—they would of course be together in person, if not for the distance.

After a few weeks, they were speaking twice a day: his evening and her morning, and then his morning and her night. It was a routine they both enjoyed and never broke, and when there was nothing at the moment for either to discuss, they were content to exist in companionable silence. Linda brought the phone with her to the garden, where she set it on top of a stool and on speaker; she cut ripe persimmons from her tree to the occasional sound of Winston's typing. Each night she carried her laptop to bed and at the end of their video conference simply rolled over and fell asleep. She discovered she no longer feared the sounds of the evening.

Winston and Linda had enjoyed sublime conversations for nearly two months—talks that she considered the most satisfying and fulfilling of her life's recent memory—before he asked her for money.

THE REQUEST EMBARRASSED HIM TERRIBLY, WINSTON SAID. AS Linda knew from their conversations, he'd been entirely self-sufficient since the age of fourteen, when he'd been shipped off by his parents to Hong Kong to live with relatives he'd never before met. It had been his one chance to escape Communism, a doom of otherwise wasting away his teenage years working in the steel mills, melting down pots and pans for the manufacture of low-quality construction supports for structures that, luckily for most of the planned inhabitants, were never occupied. Once Winston was in Hong Kong, the plan was for him to study and gain acceptance to a top school in the United States and piece together the funds to cross over. He could then send for the rest of the family.

Winston's aunt—his father's sister—had greeted him at the door with a glassy-eyed stare he'd only decades later been able to identify as indication of an opioid addiction; the two adult cousins his parents espoused as wells of career guidance turned out to be unemployed and addicted to gambling. As it turned out, the entire family didn't

work, subsisting on small handouts from their grandparents; the day
Winston arrived from Guangzhou, his grandfather shakily informed
him there was just enough in the budget to support an additional
mouth for one meal per day. For everything else, he'd have to fend
for himself.

Winston eventually found a line job hand assembling artificial
flowers at a factory not significantly less hazardous than the steel mill
he'd fled, though at least the odds were lower for cadmium poisoning.
The glue used to attach the silk rose heads to their stems did turn out
to be mildly toxic: within a few months the coughing fits started,
and in a year he had his first eye infection. He was given a half day
off and a referral to the company doctor, but even at the tender age
of sixteen Winston knew better than to relinquish his earnings back
to the very parties who'd maimed him to begin with. He visited a local herbalist instead, who charged one-fifth of the doctor's quote and
prepared a small sachet with foul-smelling leaves to steep and place
over his eyes, with strict instructions not to move for at least an hour
after application.

"You need to find another job," the medicine man advised. "You
can only do this for another year. Maybe two, because you're young."

Nearly nine more would pass before Winston made it to the
United States, and what followed was a cloudier version of the im-
migration saga shared by Linda and her peers. He earned a degree
from Baylor, not Berkeley as originally planned, and bought a home
in Houston instead of moving to San Francisco. His job as a systems
engineer at Exxon provided a steady salary, but it was barely enough
to counter a stay-at-home wife and two daughters whose private high
school tuition ate through savings like a ravenous weed.

When his youngest daughter started at Yale, Winston took a job
in Lebanon as the on-site technical administrator for Black Sun, the
military contractor. The gig paid 40 percent more than Exxon, and
housing was free—a welcome bonus, as he was now divorced and had

relinquished the house to his ex. Even meals were paid for, since the company didn't want employees wandering off campus.

Now there was an issue with Black Sun—some uncovered violation dating years back in relation to Iranian trade embargoes—and sanctions had been imposed. Winston didn't particularly understand what that meant or its significance for the company's bottom line; all he really knew, or cared, was that his accounts were now frozen. Tuition for the next semester at Yale was due in a few days, and after cobbling together the money he was able to access, he was still thousands short. Winston was fairly certain the school would grant him an extension—surely a top-tier academic institution like Yale wouldn't be so cruel as to throw out a hard-working young woman and blight her future irrevocably for something as minute as a few late payments—but it was also a risk that, as a responsible father, he couldn't bear to place onto his own blood.

"But I understand," he said, "if you cannot provide assistance."

And the silence had hung, stinking like a dead fish.

The morning after his request, Linda wired the money. She didn't give the full amount but merely a third, figuring her generosity should spur Winston's family and friends for the other portions. Earlier in her life $9,000 would have felt crippling, though parting with the sum was still painful. As it left her account it was as if she had discovered a hole in herself, one of those vestigial organs she never used but which until then had always been there, holding its place in the layers of her body.

She forced herself to recall how much more Winston had endured compared with her. Linda's struggles in the United States seemed so significant compared to the cushioned lives she had provided her children, but with Winston she was reminded of the fact that there were many layers of poverty and poor fortune beneath her own, stratas that in Asia seemed to have no bottom. She felt fortunate she could part with the money without serious consequence, and it really wouldn't be missed in any significant fashion before Winston paid it back. Linda sent a note when it had been transferred, and the phone rang minutes later.

"Thank you so much," Winston said. "I cannot begin to describe how this event shames me. My whole life I worked hard for everyone else, but does anyone care or remember? Why didn't someone tell me that raising a family in a rich country could bring such agony? My ex-wife, whom I supported her entire life, to whom I gave nearly everything when we divorced, all because I didn't want her to suffer for refusing to work all those years . . . you know what she says to me now, when bills come? *Winston, I will not pay a cent*, she says. Because she thinks I should pay for everything, even though we're no longer married! She thinks I should pay for her clothes, her car, her insurance, and of course the girls think so too! You know that when they were younger, they wanted to play tennis? All my life I thought I might one day want to learn, but I told myself I would wait until retirement, I didn't want to spend the money in case my family needed it. But when Tina and Cindy asked, I said yes, of course! And I went with them to every lesson and ran around the courts picking up all the balls, so the coach didn't waste any of my money. I wanted him to spend his time teaching! By the end of each lesson, I was panting, sweating so much, I was already past fifty, after all. My doctor told me, *Winston, please stop!* But still I did it, every week, for all of their high school. But what for? Nobody remembers. Now the only bright light in my life is that I finally met my soul mate, the woman I should have spent all my years with."

Linda squirmed. She was in the kitchen, unwrapping the packet of hand-cut fat rice noodles she would later use in a seafood stir-fry. As a general rule she didn't approve of excessive pronouncements of affection. While she had come to accept that Winston's flowery declarations—usually peppered with the more complex English he had acquired since his arrival on American soil—were a flourish he was proud of, she still preferred the soliloquies be at least kept more succinct.

This last bit, for example, had gone on far too long. Thinking he'd reached the climax, she'd finally released a sympathetic *mmm* she'd been holding in, only to have him work himself up on another tangent. The only part she'd found of any particular interest was the bit about his family. From what Linda had gleaned so far, Winston's ex-wife and children were all cut from the same cloth: lazy spoiled brats who depended on him for too much, and too often. But so far, he'd only referred to his daughters in angelic terms.

"You know what they say," she ventured. "Children can be a blessing and a curse."

"Except for you, my whole life is a curse. A curse to be punished and to give until I have no more."

"Yes." Linda unwrapped the wild shrimp she'd purchased that morning for an outrageous sum, sniffing it. "My children, they have been such disappointments lately. My son is divorced, and my daughter, did I tell you? Her husband doesn't even have a job! Not a real one, at least. Tell me, Winston, what is an entrepreneur? I used to think it was someone who worked hard all day at their business, going in early and staying late, like the Koreans with their dry cleaning. Until now I didn't know that there was this whole other kind, where you get to sit at home in front of the computer all day, doing God knows what! You know that every day, my son-in-law takes a break and leaves the house to drive to a special coffee shop? He and my daughter talk so much about this coffee, how it's organic and much, much tastier than any other kind.

"So finally yesterday I decide to go buy myself a cup, because I don't want to be so stubborn and not try new things. And, Winston, I swear, the coffee tasted exactly the same as McDonald's. But smaller! And even worse, it took half an hour to come out and cost $6. I was almost late meeting my friend Yvonne for lunch. But when

I say anything to my daughter—about how maybe they should brew their own coffee at home, since after all they only have one income— she treats me like the enemy. When I'm the only person who will tell her what everyone else really thinks!"

"Oh, I can't imagine my daughters would ever marry someone unemployed," Winston said. "Tina and Cindy, they are both very smart, beautiful too. Did I tell you that on our last trip to Shanghai the hotel concierge thought Tina looked just like Fan Bingbing?"

"You did." Linda pickled her voice slightly, to warn Winston off from recounting the anecdote, which she'd found rather unbelievable upon first telling. She had never seen photos of his children, but neither Winston nor his ex were particular beauties, and only by marrying another race had Linda ever seen an ugly Chinese woman negate the gravitational pull of her own genetic forces and pop out an attractive daughter. Winston had also violated a key tenet of polite conversation, that one should never compliment his own children when the other party had maligned her own.

Winston took the hint or had simply exhausted the topic. "How's your ex-husband?"

"Oh. He's doing fine." Linda had completely forgotten about Stanley the past few days, though it might have been closer to a week. If this was thirteen years ago, Stanley's illness would have consumed every waking moment and invaded her sleep; she would have been expected to conduct her daily activities in a state of forced optimism and quiet mourning. Now Linda barely thought of Stanley at all, except for when she heaped more greens onto her plate at mealtimes. She struggled to recall what news Kate had told her, the last time they spoke. "I think he will begin chemotherapy soon. We may have divorced, but I don't wish for him to suffer," she added piously.

"At our age, health is truly most important," Winston said.

"Yes, without a doubt. Please take care of yourself."

"Only if you do. I would die if something happened to you. Linda, I love you."

She couldn't say it back. It was too much a departure for comfort; the words would ring false, and she knew she'd relive them, wincing, the rest of the day. Instead, she told Winston she couldn't wait to see him and hung up. The vegetables needed blanching.

CHAPTER 7

KATE

Halfway through the first semester of his senior year at Stanford, on a prematurely cold November evening, Denny McCullough went out for a late dinner, some birthday party of a friend of a friend, then drove back to his apartment off campus. There'd been nothing remarkable about the night, except that it was his first time being social in a while. He'd been holed up in his room for weeks, slaving over a final project for his computer systems class, and the outing at a local Japanese restaurant had been a welcome relief, a chance to blow off some steam. On the way home, at the respectable hour of midnight, the thought crossed Denny's mind that the lights flashing in his mirror might actually be signaling *to him*; he pulled over just to be safe, and the cop had ended up being kind of a jerk, one of those real "getting off on authority" types, and that's how he ended up with a DUI.

Denny had been barely twenty-one, in trouble with the law for the first time in his young life, and terrified of the consequences. Would he be kicked out of school? Assigned a parole officer? The computer science department at Stanford was hardly the sort of place one went for institutional knowledge of police procedures, and there was no one around to share what would surely have been the comforting knowledge that a DUI would be no big deal on his record—a distinction achieved by more than a million other Americans that year. He paid a hefty fine and was required to attend classes where the widows of drowsy truck drivers and parents of deceased teenagers lectured and wept. He shunned the bar and party scene and began to frequent the gym, running miles on the treadmill during the less-populated evening hours as he slowly reshaped his body. Without the smoothing effects of alcohol, he found himself unable to tolerate certain acquaintances whose annoying quirks he used to absorb with ease, and for a while his social landscape altered so much that he assumed there was no going back to his life pre-DUI. He was the new Denny now, older, leaner, sadder; while he might live a less thrilling existence overall, at least he knew he would never again end up arrested and in the back of a cop car, which to him was a worthwhile trade-off.

Of course if Denny had actually possessed the emotional maturity he assumed he did, he would have known that this was just a passing period. That very soon the same friends whose calls he was currently screening would shortly reenter his life; that in fact in just a few months he'd once again be downing sake bombs at the cheap Japanese restaurant on University Avenue and at the end of the night forcing down ten California rolls to soak up the alcohol before driving home. But Denny didn't know, and the phase lasted just long enough for him to turn down an uncertain job as the ninth engineer at a small start-up and go work for Cisco instead.

"And do you want to know what that start-up was? A little outfit called Google."

Denny was reciting the tale for Erika, who had never heard it before, and Fred, who Kate was pretty sure had. The last line was the mic drop, the bit that was supposed to make listening to everything that came before worth it, and as they were in the presence of outside company, Kate made the effort to appear captivated. But she was so tired.

Kate blamed the emotional surge immediately following Stanley's diagnosis for the impulse that had spurred her to call Fred; *we ought to get together*, she said, *and spend some quality time.* She had felt good when she extended the invitation, forgotten all about it for the interim period, and then frantically regretted it the day of. If only she'd bothered to check her calendar and caught it just a few days earlier! Then she could have canceled and would already be at home, braless and in pajamas. Instead, they were at some bougie restaurant, the sort that specialized in serving many small plates half an hour apart, that people without children (like her brother) thought nothing of booking. She had kicked off her right shoe, which pinched her big toe, sometime after the seventh course. Now she stealthily hunted for it, waving her bare foot as she tried to avoid touching the floor.

"Really? Google." From her breathless focus it was clear Erika appreciated the anecdote; the company's name drew her attention in the same way a celebrity's entrance sucked all available sound toward them in a room. "Did you meet the founders? Do you know them?"

"Yes indeed. Interviewed with Sergey and shook hands with Larry."

"What a story. Unbelievable." Erika took a deep breath, as if to allow the full weight of the names to sink in. "And how much do you think the ninth employee of Google is worth now?"

"He wasn't the ninth employee," Fred interrupted. "He received an offer to be the ninth engineer."

"Well in the early days most employees at start-ups are engineers," Denny said pleasantly. "The business guys don't come until later."

"So how much?" Erika pressed.

"Wow. I don't know. One of my friends from Stanford, Devlin Rose, was employee number forty-eight. And he just bought an $8 million vacation home in Deer Valley. That's *vacation* home. So the ninth, or let's just say for the sake of it, twentieth? Probably hundreds of millions."

"My God. Riches beyond belief."

"Not really," Fred said, as he rubbed savagely at an invisible spot on his arm. "It's very believable."

Kate heard in his tone the pricklish buds of agitation, a milder version of one of Stanley's own warning signals that the mood was about to turn sour. "When's the last time you saw Dad?" she asked in a low voice.

"Two weeks ago. We were supposed to meet last Wednesday, but then he canceled to go to some vegan-eating seminar at that temple instead. What a crock of shit."

"My, my." When Fred was in this state, she knew the best course was to slowly needle, then drain the ill temper. "Aren't we grouchy."

He shot her an evil eye. "I'm stressed."

"I hear you. Isn't talking about how stressed we are the siren song of our generation?"

He ignored this. "There's a lot of pressure at work, and now both Mom and Dad are breathing down my neck."

"I can guess what Dad wants. Family dinner?"

Fred groaned. "He's obsessed with getting everyone together. You, me, Mom, him. Of course whenever I bring it up with Mom, she acts like I'm signing her up for a joint colonoscopy. But Dad won't let it go. It's his greatest wish, as he keeps reminding me."

"I know. I think he thought that after the divorce, we'd still have dinner together all the time. I'll work on Mom, though; she should be able to make it at least one night, given the circumstances. Now what's *she* going on to you about?"

"The will, of course. Always the will. The nonexistent trust. I'm sure she's mentioned it?"

"No."

"Oh." He took a long swig from his glass. "Well, it's no big deal. She just wants to make sure we get our fair share, that's all."

"Fair share? As opposed to what?"

"I don't know." Fred looked defensive. "It all going to Mary or something."

"Dad wants to give it all to *Mary*?" A stale memory rumbled forward: Stanley, boldly proclaiming over dim sum that he could always bankroll Denny's start-up, if financing was an issue. "It's your inheritance, anyway," he'd said. "My legacy to you and Fred. You can just take yours early." That had been almost two years ago, when Denny first quit, and she'd been so excited by the possibilities of his work and CircleShop, delighting in what a genius her husband was.

"Mom's paranoid that's what will happen if he doesn't get his estate in order," Fred said. "That we'll get nothing."

"That's ridiculous. Besides, Dad already told me how much we're supposed to get. A million, each."

There was a short burst of surprise on Fred's face. Did he not know the sum? The number had just slipped out; she shouldn't have said anything. "Right," he said, and she relaxed. "One million." He stated it with emphasis, and Kate looked over at Denny to see if he'd heard. She hadn't told him about Stanley's offer when it was made, not being sure if her father actually meant it. She felt guilty about the omission and tested herself: Would she still give it all to Denny now, if he asked? Yes. Probably.

The waiter was back at the table, a cheery twentysomething with a massive beard, the sort of San Francisco resident who always made her feel old. He'd announced at the beginning of dinner that he was graduating from art school that month and then poured himself a glass from their pitcher of sangria when they congratulated him. Was that normal? Would they be compensated for the glass? The questions made her feel like Linda.

"Hey, you guys ready for dessert? My favorite's on tonight. A shot of peanut milk, with paired ice cream on the side. *Mucho delicioso.*" He kissed the tips of his fingers.

Now was her opportunity! Her chance to finally escape this over-wrought dinner, a meal in which she'd already been assigned at least two unpleasant tasks to manage with her parents on top of her already heavy load, and go home and collapse in bed before her 6:00 a.m. call with Europe the next morning. But before she could utter those miraculous words to signal an end to the evening—*check, please*—Denny intervened. "Actually, can we see the regular menu?" he asked. "I think we might want to add a few more appetizers, maybe another order of that chicken with the aioli sauce."

Denny wanted to stay? And *linger*? Didn't he know she wanted to leave? Kate thought they had made meaningful eye contact commu-nicating exactly this, several times. Wasn't he as tired as she was? But she saw now that he was having a good time, making moon eyes at Fred's girlfriend while she spoke in that husky lilt Kate suspected was partially manufactured.

"Do you ever think about it?" Erika asked. "What would have happened, if you had picked Google?"

"Oh sure." Denny sounded so casual, Kate thought, strikingly different from the mournfully reverential persona he usually assumed when recounting this particular tale. "It's always fun to think of what could have been. But even if it was a mistake not to have taken the job, I'm still thankful for the experience, for giving me the confidence to be an entrepreneur. I don't want to have those sorts of regrets again, not in this lifetime."

"If I had a chance to be one of the first employees at a company like Google and didn't take it, I think I would not get out of bed for an entire year," Erika said. "Too depressed."

Denny smiled. "I'm sure that's not true."

Kate slumped in her chair. She remembered she was still missing her shoe. Where the hell was it?

"Maybe. But then I would feel that my next project would have to be a success. So that I would not always regret the past."

Denny nodded. "It takes a certain kind of person to understand that," he said quietly. He sounded so wistful that Kate experienced a rush of intense love, a tender sentiment shortly overrun by righteous indignation. Did Denny think she didn't understand him?

Kate knew her husband in many ways better than he knew himself, in the form that only two people who had lived and slept together for years could comprehend. That he pretended not to care about Devlin Rose, his friend of the $8 million vacation home, but in actuality secretly tracked his career progress with brutal intensity. That he watched porn at least three times a week, retreating upstairs to jerk off whenever the reality of two young children became too much, usually right after dinner. His hidden habit of trawling online gambling forums, which he read for hours at a time, relishing the stories of those who had lost fortunes.

How many PowerPoints had she assisted with over the years, pitch decks, business plans? How many times had she claimed the very desires he secretly yearned for as her own, to save him the embarrassment? Insisting herself that they spend $25,000 of their savings on the services of a top PR consultant in San Francisco, a speed-talking pro with a Cher Horowitz accent who managed to garner a mention of Denny and CircleShop as one of *Fortune*'s "45 Under 45 to Watch in Retail" only after Kate's forceful hounding? All that so he, too, could partake in the rumbling machinery of Valley hype he claimed so emphatically to hate.

Yet here he sat—Mr. Fortune #38, smiling not at Kate but at a near stranger. As if his very soul had been a parched plant, neglected for all these years, now basking under a rare shower.

What was Denny up to in the attic? What was her husband doing with his life?

———————

The park closest to their neighborhood had an official name, but everyone who lived nearby and had children called it Jade Mountain. It was considered large for the area at twelve acres, and ample parking meant it was frequently packed on weekends with oversize vehicles bearing sports equipment and zealous parents claiming tables for single-digit birthday parties. At one point there had been rumors it was to be razed to make way for a charter school, but the neighborhood parents had put an end to the initiative. The area had a surfeit of stay-at-home moms with dormant legal degrees; the nascent proposal was quickly shot down in city council.

One of the more popular features of Jade Mountain was the multiple play structures, meant for different age groups, on the north and south sides. Off to the east was a man-made hill with four slides of different-size rollers. The rollers hurt your butt going down; all the regulars brought collapsed cardboard boxes, which functioned as makeshift sleds. The grass on the hill wasn't real but rather some advanced form of turf, soft and eternally durable in a distinctive shade of deep acid green, which had earned the park its nickname.

Kate hadn't visited Jade Mountain in months, as her weekends were now occupied by children's birthday parties of an average size and lavishness that filled her with a mixture of pride and shame, but Denny still came each week with Ella. Her preschool ended early on Wednesdays, and his usual strategy, Kate knew, was to swing by the playground to eat up time and energy on the way home. Their routine was to park the car in the farthest lot and meander the long way in, until they eventually made their way to the toddler area, directly across from the bathrooms. Kate had always hated the crude structure, which she found intolerable even by the considerably modest hygiene standards of public restrooms. So it was fitting that it was here where she now found herself crouched, hidden behind a grouping of tall trees and besieged by what she was convinced was the faintest aroma of raw sewage, waiting for her husband and daughter to appear.

SLIPPERS, KATE KNEW, WAS GOING TO BE A MASSIVE SUCCESS. Even though she'd checked its footage every day now for more than a week, each time she watched the feed she'd been impressed anew by the technological feat achieved by Ron Fujihara and his team. Considering the generous size of the attic, there was still no degradation of sound quality, and the lens—which had appeared unremarkable when she made her initial evaluation—produced startlingly sharp video, even under dim lighting conditions. Despite the fact the units had not yet been back to base, they still reflected a half charge; due to their built-in sensors, they recorded only when there was sound or movement.

Unfortunately for Kate, while Slippers was functionally brilliant, it had yet to capture any content of relevant interest. She'd viewed nearly eight hours of feed so far, forwarding through most of it while being intermittently struck by the malodorous scent of her own betrayal as she watched Denny pick his nose or scratch at his balls in private confidence. From what she'd observed, most of his time was spent silently hunched over his laptop or tapping away on his phone. Though there'd been several promising leads—once Kate had glimpsed what appeared to be a multiplayer fantasy, and in another instance she'd caught the echo of a woman's voice, its sexy timbre reverberating on speaker—neither had panned out. She'd never seen Denny play the game again, puncturing her Warcraft addiction theory, and after multiple viewings, the mysterious temptress ended up being one of his engineers in Romania, who appeared deceptively young due to stylish glasses and an adorable voice.

Still, Kate was desperate. She was convinced the atmosphere was off in the house, as if a natural disaster were lurking on the horizon; it was driving her crazy, in a way she couldn't explain without she herself appearing hysterical. Jade Mountain was on the way home from work, an easy stop that didn't require advance planning. The only small hiccup had been a chance encounter with Sonny while sneaking out the back entrance; she'd been stalled for nearly twenty minutes while he ranted on about the poor social skills of their program managers in Asia. By the time she settled into a comfortable peeping stance, she'd been afraid that she was too late, but only a short while passed before Ella came along the path, pushing her doll-size stroller. Kate took her in for a greedy minute, enjoying every detail of seeing her daughter as an observer would, the childishness and energy and beautiful skin.

Where was Denny? He wasn't within eyeshot, though hers at the moment was admittedly limited. Kate knew he often let Ella and Ethan run ahead, especially in familiar territory. He had probably stopped on the path to read some email, she thought. They'd had minor spats over this in the past, when Kate had found him not as watchful as she might have liked; he was always staring at his phone like some recalcitrant nanny.

Ella had reached the sandbox and eagerly dug in with her trowel. Kate leaned forward to see if she could spot any poop. There was an old Pakistani grandmother who lived with her son and daughter-in-law nearby and took their bichon frise every day to the park. The woman spoke no English and was possibly under the impression the sandpit was a giant litterbox meant for small animals; yet another luxurious Western indulgence she couldn't fathom but took full advantage of—each morning—when her dog shit in the box. An acquaintance whose daughter also visited Jade Mountain, Sandra Mays, had implored Kate to speak with the grandmother. There'd been the delicate insinuation that because Kate was Asian and the woman Pakistani, the two might be able to achieve common ground; for lily-white Sandra herself to confront the wizened woman, it was implied, would put her at risk of being perceived as racist, the gravest of insults.

Kate squinted to see if she could identify any of the more sinisterly shaped lumps. An older dark-haired woman wearing a velour sweater had materialized in the sandbox. She held a small plastic bucket in her left hand and a sifter in her right, using it to catch pebbles. "Ella, look," she said, in accented English. "We should do this carefully and try not to get any in your shoes. Otherwise, we'll have to clean your feet in the car." And Kate was struck with the breathless shock that this woman not only knew her daughter but had arrived with her.

Ella grabbed the woman's hand and stood up, pointing at something ahead. "Look, look."

"Hmm?" The woman was bent over, gathering strewn toys. Who *was* she? Could Denny be having an affair? But she was so much older, nearly his mother's age, and not his physical type. "Sweetie, are you done? Let's clean up, then. Clean up! Clean up!" She sang the words in a familiar melody.

"It's my mama's bag."

"Ella, we talked about this, remember? It's a no-no to look through strangers' things. Want to go on the swing?"

"It's my mama's bag," Ella repeated.

Kate looked over and to her horror spotted her tote, which in a moment of extreme stupidity she had set down on a bench several yards away. Her keychain lanyard was wrapped around the handles, with a very recognizable yellow pom-pom attached. By the familiar stubbornness in Ella's voice, she guessed it was only a matter of seconds before her daughter and this woman made their way over. She would definitely lose some leverage, she thought, should Denny suddenly emerge and find her squatting behind a bush.

Slowly and methodically Kate stood from her crouch and then casually strolled to the bench and retrieved her phone.

"Mama!" Ella cried.

"Oh, hello!" Her voice sounded false, too high. She felt Ella wrap her arms around her leg. Kate knelt down to give her a kiss on her cheek. "Fancy seeing you! Are you with Papa?"

"I don't know," Ella responded in her tiny voice. "Is he here?"

"Hello," Kate said to the woman. She smiled encouragingly. "I'm Ella's mother."

The woman looked anxious. "Ella, Ella," she cooed. "Can you sing the new song we learned?"

"Hello," Kate repeated. "I'm Kate." *And who the hell are you?*

Her hand was accepted with reluctance. "What a wonderful girl Ella is."

Kate waited a beat. When nothing additional appeared to be forthcoming, she asked pointedly, "What is your name?"

"Isabel."

"Who are you? Do you work for my husband?"

"Oh no. No, no. Of course not." The woman seemed to view the question as an insult. "I'm an accredited childcare provider."

"So you're a nanny?" But her family didn't have nannies, hadn't employed one since Denny quit Cisco and Ella started preschool. "Why are you here with my daughter? Where's Denny?"

Isabel hesitated. "He isn't here," she said. "We came alone."

"Then where is he? Do you have his permission to be here?" A stream of questions hurtled forward. "How did you get here? Do you have Denny's car?"

"I don't . . ." There was a brief struggle for words. "I don't want to get in the middle of things."

Kate could feel the heat flood her face. "It's a little too late for that. You're a stranger, standing in the park alone with my daughter, and *I've never heard of you before in my life.*" Ella, bored by the conversation and not old enough to catch its interesting overtones, wandered back to the sand. Kate stood facing the woman in a stalemate, her breath suddenly jagged.

Isabel groaned. "I really can't," she said in an agonized voice. "Listen, your daughter's safe, she knows me, your husband gave us permission to be here. You should speak to him about it yourself. Why don't you take Ella? I was about to bring her back soon, anyway."

"But bring her back *where*? My house? Is that where my husband is? Did he hire you?" That seemed the most likely explanation, but where had Denny found the money? She managed the finances and certainly would have noticed a helper on the payroll.

"I can't say."

"What exactly *can* you say?"

Isabel raised her hands, as if in apology. "Nothing, nothing."

Kate waved her phone in the air. "If I don't hear a satisfactory explanation for how a person I've never before met or heard of ended up at a park alone with my daughter, I'm calling the police."

Isabel sagged. "Please," she said.

"Right, okay. I'm calling now."

Defeated, the nanny slumped on the bench. "I work for a woman, Camilla Mosner," she said. Her voice was miserable. "Your husband knows her. Please, that's all I have. Your daughter has never been in danger with me. I'm a very responsible person. I drive a 2014 Toyota Sienna. The car seats were checked by the fire department! Can you please just go home and call your husband? I want to go. I really have to go."

"Who is Camilla Mosner? Does she run some sort of childcare agency?" Understanding the question was pathetic even before she'd asked.

"She's . . . she's a private citizen." Isabel seemed resigned to her fate. "Your husband, he spends some time with her. And so they ask me to watch the children."

"The children? You see Ethan too?"

"Ethan?" Isabel looked confused. "I don't know an Ethan. Who is Ethan? I know an Edgar."

Kate took a deep breath. "Just how many people is your employer sleeping with?"

Isabel gasped. "Oh my Lord, it's not like that! I don't want to get involved, I *told* you, I'm a good woman, I love children. Edgar is my nephew! Camilla is a nice person. I would never work for someone who wasn't. . . ."

"She just has you watch other people's kids for her while she sleeps with their husbands."

"I'm a *professional*!" Isabel cried. "Take this, look!"

She thrust a hand toward Kate, who recoiled. A card dropped to the ground, which after a few seconds Kate picked up and studied. *Isabel Gorgas*, it read. *Professional Childcare and Housekeeping*. A phone number was on the bottom, and the border was filled with pink and orange flowers.

"You see?" Isabel pressed. She seemed intent on being recognized as a paid service provider. "This is my work! You understand now, right?"

"I can't talk to you anymore," Kate said. The blood was rushing to her head; any moment now she would drown.

———————

Growing up, there was a weekend when Linda went away to visit a friend in Southern California Kate and Fred knew as the Happy Meal Queen. The friend, whom Linda had known since high school, was rich. Her family owned the factories in China that manufactured the toys placed in children's meals for two of the world's largest fast-food chains; she lived in an impressive mansion in Laguna Beach and drove a metallic burgundy Bentley Continental. Usually when

Linda visited it was a family occasion—complete with harried lessons on appropriate comportment and threatening exhortations to behave on the six-hour car ride—but this time she had gone solo, citing the all-powerful and suspiciously American reason of needing "me time."

Fred took the opportunity to ditch school on Friday and spend the entire weekend with friends, leaving Kate and Stanley alone. Even when older, Kate would never be the sort of student to skip class, and she felt a certain unstated pressure from Linda not to ask friends over when only Stanley was home. There'd been an incident a few years back, when he'd berated a "study buddy" of Fred's for accidentally spilling orange soda at the foot of the stairs; the girl, whom Kate suspected Fred had secretly liked, had cried and cried. So Kate spent all of Saturday by herself in her room and in front of the TV, eating Japanese snacks, until Stanley announced in the late afternoon that they would eat dinner in Oakland.

The drive took a little under an hour, and when Kate entered the restaurant, she was immediately confronted by a massive display of stacked jars of kimchi. "This place is Korean owned, but they serve Chinese food," Stanley explained. "You will like it. The food is spicy." Once they were seated, he asked for a menu and handed Kate a credit card. "Wait here," he said, "and order what you want."

He left the restaurant, and she watched him walk across the street to a row of houses. They were an erratic mix of residential and commercial, the sort of neighborhood where children played underneath clotheslines and neon signs in windows advertised next-day clothing alterations and pawn services. The homes themselves were all of a similar shape and size, except for the one farthest to the right, at the end of the street. That residence was the largest, a squashed version of the salmon Spanish-style McMansions popular in their own neighborhood. Outside its entrance, numerous video cameras were on prominent display, and dark blinds were drawn over each window.

There was a small white-and-black sign above the entrance, which read *Sasha's Massage and Spa*. It was through this door that Stanley entered, and then eventually exited, two and a half hours later.

On the drive back home, they sat in silence for some time before Kate began to complain. She was eleven, old enough to harness the full righteous ire of a teenager, and Stanley had left her alone in the restaurant for close to three hours. During that time, she'd eaten the entirety of her seafood noodle soup, slowly spooning the soggy remnants as she reached the bottom of the bowl, convinced that Stanley would reappear by the end. When he didn't, she added an order of pork dumplings and onion pancakes to stave off the resentful looks of the waitstaff and sat in bored mortification for an additional ninety minutes. She wanted to know: What had Stanley been doing in that house for such a long period? As Stanley drove his face grew crimson, though Kate knew he wouldn't be dangerous to her on the road. And so she continued to heckle, deliberately baiting, as her father's hands gripped the steering wheel, knuckles white.

Back at the house, Stanley changed into pajamas, brushed his teeth, and gargled with mouthwash. He then walked to the kitchen and selected the nearest useful item—in this case an answering machine, one of those hefty models that held an actual cassette tape, with phone attached—and lobbed it at her with full force. It struck solidly on the side of her head, and when Kate came to, she lay alone on the ground, with the unpacked takeout containers next to her.

Only when she was absolutely certain there was no one else in the room, no silent pulse of someone trying to breathe without being heard, did she slowly slide up against the fridge. In her unconscious state she had heard music and enjoyed the sort of vivid dream that made it seem as if hours had passed. She settled into a slouched position and stared dizzily at the clock, discovering that it had been only minutes. After she placed the dumplings in the fridge, she quickly

packed a bag and walked to a neighbor's, an elderly Chinese couple whose only child had passed away from a cause Kate had never
learned, and who understood a little of Stanley's temper from the few
times she had run away to their home.

At their door, the couple took in Kate's swollen face, and the
woman patted her hand, murmuring in a dialect she didn't understand. They let her watch TV and made up a bed for her in their child's
old room, decorated with sports trophies and team photographs. She
sat at the small wooden desk and stared at a framed image of their
son holding a soccer ball. It was her first time staying there overnight,
and when she climbed into bed the flannel sheets felt foreign and
cold. She held a hand against her left eye and cheek, slowly pressing
into the pain and then releasing in a cycle, until she fell asleep.

The next morning Kate straightened the room and waited at the
window until she saw the taxi arrive with Linda. On her way out, she
thanked the couple, who avoided looking at her. At first she thought
it was her face, which had begun to purple on one side, before the
thought dawned that they were embarrassed by the situation, though
she didn't know who they were uncomfortable for.

When she opened the front door and saw him exhale, she knew
that Stanley had believed he might have really injured her this time.
He stared at her with open relief, and she felt a new sort of fury begin
to gather. She held her father's gaze. Who was he really, she thought,
but just some old man, an ineffectual bully who alternately treated
women badly and was frightened by them?

Stanley was the first to break eye contact. Kate told Linda she'd
suffered a nasty fall out running, and her mother tsked and made her
chicken noodle soup with goji berries. In the following weeks, the
swelling flattened and the bruising slowly turned darker purple, then
red, then a sickly yellow. By the time it faded completely, Kate found
she missed it—she almost wished a little bit had remained, a mark to
remember things by.

IN THE CAR NOW, KATE FORCED HERSELF TO BREATHE. SHE TOSSED her old tablet, which had been repurposed into a toy and normally only allowed at restaurants, into the back. "You can watch whatever you want," she called to Ella. She needed a few minutes to compose herself.

So Denny was taking a break from work or had possibly given up altogether—that was unclear. What *was* obvious was that he was cheating on her. She searched herself for indignation, diagnosing the roots of her shock. They had been married for eight years, with all the corresponding fights and resentments of a relationship of that length; there had even been—as she now recalled—a suspected dalliance during his Cisco years, a twentysomething Lithuanian Denny had described as "charmingly naive," which even at the time Kate had known was a descriptive to find alarm, not solace, in. He had always denied it, however, and she hadn't pressed. She'd had multiple friends with husbands who'd undergone midlife crises by then, and she wanted to avoid the mistake of badgering her own to a premature decision, especially one disadvantageous to a household that at the time contained a toddler and a three-month-old.

But now?

Ella was making whimpering sounds, mercilessly employing the instinct of young children to demand their parent's attention at the precise moment privacy is desired most. "Mama!" she called. "Play my music. Please!"

"Mama's finding it," Kate replied automatically. She fumbled in her bag for her phone to bring up the songs, some grating series featuring tambourines. She called herself Mama all the time now, even when children weren't around, a habit she'd first been embarrassed and later proud of, as Denny waxed lyrical on the sexual appeal of the mommy. Mama. Mother. Women who dedicated themselves and their bodies to the birth and raising of children. Like her and Isabel Gorgas, she thought, the thought smacking her with unanticipated humiliation.

She scrolled to the selection on her phone, which Ella had already begun to hum to in anticipation. Before it began there were a few seconds of empty noise, and Kate was struck by a calm she hadn't experienced since that morning more than twenty years ago, when she'd stood and locked eyes with Stanley. The heat from her face faded, her headache receded. And she let the chill wash over her, welcoming it as a familiar friend.

CHAPTER 8

LINDA

A ll her life, Linda thought, Stanley had given her a raw deal.
The first time they'd met was at what had been a local gathering of Chinese graduate students in Menlo Park—which she'd arrived to an hour late, after her part-time job cleaning houses to pay for Stanford tuition—and she could still recall the way he had swanned up to her, a felted bowler hat in hand like in some old American movie, to say how pleased he was to see her again. She'd never met this slightly short but curiously appealing young man with a mustache before, she was sure of it; yet he was so insistent that she considered there might be a possibility she was wrong, and before she knew it she had her first boyfriend. And so there would begin a trend that would last throughout their entire marriage, of Stanley misrepresenting himself.

Convincing her in the early years that he was ambitious and

bright, when he was in fact lazy and incompetent. Singing promises that he'd buy them a fine, beautiful house, only to move her into that deafening hellhole by the freeway. Complimenting her ability to work, work, work—she'd never left IBM as so many of her female colleagues eventually did, to stay home with Fred and Kate, never lost her temper and rashly quit her soul-numbing job in systems management, as he himself did, several times—then ruthlessly snatching away her paycheck, flushing it down the drain.

Even thirtysomething years later, when she'd finally located her courage, had gone and left *him*, told *him* that they were going to divorce, leaving him openmouthed and speechless, helplessly steaming in his armchair—even then, he'd managed to come out ahead. Stanley had recovered quickly enough from his brief period of depression, signing up for a series of elite gym memberships a month after he'd moved out, rebounding shortly after with a sequence of increasingly embryonic girlfriends. A series of events he'd then capped off by getting remarried with undignified speed. A marriage he couldn't help but publicize by braying to everyone about how happy he was, making it appear as if he was the one who'd left *her*. Because she was still alone, of course.

And now, even in dying, he was still cheating her. Linda understood this to be the indisputable truth, as she sat in the dingy red felt–backed chair at Golden Dynasty, the din of the poorly insulated restaurant clattering into her ears. Waiting (waiting!) for Stanley to walk through the entrance, as he was late (he was late!). The day her divorce had been declared final, she'd made a vow that never again would she find herself following a command from a man. And yet now here she was, once again obeying one's wishes. And not just any man, but Stanley, *again*!

Her children flanked her right and left sides like a pair of jailers, the two Judases who had foisted this predicament on her in the first place. "It's so important to him," Kate had pled on the phone. "Dad really wants to see you, have a meal together. Like old times."

Linda didn't know what Kate was talking about. They'd barely ever dined out at restaurants as a family, except for a handful of occasions at Marie Callender's or the inexpensive Taiwanese noodle shop in Cupertino. It annoyed her, this revisionist history her children had indulged in ever since Stanley's diagnosis, as they selected the few moments he'd been pleasant and charmingly self-deprecating and then peanut buttered them across their entire past landscape. But it wouldn't be seemly to bring up the difficult times at the moment; she knew it would only make her look bad. "Why a *meal*?" she asked instead. "Why can't I just meet you after?"

"Because Dad loves to dine out, you know that, Ma. Come on, it's his one request, you know everything he's been going through. It'll be great for his spirits. We want him to stay positive."

"What about me? Don't I deserve to feel positive?"

"Are you really that hardhearted?"

Linda hesitated. She could always agree and then delay, a cycle she could keep up indefinitely. "Fine. I'll go."

"*Thank you.* Now in terms of timing, I'm thinking it makes the best sense to do it this Thursday or Friday. Fred has to travel to Asia after."

Now that she was here, unable to extricate herself, it occurred to Linda how unfair the situation truly was. To be dragged into this ordeal out of guilt because Stanley was sick, stricken by a solemn diagnosis—but simultaneously for the point of being cheerful! To convince him he *wasn't* dying. That everything was fine! What sort of insanity was that? To get to have it both ways, as he always had, at the cost of everyone else . . . well, she was sick of that. She didn't have to put up with it anymore. She was going to leave right now, head directly for the door; she could claim she was going to the bathroom and then quickly pivot, duck out to the parking lot and flee, deal with the kids later. . . .

Goddamn! And here was Stanley tottering toward them now, with perfect timing to sabotage her plans, as always. He plopped down with satisfied aplomb, yet another notched win in his eternal quest to ruin her life.

"You came!" he exclaimed. He wore a white sweatshirt that had *PARIS!* printed on the front in alternating primary colors, a souvenir from their first trip to Europe. Linda chewed the inside of her cheek to keep any nostalgia at bay. "Don't you like this restaurant?" he asked. "I remember it was your favorite. Did you know that on Fridays the lobster noodles are only $20?"

"The dish isn't as good on Fridays. They give less lobster."

"Ha-ha. Always so smart." A bony shoulder protruded from the sweatshirt, and Linda gulped down an involuntary wave of sorrow. He was even smaller than the last time she'd seen him.

He eyed her in expectant silence.

"How is your chemotherapy?" she finally asked.

"Oh, it's okay. But I'm very tired after. The room I go to in Kaiser, it is too dark, very depressing. But I have a friend, one of the nurses. The head one. He is a *man*, can you believe? And black! He says not to worry, because I am very strong. He likes me the most."

"You are strong, Dad," Kate interjected. "You're doing excellent. Right?" She looked directly at Fred and then Linda, for reinforcement. Linda ignored this. She'd never understood the point of these platitudes, which were meaningless without defined parameters. Stanley was strong? Compared to what? An ant? A bear?

"Stanley," she said. "Did you start the will yet? How much is everyone getting?"

"Ma!" Kate dropped her chopsticks with a sharp crash.

"I have," Stanley replied, in a shaky voice.

"Very good. You're doing a trust, yes? With Kate and Fred as the beneficiaries? You know that's what fathers are supposed to do. Take care of the younger generation. And by younger, I don't mean your wife."

"Of course." For all their righteous indignation, the children, Linda noticed, were listening intently. Good. How else did Kate think she was going to pay for two college educations with one income? Not to mention Fred and whatever palace he fantasized about purchasing. Woodside, ha! Better for him to understand reality now, so he could adjust his real estate expectations accordingly.

"What does *of course* mean? I want to know the plan, Stanley. And exact numbers." Since Linda saw no way out of the well of human misery that was Golden Dynasty for the next hour, she might as well get some work done. She removed her favorite Pilot pen from her bag, along with a leather notebook. "So? Let's start at the high level and work down. What's your liquid net?"

"Oh, it's enough." Stanley coughed into a napkin. "I hope that everyone will be satisfied. Happy." He gave a beam around the table.

Why were Kate and Fred smiling back? Did they think that was anywhere near an adequate response? Stanley was like a slippery eel—he had to be badgered into a corner until there was no room to escape or breathe. Then, only once he'd surrendered the necessary information, did you allow him oxygen.

She clicked the pen impatiently. "I want to write the numbers down, so that there's no confusion. It should be very simple. First, you determine your net worth. Then you define a token—that means small, Stanley—amount you give to Mary. Everything else goes to the children."

"I have to take care of Mary," Stanley said. "I am everything to her."

"Ma." It was Fred. "Maybe we should do this later."

Linda was surprised. Fred was going to be the roadblock? Mr. Future Mayor of Woodside? She crossed her arms. "There is no later," she said. "We are already too late."

"Ma," Kate warned. She tilted her head quickly toward the left, in the direction of the entrance. Linda looked over.

Mother of God. It was Stanley's wife. Before Linda could prime her next move, Mary had already reached the table. "How are you?" she called out, in that fake Beijing accent of hers. She was limited to only the most rudimentary words in English, though in Linda's opinion Mary's Mandarin wasn't much of an improvement. "It has been far too long. What sad circumstances bring us here today! How upsetting, that a good man has to endure this!"

Linda suppressed a bubble of supreme irritation and deleted those words—*a good man*—from her brain. "How come you didn't arrive with Stanley?" she asked. If she had seen the two of them walk in together—Stanley in that sweatshirt and Mary in . . . dear God, what was she wearing, some sort of sheer netted item—she would have definitely fled. Dashed right past them at the door, slowing to give a brief wave but not stopping until she'd reached her vehicle. Some things in life were worth being rude for.

Mary took a seat on the other side of Kate. "We did come together. I dropped Stanley off at the entrance, so he didn't have to walk far, and then parked by myself. I got my license two years ago. Isn't it fortunate that Stanley has such a team of capable people to help him? Especially the women."

A *team*? She and Mary were a team in the same way Warren Buffett and Stanley could both be considered investors. Linda glanced desperately to her right, and then left. Who was going to save her from this idiot?

Kate spoke up. "Are you cooking a lot of new foods lately? I know you're a very good chef. Dad always tells us about all the dishes you make. Did I hear that you mastered sweet taro balls? Though I'm not sure if that's what he should be eating right now. . . ."

As they chattered, Linda took the opportunity to study her opponent. The tight black blouse Mary wore, she now saw, wasn't actually that sheer—there was a layer of nude fabric underneath, which made it less provocative but somehow even more tacky. Her hair was nice—that she would admit—though most of it would probably go by the time she passed fifty-five, with all that dying and perming. Of course, of greatest concern was the way she managed Stanley. She watched as Mary ladled beef with stir-fried flat rice noodles onto his plate, a dish everyone knew not to order at Golden Dynasty because they used too much oil. Stanley selected a piece of glistening meat with his chopsticks. His hand shook as he brought it to his mouth, which drooped open like a fish gasping for air. When it finally made its way in, Mary rubbed his back in circles and motioned for him to have another. Was she trying to kill him? If so, food was her accessory of choice.

Fred leaned over. "What do you think?"

"About what?" Linda said flatly. She knew very well what he was asking, but if he and Kate were going to treat her like a leper for saying out loud what they all secretly thought, she was going to make him spell it out.

"About the will." Then he added, in a private voice: "And what he said about Mary."

She shrugged. "Your father makes his own choices, eh? Didn't you say that earlier?"

"Come on," Fred hissed. "You feel the same way I do."

"Oh? So now we are thinking the same? I didn't know."

"Fine." He sat back in his chair. "Then he should give it all to Mary."

"Of course not!" Despite her efforts to remain aloof, the idea was instantly maddening. "That's why you have to act quickly. Push him! He has to finish his will, and then you must insist on verifying it, what your inheritance will be. Know all the numbers! Before it's too late."

She watched with open disapproval as he tipped back his glass of beer. "I tried to talk to him a little the other day," Fred said. He wiped his mouth. "Dad said Mary's never once mentioned the will, so I shouldn't be concerned either. How can I keep asking after that? It makes her look like a saint and us like the greedy ones."

Sometimes Linda wondered whether she had taught her son anything. Didn't Harvard Business School have a class on second wives and end-of-life estate planning? For the tuition it charged, it should at least have offered it as an elective. "Of course *Mary* wouldn't ask; that's not her place! She hasn't earned any of it! Does your house cleaner ask whether you paid your taxes this year? This is something between the family, the parents and children. Your father, he should understand this." A pinprick of guilt flared; Stanley, of course, wasn't very understanding. But Fred should at least try.

"Linda, Linda." That woman was babbling at her again. "Have you been to Chung Herbal Supply, in San Francisco Chinatown? I went with Stanley last week."

Why would she ever go to Chinatown? The restaurants in the South Bay were much tastier, without the loud crowds or exasperating parking challenges of San Francisco. Was Mary actually attempting to navigate the maze of one-way streets of the city with Stanley in the vehicle? There was a good chance he'd die of that, way before the cancer. "No."

"Oh, it's very good," Mary yapped. "I've visited a few times now. Last week they brought in a special tree bark I ordered; it had to be sent from Hong Kong. I've been brewing it into a tea for Stanley. It's supposed to be very powerful against cancer. For many people, it is a near-instant cure." She prattled on, detailing all the various acupuncturists, healers, and meditation gurus whose skills were being summoned. Next to her, Stanley preened, lapping it all up.

Linda decided she'd had enough. "Please inform your wife that I am a full supporter of Western medicine," she said to Stanley in English. To her left, she heard Kate sigh. But she didn't care. Lunch was over.

CHAPTER 9

FRED

I f there was a hell at San Francisco International Airport, Fred
thought, it existed in the American Pacific business-class lounge.
Of course that was the case with most lounges these days, at least the
US-operated ones, which unfortunately—due to Lion's policy of flying the lowest-cost carrier and his own desire to accumulate airline
miles efficiently—Fred usually opted to fly. But there was something
particularly sordid about the American Pacific location in SFO, situ-
ated in between a Yankee Candle store and one of the identical news-
stands that constituted a third of the terminal.

Each time Fred visited he was invariably confronted at the
entrance by the same two ill-tempered dragons, each with a highly
developed radar for unsanctioned social climbing, who together managed their roles as if guarding the gates of Valhalla. No matter how

he gamed the line, Fred always got the meaner one, the one who, contrary to logic, was slightly younger and prettier. When he arrived at the front, her usual routine was to ignore him for several minutes while she stared blankly at her screen before eventually taking his ticket and staring at it with resentment. A few moments would then pass before he was allowed in, only to inevitably encounter crowded bedlam and a food display resembling an end-of-shift Costco sample station.

Better fare, Fred knew, was actually in the food court, where there was at least a decent ramen restaurant and half a dozen organic salad purveyors. But due to a pressure to conform—and the bourgeois inclination to indulge in the most luxurious option regardless of actual preference—Fred always visited the lounge when his ticket allowed. Which was where he was now, waiting for his flight to Hong Kong, where he and Erika would spend two nights before connecting to Bali for the Founders' Retreat.

For several precious minutes now Fred had been silently debating the effort to unzip his luggage to confirm that he'd packed a phone charger. It would be a difficult operation, as his bag was sandwiched between the wall and his chair, where even closed shut it stood slightly in the way of foot traffic and was glared at indignantly by fellow travelers. He had quickly claimed the very last table available, shoved in an undesirable corner near the toilets; next to him, parked in the grouping of soft chairs he would have preferred, was one of those enormous families where the ages seemed to span four generations. They looked to have been settled for a span ranging from half an hour to overnight: Fred could see travel pillows strewn about, trolleys in various states of unpack, and an enormous makeup valise open on the low table. Closest to Fred sat a morose-looking teen wearing padded earphones, while next to the teen several cushions had been strategically arranged into a makeshift nest, where an overweight man in his sixties leaned in repose. A great-grandmother slumped in a wheelchair nearby, picking miserably at lint on her sleeve.

"I don't understand," Erika said.

She sat across from him in a black jersey dress and mink-trimmed coat, an effortlessly chic look Fred knew from considerable experience had taken significant effort. Now that they were here, surrounded by ramshackle, he realized he should have warned her in advance about the lounge. He often forgot how inexperienced Erika actually was with the society she pretended to inhabit. The first international flight she'd ever flown was when she moved to the United States from Budapest; now she sat wide-eyed, fur collar pulled tight around her neck, as she observed their surroundings in horror.

"You said this was going to be a first-class trip," Erika said. As she spoke her eyes continued to rove, settling briefly on an unattended janitorial cart by the coffee machines. "How can everyone here be in first class?"

Had he really said those precise words? "We are," he reassured. "Business."

Erika gave him a hard look. "Business? So there is not a first?"

"Well, not anymore, not on a lot of planes. They've eliminated first on a lot of routes. On ours, there still might be that, ah, class— but we're in business, which by any standard is a top luxury experience. The tickets alone cost $8,000. *Each.*"

This was true in the most theoretical sense, though Fred had used miles to upgrade his own and to purchase Erika's. He had cursed Leland Wang a thousand times when he made the booking, for being such a cheap bastard. Aside from Leland himself, only employees with dire health restrictions documented with at least two pieces of (signed) supporting evidence from accredited health professionals were qualified to fly business for corporate travel, and Fred hadn't yet stooped to begging the favor of Uncle Phillip. Thus not only did he fly economy when traveling for work, but it was usually on cut-rate fares, which meant an arduous number of plane hours was required to cobble together the miles for free flights. This trip had cleaned him out; he only had forty-eight miles left in his American Pacific account.

"In business, you still lie flat to sleep," he continued. With Erika, it was important to be authoritative. "You have the same fluffy pillows and unlimited champagne, and the only difference is the toiletries. You brought all your own creams and lotions, anyway." The process of whittling down her favorites into a quart-size bag had taken Erika the better part of an hour, though he hadn't complained. There was no way Fred was going to check baggage only to have his prized Loro Piana Traveller Jacket thieved by some enterprising Indonesian customs official.

Though Erika appeared to accept this explanation, her mood once again soured when it came time for lunch. She threw a brief glare at the misshapen rows of crackers and skeletal grape bunches, before announcing she would seek alternatives elsewhere. "I will not risk food poisoning before air travel," she declared, as if this was a long-standing policy of hers. Fred knew she expected him to follow, but he thought it unreasonable to expect him to cart their bags through the food court, where the tables were even more cramped. Instead, he fixed himself a plate with some of the less aggressively tinted cheeses and whole pieces of fruit. This would save him at least $15 compared to a food court meal, which he could mentally apply toward a charger if necessary.

Once aboard the plane, he was secretly relieved to find ample space in the overhead bin. Erika had wanted to line up early, to ensure it, but at the last minute he'd made her wait in the general seating area instead, far away from the front. He was four levels removed from the top status on American Pacific (Agate Class, which allowed one free piece of checked baggage); he didn't want to spend the first twenty minutes of boarding penned behind dilapidated red ropes while first-class fliers and million-milers strutted past, delighting in their avoided eye contact. "See?" he said. "Plenty of space."

Erika ignored him. She had set down her tote on the window seat and was making her way to the bathroom, toiletry kit in hand. Fred already dreaded what would surely be complaints regarding the service—since this was American Pacific, the flight attendants were either preemptively hostile or undergoing the slow inertia of death. Across from them on the aisle sat a tall man speaking on his phone in what sounded like French. He was fat in the way only Europeans seemed to be, with the heft concentrated around the torso, like an oversize bear. He wore a starched shirt and smelled strongly of cologne.

As the flight hours passed, Fred eyed their neighbor. Like him, he hadn't slept straightaway but had eaten dinner and now looked to be in the middle of a movie. Could he also be going to the Founders' Retreat? Since his had been a pity invite, nearly anyone else he encountered represented a networking possibility. The man had the right girth for an investor, and Europeans in Silicon Valley always were a little dressier.

Fred had never before been seated next to any combination of either attractive or important on a plane, a fate he felt was long overdue. The man belched and stood, and Fred prepared to lob a greeting. But after a quick stretch, the man placed his headphones back on and settled into his seat.

When Fred woke, they were already in Hong Kong and the plane was taxiing to the gate. Next to him Erika sat facing directly ahead wearing large black sunglasses; he couldn't see if she was awake or sleeping, and she made no response to his movements. His neck ached and his breath was stale. By the time he had retrieved his and Erika's bags from the overhead bin, the Frenchman was gone.

"A few months ago, Reagan Kwon calls me," Jack said. "You remember Reagan from school, right?"

They were eating breakfast at Maison, the in-house French restaurant at the Dorchester Hotel in Hong Kong. The space was far more majestic than Fred's modest "Superior" lodgings, which had been the lowest tier available at booking—while his cramped room featured pastel chintz wallpaper and faced the fire escape of the office building next door (the so-called Hong Kong city views), here they were surrounded by floor-to-ceiling glass windows, and the tables were separated by an extravagant distance. It was a rare clear morning where the pollution had been washed away by the rains the night before, and the beauty of the Kowloon Peaks was set in high contrast by the brash golden panels of the restaurant's interior.

More than ten years had passed since Fred had last seen Jack, at the HBS reunion. In the natural light of Hong Kong, Fred could see how Jack's face had puddled and softened since then, his hair beginning to thin in the same half-moon pattern as his famous father's. His dress sense hadn't changed—a perk of being a billionaire—and he was clad in loose jeans and a dingy light blue sweatshirt, an item he had clearly been wearing all week and to bed.

"I knew Reagan," Fred said. "But not well. He was a year above us, so we didn't share any classes, remember?"

"Oh. Right. I forgot he was in a different year. That's weird, I feel like we hung out all the time."

"Yeah you did," Fred said, without further explanation. He tapped his foot restlessly out of sight under the table. He wondered what it was like to be Jack and have the beautiful and glamorous clamor for your acquaintance. How kind did he believe the world to be?

"Reagan, he's living in Bangkok now," Jack continued. "Well not *living* living. He technically has a place, but he's gone most of the time. His family is in Thailand half the year, though, so.

Anyway, one afternoon Reagan calls and says he's got a new project he wants to work on, and right away I know I'm interested. Because between you and me, my job isn't the most exciting. Yeah, the numbers are big, but since I'm managing the family business full-time now, I'm pretty constrained in terms of risk. If anything goes wrong at Hu Land and Investment, it's me who has to deal with the fallout. Not to mention all the aunties and cousins who are then immediately on my butt. Who wants to deal with that? So naturally I'm dying to know what Reagan has planned, but with him everything has to have this big buildup, where he strings you along until there's this dramatic unveiling at the end. And we're chatting for what feels like forever, until eventually he asks if I've heard of this huge new development fund the Thais are launching. Of course, I say. It's all over the financial news here, supposedly a crazy amount, multiple billions, all to make Bangkok the technology hub of Asia. 'Silicon Valley of the East!' or whatever. The rest of Asia is booming, everyone's getting rich, and they don't want to be left behind, plowing rice and giving tuk tuk rides. And then Reagan finally lets the bomb drop, that he's getting some of that money to manage. Most of it."

Jack picked up a piece of toast. "Isn't that amazing?" He crammed the food into his mouth.

As Jack slathered marmalade onto another slice of bread, Fred took a moment to contemplate the spectacularly unfair nature of the universe. "Why would the Thai government give their money to Reagan?" he finally asked. "Last I heard, he was trying to be a movie producer in LA." There had been at least two attempts Fred knew of, a reboot of a cult Korean horror starring a beautiful but untalented actress, which had flopped, and another about World War II pilots that appeared destined to soon meet a similar fate. Reagan had been rumored to have been dating the actress from the former at the time of shooting, with gossip of a twenty-five-carat canary diamond gifted for her twenty-fifth birthday; she had since moved on to a minor sheikh.

"You know how these things work." Jack turned up his palm and gestured toward the window, as if to say, *Asia*. "Reagan is insanely connected. As is his family. Did you ever meet Regina? His sister?"

"Her name is Regina? Regina and Reagan? Jesus."

Jack laughed. "She's a fruit. When you first meet her, you think she's one of those girls you see lined up outside clubs in Hong Kong, all tight dresses and little Chanel bags. Tons of makeup, basic plastic surgery with the huge eyes and skinny nose. The gold-digger look, not that you could even kiss Regina without showing her an ATM receipt. But Reagan's parents, they've been on Regina to do something with her life. She finally finished her master's in art history at Yale, which is kind of ridiculous, since when does she care about art? Or, for that matter, history? She probably did it because she went to some Art Basel party and thought it was fun, but anyway, she got her degree, and now her parents can say she went to an Ivy League school. They expected her to get a job at one of the auction houses after, but you know what she did instead? Opened a luxury candy shop! What's a luxury candy shop, you ask? Nobody really knows, but we all go to the opening to show support, more for Reagan, really. When we arrive, we learn that not only do there exist organic lollipops, but they cost $12. That's US dollars! I mean, come on . . . and Regina is dressed like Katy Perry in that music video, wearing a bra made out of cotton candy and these slutty hot shorts with edible buttons all over them. She gets herself photographed a bunch of times—I don't, of course; my parents would kill me—and I guess that's the last straw for Mom and Dad. The next month, the Sugar Suite is on temporary hiatus and Regina's somehow Thailand's new secretary of education. Meanwhile, all of us are asking, has Regina ever even read a book? I don't even know if she can *write*. That's the kind of pull Reagan's family has."

Fred tried to conceal his admiration. "I'm sure yours could do the same for you."

"Maybe once upon a time, but these days? People are going to actual jail for that, in Hong Kong. I'm not going to prison! I'm a father now. And I'd rather be behind the scenes anyway, you know how my family is. It's more than enough to participate in some fun projects here and there, which is why I like to keep in touch with people like Reagan." He coughed. "So, back to the Thais. Right now I heard they're looking at around $6 billion. But Reagan says they'll do the full round once they settle a few open budgetary items, and he expects the total to settle at just around $45 billion. The money they're allotting him, apparently the Thais want it all earmarked for technology investment. Some of it is internal, the sort of stuff China is doing—they all want their own Apples and Teslas and Amazons, though to be honest that's a pipe dream, since even China can't always pull it off, and they have a zillion times more money and really excellent corporate espionage. I think the Thais understand that, though, because they want most of it invested in Silicon Valley. Have some markers at a few companies they can hopefully get great returns from, and maybe one day rip off and copy for themselves. The Valley side is where you'd come in. I'd be helping out on the Hong Kong/mainland end, and you'd be on the ground in the US sourcing deals. What do you think?"

Fred felt as if he'd just finished a glass of beer on a hot day and was licking away the last bits of foam. The numbers were outrageous. Six billion? Forty-five? Lion Capital was a mere $300 *million*. "Hmm." He stretched his arms. "Sounds like sovereign wealth." When he was younger he had thought the idea of investing money for the government sounded cool, but he had since learned it was compensated the same way as corporate venture capital: shittily.

"The money's technically sovereign, but it's being managed like private sector. The Thais are committed to paying for the best talent. No good investor is going to work for them unless there's long-term capital incentive, at least that's what Reagan says they're thinking, and I can't imagine he'd be involved otherwise. They're even letting him choose the name for the fund. He told me he wants to call it Opus."

While his heart gave a merry cheer at the words *long-term capital incentive*, Fred fought to keep his face level. "What made you two think of me? There's a lot of *Asia guys* in the Valley." Releasing the words with disdain, so Jack would know exactly how to regard his potential competition.

"Actually"—Jack looked uncomfortable—"it was Reagan who brought it up. Once he said your name, of course I knew it was a perfect idea, but at the time you and I hadn't spoken for so long. I didn't even know where you were living! Charlene was always the great connector, you know, she used to send out those emails. . . . Once you guys split, I didn't get my Fred Huang holiday updates anymore."

Fred had forgotten about those emails. Somewhat illogically he cursed Charlene for not continuing to keep their friends up-to-date on his developments. Who knew how many opportunities had been lost, left uncharted due to her pettiness? "But I just said that I don't really know Reagan. I didn't even think he knew who I was."

"I know, that's what I kind of thought, but then, when Reagan brought it up. . . ." Jack shrugged. "I thought, well, you guys must have gotten to know each other somewhere. Plus Reagan, he's got this crazy index in his brain; he knows everyone and what they're doing and what they've done. He's always talking people up, collecting the latest news, trading a little here, whispering some there. You know what we call him in our poker group? Asia Facebook, because if you tell him a rumor, it's sure to spread to all of mainland by the next morning!" He cackled.

Very interesting. Reagan may have heard of him through mutual industry friends; Fred considered the idea that he'd been overly harsh in his assessment of the relative prestige of Lion Capital. Its parent *was* one of the most famous technology companies in Asia, and he was second-in-command in the office and really the brainpower of the entire operation . . . but he should be modest with Jack; he liked that sort of thing. "Reagan doesn't know anyone else in Silicon Valley?"

he fished. "There's probably a hundred guys he could call with better pedigrees than me."

"Aw, come on. You're way too humble. He probably knew you better than you thought. Aren't you excited? Working with Reagan is a real head trip, you'll see. A fun kind. Party party party."

Fred forced a smile. Inside, his stomach churned. Now that he knew the details of the Opus job, he was hit with abrupt panic over how many others—with his exact same credentials or better—might want it too. How many dissatisfied Harvard Business School graduates with excellent finance backgrounds existed out there? How many men who felt the same as he, entitled to important and moneyed careers, just a lucky turn away from becoming real men of means? Even narrowing it down to merely the Asians—as this looked to be one of the few instances where a last name of Huang might actually be considered an asset on the résumé—didn't provide particular comfort. Dissatisfied, highly educated Asian men in Fred's age group had become almost a sort of cliché. He observed them each weekend: as they meticulously tended to lawns to maintain home values; at the grocery store, as they steered Teslas into remote parking spots without cars on either side; in the evenings for poker, as they debated endlessly over the merits of expensive whiskeys. Fred was certain these enemies dotted plentifully throughout Jack's and Reagan's orbits, just one or two relationship layers removed.

And that wasn't even counting the women! Asian women like Charlene, with their Stanford degrees and high metabolisms and cunning hearts, who toyed with jet-black hair and had the unfair advantage of looking hot in a cocktail dress, at least from the back. Sure, Reagan and Jack wanted him now, for reasons he still didn't fully comprehend—but what about later, when word got around?

He wouldn't miss the golden ring this time. He'd sat out on enough in the past decade, plodding along in dutiful impotence while everyone else took risks and got rich. No longer would he serve as some banal paragon of the model minority, banished to an existence of mediocre achievement. His person now was a significant upgrade, a leaner, more aggressive Fred Huang. A man who went after what he wanted, who took what he deserved.

A man of significance!

"WHAT'S THE MOST EXPENSIVE ITEM YOU EVER SOLD?"

Jack rested his cheeks in his fists and beamed at Erika. She'd made her appearance completely unannounced at the hour mark, strolling in with a radiant smile as Fred scrambled to mask his annoyance. Descending into a chair that had miraculously appeared at their table just in time by a quick-thinking server; buoyantly confident in her greetings as if she weren't in fact rudely interrupting his last chance to speak with Jack privately before Bali. It was the sort of power move she was always pulling, Fred thought —blithely inserting herself wherever and whenever she felt, always so confident that his friends and colleagues would love her.

Erika paused as if to ponder, though Fred knew she already had the answer. "A watch, a Patek Philippe," she said. "Half a million. One of my best clients, and then afterward he wanted to buy another, for almost a million. He'd already wire transferred the money, but then last minute Patek wouldn't ship it over. They said he had to fly to Switzerland first, and interview to prove he was a real collector."

"I've heard of that," Jack said. "They don't even pay for the flight or hotel, do they? It's outrageous!"

"Oh, so you know all about it then. Yes, it's true. My client, he was so insulted that he immediately canceled the order. Almost returned the other watch as well."

"But he didn't?"

"No, I convinced him not to." Erika smiled coyly. "That's why it's still my biggest sale. Since then he's ordered a few more, but I

always check now to make sure he can take each piece home immediately. Once I heard there might be a problem, limited inventory, and
I swapped the model to a different one, very nice and even a little less
money. I thought my client would be so pleased about the savings, but
you know what?" She flitted her hand. "He didn't even care!"

Jack clapped in delight. "Is this dude single? Fred, you've got some
competition! This guy is spending a million a year to impress your
girlfriend!"

"He was single," Erika said. "He has a girlfriend now, or perhaps
they are married. His name is Will Packer."

"Will Packer!" Jack whooped. "Fred, you've got an even bigger
problem than I thought!"

Will Packer was a founding partner of Tata Packer, one of the
oldest and most esteemed venture firms in the Valley. Fred had never
met Packer, though he glimpsed him regularly at the Starbucks on
the corner on El Camino—they did, after all, both have offices on
Sand Hill, though that was the extent of their similarities, he thought
sourly. "Erika, do you know who Will Packer *is*?" Jack continued. "He's
one of the richest guys ever! Our friend Reagan knows him; they're on
the advisory committee of the same climate change gala."

"Oh I know," Erika said, with a flutter of the lids. "He doesn't
make it a secret, his achievements, when he speaks to me. I think he
is a little . . . infatuated."

Though she spoke to Jack it was clear who was her actual intended
audience, and Fred was hit with a wave of repulsion, followed quickly
by shame. It wasn't Erika's fault she wasn't a native English speaker,
which often made her attempts at summoning jealousy clunky and
uneven. She didn't know not to use words like *infatuated*, which was
much too strong an adjective, particularly in regards to Will Packer,
who, Fred already knew via perfunctory online stalking, was in the
heady early months of marriage to his fourth wife, a Vietnamese cocktail waitress Packer was rumored to have met at a shady hostess lounge

in Southern California. The woman had once played last chair in her high school orchestra; the Tata Packer public relations team was actively remarketing her as a "stunning concert violinist."

Fred used to hate hearing stories like that, anecdotes of those reborn in a stroke of luck, soaring directly to the top without having slaved over the individual steps along the way. Friends of friends and brothers of roommates who, through the most fortunate of connections, got in on the ground floor of future unicorns. Low-level analysts who, after the right marriages, became lifestyle gurus. He had cheered each time one was toppled, felled by the hubris that the status they'd previously occupied had been earned, instead of bestowed by random chance.

Fred realized that Jack and Erika, who had both fallen quiet, were waiting for him. "Sorry, brain fart. What'd you say?"

"Pervert venture capitalists!" Jack boomed. "Going after your girlfriend, man."

"Who could blame them?" He stretched an arm around Erika. "But she's taken."

And Fred could see from the mix of pleasure and relief on their faces that he had answered correctly, another small trial passed in the most important week of his life.

A feeling of contentment settled over him, which extended to Erika and Jack and eventually the entire restaurant and even Will Packer and his coterie of partners. Packer had known his current wife was a cocktail waitress when he initially met her, after all; perhaps it was just unlucky circumstances that had prevented her from pursuing an early passion for music. With her new resources, the woman could hire private tutors and purchase the very finest of instruments; who was to say that without some time and dedicated practice she couldn't learn to play at the level of a virtuoso? And then none of what she had done earlier would matter; the world would know her only by her new name and all that had come before would fall away.

————————

That night Erika and Fred ate back at the Dorchester, at Silver Lotus, the hotel's Michelin star, which served braised abalone and suckling pig at breathtakingly high prices. Erika had been in a precarious mood since they first left the hotel; the air outside had been wet and hot, and her hair had instantly frizzed from the humidity. Sensing danger, Fred suggested they return to the hotel early, via the endless stream of indoor malls that appeared to constitute the majority of Hong Kong. As they passed each luxury boutique Erika stared at the patrons as if being challenged; at Chanel, where the shoppers were actually cordoned off in a line outside, she sneered at the swarm of mostly mainland Chinese waiting to enter. "They are ruining luxury," she declared.

At dinner, they opened a bottle of Krug Jack had left as a gift ($75 corkage, reasonable); then, when Fred was in the bathroom, Erika downed the remainder of the bottle and ordered another ($1,200, a moral outrage). By the time they returned to their room he was noting a familiar glitter in her eye; she began to trip toward the toilet, before abruptly pivoting back in his direction.

"Why aren't we married?"

Fred had been anticipating the question with dread since dinner. "Erika, *please*." He rubbed his scalp. "The timing, it has to be right. Do you know how much work it is to plan a wedding? Especially the sort you want." He'd picked up on various hints over the years: a view of the San Francisco Bay Bridge and massive displays of peonies; dozens of relatives flown in from Hungary to gape at the unimaginable luxury. Even if he did want to get married again—a concept he still wasn't completely sold on in isolation—he knew from prior experience with Charlene that the expense would be crushing. Fred doubted that Erika even knew how much weddings really cost; simply that they were something women like her in serious relationships demanded, and summarily received.

She glowered, her arms crossed. "Then why aren't we engaged?"

"We will be, in good time. I'm begging you to please have a little more patience right now. Can you do that?"

"I've had enough patience. I'm always patient, patiently waiting." She kicked off a sandal and slowly massaged her ankle, an erotic habit she'd picked up from barre class. "I'm waiting for you to decide what you want to eat for dinner. I'm waiting for you to come home from work. I'm waiting for you to fuck me, which you can't even do these days, because you're always too tired. I'm waiting for you to propose, but I will tell you this now, and you will take me seriously." She wagged a finger. "I will not wait much longer."

"I'm not having a conversation when you're in this state." Fred closed his eyes and flopped backward onto the bed. "You're clearly drunk."

Erika slapped him on the side of his head. "Do not think you can sleep." She began to undress, in her fury accidentally flinging her long pearl strand under the wardrobe. "Look how your friends like me. They admire you because of me! Can't you see this? Doesn't it make you feel good?"

"Of course, you're a very desirable and beautiful woman. Don't I already tell you that all the time? Can we please discuss this in the morning? You should have some water. From the tap," he caveated, hurriedly removing the glass Voss bottles the Dorchester wickedly placed each night by the bed. "Hong Kong water is very clean."

"You should have some water," Erika mimicked. "You are so boring. Poor, stupid, boring, tired Fred."

Fred yawned and tried to drown out her voice. Drunk women were only attractive when you were trying to sleep with them; afterward, they were just about the worst thing in the world.

Erika climbed onto the bed in just her slip and straddled him, on all fours. "You know what your problem is? You're *old*. Always complaining that you need more sleep, that your muscles ache, that the music is too loud. Only senior citizens say these things."

The words stung. He was *old*? Forty-four? He was in his prime! On the cusp of managing billions of dollars! But then a river of fatigue overran his indignation.

"Why aren't you saying anything?" She banged on his chest. *"Are you listening to me?"*

"I'm very tired. I would prefer not to spend any more time on this topic tonight." He laid down his head and pretended to sleep. The exhaustion of the day flowed over him like water. He prayed Erika wouldn't start crying. If she did, he was in for at least an hour of tearful consolation, as well as what would surely be a resurgence of violently contained sobs right as he entered the comforting bosom of REM sleep.

When he opened his eyes a few minutes later, Erika was gone.

Fred forced himself to sit up. He made his way to the bathroom. Excellent oral hygiene was essential to staving off disease—he had finally started the cancer book Stanley asked him to order. He found he especially liked the flosser sticks it recommended—he was catching so many items just around his gums. After he finished, he changed into a new pair of boxers and on the way back to the bed, he looked under the wardrobe. The pearls were gone.

Fred understood Erika was extremely drunk, a top five for a relationship that for the first few years had been filled almost every weekend with booze. She had likely gone downstairs to the lobby bar, with the expectation that he'd soon follow. Were they back in San Francisco she'd be strolling in her designer heels and a revealing dress right now, idly wandering through clubs and lounges. Erika never traveled past the first five or ten closest to the apartment, because she wanted to be found. Fred was always meant to appear in a frantic state at the door,

worried out of his mind that she was being date-raped in a corner—
only to discover her at the bar, calmly charming whichever man had
reached her first. The flirtations were never intended to progress past
talking, though it was ideal if Fred could catch the man looking at her
breasts or eyeing her legs. The thought of someone else—a *stranger*—
placing his mouth on her tits, sliding his fingers into her underwear,
always serving to simultaneously enrage and excite him to such a point
where he would then rush over and rudely yank her away, his fury
now solely concentrated on the blood rushing to his dick. The evenings usually ended in the hallway, or on the kitchen counter, or once
in the elevator—and afterward their relationship would hit reset,
Erika's bad behavior earlier in the night evening with his own later on.

Fred could imagine her downstairs now, testing her allure, cast-
ing a net for the fattest and richest to spur his regret. Erika was tall,
white, striking; in Hong Kong, in a sea of mostly unattractive faces, she
particularly stood out. (Linda: "Chinese women in Hong Kong are
the ugliest. Though the Taiwanese are more money hungry.") Perhaps there was someone talking her up right now, a faceless man who
thought she was a lawyer on a business trip or the moneyed estranged
wife of some minor bank executive. Maybe it was Jack, who had returned to the Dorchester for just this very purpose. At this, Fred felt
the stirrings of an erection. Still, he didn't move. He had forgotten
how terrible the jet lag going East was.

The longer he lay on the soft duvet, the less acute the dull ache
in his groin, its flaccidity diverting sharpness back to the brain. Erika
was the one truly getting old, he thought. She was thirty-four. When
they first started dating she had ridiculed single women that age,
laughing with satisfied confidence that she herself would never arrive
at the same life station without at least an ostentatious engagement
ring (her preference, as she repeatedly reminded him, was vintage As-
scher cut). When Erika learned a colleague over forty was having a
baby, she'd returned home and sniggered about what they called such

conditions in the medical profession: geriatric pregnancies. Geriatric! That was one area where overly politically correct Americans were completely right, she said. To have a baby at such an age was unnatural, a condition that deserved an embarrassing name.

At the time Fred had loved her attitude, the sort of confident *bitch* Erika was. He had long grown past his schoolboy convictions that he was looking for a nice girl and recognized that what he was really drawn to were the mean spirits, the ones who thought they were above it all. Why weren't more white women bitches? There were plenty of Asian ones; Fred could recognize a leaden heart and a whirring calculator of a brain under a batted pair of demure eyelashes any day. They went Ivy League or Stanford and called everything else "state school"; they picked a road—beauty, smarts, or wealth—and then obsessively competed in their particular pageant down to the bone. Why didn't Caucasian women have this excellent affliction? Was it because they had been told they were special all their lives and thus genuinely happy about the world? Or maybe they were mean, too, the way he liked, and he just didn't know how to recognize it.

THE NEXT MORNING, HE WOKE TO THE SENSATION OF AN AUDIENCE. When he opened his eyes, Erika's were closed. Coral blush and dark red lipstick was smeared violently on her pillow, and a row of false eyelashes hung askew toward her cheek. Thanks to his melatonin, he had slept so soundly that he had no sense of when she had returned.

Fred waited in stillness, timing his breath as if in deep sleep. She crept open an eye, and he immediately saw she knew she had miscalculated. To put her at ease, he gently brushed an eyelash from her nose. The gesture emboldened her, and an expression with which he was all too familiar crept across her face, an attitude so frequently utilized by his mother that Kate had christened it with its own name: "Let Us Pretend This Never Happened."

"Bringing you here was a mistake," Fred said quickly. He wanted to cut off any overture she was gearing to launch, as what he had to say was important.

And as her smile died, he told Erika what he had decided was necessary, in his last beats of consciousness on the truly excellent Dorchester mattress. He no longer wanted her with him in Bali. And since he was paying for the flight and hotel and everything else on their trip, what he really meant was: he was sending her home.

Fred was aware that what he was doing was the equivalent of pushing a red button on the relationship; that in an uncontrolled environment, the full ramifications of a potential explosion were unknown. But he also saw now that there was no way he could have ever brought Erika to the Founders' Retreat. How could he have not realized this earlier?

Fred had always understood Erika's behavior. How she furtively studied clients and their wives, to identify small markers of status that could be emulated (the word *lovely*, scuffed soles on expensive shoes, white clothing). How she'd reworked and perfected her family tree, to better reflect preferred American sensibilities for its white immigrants (the invention of a wealthy uncle, the elevation of György and Anna to academics). Her persistence as she plodded through the *Wall Street Journal*, dedicating herself to the rote learning of global economic trends that were out of date by the following weekend. How could he not admire and love such a woman? But now Erika was sinking him. Her desperate hunt for a tangible return on four years of investment in the relationship had rendered her unpredictable, and given the importance of the week ahead, he could no longer shoulder the neuroses of a thirty-four-year-old saleswoman dressed in Chanel. In the days ahead, Fred would need all his faculties. He had to be flying, in top form.

It was his time.

CHAPTER 10

LINDA

The Whole Foods in Cupertino took up nearly half the entire city block of a busy intersection, a sprawled arena that lay flat in repose against the continual stream of vehicles buffering it. Inside there was a gelato station, sushi stand, dosa maker, burrito bar, wines by the glass, olive sampler, and cheese emporium, while right outside the entrance a seasonal array of fruits and vegetables was stacked head-high, as if the store's elephantine interior weren't quite adequate to contain the fullness of its bounty. Since its debut there had been more of these coliseums erected nearby, the buildings even larger and more exuberant in design and assortment, but the Cupertino outlet still stood in staggering majesty, confident in its position as the area flagship for healthy living and the surrounding community's inelastic consumption of it.

In Linda's educated opinion, the only aspect not oversize about this particular Whole Foods was its parking lot. Whenever she went shopping she had to steel herself far in advance for the experience, especially during peak hours. Why would a superstore located in the midst of one of the highest concentrations of Asians in Silicon Valley build such cramped lanes? Didn't its management anticipate the endless traffic jams and accidents they were sure to unleash on their own treasured clientele? Even the ethnic supermarkets in the area—which almost exclusively employed workers off the books and brazenly violated earthquake codes to jam more merchandise along already precariously tall and tightly arranged aisles—invested in regular-size parking. To do otherwise would be to generate a never-ending string of vehicular pileups and minor collisions, all of which would then surely impact customer flow, and thus the bottom line.

When Linda arrived at the mega-shop, turning the familiar corner, she impulsively chose the wrong lane and found herself trapped in a string of cars at a complete standstill. The culprit, of course—once she managed to catch a glimpse—was a dour Asian woman in a bloated Mercedes SUV, the most expensive model, wearing one of those ridiculous oversize sun visors. As Linda idled closer, she saw that the woman had on a quilted jacket, a halfhearted Burberry imitation made all the more lurid by its contrast with the opulence of the vehicle, and gave an involuntary shudder. She knew exactly how Americans saw women like the Mercedes driver—as indistinguishable from herself. An Asian lady consumed with the creation and consumption of money, who neglected to hug her children. Why did white people like to pick and choose from cultures with such zealous judgment? Of course they just *loved* Szechuan cuisine served by a young waitress in a cheap cheongsam, but as soon as you proved yourself just as adept at the form of capitalism *they* had invented? Then you were obsessed. Money crazed. Unworthy of sympathy. And God forbid your children end up at superior schools; then it became all about how much they must have been beaten, the investigative conjecturing over what creative instincts had been snuffed out in order to achieve such excellent test scores.

As she crept toward the Mercedes, Linda could clearly make out the woman's terror. She seesawed between reversing out of her spot and then lurching back in, petrified of hitting one of the cars waiting increasingly impatiently for her space. A man in a red Toyota truck and a *Hillary Clinton '08* sticker leaned out his window. "Hurry the fuck up!" he called.

The woman ignored him. Didn't he know none of them had taken driver's ed in high school? Though they had—at least at the #1 Girls' School—practiced target shooting with rifles, which you'd think Americans would approve of, Linda thought. Eventually, each of the cars in front of her gave up, the red truck zooming off with squealing vigor, and she turned on her signal and dawdled, giving the woman a good thirty feet. And snagged the spot.

"WHO MANAGED THE MONEY, WHEN YOU AND DAD WERE MARRIED?"

These days, Kate only asked to spend time together when she already had plans for something else—errands, or shuttling the kids from one of their myriad expensive activities. This was something that usually bothered Linda in theory—wasn't she worthy of a solo lunch or dinner date?—but she rarely minded in execution. The tasks were typically something she needed to get done anyway, like the pharmacy or library, and sometimes they were even interesting. Linda had meant to go to Whole Foods ever since Stanley's diagnosis. Why was green juice so expensive, and why couldn't she just make the same at home for far less?

"Your father did, of course. He wanted complete control of the finances."

Kate frowned. "But you always said he was bad with money."

How quickly children could sway from protective to critical! Kate had chewed her out just last week, when Linda had lightly suggested that she and Fred prod Stanley for updates on his will; as far as Linda was aware, no progress had been made, typical of Stanley.

"He's sick!" Kate had cried, as if being seventy-five with a fair chance of dying that year was so much more significant than the conditions everyone else their age toiled under on a daily basis. That was why Linda had long since finalized her own estate plan, moving all of her assets into a family trust, with clearly marked copies and supporting documentation in her file cabinet. A heart attack could happen at any moment; a stroke could reduce one overnight to a jabbering simpleton. And then where would you be, if you hadn't planned ahead? There was the regular truth, and then the economic reality—how foolish she was to have assumed that her son, who had chosen a career in finance, and her daughter, who worked for one of the most profitable companies in the Bay Area, would understand this.

Linda let it go. They were having a nice time and were going to eat lunch after. She also had some questions about probiotics she thought Kate might be able to answer. "I didn't always know your father was so stupid. You have to remember, he's a few years older than me. When we met, he was already getting his PhD! How was I to know he'd never end up finishing? He was an engineer, so I thought he would be good with numbers." She shouldn't have said *stupid*, she realized. Kate would take offense; it probably wasn't a word allowed to be used for those with cancer.

"And how much did you guys save of your income? What percentage?"

"Well, we both worked, so there were two paychecks coming in. Of course, that was just *our* situation, I know every household is different these days," Linda added piously. "Each person's paycheck was deposited into their own separate account. Your father wanted things that way. Probably to be sneaky. From my account, I paid the household costs, any bills for you and Fred. And then once the money left over reached $5,000, I wrote your father a check. Then he'd go and *manage* it, since of course back then I didn't know how stup— uneducated he was with money. Still, we probably saved around fifty percent that way."

The figure was actually closer to 65 percent; the separate accounts were how Linda had been able to steadily squirrel away for so long without Stanley's knowledge. She probably should have realized earlier how incompetent he was—what sort of so-called financial genius didn't notice 15 percent of the household money disappearing, for decades? But he'd benefited handsomely in the end. Only Stanley, Linda thought, could manage to conjure money out of ignorance.

"What if one of you wanted to make a big purchase? Like a car or house remodel?"

"Why? Denny wants a new car?" It would be just like her lazy son-in-law to dream up more ways of spending money, instead of earning it. She would have to find out the make and model, which Kate would surely be cagey about. A BMW? Porsche? Or dear God, a Tesla? Linda saw them everywhere and still hadn't figured out why they were so expensive.

"There is no car. I was just wondering. Doing some basic planning." Kate had a faraway look. Could she and Denny be having financial issues? Linda waited patiently, but Kate didn't elaborate. She filed this nugget away under To Be Investigated Later.

"Well, your father and I, we didn't really spend much, *ever*," she prompted. "And things like a car or roof we would save a little for each month, so there were never too many surprises. We didn't have all the luxuries our children do, these days." She darted her eyes over to catch Kate's reaction, but she was still. Linda tried again. "Did I tell you about Yvonne Cho's daughter? She is having her third baby and is a vice president at Facebook now. Isn't Facebook the same size as your company? Their stock has been doing very, very well. I bought a little for myself. Already up thirty percent!"

"You did tell me about your friend's daughter." Kate yawned. "Facebook is a very successful and large company."

"You could always have another baby, you know. But soon, before you are too old. I wish I had."

"I told you, the train stops at two. There's no way we're adding another child. Especially not now."

"Why? Your health? You've always been delicate, eh?" Which to be honest was probably from her side of the family, seeing how Stanley's entire lineage was comprised of healthy peasant stock.

Kate fingered boxes of green tea. "Don't buy any of those," Linda commented. "Very overpriced."

Kate put back the box she held and turned toward Linda. "Do you remember when you used to say that one bad decision could change your life?"

"I did?" Linda couldn't remember. Lately, she'd had the overwhelming sensation that there were no single, seminal moves that completely altered the course of one's destiny. Instead, life just seemed to be a series of small mistakes, which you continued to make over and over again.

"When we were growing up. You said it all the time."

"Maybe I was talking about Stanford admissions."

"Like Dad," Kate persisted. "Why did you even marry him, and then stay together for so long? It kind of seems like you always hated him."

"I didn't *always* feel that way. I was very young and naive when we married. I believed everything your father told me. It was only after many years that I saw who he really was. And then before I knew it we were already old, and I realized that if I ever got sick I couldn't count on him to take care of me. He would always put himself first, even if I was dying, so it'd serve him right if— Well, anyway, life can be very funny. And he had such a bad temper, with you and Fred. The way he used to yell and go crazy!"

"He never lost it with you?"

"Never. He knew I wouldn't stand for that." She felt a hot pang of regret, the stowed memory of Stanley's erratic violence with their children. Maybe she should have done something more about it back then, really threatened to leave him if he didn't stop, but at the time it had seemed impossible. As it was it had taken her decades to assemble her courage. Besides, what could be done about it now?

"I will speak to your father about his will," she declared.

"I'm not interested in his money."

"Why not? I earned most of it. You don't care that I worked so hard? You have enough already for Ethan and Ella, their college? Your retirement?"

"Of course I care. I know how much you did for him." Kate looked cross and then confused. "The college funds—I'll have to think about that later."

A woman approached, a tall brunette with two miserable-looking children in tow. As she and Kate exchanged greetings, Linda unconsciously took a step back and stood silently. It was a habit she had acquired when her children were teenagers and embarrassed by her.

"This is my mom," Kate said. "We're doing some shopping. Ma, this is Sandra Mays. Her daughter goes to Children's Academy with Ella."

The woman smiled toothily. Linda bobbed her head and stared at the ceiling. It was useful, for an introvert, to allow white people to assume you didn't speak English.

"So funny to see you here," the woman exclaimed. "This isn't my normal Whole Foods; we're here because Kayla has a class nearby. Didn't I see Ella at Jade Mountain the other day? The new nanny seems nice."

"The park? Ella goes, but usually with Denny. Maybe it was one of the other mothers."

"Ah! Well, my mistake." The woman smiled silkily. "And how *is* the hubby?" she asked after a moment. "You're so lucky Denny's such an involved parent. Brian would expect a parade in his honor if he ever took the kids outside."

"He's fine," Kate said curtly.

Linda was taken aback by her tone, and studied the woman more closely. This Sandra person was a crafty witch, she decided, and was deliberately making the point that Denny's shiftlessness meant they had no need for paid childcare. It was the sort of stunt Shirley Chang was always pulling, loudly exclaiming her well wishes for whatever she found most worthy of disapproval in your life, thus announcing to everyone your misfortune.

Despite Kate's rudeness, the woman continued to linger. "Are you going to the gala?" she asked. "We pay so much in tuition already, why these schools need even more is beyond me. I might end up attending solo, since Brian just transferred to a new job at Google. It's more internal, but of course they've still got him signed up for all sorts of public events, symposiums and the like. . . ." She glanced at her phone, and then jammed it back in her pocket. "The other day Julie Reznikov comes up to me at pickup, you know who she is, her son's that husky shouter, the one always swaggering around the swings like a little bully. Her husband works in Brian's new group. And she starts talking about the Founders' Award, as if I had *any* control over who gets that. Well, to be honest, I could probably try, since Brian depends on me for so much. I basically dictate all his white papers. But Julie Reznikov? Fat chance."

"I'm not sure if I'm going," Kate said. "Work."

"Well if you are, let me know. I'm happy to pick you up; our neighborhoods are so close. At least until our new place in Los Altos

Hills is finished. Austin!" The woman gave a tug at the boy, who had batted down a row of boxes. "We can text," she called back.

Kate gave a wave. After she was gone, Linda sidled closer. "Who was that woman?" she asked in Mandarin. "She said she lived near you. What do she and her husband do?"

"Sandra?" Kate quickly glanced around. "Don't worry about her, she's harmless. Kind of an idiot, actually. The husband too." She grimaced, and for the first time Linda could see small lines around her mouth.

She patted Kate on the shoulder, an aggressively affectionate gesture. "You want to talk any more about your dad?"

"No, it's okay. I'm going to sit with him tomorrow during chemo. You don't want to come, do you?"

"Why would I? He has a wife, doesn't he?"

Kate exhaled, with a look that indicated she was exercising infinite self-control. "Why don't you tell me what's going on with you?"

Linda considered this. So far, the only person she had confided in about Winston was Yvonne. They'd met for lunch at Lemon Fish, one of those pleasurable meals where there were endless topics to discuss and the day seemed to yawn ahead with nothing but empty hours. When the restaurant closed they'd moved down to Starbucks to continue, commandeering a small outdoor table as far away as possible from a group of smoking teenagers.

"Jackson is driving me crazy," Yvonne had confided, kicking off one of their most popular topics. "I'm thinking of finally leaving. You know what he told me yesterday? That going forward, he will no longer vacuum the house. Apparently, for the forty years we've been married, each time I've asked him to vacuum I've been demeaning him! And you know what his reasoning is? That PhDs shouldn't vacuum, because it's a waste of their time. As if sitting in front of the TV in your robe is so efficient."

"You have a master's," Linda pointed out. "And you were always the better student. Remember how Professor Shih said it was you who should have won the department math award, not Jackson? And you have your children, your grandchildren." *And Jackson his other family in Taiwan*, she added in her head, a little tidbit everyone knew but nobody spoke of, at least not to Yvonne. Though Yvonne wasn't as pitiful a doormat as everyone assumed—Linda was one of the few privy to the knowledge that as a condition of future matrimony, Yvonne had negotiated that the entirety of her and Jackson's current and future assets be placed in a trust in their children's names. The wife and child in Taiwan, Linda assumed, would get nothing when Jackson kicked off—which is how it should be and how responsible heads of households conducted affairs, unlike her idiotic ex-husband, who would probably end up leaving it all to some trashy villager.

"Oh, I don't know about that. Jackson is very smart." Yvonne never missed a chance to worship her husband. "But I am getting tired of him."

"Being divorced isn't so difficult. I much prefer it to being married to Stanley. And I'm not lonely. Why—" Linda hesitated, and decided to push forward. "I even have a boyfriend."

"A boyfriend?" Yvonne leaned in. Romantic gossip was a rarity in their group. Linda, as the only divorcée, had already provided conversational fodder for years, a fact she'd always loathed. "Where did you meet him?"

And then, within minutes, Yvonne, the most gentle of all of Linda's friends, had managed to extract that Winston:

a. owned no property in the Bay Area or greater California region,
b. had not attended any of the top colleges in Taiwan or Hong Kong or mainland China, and,
c. had still never met Linda in person!

She should have lied about the last part, Linda realized, when the merits of a virtual relationship became impossibly difficult to explain to a technology blockhead like Yvonne. Being forced to expound on what she wore on camera, or how she was certain Winston wasn't some imposter, or (most shame-inducing) how they managed to be intimate, had been her most humiliating experience in recent memory. Yvonne had deftly excavated for details under the feigned guise that she, too, might one day discover herself in an online relationship and in need of such knowledge—no doubt revenge for all the times Linda had done the same with detailed inquiries into Jackson's shadow family.

Finally, unable to take it a moment longer, she had blurted that she wasn't feeling well and had to go. Yvonne grasped her hand. "Linda, you are so smart and capable. I know you will take care of yourself."

When Linda returned home, her answering machine flashed eight missed calls and her cell phone another six. She prepared dinner and carefully watered each of her orchids before deigning to answer the ringing handset.

"Why didn't you pick up?" Winston roared. "I called many times. I was so worried!"

"I was busy."

"Whenever you don't answer, I'm so frightened something happened to you. That maybe you were in a car accident, or someone broke into your house. Can't you have some sympathy for how I feel? I would die if something happened to you."

"Why would you die?" Linda snapped. "We've never even met."

LATER, AFTER SHE'D APOLOGIZED FOR HER MOOD, SHE TOLD WIN-ston about her lunch with Yvonne. "She said I should be very careful with you," Linda said, even though Yvonne hadn't, not exactly. "She thinks it's strange, that we haven't met."

"There is nothing more I would like than for you and I to see each other. I told you, just say yes and I'll buy you a ticket. Business class, of course."

"I don't want to go to Lebanon." Western Europe was the least-civilized destination she was willing to travel to these days, and even Paris or London could be tolerated only once every few years. "Why can't you come here? The weather is so nice, and Din Tai Fung just opened."

"I would do anything for a bowl of spicy pork and vegetable dumplings." Winston groaned. "Please, my darling, just wait a little longer. Once the sanctions are over, I'll be able to travel again. And then the first thing I'll do is send you the beautiful Buccellati bracelet I saw last week in *Vanity Fair*."

She unconsciously touched her fingers to her wrist. "That's another thing. I don't think it's responsible to keep offering to buy me expensive presents when you're having so many cash flow problems."

"How many times can I swear that I'll never ask for money again!"

There'd been a second request just last week after another tuition issue with Yale, Winston abruptly requesting $24,000 at the tail end of a three-hour-long marathon call during which they'd confessed to each other the worst of their childhood secrets. Linda had taken half a week to mull it over and then said no, allowing a frosty silence to descend for an additional day while ignoring all his attempts at contact. When she finally relented to a video chat, Winston had broken down out of relief and shame, a grayed man in a sweater-vest with twin waterfalls of tears streaming down his cheeks. "I will provide for you, I promise," he cried again now. "I've always believed that a man should take care of a woman."

"I just want you to adequately manage yourself and your own expenses."

"Why do you sound so angry? Is this because of your friends? I told you, Chinese our age, they can't stand to see others happy. Especially the women. They will always try to sabotage. What we have is so unique, so special. Isn't that so?"

The day before a bouquet of mixed flowers had arrived, followed by a large package. When Linda opened the box, she found it packed with paper confetti. Nestled in the middle, occupying a tenth of the space, was a smaller container. From that Linda had unwrapped a thin gold chain from Tiffany, sprinkled with small diamonds.

She'd held it up to herself in the mirror. It was the sort of item she would have been overjoyed to receive when she was decades younger. Larger, chunkier pieces seemed to suit her better now; delicate jewelry only emphasized the flimsy nature of her body, disappearing in the tissue paper of her flesh.

If Winston had overextended himself with the purchase, she'd thought, it was his issue. She was tired of burdening herself with the problems of men. And the necklace, after she'd toyed with it, was more versatile than it first appeared. She could double it up to choker length, or wear it with a turtleneck, and it wouldn't appear so fragile.

She would tell Kate about Winston the first time she wore the necklace, Linda decided.

———————

Each year, after a carefully considered interval following her birthday, Linda sent an email to her college class.

The tradition had started with Leonard Chan, a fellow Taiwan University classmate and mechanical engineer at Apple, one of the few who still worked a real job (one-man consulting shops, in Linda's opinion, didn't qualify as employment). Leonard had long established himself as the technology expert of their group, the one friends went to when they wanted to play DVDs of Chinese dramas on their iPads, and to whom late-night phone calls were frantically placed when laptops abruptly ceased to work (the diagnosis in most cases was porn, a fact Leonard kept gleefully to himself). Five years ago, Leonard learned from his son that each person in his high school class sent an email update on his or her birthday. It was a wonderful way to stay in touch, his son claimed, a method of cutting through all the unreliable noise of social media. Inspired, Leonard initiated the same action for the Taiwan University Class of 1966.

Initially each person was simply supposed to email the group list he set up, every year on his or her birthday, but that system quickly descended into chaos. First there was the issue that no one knew or could remember what a group email list was, or how to send updates, which resulted in more frantic calls to Leonard. Then there was the complication that while nearly everyone relished reading gossipy updates about their peers, a much smaller faction actually wanted to furnish the same information about their own lives, leading to a dire asymmetry of data.

Leonard eventually solved both problems by assuming a dictatorship over the process, where each person sent their email directly to him, which he then forwarded on to the group. He then issued an edict that anyone neglecting to provide an update would summarily be kicked off the list and not allowed back on until a full year had passed. This resulted in a flurry of communications, including Linda's first participation—a brief three-line paragraph that confirmed she was alive.

Since then, Linda had perfected her technique. She never sent an update on her actual birthday—to do so smacked of self-congratulation and also alerted everyone that you had nothing better to do on the auspicious day than to manage correspondence (delaying a week or two also allowed for a mention of how you were feted by children and grandchildren). And while it was true that one should never be seen as bragging, the same went for deliberately forgetful. Shirley Chang's volleys, for example, never failed to mention the newest renovations on her Atherton home or the latest updates on her Ivy League daughter (as if Cornell counted!) but glossed over the shut-in son entirely; since everyone knew about him anyway, all her omission served to do was highlight the extent of her shame. It was a difficult task to strike the exact right balance of success and fulfillment without the putrid stench of boastfulness, a delicate art that required her full faculties.

Linda prepared a cup of tea, the best loose leaf she had from her last trip to Hong Kong, and opened her laptop.

To: Leonard168@apple.com
From: LLiang1945@gmail.com
Subject: Linda Liang's 71st Birthday Email

Dear classmates,

I have been excited to read each of your updates. What interesting lives you all are leading, with so many fortuitous announcements! Of course at our age, living in good health is the greatest fortune of all, wouldn't you agree?

As most of you know, I divorced my husband, Stanley, more than a decade ago and continue to enjoy my freedom. Retired life is very satisfying. Every morning I take a brisk hour-long walk, and then in the afternoon I garden. I keep up with my stocks and do some light cooking. My son, Fred, works in venture capital and often travels overseas. My daughter, Kate, works at X Corp, where she has been for many years, and has two children, Ella and Ethan. I have attached a photo of me and them, at my house. The grandchildren love to come play with their Wai Po on the weekends!

I am lucky to see many of our good friends regularly for mah jong and lunches and am enjoying the company of new acquaintances.

Best regards,

Linda Liang

CHAPTER 11

KATE

What did it mean, to be nice? *Nice* was a label that had been foisted on Kate since childhood, one she hadn't known she was campaigning for but which, once anointed, she found difficult to part with. "You're great," Denny had said, way back then. "Like, actually nice. Not like so many other Asian women."

It'd been a lifetime ago, before kids or marriage but far enough along that they could make fun of each other's races, say things like "that's something white people would do," or "only Asians would be so insane." The two of them had been on vacation—their first together, a modest weekend getaway in San Diego to celebrate Denny's birthday—and she'd asked their hotel to have a private chef prepare and serve an assortment of Denny's favorite foods in their room, beef brisket sandwiches and coleslaw and garlic fries. The hotel hadn't exactly been the sort of establishment that regularly provided such services—it billed itself as three star in its own promotional materials, and touted features included working telephones and extra deadbolts— but it rose to the challenge, producing a line cook from the breakfast buffet who obligingly made the sandwiches and then charged $160 for the privilege. The meat had been dry, but Denny delighted.

"Seriously," he said, in between mouthfuls. "Just the fact that you *thought* of doing this means so much. Most girls wouldn't. You're one of the good ones."

When she'd demurred, he'd been insistent. "It's ingrained in you," he'd said, and she had supposed it must be so, since she wasn't particularly trying.

What had being nice brought her over the years? Kate used to think quite a lot: two wonderful children, beautiful home, successful career, devoted husband. Recent events, however, had proven the last assumption incorrect, and like a math formula in which just one constant has been altered, the entire equation had come tumbling down.

It was the times she had been a bitch, Kate thought now, that she had really excelled. Going toe to toe with Sonny, batting down ridiculous last-minute feature requests. Wrangling engineering and operations to cease sabotaging each other long enough, to do their actual jobs. Screaming on the phone at their factories in South Korea and China to meet promised deadlines—the only method of communication the reps (who, come to think of it, were Asian bitches themselves) took seriously.

Kate's mentor at X Corp was a bitch too. Eleanor Thoms, the humorless former director of a Virginia-based think tank, was a midlevel vice president of the sort assigned to so-called high-potential achievers—which at X Corp included any woman who'd managed to make it above a senior manager level—who met with Kate once a quarter for scheduled half-hour intervals. Eleanor had read *Lean In* and at one point been genuinely enthusiastic about the idea of mentorship, volunteering herself for the much-extolled in-house program. She had quickly tired of the responsibility, however, when no corresponding uplift was karmically bestowed from above, but then was left with no easy exit without seeming like an even bigger bitch. So she continued to meet with Kate, though as time passed these became perfunctory checkpoints, both of them wanting the ordeal over with quickly so they could continue on with productive work the rest of the day.

On one lone occasion, however, Eleanor did drop a useful tidbit. Executive-round promotions had been announced that week, and once again her name had been left off the Committee Select, the powerful steering group within X Corp known to be the politburo's top-ranked table. The omission was widely considered a slap in the face; Kate had been prepared to avoid the topic altogether in their meeting. Eleanor, however, brought it up immediately.

"People say I shouldn't have pushed out Brayers," she commented bitterly, referring to Paul Brayers, the genial former chieftain of supply chain whose departure she had engineered within months of her initial arrival. "Because he looks like a giant teddy bear. Who cares if we never chose the most qualified ODMs, right? And that the bid process was totally fucked up, nontransparent, and that we were definitely overpaying? Why should any of that matter when management throws a great Halloween party at his house every year?

"Well, I don't regret it." She seemed to be answering to a third person in the room, an invisible body behind Kate's own. "I wasn't going to make compromises so early on. Don't forget that you set expectations on the first day. So if you're too accommodating, or let others take credit for your projects, or don't speak up in meetings, that will become your new baseline. And it's a real bitch to get out of that box."

THAT'S WHAT DENNY HAD DONE TO HER, KATE THOUGHT. PUT HER in a box. Made it cozy, with just enough air to breathe and a clear view of the sky. And then she'd done him the favor of nominating herself to serve as the simpering bottom of the pyramid, where she'd stood as the thankless base for his endeavors. Because what was more important for a house than its foundation? What device more crucial in a bathroom than the humble towel rack, since without it linens would fall to the ground, rendering the entire function of the space useless? That bizarre reasoning had come from their contractor, whose extended colloquialisms and rants on vitamins Kate had indulged and Denny had no patience for. She was the one in the family, he said, who could deal with these hopeless personality cases, the implication being that she was sympathetic and kind, the sort of person to accept small flecks of shit as long as the overall picture remained positive.

That was what Denny had told her, and she had believed, and then he had rewarded her with exactly what she deserved, which was nothing.

Years ago, on her way to a restaurant in Woodside, Kate took a wrong turn. It had been peak rush hour, so she was driving on local back roads, a route she normally avoided at all costs because of the impossibly narrow streets and steep, unbarriered cliffs. Theoretically she knew that the roads were made to fit multiple vehicles, that the zillionaire denizens in the houses along its way would never stand for lanes that didn't allow enough space for two cars headed in opposite directions. But Kate didn't understand why the zillionaires didn't just have larger roads to begin with. There was, after all, enough land to spare.

That day Kate drove with her hands gripped on the wheel and eyes faced firmly ahead, until she made an incorrect turn. The street she ended up on had been larger than the one she'd missed, so she'd assumed she was still headed in the right direction, back toward commercial enterprise. She thus continued until it became obvious that the street was actually *not* a street but a private road, and that it led to a home.

The structure Kate eventually reached was the largest residence she had ever seen in real life, the sort heads of movie studios lived in, at least in the movies. It was impossibly white, and the lawn was green and even. The building itself resembled a miniature version of the San Francisco Opera House, with endless paired columns and three rows of high arched windows, and a great circular fountain pulsed up front. The home's largeness was such that it surrounded her from all angles, and Kate was struck by the thought that while the houses in her neighborhood might have been trying for French Country, this was true château.

As she drove up, a man in a gray Nehru jacket and matching trousers came rushing out. He delicately indicated for her to roll down her window and then, just as gently, made it clear that she should immediately vacate the premises. The man had a Russian accent, and as he waited with a patient yet nonproprietorial air, she suddenly understood that he was not the owner but an actual servant. Kate had theoretically known that such luxuries existed in the Bay Area but had yet to actually witness such a phenomenon in person; she had friends with household incomes in the low seven figures who still mowed their own lawns and exclusively shopped at Costco to swing the costs of four children in private school. After a brief wave of apology, she turned her car.

On the way out, she noticed a row of lanky saplings on either side of the driveway. They hadn't yet grown most of their green, and the few visible branches were thin and spindly. Young plants, new money, she thought, and then chided herself. Who was she to label anything as nouveau? Over time the saplings would bloom into graceful trees; they would bend and curve and hold sway in a manner befitting the rest of the extraordinary estate.

CAMILLA MOSNER, THE WOMAN DENNY WAS FUCKING AND WHOSE
nanny he was making ample gratuitous use of, lived in a house like
this. The fountain was missing, and there was less of an energy oli-
garch's sense of landscaping, but otherwise the two were quite close,
first cousins of the Impressive Mansion genus. Enormous doors, which
matched their enormous entrances, which led to enormous gardens,
front and back. The same lengthy driveways, deliciously wasteful in
their use of space, curves wherever straight lines would more efficiently
serve. The gate had been open as she drove up—to make it easier for
package deliveries and staff, Kate guessed.

Since the Jade Mountain incident, as she'd started to refer to it in
her head—in a series of internal monologues that had been growing
both in frequency and length at an alarming rate—Kate had yet to
say anything to Denny. She'd initially assumed that the news would
travel to him quickly, perhaps even before she arrived back home that
day from the park, a quickly typed text or frantic phone call sharing
the calamitous knowledge that the wife—hey, that was *her!*—now
knew what he'd been doing, sexual relations and job abandonment
and child endangerment and all. Kate had wanted Denny to suffer on
his way home as she had, in quaking fear over his silent phone and the
righteous stance she had earned, unequivocally so, as the Wronged
Wife. But when he arrived there'd been no change in his demeanor,
no apologies, no anger. It was just the same old Denny, regular as
always, and she had felt her insides knot.

To confront him, she knew, would be to toss him the competitive
edge—the same error she had made when she was a teenager and
threatened Stanley with killing herself, after he'd smashed her Walk-
man following a confrontation over what constituted an acceptable
time frame for washing a pan used for scrambled eggs. She'd locked
herself in the bathroom for hours with a paring knife, running the tap
for authenticity, as she excitedly envisioned Stanley in a panic on the

other side of the door. Only to emerge hours later, to find him watching TV in the family room, a box of stir-fried udon noodles in his lap.

"I knew you wouldn't do it," he called over his shoulder. Kate understood then that it had been a mistake to crack. She should have at least cut into her wrists, drawn blood. The suffering would have been worth it.

As the week drew to a close, little changed with Denny. Each day continued undisturbed in its routine banality, and even Slippers on maximum sensitivity failed to track anything out of the ordinary in his movements. Kate was almost certain Camilla knew—she questioned Ella closely every night now about her day's activities, and each time her daughter had been emphatic that she had not seen her "Auntie," aka the nanny Isabel, who, much to Kate's chagrin, she seemed to miss. For Denny to continue to exist in ignorance had to mean that all other parties possessed full knowledge, and Kate had become intensely curious about Camilla Mosner, who, on top of sleeping with Denny, was actively depriving her of the satisfaction of going batshit in the exact manner she felt she deserved. Camilla Mosner was someone who would have slit her wrists, Kate decided. She would have sliced deep, to ensure an impact.

Finally there came the point where she could no longer take the waiting, and she freed herself to search online with abandon. She found only a few images, all from the same event, the 2014 Breakthrough Prize Ceremony. A tall, thin, blonde in a silver asymmetrical goddess gown serenely posed next to a bearded older man in a gray suit. *Camilla and Ken Mosner*, the caption read.

When Camilla emerged from her front door, she didn't look surprised to see Kate in her driveway. Perhaps, Kate thought, she'd already been alerted by some unseen presence—a security guard or an array of high-definition cameras (another use case, she noted, for Slippers).

"Want to come inside?" Camilla offered. Up close, she had hints of the look Kate had long dubbed "Peninsula MILF"—the certain breed of moneyed housewife who could be found dotted up and down between San Francisco and Palo Alto. A muscled and thin body, hair blond but dry, a general banishment of fats in the diet, resulting in a slightly papery skin everywhere but the face, which appeared perpetually shiny, slightly taut, plumped. A good friend from high school, Rosa Sachs, was married to one of the top plastic surgeons in Los Angeles. The husband had once explained to Kate that in terms of procedures, Silicon Valley was decades behind Beverly Hills. "You've got these billionairesses who are getting thread facelifts I wouldn't let an incontinent D-list soap actress go under the knife for, let alone someone whose husband owns his own 747."

"What's a thread facelift?" Kate had asked, intensely curious.

"You don't need to hear the details, believe me. Just know that as the skin ages, it's like a metal string cutting through cheese."

Camilla didn't look like someone whose face would be cut through like a piece of triple-crème however; she simply had beautiful skin, which looked expensively young. She wore makeup, but it was applied in such a fashion that Kate was certain Denny thought she used none. She also, in Kate's opinion, didn't appear particularly contrite. But to be fair, she was the owner of this particular piece of property—here, it was Kate who was the intruder.

Was there a dignified manner to accept someone's invitation into their home while silently telegraphing your most ardent desire that they go fuck themselves? Kate settled for clenched fists and refused eye contact. She followed Camilla through the front door to the predictably gargantuan kitchen, which featured cream walls and dark brass fixtures on three separate islands. Camilla caught her eyeing the backsplash behind the burners, an oversize panel of copper, carved with Romanesque angels and figurines.

"Don't judge," she said. "The ex."

"Okay." Kate's first question, answered.

"Do you want some tea?" Camilla filled a kettle and stood with her back to her. She was casually dressed for a day at home, though in the sort of polished getup Kate had always assumed possible only in romantic comedies: a camel sweater with a shearling vest layered over it, loose jeans. Her hair was blown out to beneath her shoulders, and her nails were short and a warm nude. Kate couldn't decide if Camilla was actually beautiful or had just maximized each of the variables at her disposal.

Without waiting for an answer, Camilla passed over a steaming cup. "I know who you are, of course. Denny showed me photos. I was very curious about you, when I learned he was married. Of course, I also felt like a sleaze—I do have a bit of a conscience—but by then we had already started. I met him at the gym. Did you know Denny goes to the gym?"

The only gym Kate knew of was a depressingly cramped 24 Hour Fitness, which Denny patronized the one morning per week he didn't visit the attic, but Camilla didn't strike her as the type to be found at such a place. She belonged in some sort of shiny Pilates studio or upscale boot camp.

"The 24 Hour," Camilla said. "That's the one. I know, weird that I would go there, right? The thing is, I used to work at a 24, back when I lived in Arizona—this was way before I was married—and I got a sort of lifetime membership deal there. So I still drop in just to mix things up, plus I'm used to the machines. You'd be amazed by how many expensive studios don't have basic equipment like arm and leg presses. They all go straight for the fancy machines and water therapy. You look familiar, by the way. Where do you work out?"

"Nowhere."

"Ahh." Camilla gave her a cool look and appraised her up and down. "Well, you look great."

Kate felt a spasm of involuntary pleasure and rushed to bury it. "Glad to meet your standards."

"No need to be sarcastic! It was a genuine compliment. I always told Denny that I thought you were attractive."

"Oh? Was this before or after you slept together?"

Camilla leaned an arm against the counter. She studied Kate for a moment, her green eyes alert. "After."

The thought of the two of them discussing her in any capacity was infuriating. "How serious is it? Are you in love?" As soon as the words fell out, Kate was annoyed with herself.

"With Denny?" Camilla appeared equally disappointed. "Well, of course not. He's just someone to spend time with. And I know everyone says this, but I really didn't think he was married when we met."

"Does he love you?"

"That, I'm not sure." She paused. "Probably not. He likes spending time with me. And as you already know, he enjoys the childcare. Poor Isabel finally had a kid to play with—she's really a nanny first and foremost, with all that baby CPR training and mother-hen instinct. She was a referral from a business colleague, and my ex hired her right away when we moved here. That was when we still thought we were going to procreate, ourselves. Instead, Isabel's made lovely salads and looked for things to clean around the house for the last five years. Occasionally, she helps out when we entertain. Entertained."

"You have a very nice home," Kate said without thinking. Then, to make up for the politeness: "How big is it?"

"Yes, thank you." Camilla rinsed a serving platter under the faucet and put it away. She washed her nicer china by hand, Kate noticed. "Around fourteen thousand square feet. The lot itself is just under two acres." She turned back and looked at Kate. "You know I barely get any alimony? Relatively, anyway. We weren't married for too long, but my ex, you've got to believe me, he could pay a hundred times more than what I currently get and there'd still hardly be a redistribution in wealth. But I really wanted to keep the house. And he knew it.

Knew I had an attachment to it. So in the end I made kind of a shitty deal, to keep this place."

"Don't you need the money?" It had to be expensive to be Camilla, Kate imagined. Normally she would never dare ask such a direct question, but the situation had torpedoed their relationship to a certain level of intimacy.

"I mean, it'd always be nice to have more—when I first heard the property tax on this place I nearly fainted—but I'm doing fine. I don't want to give the wrong impression; I'm not *starving* or anything. And aside from the house, I'm a very rational person. Even when I was going after this place, I had my own logic. After all, a house is where you live, where you spend the majority of your waking hours, right? It's always there and keeps you warm and out of the rain. It's kind of the most loyal presence in your life, don't you think?"

Kate didn't answer and instead stared dizzily at her hands. For the past few weeks, the woman facing her had played the marquee role in her most vivid of waking nightmares. She knew she would be reliving this conversation many times over in the coming days and tried to summon some of her earlier rage. The sad truth she was growing to accept, however, was that she didn't find the thought of Denny having sex with someone else particularly inciting; it upset her more to imagine Denny eating a meal with Camilla, confiding in her, than their sleeping together did. As she searched, what she found herself returning to was the enormous blocks of time Denny had deemed himself entitled to, hours he'd apparently pissed away lolling about in some workout dilettante's palace. When was the last instance she'd had a free afternoon, a *weekday* at that, to indulge in something delightfully wasteful?

"What did you guys *do* all day?"

Camilla nodded, as if she finally approved of a question. "That was the big problem. We never did anything! We couldn't go out locally, of course, since apparently you have a lot of friends. Denny always liked to remind me of that, you know, since I barely know anyone in the area. He can be quite passive-aggressive. He brought it up out of nowhere once, right after I'd had some workers over to repair the French oak in the wine cellar. I told him, I don't even *drink* wine, it's just something that houses of this size are supposed to have, like a nanny apartment or safe room. It was basic maintenance, for Christ's sake! But he just muttered something about pretentiousness and stalked off. He likes to nitpick at the little things, whenever he feels threatened. You know?" When Kate grunted noncommittally, Camilla drank some tea and continued. "Anyway, I guess we could have theoretically gone out more, but both of us were usually too lazy to drive far. So in the end most of the time we just ordered delivery. Which gets old, fast. I don't think I'm necessarily high-maintenance, but sitting at home, eating cheap Chinese food and having sex? Oh, sorry."

"Whatever. Continue."

"That's basically it. I mean, I knew we were never going to get married—though I'd love to be married again, I think I make a very nice spouse—but with Denny, there was never even that excitement that comes with cheating. Have you ever done it? Cheated?" Kate shook her head. "Well, I have, and the best part is going out together and acting like a regular couple and the little thrill of knowing you're not. Checking into hotels with the same fake last name, paying cash, that sort of deal. But we never had even that, because we were stuck in my house eating Chef Wong's."

So that's why Denny had barely touched the orange chicken the last few times she'd picked up takeout; historically it'd always been a favorite of his. "You're making an affair sound pretty shitty."

Camilla snorted. "It's not like regular dating is so much better. My friends, they're mostly in similar life situations." She motioned with her arms, apparently in reference to the extreme wealth that surrounded them. "We talk about it all the time: how at this stage, the conversations become *hard*. A lot of the more successful men, they've got barely anything to say, they're so used to being escorted from room to room, given an agenda right before by their minions. One on one, on a dinner date? No idea what to do or talk about. They spend most of their time craning their necks around the restaurant, seeing who else is there they might know. You know the last guy I went out with actually bragged about doing a PowerPoint presentation at Benu? They had to set up a special display for him on the wall."

"Wait. You're still *dating*?"

Camilla tilted her head. "Well, yes. Of course."

"Does Denny know?"

"We haven't talked about it. I mean, he's still married, isn't he? Unless you're thinking of divorcing him now." When Kate failed to respond, she went on. "I'm just making the point that the dating scene is difficult. It can get very lonely. But at the same time, I don't want to settle either. Is it too much to ask that someone not describe himself as either a *mogul* or *visionary* in our first meeting?"

Kate was quiet. She was still in shock Camilla had dropped the d-word. She hadn't yet allowed herself to think of a separation; had so far postponed the worst-case-scenario analysis she normally immediately performed in difficult situations. Camilla studied her curiously, as if she knew what she was thinking. "Maybe someone poor would provide the excitement you seek," Kate deflected.

"Oh, men without money are the same, except that then they just want to talk about life *with* money. They're all obsessed! And I understand what they're going through better than most; I used to work at 24 Hour, remember? But even I get tired of it." She turned to the fridge and removed a glass bowl containing what looked to be a precisely assembled Cobb salad. "You want anything to eat?" Kate shook her head.

Camilla began to spear and eat. "Hey, can I ask something? How come of the two of you, Denny's the one who doesn't work?"

"Denny works," Kate said automatically.

Camilla peered at her. "Right . . . ," she said, drawing out the word. "I mean, how come he's the one at home? Everyone I know with multiple kids, the woman stays home."

Somehow Kate was surprised to hear that Camilla had friends with children; she seemed the sort to be acquainted with only the fully formed. "I was at home when Ella was born. For a year. I took a leave of absence, and at the time I wasn't planning on going back. It was great, actually. I loved that period."

"Really," Camilla said. She twirled her fork. She looked fascinated, as if learning about the behavior of a newly discovered insect species. "So why didn't you continue?"

"Deep down, I still knew I would be happier if I went back to work. Though it was a long, miserable path to get there. You can't imagine the guilt that comes after having children. And then afterward Denny said it was time for him to have his chance, and I was happy to let him quit and start his own thing."

It was a good memory, the day Denny left Cisco. They'd gone out to dinner at their favorite Afghan restaurant, and then, after they'd pulled into the garage and discovered that there was still half an hour left of the babysitter, they'd had clumsy sex in the back seat of the car.

"Why?" Kate asked. "Did Denny ever say anything about it? About me . . . at X and him launching a start-up?" She was still loyal enough to use the words *launching* and *start-up*, which she'd learned were infinitely preferred to the phrase *working on your own business*.

"He said you were supportive, but not in a real way. I asked him once what that meant, but he didn't elaborate."

That stung. "I don't know what more I could have possibly done! Denny had every opportunity to be the partner with a regular paycheck. Walking away was his choice."

Camilla shrugged, bored with the topic. "Are you going to tell him we met? I assume you haven't said anything yet. If you want, I can swear that I'll never see him again. We haven't talked since that day in the park, you know. He thinks I'm on a girls' vacation." A giggle escaped, and she put her fingers delicately over her mouth. It was the sort of gesture Kate used to practice by herself as a teenager but could never perfect; the charming, effortless movements of the expert geisha.

"You can do whatever you want, though it stands to say Ella's playdates with your nanny-chef are permanently over."

"Do you think we could keep in touch?" Camilla looked down at her bowl. "I wish I'd met you before Denny. Does that sound weird? I'd love to get a drink sometime." She met her eyes with abrupt sincerity.

"I don't think so," Kate said. "That sounds beyond weird."

"But why? I've told you more in the last twenty minutes than I've confided in anyone for a long while. Even going back to when I was still married. Isn't that kind of amazing? When was the last time you actually really shared your intimate thoughts with someone? I mean, have you even told anyone else what's going on with Denny? I bet you haven't. It's not the kind of update you blast on Facebook."

"I don't post there. And you're wrong. I have told people."

Camilla's gaze was unwavering. "I don't think so," she said quietly.

Kate kicked her legs against her chair. "Maybe. But that doesn't mean I want to discuss it with *you*."

"But we already are discussing it, don't you see? Isn't that great? Our situation is so unique. You asked me if I needed *money*! And I actually *answered*! Talking about that is even more taboo than sex!"

"Fine. I'm sorry if that came off as rude."

"But it wasn't! That's my point. I've been dying to talk to someone about my financial situation. Isn't it crazy that everyone here is obsessed with money but you can't actually come out and say anything about it unless it's related to your work? God, if I had a job, I bet I'd talk about money all the time. Or maybe not. It does get vulgar after a while."

"You have those women you mentioned. The first wives' club who compare jet interiors."

"Oh, them." Camilla waved a hand, as if dismissing a single item on a long checklist of tasks. "They're not really friends. We're just people with the same socioeconomic and romantic status. That's not so easy to find, you understand. Plus, not everyone's a first wife. There are plenty of seconds, even thirds. You can't imagine the tiering that goes on. Of course, I'm a first, which would make me higher, but I occupy a weird position because I married Ken when he was already rich, and plus we never had children."

"Tiering?"

"Oh yeah. At the very top are the wives who actually met their spouse at school or work. *Before* they made it big. I guess that's considered the most pure, true love and all that. I don't know too many of those. I'd like to, but they largely keep to themselves. I understand how they see me, but we all ended up in the same place in the end, so." Camilla gave a shake of the shoulders. "After we moved here, I always thought I would have more friends who worked. I mean, I always had a job myself, right up to when I met Ken. They were never terribly prestigious or anything, but still, I was earning money. It's strange now, to be with all these women who don't work and know I'm one of them. Denny told me you're a director at X Corp. And you did that yourself, didn't you? It's not one of those positions that your husband set up for you. I remember how impressed I was the first time he told me. I wanted to hear more, but he always avoided my questions. What do you do there?"

"I've got to go," Kate said. She knew she needed to extract herself before she got pulled in further. A portion of her was softening toward Denny; she could see how anyone might be sucked into the vortex of someone like Camilla Mosner. And she felt a horrible sort of growing pity for the fact that Camilla apparently found him quite disposable.

"Five more minutes?" Camilla pled. "Just five. Five real minutes."

Kate gathered her things. She was struck by an absurd sensation that she had been rude. "I hope things work out for you. You seem like a decent person, when not abetting adultery or mild kidnapping."

"See you," Camilla said, in a clouded voice. "Drive safe."

KATE WAS ALREADY IN THE SUBARU, DRIVING FORWARD, WHEN THE large shaggy object came hurtling at her. At first she thought it was some sort of animal and automatically braked, with force. Strands of blond hair flew at the windshield, as tufts of shearling excitedly bounced. A set of hands materialized in front.

"Jesus!" Kate yelled. She rolled down the window. "Hey! *Stop! What are you doing?*"

"Kate!" Camilla cried. She waved frantically. "I won't talk to Denny again, I promise! I realized I maybe didn't even say sorry to you, and that's why you left. I'm *sorry!*"

"I know you're sorry," Kate said. She was still breathing heavily, the shock of thinking she'd nearly hit an animal not having yet departed. It had started to rain, and she turned on the windshield wipers. "Thanks," she said. "Now I have to go home."

She kept her eyes firmly forward, concentrating on the back-and-forth movement of the wipers, until she heard Camilla turn away from the car. Then she counted to twenty and began to drive.

When she was almost completely down the long driveway she gave in and took one last glance in the rearview mirror. But she was already too far away, and it was already too dark to make out what she really wanted to see: whether Camilla Mosner still stood out front, waving good-bye.

CHAPTER 12

FRED

F red always felt better about himself in a foreign country.
For starters, he was usually richer overseas, the benefit of
holding American currency in an era in which oil prices continued
to crater and the Greeks lurched ineptly from one economic disaster
to the next. There was also China's unprecedented rise of the last two
decades—equipped with his Lion credentials, Fred did an excellent
imitation of a moneyed mainland businessman on an acquisition
spree, armed to spend recklessly abroad. Then, since he was good at
selecting clothes, had an expensive haircut, and always meticulously
researched the trendiest restaurants in a new city—the ones with the
hardest-to-land reservations and hostesses who looked through you
like water—Fred was almost always a far more splendid personage
overseas than at home.

This was especially true in Bali, a destination that warped the rules of reality. Here, slurring Russians in singlets playing grab-ass were revered gentlemen, while pasty Germans bearing vague resemblances to composite sketches of pedophiles were feudal lords, come to visit for their customary fortnight. Labor was so inexpensive that the title of managing director on one's business card indicated a staff of hundreds (Fred had 2.5, a team of junior analysts who constantly hinted they were searching for other jobs, and a disloyal assistant he technically shared with Griffin Keeles who considered it beneath her to book his travel).

He was staying at the Biasa in Seminyak, a luxury resort markedly nicer than what he ordinarily would have selected, especially as it fell outside the bounds of Lion's stringent travel policies (he was thus absorbing the entire cost himself, yet another gross injustice perpetrated by that cheap fucker, Leland). When he'd made the booking Fred had naturally assumed Erika would be with him, and an extravagant hotel ranked high on her list of Important Details. The Biasa's onerous cancellation policies meant that it made no financial sense to change the reservation; as such, he was determined to enjoy himself.

Upon arrival he'd been upgraded to a villa, a small free-standing structure with a private pool and outdoor bathtub, filled with dark wood furniture and lighting that even at maximum power cast a seductive atmosphere. Fred had never before stayed in such lavish or spacious accommodations, save for a few bachelor parties at the MGM Skylofts, and on those occasions they'd been stuffed at least two per bedroom.

The villa even came with a personal "butler," a steward supposedly solely dedicated to the comfort of his charges. The manservant, a portly local named Bawa, greeted Fred effusively upon check-in and then disappeared. He reemerged once per day to obsequiously set up the complimentary afternoon repast, pouring the ginger tea with great care. On the second morning Fred inquired if Bawa might venture out and purchase some local souvenirs for him, inexpensive trinkets to bring home for colleagues, but Bawa replied with toadying servility that the concierge might be better equipped to assist in such matters. The concierge, in the same fawning manner, pointed him back to Bawa.

In the end Fred walked to town himself, where he found some inexpensive sarongs and painted masks. The three-block return journey felt agonizingly long due to the heat, and as he passed couples and families along the way, he was lonely. Aside from Jack, he didn't personally know a single person attending the retreat. And even if he were to spot one of tech's famous faces milling about—which so far he hadn't—he couldn't imagine actually instigating a conversation, like some ridiculous founder hounder.

Fred planned on striking out that evening, at the very least to buy some stranger—preferably a stunning yet impoverished local—a drink, but back in the room, he was struck by an intense misanthropy. He canceled his dinner reservations at a trendy Italian restaurant on the beach he'd had the concierge make months in advance and ate at the Biasa's outdoor restaurant instead, staring gloomily at the ocean.

———————

Just another five minutes, Fred thought. Then he'd call Jack.

He removed from his pocket the now-crumpled itinerary that had become soft with sweat and again verified that he had the correct time and place. For an hour so far that morning he'd been checking and rechecking the paper, circling the beach as he attempted to conceal his growing panic. Where the hell was everyone?

While in earlier years Fred had assumed a high barrier to entry to be a reliable indicator of the nature and quality of the corresponding assets being shielded, he had long since learned his lesson, both personally and professionally. Newly opened clubs with costly drinks and

power-crazed bouncers turned out to be half empty and filled with
other disappointed men once you'd bribed your way inside; snooty
women who rejected you at first approach were just as vapid in bed the
next morning and resembled ogres with their makeup off. Thus Fred
had expected the Founders' Retreat to be like other conferences he'd
attended, only with better attendees—packed with boring keynotes,
mediocre lunches, and useless networking; casual discussions on favored bolt-holes, should the unwashed masses revolt after automation
had taken all their jobs. The events entirely located at some massive
resort, its amenities largely ignored by the men in dark suits parading
into conference rooms.

Instead, the instructions on the personalized agenda couriered
to him at the hotel (the cover page stamped *Confidential, Not to Be
Forwarded or Photographed*) had led Fred to this dirty beach, to which
he'd arrived half an hour early, via the hotel's complimentary shuttle.
In contrast to the pristine scenery surrounding the Biasa, the water
here was oiled and murky, and the rough sand was heavily strewn with
misshapen plastic and latex objects. Behind him, tanned Indonesians
hawked umbrellas and sun chairs of marginally clean appearance; the
prices lent confusion as to whether they were being sold or merely
rented. The only other parties present were holiday goers of a look
and caliber Fred had identified as definitively Not Founders' Retreat
material. A group of retiree-aged Australians lay naked under towels
with their torsos exposed, as masseurs lazily slid elbows down their
backs; nearest to Fred was a group of well-endowed British girls in
crop tops, who appeared to have just landed from a connecting flight.

"I said to Liam, where's my facking suitcase?" one of the girls
spat, as she dug dirt out from under her nails. Next to her, a thuggish
friend puffed miserably on a cigarette.

Fred was hit with a fresh wave of despair. He felt alien and out
of place, dressed in loose linen pants and a matching ecru shirt. The
outfit—touted as ideal for the climate given its natural fibers and

protection from the sun's aggressive rays—had been purchased from the hotel gift shop the night before. Even though he'd studied the weather forecast and packed multiple suits, in his zealousness to avoid checking baggage he'd omitted anything that could be qualified— using the given Founders' Retreat terminology—as *High Resort Casual*. In a ridiculous inversion, the getup cost more than he would have ever paid in the United States, but the boutique proprietor had whispered that Christy Turlington was part owner and did its purchasing, an outrageous and irresistible lie.

Finally, eighty minutes past the designated hour, Jack appeared. He made no apologies and instead unhurriedly led them to a small cruiser manned by staffers wearing white polo shirts with *Killer* in embroidered script on the chest. Fred had assumed it was the name of the boat, which was a glossy black and white, but it turned out to be the much larger vessel the tender eventually sailed up to, a sleek and elegant mega yacht trimmed in dark wood with a striking orange hull. As Jack and Fred walked the treaded shallow ramp, staff members waited along its sides, backs ramrod straight. When they reached the top, a porter pointed to Fred's shoes. "Yes?" he asked. The man repeated his motion.

"Thank you," Fred said. "They're very comfortable." They were also Gaziano & Girling, but he saw no point in sharing that.

"Actually, he's telling you to take them off!" Jack shouted over the wind. "I completely forgot Reagan doesn't allow shoes. I can't remember why. Maybe the wood!"

"This is Reagan's boat?"

"Yes! Only my second time on it. One day he just randomly asked to meet here. Apparently there are hidden rocket launchers. Isn't his life crazy?"

Reagan was already on board, in conversation with two men Fred recognized from their Facebook executive bios. Both were younger

than him, he recalled grimly. He was at the point where age was the
first metric he checked of anyone successful, scrolling immediately
to the college graduation year on LinkedIn (he'd long removed any
indication of his own).

There was a current of excitement in the atmosphere, undercut
with confusion. There didn't appear to be any indication of an expected order of events, and given the lack of shoes and ambiguous
dress code, many of the attendees looked to be in a state of slumped
undress. It was as if everyone had shown up to an orgy that had been
prearranged in advance, only to arrive and find the hosts missing. The
boat was crowded, though Fred and Jack were thankfully on the lower
deck, where there was still enough space to maneuver; on the level
above there were at least another hundred people. A few dozen model
types were peppered through the crowd; they moved with languor,
not bothering to disguise their boredom.

Fred tried not to gape. He had become so accustomed to the situation in the Bay Area—where any woman in possession of the merest
sliver of attractiveness strutted around like a harem master—that the
sheer appearance of so much physical beauty stunned him. Say what
you wanted about an Ivy League education or ferocious ambition; all
of that receded in the face of these faces—unwrinkled, unblemished,
and even when irregular still perfect. As Fred watched, a young brunette in dreadlocks linked arms with Mason Leung, the diminutive
sixty-two-year-old Chinese-Malaysian head of TelBank, who in the
last five years had released three hip-hop albums. Mason, Fred noted,
had been allowed to keep his shoes—a pair of forest green loafers that
looked to have hidden lifts.

He realized he had unwisely lost track of Jack and now found
himself mired in the most loathsome of social situations: adrift, literally at sea, with everyone in eyeshot engaged in conversation. Even the
porters were batched together. No way he was going to be that guy,

the one who sidled up to a group, quietly lurking, nodding with vigor at the occasional stray factoid. He'd rather be solo, aloof in repose, a stance several of the less-popular model types had also adopted.

Luckily just a few minutes passed before Reagan appeared, Jack in tow. He led them to a small setup of a few lounge chairs around a table, a short walk made considerably longer by his pausing every few seconds to call out to various acquaintances and best friends. Reagan had definitely aged less than Jack, Fred saw, though some of it was because he'd always carried an extra thirty pounds on his frame. Fred noted with relief that Reagan was dressed similarly to himself in a linen long-sleeved shirt and pants, the clothes perfectly tailored to graze his rotund body. He no longer shaped his hair with handfuls of gel; now it was soft and parted neatly, a peppered black-and-white marriage of Mao and American WASP. Though for the straight patrician look the hair was too long. A bit from the front had escaped, forming a kiss curl across his forehead.

"Nice boat," Fred said.

Reagan gave him a back slap, as if they'd always been the best of friends.

"Yeah," Jack chimed in. "I was just telling Fred you've brought the term *obnoxious Asian* to a whole new stratosphere.'

"Stated by the guy whose parents own half the malls in Singapore and a good portion of the largest developments in Hong Kong. And what's this I'm hearing about Project Carton?"

"I don't know what you're talking about."

"Right." Reagan snorted. Then, to Fred: "There's an egg being erected right now in China. Know anything about it?"

Fred shook his head.

"Well, there is one. A giant egg, in Hangzhou. A literal fucking egg, though I guess not so literal, because this one's actually a building. An egg encircled by five smaller eggs, each intended to house a select number of the wealthy bourgeoisie I'm so callously being accused of being a member of right now. A whole carton of them, each decorated with gold and silver reflective windows, with so much crystal that they make Versailles look like a Chinese official's cheap imitation. And each one is named after a specific gem."

"Reagan, come on—" Jack groaned.

"There's the ruby egg, the emerald egg, the sapphire egg, the jade egg, the pearl egg, and, of course, the diamond egg," Reagan said, charging forward. "And inside each of their lobbies, behind bullet-proof glass, is an actual jewel, a twenty-carat sapphire here, thirty-carat ruby there, the best that Graff could source. A carton of Fabergé smack-dab in the middle of China, with parking spots that start at $200,000 each. If you've been living in the United States, you really can't imagine the ostentatiousness. Vegas would be the closest, but even that barely compares." Reagan abruptly stopped and scrutinized his champagne. He seemed to be searching for something within the bubbles; he squinted an eye and then moved the glass under his nose and inhaled the scent. Fred could see that Jack hoped he had finished, but Reagan downed the drink with a quick tilt and then went on.

"Of course, given the current environment—scrutiny over income inequality, disturbing chatter about the government on social media, CEOs disappearing overnight—you'd think these eggs might be a problem, a convenient symbol for the serfs to glom on to when they rise up, right? That's what one might think, unless a certain ranking politburo official's grandson was enticed into buying a unit early, *real* early, on a floor so private no one else had moved in yet. The perfect place to stash a secret girlfriend who might be pregnant with triplet boys, eh? So now the project rumbles on—no permit delays, no nasty media coverage, no peep from the local mayor, who I hear normally is a real shakedown artist. And do you know who the genius is behind all this, albeit through several layers of shell corporations? The big fat goose that's laying all these golden eggs, the birdie that's secretly way richer than the rest of us?"

"*Reagan.*" This time Jack's voice held a distinct warning.

"My man." Reagan wrapped an arm across Jack's shoulders. "The greatest. So humble. Anyway, yeah, this is a great boat. I've wanted one for a while. At least I can swim! You wouldn't believe how many guys own these things who can't even do that. You really think Paul Allen's doing laps in the Atlantic?"

"As if you know Paul Allen," Jack sulked.

"Well of course I do," Reagan said good-naturedly. "Though I'm not sure he would say the same for me." He turned to Fred. "Fred Huang. Really glad you could make it. You been to this thing before? And I assume Jack already told you a bit about our little project?"

"Yes," Fred said, leaving it vague which question he was answering in the affirmative. "I know the general background."

"And? What do you think? What about the name?"

"Opus?"

"Yeah. Too douchey?"

"I think it's fine, for now." He was suddenly impatient. "Can you confirm what the number is likely to land at? For whatever we—you—are managing? How much do the Thais want invested in North America?"

"The first year, just around ten billion," Reagan said.

Jack whistled and nudged with his elbow, past annoyances already forgotten. Fred could feel Reagan's eyes on him, beadily gauging.

"Of course, I'm sure Jack's already told you the total they're looking to eventually fund," he continued. "Somewhere between fifty and seventy billion. They're thinking at least half that concentrated in the US, and the rest in Israel, Europe, and of course Asia. But of the US piece, the vast majority will be in California. Silicon Valley, you guys are minting money. And all you want to do is spend it on bicycles and bunkers in the desert!"

"There's a lot of empty hype," Fred said modestly, as if he were an active participant in it all. "But of course there are also real opportunities. Fewer unicorns want to go public these days. Just look at Uber, Pinterest, Airbnb. Everyone wants to stay private, maintain control, but the capital requirements are significant. The amount of money you're describing, if managed correctly, would quickly establish Opus as a major player."

"Good, good." Reagan pumped his fist. "The Thais will want to get in on at least one big name investment, a marquee they can wave around to the public. Preferably consumer facing, so people will have heard of it. They want to emphasize that they're spending on innovation, building up the next Samsung instead of flying their lapdogs on Gulfstream G650s and getting tattoos near their dicks. Bonus points if the company has a founder who can visit and suck up, do some laps around the capital, Zuckerberg-style. You know, a Hugo Menendez sort."

Hugo Menendez was the youthful but semi-balding CEO of Gadfly, a data-compression company rumored to be closing on a staggering new round of funding. "You know Hugo?" Fred asked.

"Oh yeah, I know a lot of those guys. They're always hanging out in Hong Kong or Beijing, they have the fetish you know, heh. Jews and Asian girls, it's an unstoppable force when you combine two groups obsessed with money."

"Hugo's Jewish? I didn't know."

Reagan frowned. "Well if he's not, he should be. I think he's here, actually." He clasped his hands together around his mouth. "Hugo! *Hugo!*" When only the head steward turned, he dropped his arms. "Maybe he didn't make it onto the boat. We had a late night. I've taken a few of them under my wing, socially. These young guys with new money, they really have no taste. One of them was telling me all about how awesome his stay at the Gansevoort was. I was like, Gansevoort? What are we, in high school? Your company's worth *fourteen billion* and all it takes to impress is a chocolate tower in your room and some washed-out cougars in the lobby?"

"Not everyone has your standards," Jack said. "We don't all need to drive the fanciest car or visit the best club."

"If you're going to go out, you should make it worth your while. Especially at our age. For example, if I know I'm going to be awake past midnight, I need to have prepared in advance. Gone to sleep early the night before, eaten a big lunch with lots of protein. What, you don't care about your time? You liked Sepia Lounge last week, didn't you?" Jack grunted. "Ha. Didn't I tell you about the girls? Strong pipeline. Although we have even better today." He leaned forward. "Don't look now, but right behind you are a few members of the main cast of *Serial Killer High*. The brunette can't act for shit, but the blonde is actually pretty good. I'm sponsoring Ace Getty's thirtieth birthday on the boat tomorrow night."

"Where's your girlfriend?" Jack asked Fred. "I thought you were bringing her. Is she still at the hotel?"

"You have a girlfriend?" Reagan bounced in his chair. "Show us a picture."

Fred found a flattering shot of Erika, one in which she wore a simple black sundress and the outline of her breasts was visible. Reagan nodded with frank approval. "White is right! Good for you, evening out the ratios. Charlene must be pissed, huh? You still talk to her?"

"Not really." He rarely thought about his ex these days, except for when he happened to be looking through old photos. "Anyway, it wasn't working out with Erika. In terms of the trip, I mean. She ended up going back to San Francisco."

"How long did you spend together in Bali?"

"Well, actually, I sent her back in Hong Kong."

"Wow." Jack widened his eyes. "Sherry would go apeshit if I did that. At the very least I'd have to make a pit stop at Verdura. How'd she take it?"

Fred shrugged. "It was fine."

It had actually been the complete opposite, albeit somewhat delayed. Erika's shock over the boldness of Fred's pronouncement had rendered her into a semidocile state until she was in her seat on the plane back to San Francisco; then, at some point during the flight, she'd gone apocalyptic. Ten minutes after the 747 landed, Fred had received a nine-page email narrating in excruciating detail his numerous deficiencies: his cheapness when ordering at restaurants; his refusal to hire a weekly cleaner for the apartment; his pornography addiction, which he hadn't realized she knew about (really, was three times a week—at *maximum*—an addiction? It wasn't like he was actually paying for it). The email's tenor and grammar implying that unless Erika was handled carefully and precisely, dire consequences should be expected. As Fred wished to maintain the status quo until he'd had more time to consider his commitment to the relationship— which he suspected would vary depending on the outcome of the retreat—he had called Erika right away, for an agonizingly long discussion in which every fifteen minutes he was accused of secretly wanting to get off the phone.

The night before, he'd still been managing the fallout, when, after she failed to reach him on his cell (it was off when he slept, to avoid unintended roaming charges), Erika had instead called the Biasa and been transferred to his room. It was late morning in California, she said, the only time she could speak without Nora overhearing, as it was when she escorted little Zoltan to swim class.

"I already took three weeks off work," Erika hissed. "Because you *told* me that we would be going on this trip. What am I supposed to do now? And don't you dare say I should just go back to Saks. Do you know how embarrassing that is, to have to explain that I am once again available for work? All because I am with a man who treats women like *garbage*?"

"No one's saying you should go back to work. Haven't you been telling me that you need a break?" Fred murmured gently. He had just fallen asleep when the handset on the desk began to ring; if he could get her off the phone within the next twenty minutes, he could still catch a full eight hours. "Why don't you sleep in, catch up on reading, get a massage? You love the Rosewood spa. I can call there with my credit card."

There was a brief silence as Erika considered this offer, before dismissing it as not worthy of giving up her higher ground. "That's exactly what I told you I was going to do," she huffed, "*in Bali*! Did I not pack my books? Did I not spend my own money to buy three Melissa Odabash caftans for the beach, which I didn't even get double discount on? And now I cannot return them, because I cut off the tags." Her nails clicked furiously against the phone. "I really am starting to believe you are deranged. The sort of man who enjoys playing with the heads of women. To invite me on a trip across the world, only to make up some *silly* excuse and send me back."

"To be fair, it wasn't entirely silly. It's not like you were on your best behavior. Screaming at me, throwing things, getting wasted. By the way, the Dorchester tacked on an extra $400 charge for carpet cleaning when I checked out. You could have told me you threw up behind the curtains. Management doesn't put up with the same shit in Asia that they do in America."

"Like you've never been drunk! Like you've never had so many beers, and wine, and shots, and then who has to listen to you brag about how much smarter you are than your mom and dad? Or how much more you make than your sister? And how about when you threw up on your Dior sneakers outside of the Battery, the ones I had to track down in the Saks in Atlanta and beg them to ship me on employee discount instead of selling full price to a customer? Who was so thankful then? What a convenient little memory you have."

"You're right, you're absolutely right," Fred said hurriedly. "I'm very sorry."

"Do you know how humiliating it is, what you did to me?" Erika exploded. "In all my years I've never heard of any man doing this to a woman! Even the worst Hungarian man does not go so low! And now you suggest that I *relax*, read a book, catch up on my news watching. You know who does that? A real big *sociopath*." And then, on the strength of that word, she hung up. Though in truth it hadn't really bothered Fred. Weren't CEOs usually sociopaths? The best serial killers? It meant you were, like, a genius.

"How's your dad?" Jack asked now. Fred had made a vague mention of Stanley's health on the phone when they first spoke—it was one of Jack's proof points of being a decent person, Fred supposed, that he remembered these things.

"Not too well, actually. It was confirmed to be pancreatic cancer."

"Like Jobs," Jack breathed.

"Yup. Just like Jobs." Steve Jobs, who Fred figured to be the closest thing running to a patron saint of pancreatic cancer. At least no one ever tried to assure Fred that Stanley would "kick this thing," since even a billionaire hadn't been able to stop the relentless march of a dissolving pancreas.

Reagan made a sympathetic noise. He sat up. "You guys have anything else you want to discuss? Otherwise I should go take care of a few things with the boat."

"Well." Fred paused, as if spontaneously recalling extraneous details. "I think once I sign on to this, I'm going to give notice at Lion. I've been there too long, and the deal flow's slowed. The amount of money you guys are talking, Opus is going to take up all my time anyway." Encouraged by Jack's nod, he continued. "And I was thinking we should rent an office. A fund this size, we've got to have our own space. Some basic staff too." He'd have his own dedicated assistant, of course. If there were head count issues, in her free time she could double as the office manager.

"Makes sense," Jack said. "You thinking Sand Hill?"

"Or downtown Palo Alto. No shortage of options."

"Office sounds great," Reagan said. "Associates, okay. The rest, no go. You've got to stay at Lion."

Hot pricks of agitation crept up Fred's spine. In any of its numerous iterations, the fantasy of Opus had never included Lion: Fred still in the same cramped quarters, furtively double-checking the expense reports filed by his ungovernable admin, Donna Caldbert, who he suspected occasionally omitted restaurant meals for reimbursement out of spite. He forced the words out calmly. "What's your reasoning?"

"I thought Jack told you." Reagan frowned, turning. "Didn't you?"

"Well." Jack hesitated. "To be honest, I wasn't fully clear—"

"Forget it," Reagan said. He was clearly exasperated. "Fred, a major factor in bringing you on *is* your employment with Lion. Surely you didn't assume you'd be advising on investments by yourself?" He raised a groomed eyebrow. "It's not as if a limited partner would ever stand for that in a traditional fund; it's way too much money for one person."

"Of course, but I assumed there would be direction from Asia, and—"

"The Thais want to partner with Lion on this," Reagan said, cutting him off. "They need an experienced partner on the ground in California. They have the money but not the expertise, so they want a local name to co-manage the fund. There's a lot of details still to be worked out, but their assumption is that Lion should go for it, because the Thais will put in most of the money. They'll ask for some more control in exchange, naturally; they don't want to be treated as just a dumb government piggy bank, which is how some of these deals have worked out in the past. But overall, it'd be a win-win for both parties."

"I could leave Lion," Fred said. "Take this to another shop." Like Motley Capital, or Tata Packer, or Andreessen. Ten billion dollars would be welcome almost anywhere in the Valley. "And—" He wavered, and then decided to come clean, even if it meant second-order implications regarding his own desirability. "Lion's not the most prestigious name. We're considered maybe Tier Three, Tier Two at best." Reagan and Jack had to know that, right? How could they not?

Reagan bobbed his head, as if he did. "But you're already at Lion. And Lion's an Asian company, which makes the cross-cultural communication way easier. The Thais, they're extremely sensitive, they don't want to deal with bombast and jokes about lady boys. Or kowtow to some prepubescent in Birkenstocks just because he wrote some sugar daddy app for politicians. They know Lion—the company has a huge factory in Korat. And Lion has long-standing relationships with Wilson Sonsini and Draper Carlyle. They're both your outside legal representation, Draper primarily so, am I correct? The Thais want a partner connected with those firms. If they have US investments, they're obviously going to need US representation."

"I know senior partners at both offices," Fred countered. "It would be no problem to arrange introductions." He could probably squeeze a few dinners for the referral as well. Erika would love it if he brought her along—she was always hinting she wanted to socialize more with a "certain tier of friends." At first Fred had taken her to mean white and been furious, before he realized she meant wealthy.

"Hey, we all know a senior partner or two. All those nerds who did the dual JD thing. But Lion does a lot of existing business with Draper, yeah? Leland's always getting sued in the news, antitrust this and trade secrets that. Sounds like you guys steal as much of your R-and-D as possible. I heard that Draper bills Lion in the high eight digits every year. That kind of pull, sorry, I just don't think you're going to have on your own. Unless you've got photos of Draper blowing Carlyle, which then by all means, let's draft your notice now."

"But I still don't understand why you need the introduction at all," Fred said stubbornly. The thought of Lion—and thus Griffin and Leland—getting in on so much free money for such an inane reason was beyond maddening. "Wouldn't any top-tier firm be happy to work with Opus? The billings would be substantial."

Reagan yawned. "You'd think so. But after '08, it's become far more challenging. There's more regulation now with overseas entities, especially when a government is involved, and law firms are leery. Of course they'd still take the business eventually, but it'd require time and energy. The Thais don't want any difficulties."

"Sure sounds like a lot of hoop jumping for legal counsel. Is *this* why you guys thought of me? Because of Lion? And the relationship with Draper?"

"Of course not." Jack looked offended. "You have the perfect background."

"Jack's right," Reagan chimed in. "You really do. Ten years at Lion, right? Managing director now? And you did the DataMinx deal, yeah, I know about that, don't accuse me of asking you just because of Draper. Your background's gold. Just hold on at Lion a little longer; is that really so much to ask? Get Leland on board, and then we'll go from there. In the meantime, we can get you set up as a partner at Opus. What's wrong with two paychecks? And I don't know if Jack already informed you, but this is no sovereign fund deal. They're compensating at the top of the bracket. Very generous. Once we've got the fund launched and have the Valley relationships locked down, you can go ahead and quit, tell Leland to go fuck himself, work full-time out of whatever office you like. Better have a few good-looking admins, though. Whenever I go to the Bay Area, the only places I see hot women are in lobbies and reception rooms."

"It's not going to be so easy with Leland; he'll likely want to dictate his own terms—"

"Look." Reagan sounded impatient now. "Is this something you really want to do? Because I was under the impression that you were in, and maybe I just got the wrong idea about your intentions, and either way it's totally cool. But you have to let me know whether you're

on board, because if not we'll need to move quickly with the next option. We have several avenues that would be acceptable to the Thais,
so no hard feelings, promise."

The whining scream of electronic equipment broke in, as an assistant on the open deck tested speakers. Presumably the kickoff for the
Founders' Retreat had finally arrived. Fred gave a silent curse. While
he was tempted to immediately agree to Opus, at whatever the terms,
he knew it was a risk to appear too eager. Now they wouldn't have
time to close the discussion; what if whatever magic existed on this
boat evaporated by the next time he saw Reagan and Jack?

"Remember when I sent the blow-up doll?" Reagan called out
above the din. "Good times."

Jack sighed and leaned back, tilting his head toward the sky. Despite his agitation, Fred looked with him. The problem with Bali, he
mused, was that it allowed too large a band of visitors to believe they
were experiencing true luxury. In a setting where five-bedroom villas
could be rented for $100 a night, even the middle class could feel
like kings. But there was no confusing the spindly crafts that dotted
the public beaches with *Killer*, this lustrous beast that announced its
wealth like a gleaming jewel deposited in the middle of the ocean. Jack
had let drop the tidbit that the Komodo Marina, where *Killer* would
eventually dock, charged $18,000 per night; there it was kept far away
from the gaping eyes of the public, shielded by other mega crafts.

The rich always stuck to their own, Fred thought. Even when
they were inanimate.

The next morning Fred texted both Reagan and Jack, to no response.
He felt he couldn't message either again without further skewing the
power balance and so next called Erika, where the phone rang without answer. The day had been left deliberately open on the Founders'

Retreat agenda, for the ad hoc discussions between industry players, which was where the real soft power of the event was supposed to reside; given his limited sphere of influence, he'd received no such meeting requests, and the one other attendee he'd recognized at the retreat—a business school classmate running an incubator fund—had punted his coffee invite to the undetermined future. To distract himself, Fred called the Biasa front desk and claimed the complimentary tour of local sights that had been offered upon check-in. He wasn't scheduled to see Reagan and Jack again until the next day, at the closing dinner of the retreat. A lot could change in thirty-two hours.

The guide for the tour turned out to be Bawa, who arrived on time with an enormous cocktail on a bamboo tray. The drink was blended with ice and began on top as yellow, gradually shifting to azure blue. "I am training to be a bartender," Bawa boasted. "This is my own creation! I call it Balinese Sky." As Fred tipped the glass he could feel the butler's eyes following him; he felt obligated to finish the entirety of the drink, which left a burning sensation as it descended.

Afterward, he followed Bawa to the hotel shuttle. Their first scheduled stop, the Monkey Village, was a popular tourist destination, and Bawa deposited Fred at the front with assurances that it would, in fact, be full of monkeys. "They are everywhere!" he called cheerily, passing Fred a small bunch of dark bananas as he himself declined to alight from the vehicle. Fred could find him in the van when he was finished, he said, and jabbed a thumb toward the parking lot, where a fleet of nearly identical black and silver vehicles stood idling.

True to Bawa's promises, monkeys scampered in abundance about the entrance, with more materializing as Fred began to walk along the marked circular pathway. He quickly encountered what appeared to be a family, a group of five, and stopped. The monkeys inspected him in return, coolly evaluating the fruit in his hands. The largest came up to his knee. Suddenly one leapt directly toward him, viciously batting at the bananas; in shock that they didn't fear him, Fred dropped the entire bunch, which quickly disappeared into the trees with the family.

Dejected by the experience, Fred purchased a small bag of crackers from a nearby vendor and began to toss them onto the ground. Only a few monkeys came for the offerings, with which they appeared familiar; one selected a shard and then daintily carried it intact to the trash, where it threw it into the can as a game. Fred bit into a cracker and found it tasty—salty and sweet, like kettle corn. The monkeys must live a pampered life, he decided.

Despite his efforts to relax, he remained in a state of high agitation. Opus was undeniably an opportunity, quite possibly his Big One—the sort Harvard was supposed to have supplied in excess but instead had shown him only brief glimpses of, denying actual consummation at every turn. All that he'd plotted and dreamed, however, had involved an exit from Lion. Now it appeared the two were interlinked, at least for the short term. He was bereft at the thought of once again being reduced to a mere cog, condemned to forever churn up an endless stream of profit to the Lelands of the world.

"Fucking Leland," Fred muttered. "Monkeys!" he called. "Monkeys!" His voice was joltingly loud, an aftereffect of the Balinese Sky. He shoved a handful of crackers in his mouth.

A young American mother flanked by children peered at him, the woman glancing at the tote he carried, which bore the logo of the Biasa. He called again to the animals in a pied piper singsong, shaking the bag of crackers furiously while being studiously ignored. "Fucking monkeys," he grumbled again, and wobbled. The mother threw him another look.

In anticipation of the day's heat, Fred had chugged two bottles of chilled water in the van, and his bladder now roused and called with urgency. He wandered the entrance until he located a sign that looked to indicate a bathroom, only to find himself off the paved path, surrounded by trees and flora. Desperate, he unzipped his pants. As he began to relieve himself, a monkey appeared to his right, baring its teeth.

"Get away," Fred hissed. He suddenly felt afraid; the monkey had an intelligent look to it, and its gaze was focused at the center of his crotch. Could some species of animals possess an instinct for when humans were at their most exposed, soft and vulnerable? He thought of Ebola and the many unknown diseases that seemed to germinate from jungles or caves, and how he had felt a light scratch on his hand earlier when the bananas were swiped. He locked eyes with the intruder, willing it not to come closer. "Angry!" he called. "Very angry! Do not approach!"

There was the sound of crackling leaves from behind, and for a moment he feared he was surrounded. He quickly zipped and in turning was confronted by a young boy, one of the three children from the family he had seen earlier.

"What are you doing with that monkey?"

Oh Jesus. "How long have you been here?" The last thing he needed was a citation for indecent exposure, especially on foreign soil. Didn't the Indonesians still chop off hands?

"What are you doing?" The boy stepped toward him.

"Stop!" Whatever tableau the current situation presented, Fred was sure it would be considerably worsened by any narrowing of the proximity between him and the minor. "Don't come any closer. There's something, ah . . . very dangerous here."

"Danger? You mean bad? What kind? Wow!" The child's eyes gleamed.

"Dangerous as in not good. Bad for little boys. Super boring. Not interesting at all."

"Then why are you there?"

It was a decent question. "I'm here because . . . because I'm very, very stressed."

The boy looked at him with doubt. Fred shut his eyes. There was a loamy, salty smell rising in the atmosphere, which he inexplicably believed had just come from the monkey's own piss. "Oh, forget it. I have problems, okay?" He breathed in and out. "How old are you, anyway?"

"Seven," the boy answered. A silence followed, and Fred opened his eyes, hoping to find him gone. Instead, he had inched closer. "Do you know any games?" he asked.

Fred groaned. He had a renewed appreciation for his own niece and nephew, who, thanks to Linda, at least had a healthy fear of authority figures.

"I have a game," Fred said finally. "It's called Mr. Hypothetical."

The boy frowned. "I don't know that one."

"Just listen. This is a verbal game, which means all words. There are two players in our scenario, I mean game. Player A and Player B. Got it?"

"Those aren't real names."

"Jesus. Fine. Player A is called . . . Lucifer, Mr. Lucifer, and Player B is called . . . Mr. Cool. And those are their full names," he added hurriedly. "They live on a different planet where everyone is called Mister.

"Now Mr. Lucifer, he's a very powerful and rich man. Because he's been given all these advantages, you see, and he happened to be born during a time when the world they lived in was expanding, and any idiot who understood certain technology trends could become extremely rich. You follow?"

The boy looked fascinated. "Like *Lord of the Rings*."

"Sure, whatever. Then, there's Mr. Cool. While Mr. Lucifer is super lazy and wastes his time shopping for ugly art all day, Mr. Cool's off working very hard. In fact, he's been working hard his whole life. Not to mention, Mr. Cool is smarter and handsomer than Mr. Lucifer. Younger too. Compared to him, Mr. Lucifer is way old."

"Why don't you like old people? My pee-paw is old."

"What did I say about listening? Old people are great, but in this world, they have an unfair advantage. Because by the time great dudes like Mr. Cool were born, people like Mr. Lucifer had already snatched up all the planet's treasures. So Mr. Cool doesn't have as much as Mr. Lucifer, but he would, if the world they lived in was fair. He'd have *more*."

"What's the game?" The boy shifted his feet impatiently. "What do they do?"

"You don't want to hear more about Mr. Cool?" Fred was hurt he wasn't more interested.

"No."

"Ugh, fine. Okay, the game is this. There's a certain princess in this world, a beautiful lady named . . . Princess Platinum. And only one man can save this princess. Princess Platinum, she wants Mr. Cool to save her. Why wouldn't she? He's stronger and younger and way better-looking. But the problem is, if Mr. Cool *does* save Princess Platinum, then he has to give her up to Mr. Lucifer. Even though Mr. Lucifer is so old and stupid that he wouldn't know what to do with her. In fact, he'd probably *ruin* Princess Platinum and all her special powers!"

"I don't like princesses."

"Me neither," Fred said, thinking of Charlene. "But this one is really excellent."

"Why does Mr. Cool have to give up Princess Platinum?"

"Because those are the rules of the world they live in. But rules can be very unfair."

"Does Mr. Cool have any special powers?"

"Well, he has a big brain and an earnest heart and was valedictorian of his high school class. So, that's the game. What should Mr. Cool do?"

"The game is answering a question?"

Fred spread his arms. "My house. My game."

The boy was quiet for a few seconds. "Mr. Cool should probably give Princess Platinum to Mr. Lucifer, then," he said. "Since it's the rules and all."

"*What?* But didn't we just cover that Mr. Lucifer is old and stupid? Why would you just give Princess Platinum up like that? You wouldn't fight at all to keep her? Mr. Lucifer doesn't deserve her!"

The boy considered this. "But we don't *know* Mr. Lucifer doesn't deserve the princess," he said. "It's just what you *think*. And if he really is so rich, then he probably did something to earn it. He can't be that dumb. My dad always says that society unfairly judges those who make a lot of money, because they don't understand the nature of risk."

"Do you even know what that means?"

The boy shrugged and shoved his hands into his pockets.

What kind of father said such things to a seven-year-old? Though the longer Fred considered it, the more it sounded like precisely the ramblings of some smug billionaire dick—a high-value attendee of the Founders' Retreat, for example. He bent down, so that he and the boy were eye level. "What's your dad's name?"

The boy shook his head. "He says I'm not allowed to say to strangers. Because of too much networking."

Ding ding ding. "Well, what's your name? Your full name."

"I can't say either. Unless you have the special password, to pick me up from school."

Fred cursed to himself. "Aren't we friends?" he asked. "Didn't I make up a great game, because you asked me to?"

The boy hesitated. "The game was weird."

"Listen, I don't know how some people choose to raise their spawn, but—"

The young mother appeared on the slope. "Lucas!" she shouted. "Lucas! *Is that you?*"

"That's my nanny," Lucas said. "Bye."

The boy navigated through the trees with slow caution, not bothering to look back. Fred watched him go until he disappeared from sight. He remained crouched for some time before his silence was broken by a hiss. He stood and turned and saw that the monkey was still there, waiting.

BACK IN THE CAR, BAWA TOOK IN FRED'S SOMBER MOOD AND AN-nounced an amendment to the normal route. Instead of the usual medicine man, he said, he would bring Fred somewhere very special. A famous water temple, to experience the region's springwater.

When they arrived, Bawa instructed him to leave his valuables in the lockbox in the car and handed him a printed sarong. They walked together to the pools, where a dozen fountains poured at a steady, leisured pace. Fred was surprised to see people in the clear water, groups in brightly colored tees and swimsuits, wading about. "People can go in?" he asked. "Isn't that dirty?"

"Yes, very much."

"Why are there so many fountains?"

"Each of them is for a different blessing. You see, look." Bawa brought out a laminated plastic card. "Guide for success. This fountain is for career, this for healing from body injury. This one is for love, this for money, this for academic excellence. You must touch the water, to be blessed."

"Which one is career again?" Fred squinted to match the card's icon to the fountain.

"Here, take with you. Waterproof, so don't lose." Bawa shoved him into the shallow water.

Fred waded forward until he located the fountain he wanted. The liquid, when he dropped under, was cool. To ensure a breadth of celestial coverage, he passed under each of the twelve and carefully wet his face and hair. He wanted to avoid accidentally drinking the water—it had to be recycled, and filthy—but when a group of teen-agers knocked him forward, a few drops fell into his mouth.

He was surprised by the taste. Its purity.

From: Kate@XCorp.com

To: Fred@Lion-Capital.com

Subject: Where are you?

Fred,

I've tried to reach you multiple times this week, but you haven't replied
to, or answered, any of my messages or calls.

If you had, I would have told you that Dad is in Hong Kong right now.
Yes, our father—who has pancreatic cancer and can barely walk—
sat on a plane for fourteen hours and is now in Asia, away from all
his doctors and against all sound medical advice. He thinks that he
found a way to cure himself and so decided it was no problem for
him to travel.

Don't you have a layover on the way back from Bali? Could you meet
with him and Mary and let me know what's going on?

From: Fred@Lion-Capital.com

To: Kate@XCorp.com

Subject: Re: Where are you?

Hong Kong? Is he out of his mind?

My schedule is already crazy busy, I'm not sure I can find the time.

Let's definitely catch up though when I'm back!

From: Kate@XCorp.com

To: Fred@Lion-Capital.com

Subject: Re: Re: Where are you?

Fred,

Make the time. Are we seriously having this discussion? Dad's condition is a lot worse than when you last saw him. The last time I visited him, he was out of breath just talking to me. When we had lunch, he almost collapsed in the parking lot. I know you're used to me and Mom taking care of everything, but you're the one in Asia right now. It'll take an hour, tops.

From: Fred@Lion-Capital.com
To: Kate@XCorp.com
Subject: Re: Re: Re: Where are you?

Right, you take care of everything. Except for when it comes to the trust, right? Then it's me who has to do all the work, since you don't seem to give a shit if everything Mom worked so hard for all goes to some random woman. You're above it all; you don't care about money. Though I'm sure you'll still collect your share at the end.
If you're so worried about Dad, why don't you fly here yourself?

From: Kate@XCorp.com
To: Fred@Lion-Capital.com
Subject: Re: Re: Re: Re: Where are you?

Fred,

When I first read your email, I wrote a response and decided to sleep on it. Then I wrote another one and called you, but of course you didn't pick up. This is my third attempt, and I'm going to finish it and then press Send no matter what.

First, I'm sorry for insinuating that you're not doing your share with Dad. I was wrong. Please accept that this is a high-stress situation. All I ask is that if you do have the time, meet with him for an hour, or even a few minutes. Anything would help, just so we could check in. Dad has already skipped one chemotherapy appointment, and another one was supposed to be scheduled for tomorrow.

On the will—of course I've considered it. It's the sort of thing nobody wants to admit they think about, but everyone does. Mom thinks that he might have made the trip to Hong Kong to close out his accounts there. Please let me know how I can help.

As for my finances, not that it's any of your business, but at the moment I care very much about money. Knowing the amount of our potential inheritance would be a massive relief, as there's currently a decent chance that I might be on the hook for spousal support, for a man who I very recently learned may not take his employment too seriously.

From: Kate@XCorp.com
To: Fred@Lion-Capital.com
Subject: Re: Re: Re: Re: Re: Where are you?

Fred,

Why aren't you responding? Can you please tell me if you met with Dad?

Also, I drank too much Pinot before I wrote that last email. Please don't mention anything I said about spousal support to Mom. Please?

———————

"I just pooped," Stanley said. "Did I already tell you that?"

They were seated across from each other in the open food court of the Elements mall in Hong Kong, from which Fred could take a train directly to the airport afterward. A steady stream of foot traffic surrounded them; Mary was off somewhere, meeting a friend she said had connections for acquiring rare and coveted Chinese herbs. His father looked so old—ancient, really—although Fred couldn't remember if he'd always appeared this way, just a little younger, or whether it was the disease that had brought it all to the surface. His face was gaunt, and the skin seemed to hang from his face and hands, as the formerly taut flesh receded.

"Are you pooping?" Stanley asked.

"Jesus. Yes, Dad, I'm pooping."

"How often?"

Fred rummaged his memory and discerned the last time had been back in Bali, the morning after the alcohol-fueled debauchery of the closing night of the Founders' Retreat. The event had been held at KoKo's, the trendy fusion bar–cum–restaurant starting to meander past its prime. The food had been gross, the lighting garish, and Don Wilkes had given a super boring speech, but that was the end of what Fred was able to recall coherently or chronologically. The rest was a series of blurred scenes: shots with Jack and Reagan, as they cheered the future of Opus; his promises to extract Lion's full cooperation, as he shouted, "Fuck Leland!" over and over. Jack disappearing sometime during the night; Reagan shoving a model slash actress slash Instagram influencer against him on the dance floor. The streaks of self-tanner on his new linen shirt, which he hadn't discovered until the next morning.

"Often enough."

"It's very important that you go regularly. I think Kate goes at least once a day, which was my own pattern until very recently."

"I highly doubt that. Kate eats like crap."

"She has access to all that healthy organic food at her company. So many fruits and vegetables. All free! Whole Foods–quality too."

Fred experienced the familiar twitch of jealousy that surfaced whenever his parents brought up Kate's job. He made more money than her (and would have for a long time had it not been for X Corp's ridiculous run-up in the equity markets) and possessed a far more glorious title (not to mention whatever lofty honorific he was going to employ on his Opus business cards), yet his parents never let up that X Corp had free food and dry cleaning. It annoyed him to no end that their approval came so cheap, just a few bags of chocolate-covered almonds and some dried apricots. Though from her last email, it appeared as if Kate was going through some major issues. He felt a brief thrill at the possibility of being the superior sibling; then he considered to whom Kate might actually turn should she have a financial emergency and be in need of funds.

"We didn't meet to talk about poop, Dad. How is your health? Weren't you supposed to start chemo again? How could you possibly think it was okay to travel so far?"

"Oh, my health is very good. I'm feeling much better. Mary was right; I needed to stop obeying the doctors' plans without thinking. It's my responsibility to push back, ask questions! Chinese medicine has been around for thousands of years. And I am Chinese! You think American doctors know how to best treat a Chinese person?"

"But you're still doing what the doctors are telling you to, yes?"

"The doctors don't tell me to *do* anything," Stanley said haughtily. "They work for me. They give me choices."

"You're still doing chemotherapy. Confirm. This."

Stanley leaned forward, as if about to impart a juicy secret. "Chemotherapy is deadly. It is feeding your body poison to kill another poison. Do you know many people actually die from the chemotherapy, and not the cancer? That's what happened to Michael Chan's wife."

Fred attempted a different angle. "Did you talk to Uncle Phillip?"

"Oh yes, Uncle Phillip, he is so nice. He says he is a patient advocate."

"What the hell does that mean?" Fred felt as if his skull were splitting in two. "Did he tell you that if you stop chemotherapy, you could die? You *will* die! That is the likely conclusion!"

"Mary has many friends with unique medical talents," Stanley intoned. "She is going to save me. She says it is her life's goal."

Why did Stanley have to be in Hong Kong at this precise moment? Why was this his responsibility? Normally this would be the point in the conversation when they would change the topic and never address it again; there were certain benefits to historically being the least qualified person in the family at managing Stanley. But there was no time now for any other option. "So this is all Mary's idea. You know she's not a doctor. She's a restaurant hostess with a shady background who appeared in our lives a mere nine years ago."

"Mary is a wonderful person. She says I am like a god to her." Stanley's voice softened. "Can you imagine? A woman like that, who says her only goal is to make me happy. What could a selfish man like me have done in a past life to deserve her?" Fred watched in horror as a single tear rolled down his father's cheek.

"Jesus. It's all Mary, isn't it? She's gone and convinced you to pursue this utterly ridiculous, completely irresponsible course of action! If you're so sure whatever she's promising is going to work, why are you in Hong Kong to begin with? Why aren't you at home, resting?" When Stanley glared at him in hostile silence, Fred pushed on. "Kate told me Mom thinks you made this trip to close out your accounts in Asia. Is that true? Why the rush to consolidate your money, if everything's going to be fine? Has it ever occurred to you that Mary might have another motive in giving you less-than-ideal medical advice? What do you even know about her, really? Who knows what she was actually doing back in China? Hasn't she been trying to move her mom over here? What's the one thing standing in her way? How can you be so blind, not to understand the position you're in?"

Fred hadn't experienced Stanley's fury in decades, but as soon as it reappeared, he knew he had been courting it all along. The air between them became thick with rancor, and he took a deep breath as if to absorb it all, willing himself to look forward. His father looked at him with what appeared to be pure hatred. "Shut your mouth," he said. "Watch what you say. Shut your fucking mouth."

Some memories were so hidden and rarely called upon that surfacing them was almost pleasurable. A bird, Fred's first pet, which had been his parents' shitty compromise for a dog in middle school. One day he returned home from school and discovered in the center of the living room an enormous white wire cage with a blue parakeet inside.

To preempt any disappointment, Linda had made a rare display of outward excitement. She brought Fred over to the cage, where she pointed at the water bottle, seed stick, and rope already installed inside. There was also a thick custom flannel cover, which she'd sewn herself, and Linda explained that when it was placed over the cage, the bird would assume night had arrived and go to sleep. The cover had featured a garish duck print, the material a by-product of the upcycling his mother was constantly engaged in around the house, repurposing torn wrapping paper into envelopes and hems of jeans into useful hanging straps for utensils.

For the first few weeks the bird had been exciting. It was fun to lift the cover and see the blue feathers ruffle and expand and shake; entertaining to arrange inside its cage various sticks and dowels and watch it travel back and forth. Perhaps to compensate for its silence at night, it was particularly vocal during the day—it circled Fred as he did homework and perched on Kate's shoulder during her daily piano practice, chattering an individual beat to the melody.

They'd been living in Cupertino by then, in the house Linda hated. It was the only one Stanley had agreed to buy in the area, for the simple reason that it'd been priced cheaply due to its relative location—at mealtimes when they looked out the kitchen window, they could watch cars zooming by on the freeway. As children, Fred and Kate hadn't been bothered by the noise, but it drove Linda crazy. She was convinced the constant din of traffic was driving her blood pressure to uncharted heights, and she continually pursued home improvement projects in an attempt to keep the clamor at bay. Her latest—a series of empty hallways across the entire south side of the house—was meant to trap sound.

Since the construction was ongoing, the contents of the living room had been placed in storage and the parakeet's quarters moved to the den, where Stanley watched TV. The bird enjoyed the space, which it'd been previously barred from. Occasionally it would perch on Fred or Kate or, once in a while, Linda; only as a last resort would it go to Stanley, and usually as a rest stop—a hop on his thigh on a journey to the remote or a bowl of grapes.

There came a rainy weekend when they were all trapped indoors. Only Linda was out, on a grocery run, and Fred impatiently waited for her to return so he could go to a sleepover (Linda always pre-ferred chauffeuring him and Kate to and from activities; it negated the chance of their friends' parents seeing the Cupertino house, which was her greatest shame). To kill time he slouched next to Kate at the desk in the den and leafed through her Sweet Valley Highs (like many boys, Fred pretended to find the books dumb but was secretly excited by the idea of pretty blond twins, who unfortunately existed in an alternate universe without Asians). The parakeet had been set off by the jingle of a cereal commercial and was cheeping loudly. Fred idly wondered if something was wrong with the bird's mental health. Was it going crazy? They called it bird brain for a reason, right? Over on the couch, he could hear his father as he rustled to get comfortable, rearranging pillows under his back.

"Shut up," Stanley said. "Why can't that bird be quiet!"

"Maybe it just wants love and attention," Kate offered. The sort of dumb treatment his sister was always prescribing. "Here, Tweety! Fly here and I'll give you a kiss!"

Stanley ignored the comment, as did the parakeet, though its chatter ceased. At the next commercial break, when it again started up, Stanley pointed a finger, and after a brief hesitation, the parakeet hopped on. Fred had read somewhere that for a bird to land on your palm you had to make the gesture inviting, slow, and gentle, but Stanley was none of these things. Maybe this one really was dumb.

Once perched, the bird continued to caw. Stanley pet it between its eyes and over its head, the way it usually liked. Unsated, it continued its noise.

"Quiet, please," Stanley said. "Quiet!" He began to lightly stroke the bird's throat, as he tapped its gray beak with his nail. "Quiet! Shut up! Quiet!" His mad voice had emerged. Stanley had been angry a lot lately, something to do with his investments and what he kept referring to as a "market correction" to a chilly faced Linda. Fred barely even noticed his furies anymore, unless directed at him; they had become part of the background din of normal life, the pitch of one of Kate's hysterical crying jags occasionally breaking through.

Eventually it wasn't any particular noise but rather the complete absence of it, that alerted them. The queer silence of their surroundings struck both Fred and Kate at the same moment. There was no interruption of an animal chime or the movement of ruffled feathers; the TV had been muted, which almost never happened. It wasn't clear how long the hush had been there, though by the time it was realized, it was immediately apparent it had existed for too long.

Fred saw it first, since he instinctively knew where to look.

His father's hand, where the parakeet lay in his outstretched palm, strangled.

IN HONG KONG NOW, STANLEY SLUMPED IN HIS CHAIR, NO LONGER able to sustain an extended rage. His finger was still pointed, but in his shriveled state it looked almost pathetic, a parody of the appendage. As Fred watched, it wavered, as if searching for an effective weapon, and clenched into a fist.

Without thinking, Fred pushed back his chair, involuntarily bracing himself. Stanley stared at him and then down at his own hand. When he finally opened it, slowly stretching out his palm, splaying wide his fingers, both he and Fred looked startled to find nothing but air.

CHAPTER 13

KATE

The intensive care unit at Kaiser Permanente in Santa Clara, where Stanley had spent the better half of the week, was nicer than Kate had expected. The room was private and relatively spacious; both the facilities and the couch she sat on were new. Kate had never used an HMO, only hearing of the horror stories secondhand: They cycle you through! Churn and burn! People die! And still there's no service! But so far, everything in her experience had been professional and organized. The doctors were thoughtful. Medical staff arrived as scheduled, once per every half hour.

It had been Kate who discovered him, her and Denny, after dropping by unannounced with organic juice and caprese sandwiches following Stanley's return from Hong Kong. There'd been no answer when they rang the bell, but the front door had been unlocked, so they'd pushed their way in. Only to find Stanley alone, asleep on the couch, covered with an enormous mound of blankets.

"Where's Mary?" Denny had asked. "Why is he alone?"

Kate shrugged, though inside she was pissed. She was already on edge, after Denny had insisted on accompanying her last-minute—given the recent developments with Stanley and his trip to Asia, she'd put any plans for a confrontation on temporary hold. From the window, she could see that Mary's car was missing from its spot out front—probably a quick errand, she thought. Though she'd call out her absence, subtly, when Mary returned. Stanley shouldn't be left by himself.

She poured herself a drink and set the food out on plates before wandering over to the couch with a glass of water. She bent and placed her hand on Stanley's forehead. When she touched his skin she instantly recoiled; it felt too hot to be real. Kate shook Stanley by the shoulders, and when he didn't respond, she screamed.

Denny ran over and began to strip off blankets. "Why is he sleeping under all of this? Did Mary put them on?" His calm turned frantic when he saw what lay underneath all the layers: Stanley, curled up and impossibly small, barely rousing. "He has to cool down. He could die from the fever; we've got to call an ambulance, right away."

"No 911," Stanley called weakly. "No ambulance. Too expensive."

"Dad? Dad?"

But Stanley was already gone, back to his fevered stupor, and Kate hadn't been able to rouse him back to consciousness. In the emergency room she stood in mute shock as medical personnel filed through. His temperature was measured at 105.7 Fahrenheit, and someone asked if he had any allergies to antibiotics, for infection. A random question then struck her, from years of watching medical dramas. "Is he septic?" she asked. "Is he in septic shock?"

The doctor looked at her curiously, and she immediately thought she must have said something wrong, the word couldn't possibly be septic, the same as septic tank. But then he answered, "Yes, he's septic. In shock. We'll need to intubate." At those words a nurse at his elbow turned to the computer, and the doctor left the room.

At one point Stanley woke and asked for his phone. "To call Mary," he said. "Where is Mary?" But his phone had run out of battery, and Kate had never bothered to get Mary's cell number. She looked everywhere to find a charger but failed, and then Stanley went back to sleep, falling into the state as easily as taking a breath. She cried then, Stanley oblivious next to her, his dead phone by his side on the bed. She was sure he was going to die too. At any moment, he would die.

But he didn't. He went into an operating room, an emergency procedure to remove some of the tumor ravaging his interior. A surgeon was called in, a redhead named Brian who looked like someone she remembered from high school, and it was a shock to Kate that people her age were now in a position to save or end people's lives. He had been paged from another location in the hospital and had rushed over in the fifteen minutes it took to get the operating room ready. It reminded Kate of when she had given birth to Ella, the twenty hours of labor during which the delivering obstetrician visited only once; the sudden scramble for a C-section when the baby's heartbeat dropped. The shock of realizing she was still awake as they were cutting her open and looking over the bloody sheet covering her torso and seeing a room filled with nurses and doctors.

By the time Stanley came out of surgery, hours later and still under sedation, Mary had been located. She hurtled into the waiting room with two pieces of rolling luggage filled with blankets, clothes, and Tupperware. "Where is Stanley?" she wailed. "Where is Stanley?"

And when Stanley finally woke, in his private room in the ICU, he found on his hospital bed his favorite duvet from home as well as his usual foam pillow. Mary was on the opposite end, massaging his foot; it was as if she'd never been gone.

———————

"You the wife?"

A Haitian nurse with short bobbed hair and burgundy lipstick had been silently bent over Stanley, checking his IV and medical signs for ten minutes. Though she asked the question with seeming casualness, throwing the words over her shoulder, Kate could sense the weight of the woman's interest.

"No, I'm his daughter. He had me when he was younger." She didn't know why she'd added the last part, since she'd been born when Stanley was thirty-eight. It was one of her problems, bending the truth to find a route for people to save face, even when they hadn't asked for it.

"You don't look old," the nurse said, as if she thought Kate might have felt slighted. "I just hear from the others that this man Stanley has got a younger wife. There was a lady earlier; I thought it was probably her. But then you showed up, and I wasn't sure."

"Aren't you my father's regular nurse?"

"Oh honey, I am. But I'm not surprised you don't know. I barely see anyone when I come."

Kate's defenses flared. "I usually visit in the late afternoon and evening. It's hard for me to come earlier. I have a job and young children." She immediately felt stupid for announcing she had a job, as if that were so special.

The nurse shook her head, not caring. Her name tag read *Aisha*. She began to clear the tray at the foot of Stanley's bed, setting aside the water cup as she efficiently stacked loose ends into a pile. "You want these papers?" she asked.

"Oh boy." Kate paused. "Not really." The papers, standard white computer sheets, had been Stanley's main method of communication ever since he had woken up four days ago from his nap to find himself no longer on his couch but in the ICU, prostrate on a hospital bed with a tube shoved down his throat. They were filled with various scribbles and demands: *Where is Mary? Does your mother know? Where is Fred?* And, *I want to go home*, which never failed to send a small lurch through Kate's gut. On a few other pages were solved sudoku puzzles, which Kate re-created by hand in large format so Stanley could complete them with a clipboard, and on the very top of the pile was a sheet with just two words, YES and NO. The word NO had been violently circled, many times.

"Everything going okay with my dad?" Kate asked. "Anything unusual?"

She'd meant about his health, but the nurse took the statement differently. She grimaced. "I don't know if I should say anything."

"About what?"

Aisha ignored her. She appeared to be struggling between a mild dislike for Kate and a greater unknown force compelling her on the other side; Kate had encountered this type of personality enough times within the engineering group at X Corp to know to remain mute and keep her face pleasant.

After a minute, Aisha cleared her throat. "Well. I suppose you're family. The woman from earlier, your dad's wife? She tried to bring some lawyer in here, few hours ago."

"A lawyer?" Kate tried to recall if Stanley had ever mentioned legal representation. "How could you tell?"

"You work here long enough, you learn how to recognize all sorts of people. This was a lawyer. The wife, she tried to walk him in, say she's got some papers they need a signature for. Was pushy, that's why I remember. But your dad said no, no guests."

Stanley could be both irrational and calculatingly obstinate; Kate wondered which of these faces he'd been wearing when he turned away the visitor and whether he'd known what the documents were. "Thank you for sharing this with me."

"Get involved in these situations, you asking for trouble," Aisha muttered, as if Kate were already thinking of making problems for her.

"I'll keep everything confidential, of course."

"Mmm." Aisha made another circle and scooted toward the door. Kate watched the nurse leave.

When she turned back to the bed, Stanley was awake. She leaned over and saw his eyes were yellow from bile. He looked immensely irritated. "Hi, Dad. Can I get you anything?"

He snatched up a marker and a sheet of paper. *when go home?*

"I'm working to get you back, I promise." She felt herself tear up again. The attending had informed her that no matter what they did, Stanley didn't have long. "If we're lucky, a few months," he had said. There would be no more operations or aggressive treatment; the medical focus going forward would be to make Stanley as comfortable as possible. To achieve that, however, they would first need to make him extremely uncomfortable, by confining him to the hospital bed. He couldn't be moved until his vitals had improved enough that there was no longer a need for intubation.

"I'm making a big fuss," Kate assured him. "I've asked to speak with management." Stanley had always demanded to speak with a manager when unhappy with service.

Another impatient tap. *how much urine?*

She bent down and examined the bag. "Lots. And good color too. Not too dark." Stanley nodded and laid down his head.

She was late for a meeting. It was a busy time for the Labs; they were close to launching an actual product, a powder called Grommix (Sonny himself had dreamed up the name—a jarring marriage of the words *grog* and *mix*, much to the marketing team's despair). Grommix, when combined with water and fastidiously consumed eight times a day, was touted to provide as much caloric sustenance as an ideally balanced diet of fruits, proteins, carbs, dairy, and vegetables; the product manager Kate had assigned to it estimated its yearly revenue as somewhere between zero and $2 billion.

Kate went outside to call Fred. The first time he'd visited the ICU, right after his return from Asia, he'd pulled her aside and whispered in heated aggravation what he'd learned from Stanley in Hong Kong. After what she'd seen in the hospital, however—the misery of the unending lights and noise, the air of desperate futility that hung in the rooms of terminal patients—Kate couldn't inspire in herself the same levels of indignation. Who was to say what continuing with chemo would have achieved? It was clear now that this was going to have been the last stop all along; the rest was merely buying time.

"I'm on my way," Fred said when he answered. "Did you talk to Dad about the will?"

"A little. To be honest he was pretty cagey about it, though I'm not sure if it was from the meds. I couldn't get any details, except that he said the 'plan hadn't changed,' whatever that means." She looked around and lowered her voice. "Did Dad ever confirm with you how much he was planning to leave us?"

She felt his hesitation through the phone. "What did he say to you?"

"As you recall, I stated he told me a million each. I was very open and clear about our conversation. What did he tell *you*?"

"He . . . he didn't say anything."

"Fred, this is ridiculous, if you can't trust—"

"Did he have accounts in Hong Kong?" he asked, cutting her off. "Mom was asking if we found out anything."

"He's incredibly uncomfortable and disoriented. I'm not sure this is the best time."

"There *is* no best time in a situation like this. Why aren't you taking this more seriously? It's almost as if you're on Mary's side!"

"Of course not! I'm as pissed as you are. I don't trust her at all. But for now I just want Dad to be comfortable. You've seen him; it's nearly impossible talking to him in this state. Can't we wait until we get him home?"

"That's where I'm coming from. It's why I'm late. Dad's office was in complete disarray when I entered; at first I thought he'd been robbed, that's how bad it was. There were papers and files everywhere. Mary must have gone through everything."

Kate stopped to consider this. "Why would Mary do that? It's not like he keeps any actual money in there."

"Who the hell knows? That's why you have to ask him about the accounts and find out about the will. Right now."

"I'm sorry, but I don't agree."

"Okay, forget it." His voice was filled with disgust. "I'll do it when I get there."

Outside the lobby entrance, Kate spotted Mary. She sat huddled with a small group on a bench, conferring over a phone. Before Kate could approach closer, Mary hurriedly stood and waved her over, introduced the strangers as her two sisters and one of their husbands. It struck Kate that she had never seen these people before. Was that normal? To have never met your father's new family?

One of the sisters looked closer to Mary's age, while the other—the one wearing a shiny leopard-print blouse tucked into tight black pants—appeared significantly younger, though in a blunt fashion that brought to mind her friend's husband's warnings on thread facelifts. Both women offered regretful murmurs while the husband looked at the ground. Stanley had always said that he preferred the prettier of the sisters; Kate assumed he meant the one in leopard. "Are you here to see my father?" she asked in halting Mandarin.

"Yes, yes," Mary said, alert. "Is he awake?"

"No," Kate lied. "He's been asleep the whole time. Fred is coming later."

"Ahh." A look passed among the women. She should stay, Kate thought. The words of Aisha echoed; there was something strange in how they looked at her and then each other, as if trying to telepathically discuss a course of action. But then she remembered she had to go home. She was horribly behind at work, and even Sonny had begun to give her the evil eye when she left early to go to the hospital in the afternoons. Fred would be there soon, anyway.

In her kitchen, Kate wiped down the counters and put away clean dishes while she assuaged Sonny's latest complaints. She needed a new headset, one in which his rants didn't come across so shrill. He was convinced it was only a matter of time before the other chieftains at X swooped in and snatched away the idea for Grommix, as they had Slippers; he had called her immediately following the end of a video conference with the sales team, right as she'd decided to open a bottle of Pinot Noir.

"Didn't you already present to Alexei? It's on record, Sonny. Grommix is the Lab's from beginning to end." She left unsaid the most compelling argument, that she didn't know who would want to steal Grommix in the first place; the rest of the executive team was too busy building cloud empires and data centers.

"I've been getting bad feelings," Sonny said with a moan. "Nasty, nasty, vibes. Grommix has the potential to be big. Like the Gates Foundation, but even more substantial. Because all they have is money, and we have *a real resource.*"

Kate gave an involuntary wince; in the past, when Sonny had pierced this level of paranoia, delusion had followed shortly after. "Alexei loved it," she cooed in her most soothing tones, as she scrubbed at a red wine stain on the marble. "You have nothing to worry about. You should be feeling good about yourself. More than good, *great.*"

"You don't think Alexei liked it a little too much, do you? Because this younger generation, they're all thieves. They think stealing ideas is just a part of business. No social code, no honor! Alexei called me old man the other day, did I tell you? Is it okay to call me dot head, because I'm Indian? Yet such ageism is acceptable from our very highest leader. Where is the accountability? The morality?

"And *then*, just the other day, I see Alexei dare show a preview of

Slippers on CNBC, just a little 'teaser,' he says, with no mention that I was the man who inspired its very creation! And after that," Sonny continued, his voice lowering ominously, "when I go to look for the sample Fujihara gave me? I find it's vanished! I know I put it in my office, I remember exactly where, but Marissa says I am mistaken, that it was never in that drawer. Do you think she's secretly working for Fujihara, to inform him of our projects? Or perhaps Alexei himself. Because that is how the Russians work. They can come to America, maybe they're even born here, but they retain the knowledge from the motherland, you can't escape it."

"I'm sure Marissa is loyal to you," Kate said. She felt a twinge of remorse about Slippers, though Sonny was wrong about the office—even Kate was too frightened to snoop through his private domain. The units had come from the supply closet. She vowed to replace them soon; they were of no use to her any longer, anyway.

AFTER SONNY, THERE WAS ONE MORE CALL. KATE HAD TO FUMBLE through her desk to find the number, which she'd stashed in the very back, among a pile of blank index cards. The phone was answered on the second ring.

"Is this Isabel Gorgas?"

"Yes." Isabel sounded joyful, as if she had just stepped away from a lively conversation. "Who's calling?"

"This is Kate Huang. We met at the park, a few weeks ago. Ella's mother."

The voice that eventually responded was firm. "I haven't seen your daughter since that day. I am at home, with my family. I have nothing more to say."

"I understand, and I'll be quick. That's not why I've called."

"Anything else, any questions, please talk to Ms. Camilla."

"Ms. Gorgas, I'm calling to offer you a job. Whatever Camilla

Mosner's compensating you, I'll add $15 per hour. And pay for your mileage to and from our house. The responsibilities would be heavier on the childcare side, but I can assure you that our home is much smaller than the property you are currently working with. We never entertain, and I'm back every day by five thirty p.m. I've just emailed you reference numbers for the past three nannies who worked for our household. Take your time, and think about my offer."

DENNY WAS STILL IN THE ATTIC WHEN SHE FINISHED WITH THE kitchen. Kate took the stairs two at a time, the way Stanley always had when excited. When she opened the door, Denny was hunched over the laptop with such an eager look of concentration that for a brief moment Kate felt remorse for the events she was about to set into motion. As she moved closer, he raised an eyebrow.

"Camilla Mosner," Kate said. His mouth opened to form an O. "Save it. You think I've never wanted to have an affair? You don't think it's crossed my mind during our marriage, like, oh, dozens of times? What is this, a midlife crisis?"

Denny stood, and then sat back down. "She's not a midlife crisis," he said. "You wouldn't understand. It's between her and me."

The fact that their relationship so obviously meant more to him than Camilla overwhelmed Kate with a mixture of pity and disgust. "What about CircleShop? Are you still working on that? If you've given up, it would have been nice to inform me."

"Of course I'm working on it," Denny said. "You have no idea what you're talking about."

"I know that to launch a start-up in one of the most competitive, well-funded spaces in the Valley, one should probably be doing more than taking extended naps during the day with his unemployed mistress, shoving his kids off with perfect strangers—"

"You don't understand a fucking thing!" Denny exploded. Kate felt herself jerk at this sudden anger. She shushed him, pointing a finger down toward Ethan's bedroom. Denny took a deep breath and continued in a lower voice. "You think you know everything, but really—" He stopped himself.

"Tell me," Kate goaded. "Tell me everything I'm lacking. This is your chance."

Denny regarded her with a flat expression. She could see the pride as it flashed behind his eyes, blinking on and off. "You know what I've been wanting to say?" he finally said. "For years now, ever since we got married. Since we met, actually. X Corp was the luckiest thing that ever happened to you. It was the luckiest thing," he repeated, more loudly. "You think you would have gotten this far at any other company? Or if you had to do it on your own, like I am? Of course you do, and I can never say otherwise, because that would make me out to be this cliché, the jerk who's jealous of his wife because she's more successful. Yes, I said it, you're more successful. I know you think you've been so sensitive and thoughtful, never bringing it up, the fact that you're a director of whatever-it-is dumb shit you work on at the Labs while I'm just some dude with an unknown company. That it makes you some sort of modern woman. You think that I care? Or that I might actually think you're better than me?"

The words took Kate by surprise. She had never thought anyone might consider her the more successful of the pair—Denny was the one with the Stanford computer science degree, the list of patents to his name. Even Linda, who never missed a chance to comment on their status as a single-income household, openly stated that Denny had superior credentials, making his choice of self-employment even more irrational. "I would never think that I'm better. I've always said that you're the most brilliant—"

"Well, that's what everyone else thinks, isn't it? Society? Because everything in life is so fair. Because America is such a meritocracy, and we've all earned our positions."

Kate took a deep breath. "I never claimed the world is fair. But to imply that I didn't earn my way, while you, as a perfectly capable *white male in America*, have suffered from some sort of unfair predicament—"

"Ah, of course," Denny cut in. He looked energized, as if he'd just been reminded of a particularly compelling argument. "That's what's always pissed me off the most. That you don't think your success was luck at all, that you think it was earned. You think you *created* it, that the fact that you ended up at a company that grew into this huge, nasty, monopolistic monster is all thanks to your skill. And that because of it, you're qualified to opine on all kinds of shit you know nothing about. Like CircleShop, or Camilla." Releasing the name with emphasis. His eyes were green and unyielding, and in that moment Kate could see how little regard he had for her.

"Well, I want to make one thing very clear, Kate. The reason you got where you are isn't because you're so smart. It isn't because you made such great decisions. It's because you and a few thousand other people got lucky. So fuck off."

When Camilla Mosner appeared two people behind her in line at Maggie's Artisanal Bakery and Café in downtown Mountain View, positioned in front of the sparse remaining loaves of the nationally acclaimed Ozark Mountain Bread that *Bon Appétit* had proclaimed one of the best in America, Kate had been surprised, but only slightly. Though she had neglected to call her after their first encounter—had in fact willfully and purposefully thrown away the scrap of paper with her phone number that Camilla had pressed into her hand through her car window—Kate had assumed that at some point, they would meet again. Camilla just seemed like that kind of person, the sort for whom events proceeded down an inevitable path; Kate was even struck by the suspicion that Camilla had been following her, as she had chosen to make her appearance at the one point during the weekend Kate was in public alone, without kids. Ella and Ethan were in fact next door, browsing children's books at Little Acorn with Linda, who insisted on giving each a budgetary limit for the visit instead of the one-book-per-trip policy Kate had long enforced.

"I just don't see why a $20 hardback and a cheap $2.99 paperback would be viewed as equally valuable," her mother said. "It sets the wrong sort of expectation for when they grow older. Shouldn't they know that different items have different values? Hadn't we already given you *Learn to Earn* by Peter Lynch when you were Ethan's age?"

After Kate purchased her small coffee and Danish ($12; sometimes she hated the Bay Area), she brought them to a bench outside. A few minutes later, Camilla sat down.

"My ex-husband, he's with an Asian now," Camilla said. She wore a light gray turtleneck and matching short trench and soft blue jeans; a pair of tortoiseshell sunglasses was perched on her head. "What do you think about that?"

Kate closed her magazine. "What do you mean, an Asian?" she asked after a few seconds. "Do you go around telling people you were married to a white?"

"Oh. I meant a Japanese woman." Camilla tittered nervously. "I'm sorry, I didn't mean to offend. Do you want to try my *pain au chocolat*?"

Kate scowled. Camilla's sudden appearance had distracted her when she was placing her order; her Danish had turned out to be both savory and vegan, filled with leeks and mushrooms.

"Anyway," Camilla continued, "my ex, I met him in Arizona. At the time he was a property developer, had done a few big commercial projects and just finished a high-rise condo, which is where I met him. I was one of the contract girls, the ones they bring in at the end to finish all the hundreds of pages of paperwork, where the guy really should read the terms but doesn't want to look dumb, so he just signs. This was before the whole housing crisis, of course. Once 2008 happened, kaboom! But by then I was married. We took a few years, did some traveling, and after that, Ken—that's my ex, if you didn't already know his name, but if you found my house you probably do—he started to get involved with data centers. Do you know what those are?"

X Corp operated seven of the largest facilities in the world; Kate had personally run the project management for Operation Lenin, an early-round feasibility study of what a nuclear-node-powered center would look like. "Yes."

"I don't look like the type of person who'd know about solid-state memory or server farms, do I? There's a lot that might surprise you about me. A lot," Camilla repeated. "Then again, you already know quite a bit, which is maybe why I find you so interesting."

"What happened with your ex?" Kate was irritated that Camilla had not only managed to involve her in her convoluted personal tragedy but then had the poor manners not to conclude the story in a timely fashion.

"So, Ken. He starts doing these data centers, right? On the real estate side, that is. For everything else, his partner is this guy, Manesh Das, whom he met through a mutual acquaintance. Long story short, the data centers do well, and then Manesh asks Ken if he might want to invest in this other company. Because Manesh, he works for this big venture firm called Motley Capital. And Manesh is kind of famous, he's one of those guys who's on TV a lot. He was also known as 'the Maid Beater of Silicon Valley' for a while. I'll let you figure out the story behind *that* charming nickname.

"Anyway, Manesh—he's got this company he's on the board of, and they need money, but they aren't in the sexiest industry. I guess they're having some trouble with financing, and Motley won't put in any more cash. And the company's desperate, and Manesh is swearing up and down, on his life, and on his wife and children, that it's a sure thing. And Ken, even though he knows *nothing* about technology, ends up putting in money, quite a lot—if I'd known at the time how much I probably would have been pissed, though I'm not sure he would have listened to me, and either way the situation would have turned out poorly, at least for me. Because guess what happens after? The company ends up getting sold to Microsoft, and a few months later Ken announces that we're moving to Silicon Valley. I guess he figures he's a technology investor now!"

"Mmm." As far as Kate was concerned, the story so far was fairly generic; the part she really wanted to hear about was the bit with the Asian.

"Before this year, Ken had never dated an—a Japanese woman before. From what I knew of his dating history—and believe me, I did my research—he was strictly Aryan, no black, no brown, nothing but white. To be honest I was the same, though I'm not sure that's something we should be calling attention to about ourselves these days. Once we moved here, though, started going out and attending events, we both noticed it. Why were there all these white men with Asian women? They were everywhere! We would be at dinner, and the entire restaurant would be filled with couples like that, except for us."

Camilla suddenly broke off and looked at her. Kate met her gaze. Was she waiting for her approval or just checking that she wasn't offended? "Go on," Kate said. She brushed some crumbs from her lap.

"Ken, he likes a certain body shape and look. Big breasts. Tall. Blond. When we first got married, I was a brunette, and then I slowly started going lighter and lighter, because it was like there wasn't a concept of too blond for him. Or too large a pair of breasts, though I never did the surgery, thank God. But that doesn't mean I didn't feel the *pressure*. The hints, they never seemed to stop! And now all of a sudden, the first person I hear that he's with after our divorce, an actual *girlfriend*—she's miniature, with black hair. Five feet if that, shaped like a tiny surfboard. Can I say that it makes me go what the fuck? What is this, a *thing*? We've all seen it. We discuss it all the time, the women here."

"The women you talk to are all white, I'm assuming."

"Well, yes." Camilla blushed. "I'll admit it's a little embarrassing. I'm from Arizona, right? The diversity profile is different there. But why does everyone here make such a big deal about not being racist?"

"Probably because they are. Who cares? Besides, you really think I would know the answer to your question about your ex? On the sole basis of, what, my being Asian? Maybe the chick is a data center expert and prepares gourmet meals." *Like me.* "Is this why you keep talking to me?"

"Of course not!" Camilla cried. "I just think you're so interesting! I've never met anyone like you here before. I'm just sorry we had to meet in such a way. I'm so, so sorry!"

Kate ignored her entreaties. "Is this, like, some sort of sexual thing?"

"No! Can't you just accept that it's hard for me to find women I like to spend time with? Why is that so difficult to believe?"

Kate groaned. Inside the store, Ella spotted her and jumped up and down. Linda was next to her, holding a stack of thin Little Golden Books. She peered at Camilla and gave a tentative wave. Linda probably liked the look of Camilla, Kate thought, since she looked educated and moneyed; her mother generally felt that most of Kate's friends were a few rungs above losers. Linda also worried that Kate's good friends were almost exclusively Asian—as with neighborhoods, she felt that an ideal balance included a good number of whites, preferably Jewish.

"Hey, how's your dad?" Camilla asked. "I heard a little about that."

"He's fine. Doing better, actually." Last week she'd finally managed to coordinate with the palliative care team at Kaiser and bring

Stanley home. The day his breathing tube had been unceremoniously yanked, Stanley had been almost happy; since then, he'd made a remarkable recovery. Key vitals had improved, and he was able to keep down three small meals of various porridges and smoothies a day. The only aspect that hadn't improved was Stanley's mood, since he was now largely confined to the makeshift hospital bed downstairs. Though he managed to get up twice a day to avoid bedsores, these excursions were limited to short walks around the house, on the first floor.

Whenever Kate visited, Mary fluttered about nervously, offering her food and Stanley sips from his water bottle, which he usually waved away, irritated. Next to the bed on a flimsy stand was a vast arrangement of various pills in their containers, which in Stanley's weakened state he found enraging to open and decipher. Kate had solved this by placing each dosage in clearly labeled plastic bags— *Tuesday a.m., with water, Tuesday lunch, with food, Tuesday dinner, with food, Tuesday evening, before sleep, with water.* She was due back this afternoon to refill the next few days; Stanley didn't trust Mary to read his prescriptions correctly.

"Don't you want to know anything about Denny?" Kate asked. Absurdly, Camilla was the only person she could talk to who knew all the intricacies of the situation.

"Not really." Camilla examined a nail. "I haven't spoken with him. Do you want to share something?"

"I told him that I knew."

"Ooh. What was that like?"

Kate flushed at the recollection: their whispered screaming match, which had continued downstairs, the two of them penned in the laundry room since it was farthest from the kids' bedrooms; Denny's departure with a packed bag, the front door slamming with a violence she'd never before seen from him. Suddenly she didn't want to repeat his words and shook her head, willing the scene to reshape itself. It was how she dealt with bad memories in general—locked away and stowed, to be removed only in case of emergency. "I asked him to leave the house."

"For good? Where's he living?"

"One of those furnished extended-stay complexes. My suggestion. I thought there would be lots of single and divorced men there, but it turns out half the people are families waiting out remodels." Kate wondered why she bothered to sound so nonchalant. Wasn't it her freebie as the scorned wife to indulge in a little melodrama? "They serve a buffet breakfast, as well as a different soup each night. Denny's probably in heaven."

"Oh. Then why is his car still in front of your house?"

"You went to my *house*?"

"Just once late last week," Camilla said defensively. "I thought maybe I'd find you alone, and we could talk. But Denny's car was there, behind a black Porsche."

That was Linda's, a recent acquisition. She'd sailed up in it a few weeks ago, the vehicle long and sleek, all black both inside and out, like a polished piece of agate. Ella and Ethan had climbed in immediately, as Linda laughed off Kate's attempts to have them remove their shoes. When asked what had inspired the purchase, Linda had said that she just felt like a new car. "I wasn't going to buy one of those Lexus SUVs," she said. "What am I, a real estate agent?" Kate felt that her mother had been acting strange lately. But her immediate priority was Stanley; Linda would have to wait.

"He dropped the car off back at the house after he moved his stuff and then took his bike. We told the kids he was on a business trip, so it wouldn't make sense if his car was gone." That'd buy them at least a few weeks, Kate figured, before they'd have to figure out something permanent. She gestured with a thumb toward the bookshop. "The Porsche is my mom's. She's been coming over more, now that Denny's gone."

"Ah." Camilla eyed Linda, who was sitting in one of the rocking chairs by the window, with a respectful gleam. "And of course you have Isabel now, to help out."

"Yup." Kate shut down the apology that naturally swelled and pushed to be released. Even if an insane series of events were to occur and she were to become friends with Camilla, she would never relinquish Isabel. She and Denny had used weekly cleaning services for years, but Isabel had brought the house to a whole new level of order. She had appeared ten minutes early on her first day with documented pay records for the past six months, reconfirmed that she'd be matched with a $15 hourly increase, and requested that direct deposit be set up as quickly as possible. She'd been horrified when she examined Kate's neatly arranged stash of store-brand cleaning supplies and had created her own in empty bottles, mixing vinegar, ammonia, and rubbing alcohol, adding lemon peels and lavender for scent.

"She's really quite excellent, isn't she? I'm glad she finally has some children to play with. Ella's a very sweet girl. I never met your son, but I assume he's lovely too. Though that wasn't very nice, what you did. Isabel told me about the additional bonus you offered if she quit and started with you *the very next week*. Of course I tried to match it; I said I'd double everything you offered, but she said she honored her agreements. What about your agreement with *me*? I asked. Doesn't longevity carry with it any benefits? I had an event that Tuesday! Anyway, I worked with an agency, and they replaced her the same week. I'm planning on adding another helper full-time, just in case, so that there's always continuity of coverage."

"Must be nice. To have such resources."

"Yes." Camilla glanced over. "It is. What are you going to do? Are you still paying for everything with Denny?"

Kate started to get annoyed, before recalling all the personal questions she'd asked Camilla. "Well, we are still married. I haven't thought much about the rest." Which was a lie. As of late, finances had occupied a significant portion of her mental stress load—the Palo Alto Home Suites charged a usurious $5,800 per month, and taking into consideration the costs of preschool, Isabel Gorgas, and the mortgage on Francie, they were now running a negative balance each paycheck. Given Stanley's improved condition she berated herself for even still thinking about the possibility of a trust; a million dollars would provide a good deal of breathing room, however, should a divorce come to pass. Kate realized she didn't know the answers to even the most basic of questions. Would she owe Denny alimony? Child support? She couldn't imagine he'd ask for sole custody.

"It doesn't seem very fair, does it? That he's sitting in a nice quiet apartment while you're off making all the money *and* managing most of the childcare. It's almost as if you're being punished, for being a working mother. I wonder what the situation would look like now, if you'd stayed home."

"Maybe the Japanese girl has big breasts." Kate couldn't decide whether she was fascinated by Camilla or wanted to claw her eyes out. "Japanese women sometimes do, you know. Maybe she's from Stanford and voluptuous."

"Oh no. I've made a study of her. Aki Yamaguchi. I told you, body like a surfboard. Good education, though, you're right about that. Caltech. I'll share something embarrassing with you: before we moved out here, I'd never even heard of Caltech. Right after we moved we were at this event that Manesh was hosting, and some guests were in a debate about what the top schools were in California. Because their children were all applying, you see, and I remember thinking, *I can't believe we're eating with couples old enough to have kids in college!* And people were saying well there's Stanford, and UC Berkeley, and UCLA, and then someone brought up Caltech. I have a cousin who went to Cal Poly in Pomona, and that girl is pretty dumb, so I mentioned how surprised I was that Cal Poly made the cut. And then everyone just looked at me with these awful blank faces.

"The worst was Ken, after we got home, he just couldn't let it go. Hadn't I ever heard of Caltech? The California Institute of Technology? He's the sort of man where if you look bad in a photograph he can't help but keep looking at it, again and again. It's not like he went anywhere special—he did his undergrad at Arizona just like me, and then an MBA at Thunderbird—but he treated it like this horrific *offense.* And the thing is, I know I'm smarter than Ken, I was always quicker than him, but he just adapted so much better to living here."

"Well, Caltech is a very small school," Kate allowed. "I think I only know a few people who went there, and I could probably list at least thirty from MIT."

"I could only name one from MIT," Camilla said. "That jerk Manesh Das." She sighed and wrung her hands, and Kate felt an ache of jealousy, that she could make a mundane gesture look so lovely.

"WHO WAS THAT WOMAN YOU WERE TALKING TO?" LINDA ASKED. They had exited Little Acorn, and Ethan and Ella triumphantly held their bounty in their hands. (While Linda had held true to her $20 allotment, she refused to pay the fifteen-cent charge for paper bags.) "No one lose their books, yes? Because Wai Po won't buy more."

"Just someone I know from the neighborhood."

"Your area? Really? I haven't seen her before. She has kids?"

"No, none."

Linda studied the bench where they had sat, as if there was still a lingering whiff of Camilla she could analyze. "Must be because of the husband," she concluded.

That night, Kate crushed a sleeping pill and downed it with a mug of water. She'd had two glasses of wine earlier, which were fast becoming a daily indulgence. Usually she couldn't sleep well after alcohol; her body would tremor and she'd invariably wake up after an hour of flat dreaming.

The pill did its work, however, and she slept until late morning. She went downstairs and found Ethan already dressed and pouring cereal for himself and Ella. The scene seemed surreal: her two children sitting calmly, eating Cheerios, no adult supervision required. "I didn't know you could do that," she said. "Did you just learn?"

"Wai Po always has me make breakfast," Ethan said. "No big deal."

"Ah." Kate looked for the kettle but couldn't find it. Then she remembered she had placed it in the sink the night before, to wash.

"Mama, are you sick?" Ethan asked. Hopeful, so that maybe Linda would come help for dinner; she usually brought over pizza and clam chowder.

"No, I don't think so." She cracked her neck. "Just tired." What was it she had dreamed of the night before? It had been so clear when she woke, but the plot was already gone, and all she could remember were insignificant pieces. Her mother dying, her father already gone. And a blonde walking away, calling out about server farms.

CHAPTER 14

LINDA

Linda had heard about Stanley's house for years, though in her opinion her children were always too stingy with the details. Kate and Fred claimed this was because they rarely actually visited Stanley at home, meeting him instead directly at cafés and restaurants (a habit Linda had never approved of—besides the health implications of excessive dining out, why marry a younger woman from China if you weren't going to get some decent homemaking?). Over the years Linda had been tossed a few mere snippets, each of which she'd carefully stored and extrapolated on.

There were the furnishings, the majority purchased during a dedicated shopping trip to Guangzhou, the selections not making their arrival until half a year later, via container ship (the cheapest delivery option). *What kind of furniture?* she'd asked. Was it wood, and what kind? How large was the bed? "Cheap" had been Kate's only response. The artwork, which on the first floor was portrayed as generic but which in the upstairs bedroom apparently included several portraits of a redhead in the nude. (Why a redhead? Stanley had never expressed an interest in them.) A baffling story about a coffee table with neon track lighting, which Linda had trouble envisioning and thus didn't fully believe.

Then there was the layout, described simply as bizarre. Upon entering one was immediately confronted with the distant view of a beige toilet, which belonged to the guest bath Stanley insisted on keeping the door open to at all times. The staircase to the upper level stood in the very center of the house, which was terrible feng shui, an ancient art Linda believed in solely for its ability to influence real estate values. Stanley had also apparently deliberately selected a home with all the bedrooms located on the second floor so that there was no chance of Mary's gouty, wheelchair-using mother moving in. On this last point Linda had agreed. Why should Stanley care for Mary's mother? He had bought himself a nurse, not agreed to become one himself. Though it was ironic that it was this very lack of accessible bedrooms that meant Stanley now slept in the downstairs family room, for all to see.

When Linda finally came to visit, the week after Stanley arrived home from Kaiser, she found his house exactly as she'd imagined it, in her most gleeful of nightmares. The living room was a vomit of cherrywood, which she recalled Stanley had always considered the finest of materials. Along its walls were built-in cherry shelves, stacked with leather-bound books whose sole purpose was to occupy the space; in the middle sat two cherry chairs and a sofa, each upholstered in the same scratchy yellow-and-red-patterned tartan. A low table was positioned in between, made out of cherry, and to the side of the sofa was a small side table, on top of which sat a desk lamp, both cherry. Tucked in the far-right corner was a tall wicker basket, which held a collection of walking sticks and canes—after selecting the most ornate staff, constructed out of a dark burled wood (possibly cherry), Linda examined its silver handle and discovered it to be made in China.

She felt safe to snoop at her leisure, at least for a little while. Mary was gone from the house—to buy groceries, or so she claimed. Linda made a note to check the receipt if there was an opportunity, after she returned. She was probably tacking on store gift cards to her purchases with the credit card Stanley provided for "essentials," a trick Yvonne had discovered via one of Jackson's paramours, back when he had a girlfriend in Santa Clara. Apparently, the hussy had saved up enough in Nordstrom gift cards for a Fendi handbag.

Linda continued her exploration. If the living room was Stanley's fantasy of an English gentleman's sitting quarters, then certainly the family room he now occupied was a modern-day bachelor pad born of the same deranged mind: shades of lunacy cast in black and reflective silver. The pièce de résistance, a seventy-two-inch flat-screen television, hung on the wall tethered by invisible hooks, while on either side of it stood two identical floor lamps, their spindly lengths forged in full chrome. The couch, recliner, and coffee table were all black leather. At one point, the lacquer tray on the table had probably held TV remotes and the books Stanley was always pretending to read; now, it was filled with adult diapers and baby wipes. When Kate began to fuss with the blankets, Linda knelt and ran her hand around the coffee table's base until she felt a switch. When she flipped it, a ring of fluorescent lighting lit the table from below. She sank down on the carpet. She found she was too depressed to move.

Once there was a time when she would have wanted their friends to see all this, the portrait of Stanley's life without her in it, how it looked when the worst instincts of his taste were indulged without a moderating influence. Now, she was glad most of them had never been over. She was loath to imagine what they might already be speculating, as estate and retirement planning were two of the group's favorite topics; they saved a particular prurient fascination for those who had failed to save adequately, or vastly overstated their wealth, or caused family infighting over their will.

Of course this being Stanley, there was the possibility of all three. He'd represented himself as a wealthy man for decades, and Linda knew that amongst their mutual friends there was the assumption that he was at least as responsible as the rest of them; perhaps no genius in the markets, but someone who earned and saved. Only Linda understood the spectacular mismanagement he was capable of, his fondness for penny stocks and fruitless property development schemes, and on this topic she'd been the very picture of discretion, hinting only to Kate and Fred that their father wasn't nearly as flush as they might believe. One million each? Two? *Three?* Each time she'd heard the figures, she'd forcefully renewed her charge that they had to ask him about his will, to pin down the facts, with evidence—a request that so far had left her sorely disappointed.

Linda knew her children's refusal to confront their father was anchored at some level by their blithe confidence that they were still central in his mind. Though Stanley had never displayed any particular passion toward them they assumed it was related to how he regarded life in general, and not a judgment on their own relationships. They didn't yet understand that as one grew older, as one's own children aged and moved away, your own self came increasingly back into focus. Life became definitively finite, increasingly so, and your desire for pleasure grew each day. Mary made Stanley feel important, like a real man, a wealthy benefactor—how did that compare with Kate and Fred, who had grubbed under his roof for eighteen years, rarely giving thanks or appealing to his ego (or, come to think of it, her own)? Wasn't it so that Candy Gu no longer spoke to her own adult children, after their vehement opposition to her young paramour? Candy saw her grandchildren—whom she had raised until preschool—only once a year, on their birthdays, and still she stated that she was the happiest she'd ever been. Linda believed her. At their age, after everything they'd achieved in coming to America, they all deserved a certain amount of reckless indulgence (she was highly enjoying her new Porsche).

The problem with Stanley, however, was that he'd never understood limits.

Linda walked over to the bed, where she loomed over Stanley's prostrate form. He still wore the same white *PARIS!* sweatshirt as the last time she'd seen him; his hair was in wisps now, nearly gone. She inspected the bed configuration, which looked to be mildly comfortable. A real mattress had been placed over the hospital pallet, with a discreet layer of plastic sheeting tucked neatly from the waist down. A duvet she recognized from the house—a thin quilt covered with a blue duck print she'd sewn herself—lay over his legs. "Stanley," she hissed. "It's me."

Stanley opened his eyes and took her hand. She resisted the urge to recoil; Mary might be back and lurking nearby, smiling in her simpering fashion while undoubtedly attempting to eavesdrop on their conversation. Why couldn't that woman shut up about her vegetarian soups? Linda reminded herself not to consume any food or drink offered to her. Who knew what Stanley's wife was plotting, what she was capable of?

Linda checked over her shoulder for Kate, who was in the kitchen, within eyesight. She lowered her voice. "Stanley," she repeated. "Did you finish the will?"

She waited impatiently while he hacked and coughed. "I want to meet with my accountants and lawyers first," he rasped. "I need advice . . . on how to structure things."

"What are you talking about, *accountants*?" As far as Linda knew, Stanley's closest interaction with any member of the bookkeeping profession was his yearly appointment with H&R Block, where he opted for the cheapest express service. "What do you have to structure? If you need a lawyer, go to mine, Ellen Lu. She's very professional, speaks Mandarin, and is based out of Menlo Park. You can have lunch at Osteria after." That had been their family's go-to restaurant, way back when.

"Does she know how to set up a foundation? I've been thinking, I want to start a foundation."

A foundation! Linda nearly fell over. It was just like Stanley to dream up such an idiotic idea on his deathbed, a final wish impossible to satisfy that would only waste everyone's time. Who did he think he was, Steve Jobs?

"A foundation is for people who are very wealthy," Linda said carefully. "You need to have a purpose, a cause that you believe in, and then you need to have a lot of money. A *lot*, like fifty million." From the way he was still beaming, she could see she'd have to spell it out. "You don't have nearly that much."

"I've always dreamed of having a foundation in my name. So I can know a part of me will live on, for eternity."

"Since when? I never once heard you mention one."

"Oh, for a while now." He waved his hands vaguely. "I've always thought about it—for my name to be out there. It's what great men do, isn't it? They have foundations, colleges, hospitals named after them."

"But, Stanley," Linda whispered, "you aren't great."

"Ah." He smiled with open lips, and from his throat came the sound of a distended laugh. "Of course you wouldn't think so, Linda, but you might be surprised. Many people come to me for advice. They seek my guidance. Because of my life experience."

Mother of God, he was completely serious. Who could possibly be crazy enough to go to Stanley for counsel? It had to be Mary's low IQ friends. Could he possibly be on drugs, hallucinatory ones? Linda looked around for medicine bottles, but Kate had taken them to the kitchen.

"Stanley, the best way for your name to live on is to *honor your children*. They are your legacy. And the best way to do that is to make sure you have a trust. A *living* trust," she added, to make it sound more appealing.

"I am, I am. I wrote it down, somewhere. . . ." He patted up and down. "Kate and Fred will each receive a third, and then Mary the last third."

There was a sudden brutal pounding in her temples. "So you think your two children, who you've known for their entire lives, who are your *blood and the parents of your only grandchildren* . . . you think that they are equal to your second wife, who you didn't even *know* a decade ago? Stanley!" she fumed, edging closer. "This is not right!"

"Mary is my life and soul," he countered. "She is my angel."

"My God! I don't know why you've become so stupid recently, but—"

"Ma!" Kate called from the kitchen. "What are you going on with Dad about? You know he's not supposed to have any stress; he needs to save his energy."

"Nothing! Just discussing the old days. We're having a nice time, aren't we?" Linda rolled her eyes and turned her attention back to the task at hand. "Just how much is there, anyway?" She kept her voice slightly above a murmur, though Kate was running the faucet now.

"Enough, but probably not to you. You were always better than me, there." Stanley still held her hand and now gave it a weak squeeze. His face turned solemn. "When I'm gone, I want the children and Mary to remain friends. They can visit my resting place together. You should come too."

An even more idiotic idea. He was definitely losing his mind. "I'll probably be dead," Linda said. Or she would kill herself, if visiting Stanley's grave with Mary were her only other option.

"The foundation will bring everyone together. The children and Mary can administer it. What about a college scholarship, each year granted to a worthy young man from Taiwan? Mary said it was a wonderful thought. I know you think she's after my money, but I swear in my heart I know she isn't. Why else would she support the foundation?"

Any foundation of Stanley's would likely only be able to pay out a semester of tuition—maybe a whole year if it was community college—before it petered out to ashes, but Linda didn't go into that now. An idea had materialized, a sprig of inspiration. "What do you tell Mary about your money?" Linda asked. "Anything?"

Even in the hazy cradle of drugs, Stanley bristled. "She knows I'll always take care of her. She doesn't need to be concerned over details."

Ah, so Mary knows nothing. Linda wondered if Stanley's wife knew just how little he was likely worth. Of course, *little* was a relative term—Stanley was still a rich catch for that so-called Buddha lover, wealthier beyond belief than any man she could have captured in whatever marshy village she'd emerged from. Still, Linda knew Stanley liked to brag. She wondered just how vast a portrait he'd painted.

"If Mary is so supportive of the idea, why doesn't the foundation come out of her share of the estate? Wouldn't it be nice to give her a concrete legacy to remember you by, and to care for in the years to come? After all, it isn't as if you two had children together." And thank the gods for that, otherwise Stanley would likely be awarding the entirety of his paltry savings to this devil woman and whatever half-wit they'd managed to spawn. Linda bent closer. "Kate is having problems with Denny," she murmured. "I think he moved out! Oh," she said, and wrung her hands. "To be a single mother with two innocent young children. . . . Stanley, you *must* think of your daughter now. She could have a breakdown any moment. I am seeing the signs, everywhere." She nodded toward Kate, who was efficiently packing vitamins. "Obsessive behavior, because she is lacking control in her own life."

"Who? Kate? They're getting a divorce?" Stanley looked out of sorts. "Out of her share . . ."

"*Mary's* share," Linda prompted. "*Mary's* share. The foundation money comes out of Mary's. Share." Who knew how much of Stanley's mind still remained? She'd have to repeat the key points as much as possible.

"Mary's share . . . ," he intoned. "She's not good with money. I'd have to make sure there'd still be enough for her to live on . . . but really, she's *such* an easy woman. She always said I was the one who wanted to travel; she was happy at home massaging my feet. So sweet, so simple."

Had Stanley really been this daft the entire time they were married? Linda made another quick, surreptitious check to ensure Mary hadn't materialized.

"You think Mary would truly appreciate the gesture?" Stanley asked. "She never mentioned wanting to manage the foundation itself."

"Of course, didn't you just say she is all about giving? And I know how much she loves meditation and temple; she told me herself when we had that lunch. As Confucius says, a gift to others is a gift to ourselves." Linda had read that in a fortune cookie at China Garden the other day. "This way, your wife will ensure your name lives on."

"It would be a true gift, one worthy of her heart. Ah, and Mary has such a big heart." A concerned look crossed his face. "But I think that if the money were to come out of her share, I'd want Mary to have her name on it. The Stanley and Mary Huang Foundation. Do you think the children will be upset?"

"I will explain to Kate and Fred how important it is to you. I like the idea of both of your names, very dignified."

He gave a weak thumbs-up. "Linda, you've always been so smart and creative. Even after all these years you're still taking care of me."

"Of course," Linda said, and made herself take his hand. "I'm happy if you're happy. And remember, to make sure it all happens smoothly, you have to get the trust done. After that, you can rest easy, hopefully enjoy many more years. I'll have my lawyer call Kate tomorrow, how about that? And then she'll work with you to determine a plan."

Then Linda forced herself to do the thing she really didn't want to do, which was bend over and give his forehead a kiss. Stanley sank his head back into the pillow as she knew he would, sighing a small noise of delight.

Linda was fairly certain that all of Stanley's assets combined, much less one third, wouldn't be enough for even the most miserably funded of foundations, but she'd leave that unpleasantness for her attorney to deal with. Ellen Lu, after all, could bill Stanley directly; in all of Linda's years with him, when had she ever received even a cent for all her helpful guidance?

The women in Linda's circle gathered easily. A few quick phone calls, and a date and time were set, a location bickered over and agreed upon. It was one of the few perks of retirement, the mutual assurance of the desire to fill calendars in advance, which suited Linda perfectly. She'd always been a planner—never the sort to dither on making engagements until the last minute, in case a better option came along.

When the get-togethers included husbands, however, they became more problematic. Even though the men were mostly retired, they all still had to invent reasons for why they were busy, off doing important tasks. To admit their calendars were as empty as their wives' seemed to be an open invitation for death to come trotting along and scoop them right up, so instead they had consulting businesses to tend to, doctor's appointments to wait on. Whenever men were involved, the events had to be scheduled at least a month out and usually ended up as dinners. Given the considerable hurdles, it was considered a major loss of face for one's partner not to show after a positive RSVP had been registered, which was why it was absolutely imperative that Winston behave flawlessly two nights from now.

In hindsight, it had probably been too hasty for Linda to sign Winston up for dinner just twenty-four hours after he was due to arrive in San Francisco. Better, she thought now, for them to have earmarked some time to settle into each other a little more, become adjusted to the physicality of each person. Because while Linda felt as if she already knew Winston, understood his story far more than she'd ever Stanley's—whose family secrets and demented personality she'd had to unravel over decades, by which point she didn't even care—she and Winston were still missing the key knowledge of each other's bodies. Not in a sexual way (though that was a topic she'd been pondering with ballooning interest and apprehension) but in a comfortable, grown-together sort of fashion. When she'd hovered over Stanley's frail form and he'd lifted her hand, she'd known instantly what his body used to be and what it had become, and Stanley had shown no surprise when he touched her dry and papery skin. They'd lived together for thirty-four years and shared a bedroom for thirty; he'd been with her naked, heard her fart, assisted her with her colostomy bag after surgery. Seen her as she'd aged, as he passively observed the gradual softening of her body.

Now Winston would arrive, a man with no memory of Linda as a young woman, nor vice versa, a situation that along with its crippling insecurities introduced a whole host of other problems. Their lack of physical familiarity, for example, would be obvious when they walked. Would he take her arm? Hold her hand? Yvonne and Jackson always did that, Jackson making a big flourish about what a gentleman he was. Would a ray of light harshly illuminate her face as she sat next to him, and could he successfully hide his surprise at angles previously concealed? When the check came, would Winston attempt to pay, and would he know how to read the situation, when to obstinately press forward, and when to retreat?

It was all so very stressful, and Linda ardently wished she hadn't invited him to dinner to begin with. It'd been that goddamn Shirley Chang who'd set the calamity in motion, she and her incessant bragging about her new husband-to-be. She'd met him on Tigerlily, of course, come right out and announced at the last group luncheon that she was once again going to be married. Another lap in her life's victory tour.

"Married!" Yvonne exclaimed. "We didn't even know you had a boyfriend!"

They had been seated in a circle, so everyone could see the shock on her face and satisfaction on Shirley's. Only groups of ten were technically allowed at the round tables at China Garden, but the owner had obsequiously made a show of seating the four of them at one anyway, insisting it an honor due to his "good friend Shirley." The rumor was she was a silent investor (another poor post-Alfred investment decision). And now here she was announcing yet another, looking as smug as a well-fed Persian cat.

"Where did you meet him?" This from Candy Gu, she of the younger husband, who was always jealously scanning for competition to her status as the group's resident Sexual Adventuress. "How old is he?"

"He's my age, my real age, and we met online. Oh, don't give me that look, Candy, you know everyone is doing it these days, even graduates of Princeton and Yale! There's even a separate site just for surgeons to meet other surgeons; these are the sort of highly qualified people who are internet dating now. I know for some of you the concept is very shocking, but what does it matter now that we are going to get married? I will bring him to the next get-together we have with husbands, so that you can all be introduced."

"Why did you keep it a secret?" Yvonne asked. "We would have wanted to meet him earlier." She darted a look to Linda, who kept her face impassive. Inside, she was roiling—that Shirley could just announce she was dating online with such brazen aplomb, whereas she'd suffered under such a heavy cloak of shame for months! Why hadn't she thought to control the conversation from the beginning? But then, she was a very different person from Shirley.

"You know me, I don't like to introduce new things until I *know for sure,*" Shirley said. "And plus, I hate the word *boyfriend.* It's so juvenile, isn't it? At our ages, we should have husbands." She couldn't help but swivel her neck once again around the table, the triumph clear on her face. Yvonne met Linda's eyes: *Can you believe this?*

Linda felt herself beset by an uncharacteristic rash anger. What did Shirley think, that she was the only one desirable enough to find another husband at their age?

"Congratulations, Shirley," she called out, before she could stop herself. "Is this the dinner next month?" She let a brief pause elapse. "I can bring someone, too, if we do it on the third weekend."

"Oh my!" Candy cawed. "Two surprise weddings! Should I be thinking about a new husband too? Seems like there are many good opportunities out there!"

"Linda, are you getting married?" Yvonne asked. She looked wounded; just the week before they'd met for coffee in Los Gatos, where Yvonne had confided the latest monetary demands of Jackson's Taiwanese concubine. She'd been too agitated to ask about Winston, and Linda hadn't offered.

"No, not that. Just a special friend." *Special friend.* She silently tried the phrase on again for size and found she quite liked it. "No hurry for me. I enjoy to be alone, spend time with grandchildren." *Unlike others here, with abnormal adult sons and no continuing progeny to speak of!*

At first she'd been nervous to tell Winston about the dinner. He had only a weekend in the Bay Area, after all, and had already spent considerable time detailing all the potential activities he'd want to partake in (staycation in Napa! Stanford sculpture gardens! San Francisco Opera!). But when Linda informed him of the event, posing it as a choice fully his to make, he'd been enthused.

"I'll wear a special suit," he promised. Linda was relieved he wanted to make a good impression on her friends; he was always going on about how most of them were saboteurs, stewing in a paranoid sulk whenever she met with Yvonne. "I had it custom tailored by a famous shop in Hong Kong."

"That's not necessary." It wouldn't do to have Winston look like he was trying too hard. "Just a pair of clean slacks and a sweater."

"If only Black Sun weren't making me return so early. We could go somewhere outside of California. Like Arizona. Have you ever been?"

"No," Linda demurred. "Stanley and I talked about it, but we always ended up in Vegas, usually Circus Circus." That was back when they went on vacations; they'd stopped traveling together after the children were in their teens.

"Oh my Lord. I don't like to speak badly about other men, but your former husband really didn't deserve you. A woman like you shouldn't be in Circus Circus. Arizona is one of my favorite destinations. It's so beautiful, and warm all year. There's a very good steakhouse that John McCain goes to. And a wonderful hotel, five stars, where you can see the mountains."

"That all sounds very nice." She quietly flipped through the morning's *Wall Street Journal*. Didn't she see a teaser for some article about U.S. Steel? She'd been accumulating shares since the beginning of the year.

"Finally, we will be together soon. I cannot wait. Do you feel the same passion as I do? Please say yes!"

Ugh. She hated it when Winston got all drippy. "Yes, I feel that we have become very close. Just remember, in person with my friends you needn't say such, ah, romantic things. You should still be a *gentleman*, of course," she added hastily. "But they are very conservative, and their relationships aren't like ours."

"Because they're in loveless marriages. Like you and I used to be. They're jealous. Remember how I said Chinese our age, they just can't stand to see happiness when they don't have any."

"Some of them are in good relationships. My friend Candy, she is very happy."

"Is she the one who owns apartment buildings in Mountain View?"

"Yes, but I wouldn't mention that when you meet her." She'd have to vet his manners carefully when he arrived; coach him not to blab everything she'd told him about her friends.

"I read that book you recommended," Winston said. "The Ha Jin."

"Did you enjoy it?"

"I finished it in one night. Linda, we are soul mates. I never met anyone who loved all the same things I do. How fortunate we are to have found each other!"

After they hung up, Linda felt a trickle of guilty relief. Winston could be so cloying at times. If she didn't answer his video chat, the mobile and home lines would ring incessantly, until she finally picked up; he was also a prolific emailer, whereas she used email purely as a basic communication tool.

She went to the guest bedroom, where she had begun to make up a bed before realizing Winston would likely sleep in the master, with her. What would that be like? Linda hadn't shared the California King she currently occupied for well over a decade, and over the period she had established certain habits she was loath to relinquish.

The connecting door to the bathroom, for example, hadn't been shut in years; she could use the toilet in the middle of the night without fear of the noisy flush or fumbling for the knob. She used to complain vociferously, and often, about Stanley's snoring. Who was to say she didn't do that now? Or, God forbid, fart?

Stanley had slept in the guest bedroom the last years of their marriage, after Linda decided he was no longer welcome by her side at night. The evening she informed him of his new quarters, she'd slept soundly, sprawled over the king-size mattress like a queen. Over time she'd reverted back to her original side, the left, but still. She wasn't sure how comfortable she would be sharing her sleeping space, not to mention everything else that happened in the bedroom. By the end with Stanley, many months would pass between the inevitable nights when she would creep open his door and lie next to him; they would silently move together, her back to his front, him barely touching her, her nightgown still on, hiked up. Though he was always responsive to her overtures, Stanley never once came out of his own accord to her bed, likely out of respect for what he believed were her wishes.

That routine, she knew, wouldn't be what Winston expected— not with his abundant *I love you*s and talk of soul mates. With him there would be the assumption of passion, a fiery spirit unable to be contained. And it wasn't that Linda was technically against such a thing; it was just that she had gone for so long without that she didn't know how it was done anymore and was terrified of being humiliated.

She went to Kate's old bedroom, where her old clothes and memorabilia were stored. After her children left for college, Linda had figured anything they'd abandoned was fair game. She'd gone through their remnants, tossing out crusted-over nail polishes and yellowed baseball cards and fruity perfumes, labeling the remainder in neat boxes: *Kate's Diaries, High School.*

In the second dresser drawer she found what she sought, a stack of silk slips Kate had purchased from Victoria's Secret when she was a junior. When she brought them home Linda had been suspicious but not in a serious way—she never thought they had been procured to actually be *used*, had simply filed them under inexplicable purchases, things teenagers wasted money on. Kate's own explanation was that she thought they were pretty, which they were, flimsily so. Linda held one up to the light, a baby blue lace confection edged in dark crocus. It was lovely but juvenile.

She wished she still had her satin nightgown and robe, the ones from that crazy period when she had thought it possible to stoop to Stanley's level and continue to be married to him. She'd never told anyone about her affair with her former coworker, a dalliance she wouldn't ever have dared consider had he not been so bold in professing his love for her, bowling her over with his sheer *lust*. He'd been American, as in *white*, a good-natured bear of a man who she imagined cheered loudly at his children's sports games, occasionally beating his chest at the referee. Clement James, a delicate name for such a rudimentary person, from whose slight caveman-like demeanor she'd extrapolated all sorts of assumptions regarding his behavior in the bedroom. Their two meals together were hideously awkward, what followed after even more so, and that'd been the end of it, the second and only other man she'd ever slept with.

Linda riffled through the bureau until she pulled out a more demure slip, in a larger size. This one was cream with ecru. She held it up to herself. She noted that each of the teddies still had their original tags on; Kate had never even worn them once.

CHAPTER 15

FRED

In Fred's opinion, one of the worst developments of the digital age was the proliferation of in-person photo sharing. It was one thing to post item after item on social media—he himself used Facebook purely for stalking, skipping directly to his intended targets—but it was another offense altogether to badger acquaintances in person, trapping defenseless colleagues in agonizingly long reveries of budget holidays and tacky remodels. As an Asian man in finance, Fred had long felt pigeonholed into one of two personas: Gentle Asexual Worker Bee or No Social Skills/Possibly Asperger's, and after a careful assessment of the associated trade-offs, he had reluctantly adopted the former. Doing so had allowed him to rise higher than certain brethren like Johnny Kim, a genius in computational models who insisted on consuming the same stinking chive-and-egg buns every day at his desk for lunch, refusing all collegial invitations to dine out while surfing esoteric soft-core porn when he thought no one was looking. But the strategy had also branded Fred as someone pleasantly innocuous, a persona he hadn't yet figured out how to shed without social consequence. So he continued to be waylaid by chubby admins as they brandished albums of their hideous babies, always so pale and fat, the girls even uglier than the boys; squandering precious minutes as he oohed and aahed over cheap Disney World getaways, slivers of dirty beach that were purportedly ocean views.

When Fred returned from Bali, the same low-level grunts had politely inquired into his travels, but he found himself sharing only the most broad and succinct of details. It wasn't much fun, he discovered, gloating about *Killer* or a D-lister's bare breasts—not when the audience was a research analyst who due to budgetary constraints still shared a one-bedroom condo with her boorish ex-husband, a deadbeat who smoked pot all day. What had transpired in Bali was a victory of the sort that could be shared only with a true partner, someone whose interests were undeniably intertwined with his own, and thus happily willing to tolerate the necessary debates over his LinkedIn profile (which title communicated power more: general or founding partner of Opus? Third-person shot of him in profile, mouth ajar and hands in the air as if speaking to an immense crowd? Or traditional headshot photo, which might require a visit to a professional studio?). Erika had always considered Fred's job one of his most attractive qualities, so it was ironic that they were still on the outs, not speaking or communicating, right as he was in the midst of the best career run of his life.

For at the same parallel moment that Fred had been clumsily stabbing at the phone in his villa in Bali, in a drunken late-night attempt to order *nasi goreng* from room service, Leland Wang had been en route to Menlo Park in a (first-class) airline seat to conduct an irate dressing down of Griffin Keeles. His specific grievance: why Lion Capital, and thus Leland himself, didn't garner more respect in Silicon Valley. After all, wasn't Leland a *billionaire*? And Lion one of the largest technology companies in *Asia*, a totally important region? Then why so little press? Why not more interviews with Bloomberg or the *Wall Street Journal*, and why no participation in the latest financing round for Gadfly, which two of their neighbors in the same Sand Hill complex had subscribed to? Why no in-person pitch from Hugo Menendez, who instead had sent a few moonfaced lieutenants in his place—a complete slap in the face? And why such shitty seats at this year's Breakthrough Prize gala? Didn't anyone consider that Leland might want to sit farther up front—or at the very least, not spend the entirety of the three hours staring at the back of some Google executive's head (not even Larry's or Sergey's!).

Leland didn't want to hear Griffin's tactful protests about money, his nervously phrased explanations that despite Leland's personal wealth, Lion Capital managed only $250 million in assets, rendering it a tiny, insignificant minnow in a sea of oversize whales. That despite all its talk of globalization, Silicon Valley was still US-centric and, as such, didn't always recognize the full groundbreaking influence of the number three components manufacturer in Taiwan. What Leland wanted, he barked, was *results*—and he wanted them *fast*. And of course, both came with the unsaid command that ran through each of his pronouncements: that he wanted it *cheap*. Thus just a few days later—when Fred's email landed in Leland's inbox, dangling $6 billion in Thai government money with precious few strings attached—it had been like a boon from above, an offering from the gods whom Leland had never doubted were in his favor.

The Thais! As it turned out, Leland adored the Thais (he had once informally proposed himself as a match for one of the princesses, a flying leap of a social elevation that even vast wads of Lion cash couldn't push forward). He loved the idea of Opus, and sovereign wealth funds. (Didn't everyone know that to efficiently conduct business in Asia, you needed the government? As if things were so different in Western society!) And most of all, he loved the idea of an additional $6 billion under his kind-of-indirect control. Sure, Lion had to put in some cash—$100 million as a starting sweetener, which Leland freed with uncharacteristic decisiveness from the company's ample hoards—but it was a shrewd bargain given the privilege of managing a pot fifty times its size. And Leland made it clear that Fred, and Fred alone (with some help from Jesus Christ), could claim credit for the magnificent bounty that had been laid at his feet.

The understanding that he had spectacularly upstaged Griffin was delectable, so sublime that Fred didn't even initially care when he learned that Leland had assigned a minder from Taiwan to periodically "check in" on Opus, a spy from headquarters who later turned out to be his own son. The scion, a loutish Wharton graduate named Maximilian, was rumored to appear any day now, to aid his father in what he was pretentiously referring to as "on the ground frontier technology scouting," and Fred had moved quickly against the encroaching tentacles of nepotism. He received verbal approval from Reagan to title himself a general partner and surreptitiously ordered new business cards, going around the normal admin channels to work directly with the printer. When the cards arrived, the final versions were exactly what he'd envisioned: *Fred Huang*, in a simple, discreet serif, followed by *General Partner, Opus Ventures*. Then an email address, no phone. Only foot soldiers made their numbers public— senior leadership like Fred filtered incoming traffic through generic inboxes, which an assistant then combed through as a first barrier to entry (he'd also have to hire an assistant).

Good news continued to accumulate. Donna Caldbert, his bad-tempered admin, put in her two weeks' notice; a well-trafficked tech site picked up the rumor of Lion and Opus and printed Fred's name next to the identifier of *Venture Capital Executive*. Executive! Fred forwarded the link to Kate, who replied with an emoticon, and then Linda, who left it unanswered. Fred followed up with his mother the next day, dialing in half-hour intervals until she picked up.

"Hello?" she answered. "Who *is* this?"

"What do you mean? It's Fred."

"Are you the one who keeps calling?"

"What? Yes." His mom was getting loopier. "Who else would it be? Did you read my article?"

"From yesterday?" He could hear rustling in the background; the unpacking of reusable grocery bags. "What is this TechCode? I've never heard of it. I almost didn't click the link; I thought it was one of those viruses Leonard's always warning us about."

"It's a famous publication, Ma. Everyone reads it in the Valley."

"Where can I buy it?"

"It's online only. Free to read."

A pause. "I see." Then, almost grudgingly—as if recalling a particularly distasteful passage from the *Sensitive Parenting* book Stanley had brought home and never read during Kate's brief teenage rebellion phase—"I am proud of you."

Afterward, alone at home, Fred consumed a bottle of Cabernet and pondered why everyone said family was so great. What good had his ever been? They'd never been happy for him at the right times; had often mourned when they should have been merry. Unfortunately, the one person Fred *did* know would be unequivocally joyous over his success was still refusing all attempts at contact. Either Erika's cell phone was off or she had blocked both his mobile and office numbers; only one of his numerous calls to the apartment she shared with Nora had been picked up, to a few seconds of labored breathing followed by the dial tone. She had snuck into his place at some point in the last few days and removed the majority of her belongings—when Fred returned, he'd been startled by the barren white of his bathroom counters. If he wanted to make nice it was clear much more was required, a dramatic show of appreciation. And nothing spoke to Erika like the physical manifestation of ardor: presents.

The next day during his lunch hour Fred drove to Union Square, where he briefly wandered between various luxury boutiques before settling on Hermès. Inside, he was helped by a young Korean sales assistant with creamy skin. He'd originally wanted to purchase a small accessory, a silk tie Erika could use around her neck or in her hair, but he cued off the saleswoman's hints that, once wrapped, the piece might seem entirely too small. Instead, together they selected a medium-size scarf in shades of taupe and navy blue she thought would go well with Erika's described complexion.

"And what color is her hair?" she asked.

"Dark blond." Then, not wanting her to have the impression that he was dating one of *those*, an Asian with tattoos and thick-winged eyeliner, Fred explained, "She's from Europe. Hungary."

"Ah. Delightful country. I visited Budapest once, right after college. Euro trip." The beautiful Korean finished wrapping the scarf and then suggested he add a small leather trinket in the shape of a padded horse. They had just arrived, she said, and were one of the store's best sellers. "Many of our customers purchase three or four. They can be dangled from a handbag." Fred was fairly certain she was attracted to him; if he wasn't clearly about to purchase an item for his girlfriend, he might have asked for her number.

After he held firm in politely refusing a silver fragrance atomizer, the assistant disappeared and was replaced by an older Frenchwoman. It was only at the register that he discovered the leather charm alone was $500, and that together with the scarf and taxes, the purchase rang up close to $1,000. "Can I remove the horse?" he asked.

"I can allow a store credit," the woman said, giving him a severe look. "Once we ring up an item, it's considered a sale."

Back in the car, Fred mapped out the most efficient route to the

Fremont apartment. He felt an anticipatory shiver over the altruistic credit he was about to receive. He could imagine Erika's face, the pout that couldn't help but lift into a repressed smile when she saw what dangled from his hands. He realized he had missed her more than he thought. Perhaps they would end up getting engaged. What was the point, otherwise? He would never be able to land anyone better. Maybe if Opus went remarkably well, but he might be near fifty by then, the equivalent of thirty-five in female years. Linda had recently discovered how to share links and had inundated his inbox with articles about aging sperm, how if you waited too long your child might turn out slow in brain and gigantic in stature. Apparently Stanley wasn't the only one whose body was capable of betrayal.

He returned a call from Auntie Deborah, Stanley's only sister, up visiting for the week from Southern California. Deborah had always been his favorite relative. Short, contendedly fat, and exceedingly confident, she was one of the few people who both knew the full extent of, and could manage, Stanley's temper.

"Fred," she whispered when she answered. "Fred. What are you doing?"

"Hi, Auntie. I'm at work." He installed an air of harried importance in his tone, insurance in case she was going to cajole him into joining them for dinner. "Things are busy. Is there something I can do?"

"Not for me. But you need to go to your dad's house, right now."

"What's going on? Aren't you there?"

"No, we're still driving from Los Angeles. We had to bring my mother-in-law last minute; we couldn't find anyone to take care of her. Big surprise. So we have to drive very slow, take many restroom breaks. I think I'm going to go crazy."

"Is she asleep? Why are you whispering?" Fred had never met Deborah's mother-in-law, but he was pretty sure she didn't understand English.

"Oh." Her voice returned to a normal volume. "I don't know. But listen, I think you need to go to your dad's house. As fast as possible. I just talked to Mary on the phone, and I think she's trying to move him out."

"Move him where? Didn't he just go home?" He swallowed a little pill of guilt; he hadn't visited Stanley since he'd left the hospital.

"I don't know, but she was asking me very many things. Questions about property values, home prices when there might be bad feng shui. She really doesn't know anything." Deborah in her heyday had been the top-ranked real estate agent in San Marino; she still harbored a healthy disdain for anyone with less than encyclopedic knowledge of the various levers of home values in California. "You know your dad is giving her the house in his will, right?"

"Yes." Kate had informed him earlier, via a cowardly text, before she left for a business trip. Something had gone wrong, she wrote. Linda had agreed with Stanley on a certain plan. Then, the plan had changed. Predictably, Linda was furious.

"You know your dad paid off the whole mortgage for her?"

"*What?*"

"Oh yes, yes," Deborah said, sounding both indignant and excited to be the bearer of bad news. "He wrote her a check. Who knew he had that kind of money? Not to say your dad isn't doing well, but you know, it was always your mom who was really smart. She's pretty tough, huh. So anyway, Stanley must have sold some stock to cover it. And everyone knows the market is no good right now! You know your dad's friend, Shirley Chang, the tall, fat one? She advised him to do it for Mary, walked him through the whole thing. I just spoke with her, right before you called. Now that Shirley has the whole story she regrets helping, of course; she says she never thought Mary would try to move Stanley. That Shirley thinks she's so smart, but look! Falling for Mary's sad tales just like any stupid old Chinese man."

"I still don't understand." How much had the mortgage been?

And why was Shirley Chang getting involved? He couldn't make sense out of the events being described. "Why would Mary want my dad out of the house when he just moved back into it? Where would she move him to?"

Deborah sighed loudly, exasperated by his slow comprehension. "The house will be completely Mary's now, when your father goes. And from her questions I got the feeling she is trying to move him so that he will not die at home and lower the real estate value. Maybe to a nursing facility. Can you believe it? Even I wouldn't kick out my own mother-in-law, though she's been here for at least two years past the date she told us she would *definitely* die, and for eighteen months now I've had a very expensive stationary bike just sitting in the garage, because her bedroom was supposed to become the exercise room. It's very important at our age to do cardio, you understand. So now I have to walk outside every day, even when it's hot! So dangerous!"

Fred endured another wave of nausea. "Is Mary out of her mind?" he sputtered. "Dad's explicit wish was to be at home. Even I know that!" He didn't want to deal with this. Why had Kate chosen this exact week to be out of town?

"Ah yes, but Mary, she is so greedy! You have no idea; you were born in the States. Some of these women from China, they can be ruthless. There are so many rich ladies there now, why couldn't he have married one of those, or some AI genius? But then of course they wouldn't want to be with . . ." Her voice broke into static. "Plus the income on the house alone, after Mary rents it out, is probably $4,000 a month! Because she *will* rent it out; her type never wants to sell right away. I keep telling her, if it is a rental, you do not have to say anything about a death, just let the tenants move in, no problem. But anyway, well, I just have a bad feeling. So better go now."

CHAPTER 16

KATE

CES, the annual Consumer Electronics Show held every January in Las Vegas, was colossal, one of those events where booths stretched out to infinite lengths and even the air smelled neon, and everyone on the floor not actively engaged in sucking up (to partners, customers, press) looked pissed. Each year X Corp blew its wad on a few products specifically for the event, frantically accelerating schedules and stretching out acceptable time frames of preorders to make their announcements. Lately other companies had moved toward private events, as they sought to avoid rubbing shoulders with the dingier Kickstarter crowd; rumor was that X Corp would soon follow suit. Until then, however, there was only CES.

The first time Kate attended, it'd been one of the first work trips of her career and she'd been thrilled with the excitement of business travel. Tasting menus and free-flowing booze, all paid for by a company that normally calculated per diem expenses via complex algorithm; acrobatic shows and lavish corporate parties, the pale and nerdish holding court in the costliest seats and booths. The temporary social reversal lending a potent fervor to the air, as executives both male and female cavorted with research analysts with whom, in the natural wild, they would never share close oxygen. Kate herself wasn't immune to the atmosphere: on the second night she took three shots of tequila and indulged in a drunken makeout session with one of the Irish sales partners who, to her ongoing mortification, still worked at X Corp.

Despite the novelty of such daily—and occasionally gratifying—excess, by the time the trip was over, Kate had felt bloated and unsatisfied. The week had left her with a sensation of smut and ill health, and she had scrambled over the weekend to make up for all the day-to-day work she'd missed while away. Each year was worse, as she grew older and the idea of free alcohol completely lost its allure; with time she had begun to recognize the sort of coworker who lived for these events, the week of riotous release it allowed from their drab everyday lives. The cubicle dweller who began moaning about the trip long in advance at home, to prepare their spouse for why they had to stay through Friday and fly out the weekend before; the sort who was always badgering everyone to linger for just one more drink after dinner, hit up another bar.

In the past Denny had joined her at CES, taking advantage of the X Corp–expensed hotel room and laxly guarded complimentary snack buffet to do his own networking on the cheap. During those periods Linda had been entrusted with the care of Ethan and Ella, a service she'd been performing with rapidly decreasing enthusiasm. She was getting older, she complained, and Kate's parenting choices meant the children regularly expected sojourns to a selection of filthy play yards and activity zones, any number of which could very well be harboring an array of germs lethal to a senior citizen such as herself. This year, Kate had expected Linda to finally make her stand, a battle to which she'd already conceded mental victory to her mother and planned for accordingly. This CES was supposed to be her out—there weren't any relevant product launches, and she'd weighed the moral implications of the "my father could go at any moment" card and found them tolerable. But then Grommix had come along, as well as what appeared to be a significant improvement in Stanley's condition. His doctors assured Kate she'd have ample time to return should any developments occur while she was gone—Vegas was only an hour away.

Linda, too, seemed to join in the conspiracy. Arriving at the house unannounced a few weeks before the event, she gathered the kids to her and cheerily pulled from her Bottega Veneta tote a variety of brochures, previewing the special grandma time to come. She'd even done her own research, locating a small farm forty minutes away, where the children could ride tractors and taste goat cheese.

"Will you play with the animals too, Wai Po?" Ella asked.

"Well, no," Linda said, wrinkling her nose. "But I'll be on the side watching so you can look for me. Wai Po has a good time when she gets to sit. And then the day after we'll go to Costco. You can have lunch there." She snuck a look at Kate, who normally viewed its food court as contraband. "You'll each have a budget and can pick anything at its value or below. Unless it's too heavy. Wai Po has a bad back."

Kate strongly suspected that Linda's energetic initiative, highly out of character, was linked to her own admittedly less than desirable domestic situation; Denny, with her blessing, had extended his contract another two months at the Palo Alto Home Suites. For the moment, the children seemed to enjoy their visits (it helped that there was an indoor pool), though Kate knew she and Denny were just kicking the harder parts—the difficult conversations and decisions—

down the road. The last time she'd seen him, during a handoff, they'd been entirely civil, with Denny guiltily but excitedly declaring separated life better suited for a start-up. "Of course it's harder when I have the kids," he said. "I never thought two would be so difficult." They were in an amicable enough place where Kate had genuinely been able to laugh, and she'd studied him when his back was turned. He didn't give off the air of someone with a new girlfriend, but she found she didn't very much care.

She told her mother the news of the separation in the very broadest of terms. Kate knew Linda had never approved of CircleShop and thus Denny; in her world, entrepreneurial activities were to be lauded only when pursued after returning home from a steady career of the sort that provided a regular paycheck and employer-matched 401(k). Conversely, however, a marriage dissolution was also a horrific event, a stigma Kate would carry for the rest of her life, torpedoing her desirability and dooming her to a late-life remarriage with some piddling state school graduate.

"But you and Dad are divorced," Kate said. "And you always conveniently forget that Yvonne Cho's daughter, the one you mention in almost every single one of our conversations, went to UC Irvine."

"Your father and I are different," Linda huffed. "And I don't forget where anyone went to school."

Overall Linda seemed to view Denny's absence as something delicate, a land mine to tread carefully around while she investigated the surrounding terrain. When Kate packed her bag for Vegas, Linda took a particular interest in the proceedings. "That jacket makes you look old," she complained, after spotting a leather blazer.

"This was extremely expensive. I bought it at Le Bon Marché in Paris. It was a zillion euros."

"It looks like something Mary would wear. And why so many ugly shoes? You used to beg me to let you wear high heels when you were a teenager!"

Now that she was in Vegas, Kate admitted Linda had been right, at least about the jacket. It was far too warm for an outer layer—the temperatures outside were in the mid-80s, and the Labs demo space was being maintained at a balmy 79 degrees Fahrenheit, to create what Sonny insisted was the ideal environment to consume Grommix over ice. Almost everyone was adorned in corporate swag or—if an executive—regular business casual, the general rule being that the higher one's seniority at X Corp, the lesser the requirement to advertise you actually worked there. Most mornings Kate paired the simplest logo tee she owned with black denim and stacked loafers and hid out in one of the makeshift conference rooms until it came time for press interviews. She was never allowed near any of the top-tier media, the national papers and online networks that were hoarded by the various public relations managers as tributes to their associated chieftains. Instead, she was shuttled off by one of the event coordinators—a Vietnamese woman named Trang who managed to pull twelve-hour days in a tube top—to meet with a series of increasingly obscure media outlets and YouTube reviewer channels at a breakneck pace.

On the third day—partly due to Sonny's refusal to enter the main X Corp conference space, where Ron Fujihara was onstage giving an early demo of Slippers—a reporter from *Forbes* writing a cover story on X Corp was ambushed by Ken Bullis while waiting for the elevators. The reporter had been headed to the forty-eighth floor, to the suite that had been repurposed as Sonny's office for the week, to interview him as the company's mouthpiece on research and development; the chief brand officer had instead proceeded to divert the captured journalist to a nearby conference room, where he issued a series of quotes on innovation and ate up the remainder of the time slot. The resulting mayhem and accusations of sabotage had exhausted Kate for most of the afternoon, to the point where she now decided to ditch that evening's team dinner. She normally never missed corporate events, considering them a form of self-flagellation for the absurdly low strike price of some of her earliest X Corp option grants. But by the end of the day, Kate felt she had earned a solo evening. The terrified communications manager who'd lost control of the reporter and subsequently been shouted at and called a dirty dog by Sonny was pacified and in his hotel room, inspecting his free new 500GB unit of the controversial X Phone; Sonny himself was a few floors higher in his suite, rehearsing lines for a video appearance on CNBC's *Squawk Box* the next morning.

With her evening open and a rare desire to avoid misanthropy, Kate decided to go to a bar. She had no particular preference of venue, and given her end-of-the-night feet, which were actively protesting in a pair of rarely worn heels, she opted for the first one she saw. The lounge was barely thirty feet from the elevator, a luxurious yet bland setting clearly meant as a stopover between more profitable destinations. The stools were too tall, and she shifted her position every few minutes as she sought the right balance between her legs dangling in the air and her butt hanging off the seat. She avoided eye contact and breathed through her nervousness.

It was only after her first drink that Kate allowed herself to admit she had descended with the express purpose of seducing someone, and only after her second that she comprehended the actual difficulty of doing so. First there was the matter of effectively signaling to the number of frightened engineers strewn about that she was, in fact, open to a proposition; then there was the issue of fending off the drunk marketing managers, who were lurching in a harassing fashion from stop to stop. She felt ridiculous and old, a tableau of some wilted cougar lying in wait for some similarly beset traveler, and she had nearly given up when someone sat beside her.

"Here for work?" the man asked.

With his tawny hair and matched features he reminded her of Charles Fennelly, the Irish fling she'd enjoyed at this very conference more than a decade earlier. She looked down past his oxford shirt and dark jeans and saw he wore expensive sneakers like the sort her brother collected. That was encouraging; this guy had probably had sex before. After she'd made casual banter and verified that he was, in fact, not employed at X Corp or any of its subsidiaries, she decided to linger.

It wasn't as if she *truly* wanted to sleep with someone. If she was being honest with herself, Kate hadn't wanted to do that for quite some time, which was sad and probably some of the issue with Denny. But she wanted something, like those high school dances where you pressed your body against someone else's for a few minutes while slow music lent a dramatic aura. If only there was something like that for adults, a brief encounter that made the heat rise to your face but didn't involve the intimate exchange of bodily fluids. If there was, Kate didn't know about it. So she assumed she'd have to have sex.

The man—who'd introduced himself as Lars Sundstrom—was already signaling his intentions in that direction, with a determined gaze that kept returning as if propelled by magnetic force to the deep V neckline of her dress (she'd bought it on a whim, thinking the Moroccan print pretty, before stashing it in the back of her closet; Linda had pointed it out and insisted she pack it, over a plain black Ann Taylor option).

"Do you ever work with Sonny Agrawal?" Lars asked.

"No, not really."

"Oh." He looked disappointed. "That's too bad. It would have been great to land an introduction. I have a meeting with the X ventures team next month; I hear he's very close with the leadership there. He advises on certain investments, doesn't he?"

"You know, I'm really not too sure." In fact Kate had penned the majority of Sonny's last missive to the group, a ranting treatise on autonomous vehicles, but she had no intention of divulging such. At this stage she saw little advantage in exposing herself to a potential barrage of networking emails in exchange for a one-night stand. "What does your company do?"

"I'll share if you try to keep an open mind." He offered a shy smile. He looked better than Charles the salesman from Ireland, Kate decided. More interesting features. She nodded.

"It's bras. Before you react, just listen. I promise I'm not a deviant. Almost every adult woman in this country wears a bra. Right?"

She crossed her arms. "I suppose."

"And they start wearing them from approximately the age of, say, thirteen, and the average life expectancy right now for an American woman is eighty-one years. That's sixty-eight continuous years of wearing the garment. Yes? Now, if you'll allow me to ask a personal question: Do you love your bra? As in, does it do everything you'd like for it to? Would you be willing to sleep in it at night?"

"No, that'd be way too uncomfortable. It's the first thing I take off when I get home." She wondered if that sounded too suggestive.

"And how many bras, approximately, do you own?"

Kate considered this. "Forty? But I probably only wear ten." The answer was actually closer to five, but she didn't want to sound gross. "I keep buying them, in various colors. Or I try a new style, wash it, and then realize I don't like it at all. But at that point it's too late to return."

"Exactly!" Lars thumped the air, excited. "We hear that same story from so many women. They buy for a certain occasion, or because the material feels comfortable, or because they like the design or print. They have a dress with thin straps, or they find they need a certain level of support. The reasons are endless, really. But what everyone has in common is that so far, they've been unable to find the perfect bra."

"And you're going to change this."

"We'd certainly *like* to. Custom lingerie, produced specifically for each woman's body, at a reasonable price. You know how big the global intimates industry was last year?"

She shook her head.

"Thirty-two billion dollars. And how much of that money spent was a total waste, just more fabric and wire sitting unused in a drawer? Not to mention the environmental impact of clothing manufacturing, which is a whole other externality we haven't even explored."

"I do like the idea," Kate said. She hated most of her bras. She had once spent more than $1,000 at Agent Provocateur out of a misguided idea of glamour and had never worn most of the pieces even once. "But how are you going to manufacture at an individual level? Isn't that terribly labor- and cost-intensive?"

"Some of that I can discuss publicly, but most of it I can't. I can tell you that 3-D printing is technology we're very excited about. And we've had preliminary meetings with some of the big brands, Victoria's Secret and the like, white label production. Of course, there's no way we'd enter brick-and-mortar retail ourselves."

"And what's your target market? Every woman above a certain age?"

"That'd be great, but too broad for us at this point. Right now we're looking at women with a certain household income, and we have to limit where we ship, at least initially. Apparently some countries are very strict about their undergarment imports. But you're right that the market is huge. And why stop at women? There are men out there who buy bras too. A very important and largely neglected audience."

"Seriously? Like a fetish thing?"

"Sometimes, but mostly they're overweight or have a medical issue. Usually they're too embarrassed to go to the store and ask for help, so they just suffer in silence. It's a highly underserved market. Something else we're doing differently."

"Hmm." In Kate's experience, *highly underserved* was the phrase typically deployed by executives when there was a pet project with flawed fundamentals they desperately wanted to push through; no woman, she thought, would describe the male undergarments market as one in dire need of innovation. "So is your founding team all men?"

Lars hesitated. "We've had only a few hires so far, since we're still in stealth. So yes, technically. But once we start ramping up the sales team, we expect to have more women."

Kate finished the remains of her drink and searched for the bartender. "Do you ever get heat for that?"

"You think that because my company is led by men, it can't address the needs of women?"

"That's not what I said."

"Because discrimination is a real problem, for everyone." His tone had turned frosty. "It exists universally, even for men. Even for *white* men. And to answer your question, we do get shit. In fact, we just had some promised seed funding drop out, after the investor learned we didn't have any women on board. Do you know how unfair that is? Do you understand how difficult it is to find a CTO or VP of Engineering who has the necessary skills, background, and education and is also a woman? Or, for that matter, an operations expert? Or let me put it a different way: Do you like this hotel?"

"The Bellagio? It's fine. Breakfasts are good."

"You know the person who developed it, Steve Wynn, is a man. And nearly the entire current management team, and board of directors, are men. Do you think that makes them less qualified to build hotels for women to patronize? Since you're obviously enjoying yourself." He stared pointedly at the neckline of her dress.

"That's an insane argument. A hotel is nothing like a bra."

"Wow. . . ." He drew out the word, making it undulate. "Are you a bitch, or what?"

Automatically Kate pushed herself off the stool and reached for her bag.

Lars caught her arm. "Where are you going?"

She jerked at his touch. "Let go of me."

He didn't and instead brought his mouth closer to her face, to a distance where the smell of what she had thought was Vegas, but now refined itself as vodka, permeated the air between them. "Sorry. I didn't mean it. Let's start over."

"Let go of my fucking arm."

He yanked her closer. "Coarse language from a woman is disgusting." His voice had gone oily. His grip tightened, and it felt as if his fingers were hitting bone. Kate felt the dizziness of shock and fright, a familiar but faraway sensation.

With her free hand she hurriedly searched her bag and brought her phone up, face level.

Lars recoiled. "What the fuck are you doing? Are you taking a *picture*? You can't . . ."

But he let go of her arm, and she took the opportunity to walk, nearly run, to the bank of elevators, which between certain hours were manned by a security guard to prevent overflow. Lars wouldn't be able to follow her, she calculated—working at a start-up he probably wouldn't be staying at *this* hotel, even if its management team did merit his approval. But she didn't feel completely safe until she had entered her room, locked the bolt, and pressed the cobalt armchair against the door. She sunk to the carpet then and leaned against the wall, breathing heavily. Her arm, which she'd imagined at the very least would be bruised, appeared unblemished.

"HELLO?" AS USUAL WHEN KATE CALLED LINDA OVER VIDEO, SHE was greeted by dark movement. "Ma, face the phone toward you."

Ethan came into view. "I got five new trucks today," he informed her. "And they move with a remote."

"Wow, really cool." His voice was like a soothing balm, and she thought she might cry from the release of so much tension. She suppressed a gasp, collecting herself. "Your Wai Po bought you *five?*"

"It was the size of the warehouse pack," Linda retorted. "I cannot control these things."

"And I suppose they just had pizza for dinner, or those chicken ranch sauce things."

"Oh no, I told Ethan and Ella, when we go to Costco, they can each choose between a toy or the food court. So they both pick toys. We had Hainan chicken and stir-fried vegetables for dinner. I used the brown rice. Sunflower oil, so not too greasy."

Her arm had begun to throb; she rubbed it against her leg. "Fine. Sounds fair."

"And very soon we are going to have Asian pear. Do we all like Asian pear?" Linda called out behind her. She peered at the phone. "Why do you look so old? What did you do today?"

"Pear sounds good. Thanks again for watching them." Kate hung up. It was comforting to argue with her mother, but she wanted to keep the flow of information limited, to negate the chance of any misinterpreted details. She knew Linda harbored some furtive hope that she might start a new relationship on this trip, evolving some existing collegial friendship (preferably senior vice president level or higher) into a bona fide marriage. That was how her mother had always handled problems, a bulldozer path to the most direct solution. While Stanley ineffectively raged, Linda was the one who calmly acted, driving relentlessly to resolution. Kate realized she wanted to impress her, and the thought was depressing.

Because how could she possibly explain anything to her mother, who already thought her life so easy—high pay, appreciating home values, loose moral standards and all? That her world was in fact not simple but filled with violent, thin-skinned men who behaved only when the threat of exposure was dangled above them? And that to wield public shame was the only reliable way to hurt them in the same tender places they wished to bring harm onto you, for no reason except that they were furious at a world they felt had slotted them in the wrong place.

How could she explain to Linda that aspect of being a woman today?

———————

Early the next morning, Kate woke to a thumping in her legs and head. Her limbs felt as if they were filled with tiny stars, a sensation that had grown familiar enough that she knew she needed to curtail her drinking. Halfway through room service she noticed the purple prints on her arm, in the unmistakable fanned pattern of a palm, and she felt a perverse wave of satisfaction. A story like hers needed evidence, even for herself.

The events team had only two styles of logo'd company tops, both short-sleeved, so Kate opted for one of her own pieces, a softly starched cotton tunic with wide sleeves that covered the bruising. As the day progressed, she noticed the lack of uniform seemed to elevate her—since she and Sonny were the only Labs employees not in branded gear, various staff seemed to assume that she, too, was senior management, privy to certain privileges. When she wandered over to the snack table, a coordinator she hadn't seen before rushed to direct her to a private ballroom, an executive-only oasis of tea sandwiches and ample seating. "You'd probably be more comfortable in here," he confided. Ken Bullis was the only person to raise an eyebrow— literally—as he walked in with a reporter from *Adweek*, but he then conducted his meeting in a back corner of the room, and nothing was said of her presence.

In the late afternoon, Sonny appeared. "I hate these MBA rotational program events," he said, as he sank into the chair across from her. "Why do I even have to speak at them? They interrupt to ask such *stupid* questions, just to hear themselves talk, and then afterward email me without end, to request *one-on-ones* to discuss their *career trajectories*. It's relentless! And why are young people these days all obsessed with being vice presidents?"

"Titles are important." Kate closed her laptop. She knew she'd have to finish her work later. "Especially with this generation. Why be a schmo with a manager title when all your friends are VPs at start-ups?"

"But you're a manager and perfectly satisfied."

"Actually, I'm a director. But I've been going through some recent life changes where a VP-level stock package might really come in handy, so."

"You're a director?" Sonny stared at her agog. "What do you *do*?"

"Are you kidding me? Do you enjoy it when your products launch on schedule?"

"Yes, but that's part of your job description. Do I receive extra for my innovation? For daring to push X Corp forward into new and uncharted technology frontiers?"

"I would argue that you do, but that's a different discussion. I manage a lot outside of my specific job. Who do you think cleans up your messes? Makes all your whims come true? Do you have any idea how difficult it was to get Curry Grommix approved on such short notice for shipment in Japan?"

"I didn't know you wanted to become a vice president," Sonny said. "Now I feel bad."

"Oh, it was a joke." She flicked her hand. "I know how stingy the company is with titles."

"Are they really? But I am an executive vice president."

Kate nodded patiently. The honorific had been bestowed as part of Alexei Sokolov's original employment offer; there were only four in the entire company.

"I could probably make you a VP," Sonny said, after a brief silence. "I've been under some pressure, to do promotions."

Was he bullshitting her? But then Sonny wasn't really a liar, Kate thought. He didn't know how. "Really," she said carefully.

"Because you're a woman," he continued. "Sokolov promised in the last board meeting that there'd be more of you. Apparently, we don't have enough! So I'm supposed to promote females, but I have only two currently reporting to me, you and Marissa." Marissa was Sonny's executive assistant, who he was actively trying to fire. "The good news is, at the Labs we at least have enough Latinos and blacks. But perhaps we should identify one or two candidates of each in reserve, for good measure."

"Well, if that's all it takes to be a VP, then by all means." Kate pushed her forehead into her palms. "Since I'm a woman and all."

"Why are you upset? You should be proud. I'm doing you the courtesy of informing you of the specific situation directly, as I would a man. It would be best if you weren't Asian, but I can't be too picky. Of course, you'll still need a project. Some initiative people will associate with you that I can use as justification to the executive committee. I can't just name anyone; I have to give a list of reasons, examples of the nominee's initiative and character. For example, I would never nominate Marissa, because she talks on the phone every morning even though I've repeatedly informed her loud voices before noon give me migraines."

"What sort of project?"

Sonny stopped to think. "An entrepreneurial one. Since we're the Labs. Something new that could turn into a real business, like Grommix."

Then she was screwed. Creativity had never been Kate's strong suit; she was always better at following through on specific directives than conjuring things entirely out of her imagination. Sometimes she could move pieces around, rearranging them so that they fit better into place, but the concepts had to exist somewhere to begin with, for her to mold and reshape. She was like Linda in that way.

A thought began to nibble at the fringes of her consciousness. She slowly cracked her knuckles, which produced a sound she knew Sonny found lulling. She needed to buy a few moments to knock loose the idea.

"I've got a bra project," she offered.

"Bras?"

"Undergarments. Uniquely designed and produced for each customer, using 3-D textile printing. It's a huge industry, more than $30 billion. There are other entrants, but they're all in nascent stages. If we execute right, we could be first to market."

She'd worried Sonny might be squeamish, but instead he removed a small notebook from his right jacket pocket, a sign of high respect. As he hovered over the pages with his pencil, he had her describe in detail all the various fallacies of the current product—pinched straps, twisted underwire, deformed and misshapen cups. "How fascinating," he commented, after he'd finally exhausted his questions, "that women are willing to put up with such aggravation. In the same situation, I would probably not wear anything at all."

"Then you'd have a whole other set of workplace problems. You realize I don't even wear sleeveless tops in the office in summer? Whereas I heard you gave your last presentation to the board in hiking sandals."

He eyed her for several seconds. "I think this could easily fall into the bucket of wearables," he said, ignoring her earlier comment. "Since we haven't had a compelling project there in a while. Ever since the sneakers that gauge barometric pressure were killed by the go-to-market committee. The more I think about it, the more potential I see. Yes, I'm very excited." A sly look crossed his face, and for a moment Kate was paranoid that Sonny was about to steal her idea and improve upon it, right as she was about to do the same to Lars Sundstrom. "You'll act as the head of the program on this, then," he announced. "Assign a product and project manager, and we'll get you the engineering resources."

"I also think we need to meet with the ventures team and make sure that they haven't made any similar investments. It might also be best if they recuse themselves from engaging with any other start-ups exploring the industry."

"Yes, good idea," Sonny said. "Send an email today."

If she could land a bump in pay, it would at the very least relieve some of the pressure of the separation, Kate thought. And help with the kids' college funds. If there was any left over they could install a guesthouse in the backyard. She'd always wanted one; Denny had never agreed. But then that was no longer a problem.

A giddiness came over her and she reached for her laptop to draft the message to the ventures team. There was an email from Fred, entitled *Where are you?*—an echo of their exchanges from Hong Kong. She opened it and read its single word out loud.

Help!!!

CHAPTER 17

MARY

When Mary Zhu had first walked into the intensive care unit of Kaiser Permanente and seen Stanley—as he lay unconscious with his head tilted at that unnatural angle, all of those tubes crawling out from his body and throat—she'd been terrified. Kate and her husband had been there, the white man whose name she could never remember because it was some derivative of a regular one, and the way they'd looked at her made it clear they thought she'd done something wrong by not being present from the start. She could sense the questions they thought they were being so tactful in leaving unsaid: Where had she been? What had she been doing for the past five hours, while her husband had been near death, in and out of emergency surgery?

Mary wasn't ashamed but felt attacked, unfairly so. And so she didn't tell them where she'd been, out shopping for disposable adult diapers and a plastic bedsheet because for the first time in his adult life her husband had urinated in bed; that afterward she'd gone to Valley Fair mall to look for sheets on sale at Macy's so he could have several identical sets, to spare him the embarrassment when his bedding was in the wash. And that it was only after she was already halfway to the house that she realized she had used her own personal credit card for the purchase, out of habit since she typically only bought clothing or cosmetics for herself at Macy's, and Stanley didn't pay for those. But since the sheets were really for Stanley, and she had trawled the bargain section to find them at 75 percent off, they should really go on his card, shouldn't they? And Mary knew that if she got home she'd never find the time or energy to go back and make the switch, so she turned around, executing a jolting U-turn, and went through the extended motions of returning and repurchasing with an elderly Japanese clerk who seemed to know exactly what she was doing and why. And by the time she arrived at the house, staggering through the front door with the bags, Stanley—whom she'd left napping on the couch, who by all accounts and routine should have still been asleep—had disappeared.

She'd searched frantically for some time—running upstairs, calling out his name in the garage, even however improbably unlocking the storage shed in the backyard—before thinking to check her phone, which she'd left charging in the kitchen. And when the news came that Stanley was going to survive, when he opened his yellowed eyes and met her gaze and gave a weak wave of his hand, she'd collapsed on her knees in front of him on the hard hospital floor and thanked the gods that her husband would live. At that moment if you'd asked Mary if she would trade a year of her life so that Stanley could have another week, another seven days to go home and be in peace, she would have made the deal without hesitation.

She'd been convinced that the hospital, with its diseased halls and deceptive sterility, was making Stanley more ill. He complained endlessly about the uncomfortable mattress and the constant noise of machines that made it impossible to sleep, the narrow confines of his shower. In truth he'd been fortunate to have a private room at all; after he was deemed no longer worthy of the ICU, Kaiser had moved him to a lower-level ward, where he was supposed to have shared a space with another patient. Mary had watched as Kate and the registering nurse in charge, an agitated Filipino woman in her fifties, argued, as Kate violently gestured toward her father and occasionally waved what looked to be his insurance cards into the air (where had she found those? Did she have his wallet?).

It all looked terribly inefficient and unofficial, and Mary had been shocked when it appeared to have worked: the administrator eventually walking toward them with an insincere smile, clearing her throat to announce to the two men transporting Stanley that he would be moved to a private room after all, a smaller one down the hall. Mary's English wasn't nearly advanced enough to catch most of the words that had been exchanged; she wondered if there had been certain key phrases used, a hint of litigiousness. Either way Mary had been impressed, though when Stanley woke after Kate left, she said nothing about what had transpired. The hospital had found a spare room and moved him while he was asleep, she told him. And left it at that.

Both Kate and Fred visited their father regularly in the hospital, far more now that his life was in immediate danger than ever before, when they might have spent real quality time engaged in the activities he loved, like going to the movies. When Mary knew they were scheduled to come, she tried to make herself scarce—run errands or go back to the house. Fred in particular treated her with a chill; his demeanor had steadily worsened to the point where he was now openly rude. He'd confronted her in front of Stanley—only a few days into his ICU stay, when Stanley had still been intubated and voiceless—about why the office in the house had been such a mess during his surprise visit. "Can I help you find whatever it is you're looking for?" he'd asked with a smirk. "I was shocked to see everything in such disarray."

Mary could sense her husband bristling at Fred's discourteousness, though Stanley had ultimately remained mute, no scratching of indignant messages on white paper, which meant that he, too, was waiting for an answer. She knew she had to be careful. "I was looking for health insurance cards," she said. "So that your father is not charged extra at the pharmacy." Fred had appraised her with a bald look that made it clear he thought she was lying, the lack of respect obvious in his eyes.

She'd gone around him then, stroked Stanley's head gently with her nails. Only one of us can do this, she'd reminded him silently. Run their fingers through his hair, kiss his palms, massage his feet. Only one of us goes to bed with Stanley every night.

MARY HAD BEEN LYING ABOUT THE OFFICE, OF COURSE. THOUGH IT hadn't been her who first entered the space but Jeylin and Grace, her two sisters.

Once, all three of them had been married to fools. Grace to Tony Wong, a stir-fry cook at China Garden, the restaurant at which they'd each at one time hostessed, and Jeylin to a real estate developer named Nicky Chen. For a brief period Nicky had been their Big Hope, the one who was going to show them how to get rich in America. Until he ended up being not a developer at all but a low-level construction manager, someone with only minor managerial oversight over three under-the-table employees from Korea, who spent his days completing easy plumbing jobs.

Then there was Ed Yeh, Mary's first husband. He'd been her age, handsome with a full head of black hair, one of the few Chinese men she'd ever seen who could pull off a beard. When they met, he told her he'd been a television producer back in Beijing, on a national talk show she had vague memories of. One of his duties had been to serve as the celebrity wrangler, and he shared stories of one B-list actress after another, making her giggle with anecdotes of their ridiculous demands.

"I'm not joking!" he would exclaim. "I'm telling you the absolute truth!" And then he'd tickle her, and she would squeal, and they'd lie together in their single room, that terrible low-income apartment Jeylin had managed to sign Mary up for a year in advance of her arrival to the United States, and eat steamed buns on the bed.

Only after they were married did she learn that almost everything Ed claimed to have had been an exaggeration at best—designed to impress her, he'd said, because she was so obviously a woman who deserved the most accomplished of partners. That flattery was expected to sustain her through twelve-hour shifts working at China Garden—sometimes eighteen if she did some massage at night (despite what Stanley's ex-wife and friends believed, she had never been *that* sort of masseuse)—while Ed himself pulled five-hour days at the local Chinese paper, cycling down after lunch to the community center for chess and backgammon. Ed had refused to give her children or save for a house; had smacked her with the back of his hand on two occasions (though both times not very hard). But it had been normal, her life: not so different from those around her and certainly not from those of her sisters, who had their own losers to contend with.

Still, she left. Why stay? There was no benefit—social, emotional, or financial. And then she met Stanley, and in a single leap she elevated her status far above her sisters', despite being the oldest, the one who'd traditionally had the worst outcome: the nastiest husband, the worst complexion, the most demeaning job.

At first, Mary had worried that Jeylin and Grace might resent her random good fortune. Because how else but through some past karma could one explain the series of events that had brought her together with a man who owned his own home, who had a pension, who could afford to take her on vacation to faraway destinations and didn't force her to work? Whose only real request was that she serve him, delight him in every manner she could imagine, cook foods for him to enjoy, and massage his body each night? Compared to her life before, it was an incredible stroke of luck, one for which there was no real explanation. And a twenty-eight-year age difference was simply an accepted part of that equation, without which the whole thing fell to pieces. Someone with all those attributes, who was actually her age or near? Not possible.

To Mary's surprise, Jeylin and Grace had been supportive, with relatively few gleams of pettiness. They immediately made her and Stanley regular partners in their mah jong games, a weekly event she'd been kicked out of after her divorce, since odd numbers in mah jong never worked. They cooed over Stanley, inviting the two of them on weekend trips to Yosemite and holiday dinner banquets. When Stanley spoke they listened in rapt silence, shushing their own husbands when they tried to interject, to better hear and absorb his advice on the financial markets. Stanley, after all, was the most successful person any of them knew, at least familially. Who else could they turn to with questions regarding 401(k) plans (scam), index funds (too confusing, stick with his broker at Charles Schwab), and real estate management? Who but the only person they knew who'd already achieved what for most still remained a distant fantasy, to come to the US and build a fortune from nothing?

Jeylin and Grace even joined in on one of Mary and Stanley's international trips, a cruise through the ports of Spain, though Mary knew it must have been a stretch for both financially. The three sisters split the cost to bring their mother along, flying her in from Beijing.

Mary's mother, while a few years younger than Stanley (a fact Jeylin always enjoyed to mention), was far less physically able, and halfway through the cruise there'd been an agonizing moment of embarrassment when Stanley had refused to push her wheelchair any longer. "I'm too tired to cater to another person," he said, his mouth set in a tight line. "I'm here to enjoy myself." He'd especially hated the stairs that greeted them at every museum in Barcelona, which meant the wheelchair had to be manually lifted up and down the steps. "She should just sit outside," he snapped. "She's inconveniencing the rest of us."

Back on the boat, in the privacy of their cabin, Mary had picked a rare fight, insisting that he had made her lose face. "What will my family think, that you can't even bother to show respect to our own mother? Not in a million years would I treat yours like this!" And immediately understood her mistake, as Stanley's mother occupied a saintly status in his mind, having passed in his early teens. His face had clouded over, warnings of a portent storm best avoided, and the topic closed.

Her sisters had been understanding even about that, however, which in retrospect Mary should have noted as unusual, especially given their normal inclinations. Grace on her own could be kind, especially to children, but Jeylin was sweet only on the outside, with her red bow mouth and almond-shaped eyes. The next morning Jeylin and Grace had their husbands prepped to split wheelchair duty between themselves, while Stanley marched ahead to take in whatever sights caught his eye, rarely bothering to check back on the group's progress. When Mary attempted to apologize for his behavior, her sisters waved her off.

"He's an important man," Jeylin scolded. "He must care for his health. How can you ask this sort of person to do physical labor? It's beneath him."

Jeylin was Stanley's favorite. "Your sister has such nice skin," he commented once. "And her eyes are so youthful." Mary had been upset by the compliment, which she felt had been deliberately suggestive. More than once she'd been struck by the paranoia that both Stanley and Jeylin wished he'd met Jeylin first. But Mary had kept her mouth shut, and the next time Jeylin traveled to China on one of her "beauty holidays," she'd gone along with her and had her under-eye bags cut away. She had fillers put in, too, some in her forehead and even more in her neck. She'd been shocked by the number of units required for that, and the nurse explained that it was a lot of space, in terms of square centimeters. But it had been worth it, because when she returned, Stanley had been so affectionate, going on about how much he'd missed her presence. He even brought dinner home that night instead of expecting her to cook, making a big show as he served it on matching plates and pawing at her as soon as he finished his own dessert. Murmuring on about how beautiful she was. "You're the prettiest of all your sisters."

TWO DAYS AFTER STANLEY ENTERED THE ICU, JEYLIN AND GRACE appeared at the house, Nicky and Tony in tow. Mary had been at work in the kitchen, and after opening the front door, returned to check the progress of her famous double-boiled soup. Although Stanley could not currently eat or drink and Mary was unclear as to when his breathing tube might be removed, she thought it best to have some of his favorite foods on hand, just in case. She stopped stirring when she heard the racket from above—she guessed the two might be in the bedroom closet, riffling through her clothes and shoes. "What's going on?" she called out. She could see only Nicky and Tony from where she stood; they were watching TV, and ignoring her.

Several minutes later she heard another bang, followed by the distinct sound of a crash. She switched off the burners and ran upstairs to the office to discover the filing cabinet tipped on its side and Jeylin on all fours next to it. Grace stood on a stool nearby, flinging down binders from the highest level of the bookshelf.

"What is this?" Mary shrieked. "Do you know how much I have to do today? How am I going to clean all this before I leave? What if Stanley returns?"

Jeylin sat up and regarded her with condescension. "Stanley isn't coming back today," she said. "Though I'm shocked you haven't realized it already. He may not be coming back at all."

Mary bristled at the implication that she was in some way less informed. Who among them lived a life like hers? How did they think she'd managed it? "You don't think I've considered the idea? I think about it all the time. I'm only forty-seven. I never imagined I might already be a widow."

"Good," Jeylin said. She continued to stare at her with that infuriating expression—a single raised eyebrow, lips parted, a mannerism lifted from a famous Korean soap actress. "So has Stanley told you how you'll be taken care of? He *is* providing for you in his will, yes? You have talked about this?"

"Of course. I get the house and half the pension, and plus there are other accounts."

"What accounts?" Grace interjected. "How much?"

"He said everything would be divided equally. A third to each of his children, a third to me." Mary folded her arms across her chest. "I don't feel comfortable discussing the details. You know how private Stanley is about his matters. *Our* matters." Then, to soften the bluntness of her words, she slid her eyes toward the staircase. "Someone could come in," she said. She meant Kate or Fred.

"You worried about Nicky?" Jeylin lowered her voice. "Don't worry, I won't tell him anything. Same for Tony." She tilted her head toward Grace, who nodded eagerly. She looked like a lapdog, Mary thought.

"I don't want to talk about this. I'm far too busy. I barely have enough time to finish the soup before I have to go to the hospital."

"I have to finish the soup," Jeylin mimicked. "What's wrong with you? I thought we promised to never keep anything from each other. Haven't I always told you everything? When Nicky lost all that money investing in that franchise scam, didn't I call you first? And what about Grace, when Tony cheated on her with that bartender, the one who wasn't even Chinese, but Vietnamese, and we found out he bought her that Burberry skirt? And now you want to keep your husband's secrets? He isn't even your first husband. He isn't your true family. You don't even have *children*." Her arm snaked under the cabinet, disappearing almost to her shoulder. She let out a cry of triumph. "I found it! Ha-ha. The manager at China Garden used to tape an extra key on the back of the cabinets just like this."

"Or maybe," Grace said, "she's worried we'll be a liability, once Stanley dies and she becomes rich."

Mary gaped. She'd never expect such a statement to come from Grace, the baby of the family.

"Is that it?" Jeylin's voice lowered even more, to a seductive timbre. "Are you worried your little sisters will take some of your money?"

"Don't be ridiculous." But inside, Mary's heart quickened its pace. Because even though she knew Grace had said what she did mostly to hurt her—she was so obvious in that way, no finesse—for once her sibling had inadvertently struck close to the truth. Stanley had money, serious money, amounts Mary theoretically knew existed but until recently had never thought possibly within her reach. And now the events of the past month had forced a voice to the question that until then had only lain in the very back of her unconscious mind:

What would life be like with Stanley gone and his money still here?

The idea was so intoxicating, so attractive, that she knew to give it oxygen would be to allow it to grow to dangerous levels. And so she'd quickly stashed it away, back in its dark corner, where it remained dormant. But not dead.

STANLEY HAD LET SLIP THE NUMBER EXACTLY ONCE, HIS NET worth. He normally refused to divulge details on anything financial— he was so mistrustful in that way, even with his own *wife*!—but there'd been that one time, at Charles Schwab. He'd taken Mary there before, and each instance she'd waited in the lobby. But for some reason, on this occasion, he motioned for her to join inside.

The advisor, an elegant white woman named Patricia, had worked with Stanley for decades. They sat in her office on the other side of the desk, Stanley in the chair closest to Patricia, since he was the actual client. Just a few minutes into their small talk, she remarked, "You know, your ex-wife was in here just the other day."

"Oh?" Stanley was always attentive when it came to news of Linda, though he tried to hide it. "How is she?"

Patricia assessed Mary with a cunning look before she slid her gaze back to Stanley. "She's doing great. You know how capable she is."

"What's she invested in?"

"Now, you know I can't divulge *that* sort of information."

Stanley took the bait. "Well, how's she doing, overall?"

Patricia made him wait while she opened a pouch of sugar and tapped its contents into her coffee. "Very well, in my opinion. Some- one her age, we usually don't advise that they have so much of their portfolio in the stock market. We like to see more diversification— CDs, bonds, good old cash. You know the rule. Take one hundred, subtract your age, and that's what percent of your portfolio should still be in equities, roughly. But Linda's one of the very few clients I have who's the exception. She has one of the greatest natural talents for portfolio management I've ever seen."

"Ah." Stanley coughed. "I'm so happy for her. Happy for all of us, that we can live so well. Of course, I'm not doing so poorly myself."

"Oh yes. You're doing a fine job."

"I'm the sort of man who likes to make his own decisions." He stretched his arms over his head.

"I completely understand. It's your life, your money. Just remember that I'm here for guidance should you need anything. And keep in mind what I said about the market and retirement. As we both know, you like to get a little daring yourself." She winked, the crow's-feet prominent around each eye. This woman might be rich, Mary thought, but even at her age wealth couldn't make up for a lack of injectables.

Though she'd said they should stay for as long as they wanted, offering to fetch them more coffee and tea, it was obvious Patricia wanted to return to her daily schedule. They passed her next appointment on the way out, another Asian couple near Stanley's age, the woman primly dressed in one of those St. John suits Mary occasionally imagined herself wearing one day. As soon as Stanley shut the car door, she could see the red beginning to web its way across his face. He sat in the seat facing directly forward, not yet turning on the ignition. "Who does she think she is?" he seethed. "Talking like I don't know anything. I know what I'm doing, more than that old bitch."

"She probably meant to insult you." Mary had been perversely cheered by Stanley's bad mood; she hadn't liked how the advisor felt she could just bring up Linda in front of her, as if she weren't even there. "Maybe Linda put her up to it, planted the idea in her head."

"Linda wouldn't do that. She's very discreet." At this Mary had been ready to finally snap; she'd had quite enough of Stanley's refusal to ever utter anything negative about his ex—as if Linda had been such a *saint*!—but then he went on. "Patricia doesn't know how much I have now, what I've done with real estate. You see, I've done some flipping, made a lot—" He stopped.

Mary was quiet. She was used to Stanley starting conversations like this, dangling the prospect of tantalizing information in the air, only to snatch it away.

This time, however, he continued. "My net worth is almost seven million now. Seven million! And growing fast. Never in my lifetime did I believe I'd have so much. Shirley Chang always says money just brings problems, but that hasn't happened to me." His voice softened. "It's only brought me happiness. Someone like you. You know that I'll take care of you, right? I've been meaning to tell you that when I pass—though I'm sure that is decades from now—you'll be in my will, as long as we're still married. Fred will have a third, Kate another, and you the last." He turned toward her. "What do you think?"

Mary had thought it wonderful, of course. More than wonderful. *Seven million*. And *growing*. Even a third of that was an unimaginable fortune: it meant that were something to happen to Stanley she could keep the house and have enough left over so that she didn't have to work again for the rest of her life.

She took his hand, placing it between both of hers. She knew what he wanted to hear. "My life is only worth living with you in it." It was the truth, anyway. Stanley was so strong, so capable; infallible, especially when compared to her own flimsy existence. He kissed her hair.

In the days after the conversation, Mary had the feeling that Stanley regretted his outburst. She felt him studying her, watching for some undefined action. So she meticulously maintained her normal routine, taking care not to startle him. Which was easy, as nothing had really changed, except for the fact that she now knew of the money, which she wished she could have told him meant more to her at that point than the money itself. Because just the knowledge of it enveloped Mary with a warm security, a constant glimmering reminder of how lucky she was to have married a man of means who loved her.

Mary didn't want to tell Jeylin and Grace any of this, because she didn't know what they would do with the knowledge. The problem was she didn't know how *not* to tell them either, so in the end she compromised.

"He has millions."

"Millions," Jeylin repeated. The envy that seeped from her voice was surprisingly delicious. "How many? That makes a difference, you understand. If it's not just one."

"What does it matter to you?" As if Jeylin had ever seen even a million dollars, much less more!

"I want to make sure you are taken care of, big sister. Do you think I want it for myself? I can manage my own affairs, thank you. But it would be nice if there was some extra, to use for our mother. She's getting older, like your husband. She could move to California, since there's better medical care here. The air in China is getting worse every day."

"If Stanley says I'm taken care of, then I am. He trusts me. He even took me to meet his advisor at Charles Schwab."

"Schwab?" Grace piped up. "I saw that one."

"Leave it alone!" Suddenly Mary wanted everyone gone. The conversation was spiraling out of control; she was afraid of what might follow next, the extraction of promises that upon Stanley's death she'd take in their mother, dooming herself to decades more of familial obligation right as the intoxicating rays of financial freedom were beginning to shine through. "Leave everything alone! This is none of anyone's business!"

"Don't you at least want to take a look?" Jeylin asked. "You used to complain that Stanley never let you into his office. This is your chance. Who knows if it'll come again? You're right; Stanley may very well recover with all that special medicine you've been preparing. But either way, don't you want to know?"

Grace already had a binder open. "It says $14,000 for the balance here," she chattered, trailing a nail down the page. "For Schwab. And then another $4,000 at Chase." Mary snatched the binder before she could stop herself.

"Guess we know how you truly feel now," Jeylin crowed.

Mary barely heard her. After she went through each of the statements, she climbed up on the stool and took down another binder. Then another. She was three hours late to the hospital that afternoon, which she told Stanley was the fault of the internet repair technician. He was half out of his mind on drugs anyway, he didn't care, and in fact he returned to sleep shortly after lifting his head to register her arrival. She sat in the hard plastic–backed chair next to the bed until nearly midnight. The nurse on call, the black one she suspected secretly hated her, asked at one point if she wanted to move to the couch. "Much more comfortable," she commented pointedly.

Mary ignored her. Long after her lower back had begun to cramp in protest, she remained still, posture erect.

AFTERWARD, A MENTAL LINE WAS CROSSED FOR HER, ONE THAT, once stepped over, could be revisited at will. The lawyer had been Jeylin's idea—some cheap hack Nicky knew from his so-called construction work, who he claimed could quickly draw up documents for a reduced fee.

Even though the lawyer was white, with a perfect American accent, the first time they met even Mary could tell he was unsuccessful. He had a shaped beard and looked as if he only wore suits when forced to for show; he did his work, however, and rustled together a will that stated Stanley would leave a set amount to Mary of $1.5 million, as well as the house (worth another million), with any remainder to be split between Kate and Fred. Mary figured it a good gamble, since so far her research had led her to believe there was going to be considerably less to his estate than the promised seven million. Of

course, there was always the chance there was more—there were all
sorts of ways to hide cash, and Stanley had made it clear that when it
came to the topic, he was worlds above her in education—but Mary
wasn't willing to bet her future on it.

It was funny, about the money. She'd always viewed Stanley's finances differently than her own. While with her personal means she
was exceedingly careful, begrudging every expense, when it came to
Stanley's she was relentless in her encouragement to spend. His wealth
sprung like water from the tap, supplied by a limitless source many
degrees of separation away, one where she never saw the bill. When it
came time for Stanley to buy a new car, she nudged him toward the
most expensive models, endorsing every option he expressed interest in.
When they traveled on vacation to China—one of those $99 pack-
age holidays during which the tour operators forced lengthy shopping
visits—she strolled him past the cheap tchotchkes and shoddy silk
garments to the displays of Grade A jadeite (and netted a bracelet
for herself out of it too). When they dined out, she always ordered a
special drink from the menu, usually plum tea or wine or, once in a
while, even a cocktail. The depletion of funds never concerned her.
She never thought, I am spending my future money.

Until Stanley had gone ahead and released a number in the air,
made a promise, become sick. Then it became a reality, and she felt its
loss as keenly as one of her own treasured possessions. Mary mourned
her one third of *seven million and growing*. It was her right to recover
as much of it as she could. So she wanted the will. She wanted it
signed and witnessed. And as soon as that was done, she was sure she
could return to her normal existence, fully inhabiting her authentic
self as a devoted wife. Which would be a relief.

THE LAWYER WASN'T ALLOWED IN. WHEN HE ARRIVED KAISER SAID
he wasn't on the list of approved visitors, and Stanley—either out of

confusion or deliberate obstinacy—refused to add him, though the man still collected his $400 fee.

"Call me when he's out," he drawled, and proceeded to provide a phone number which he never answered. Afterward, Jeylin chided her for writing him a check in the first place. "You only pay for results," she said in a superior tone. "That's how these things work."

But by then it didn't matter. Because Stanley was coming home.

The days after Stanley's release were filled with a sort of euphoria. His condition improved markedly—within a day he was able to sit propped against pillows and was demanding to watch their favorite TV show, a Chinese drama set in the Qin Dynasty. Mary made him special egg drop soup, soft foods like the lamb dumplings he liked so much (she adapted them to have less meat and more cabbage), and allowed a small piece of dark chocolate with dinner. The palliative care team who set up Stanley's medical equipment were friendly. They helped him in the shower and monitored his vitals.

"We're always happy to see situations like this, where there's an energetic spouse who cares," one of the nurses, a Filipino-Chinese named Paolo who spoke Mandarin and who'd visited twice so far, said to her. He murmured quietly to avoid waking Stanley, who was lightly dozing, and bent over and delicately wrapped a blood pressure cuff around Stanley's arm. "People often think that having their kids nearby is enough." He grimaced. "It rarely is."

To be fair, Kate had visited regularly since Stanley's return. Mary had followed nervously the first time she went barreling upstairs—it still irked her that Stanley's children felt entitled to charge through the house as if it were their own, never asking anyone's permission before entering a room—but Kate had given the office a cursory glance and didn't mention if she noticed anything out of place, just straightened a few papers and located a laptop charger. Still, Mary had been relieved when she left. She had tried to re-create the setting as it was earlier, but she knew she must have missed a few details.

Kate spent most of her time in the kitchen or by Stanley's bed, watching TV with him. Mary had been surprised by the sheer number of hours she was able to dedicate, though she'd gathered in snippets that there was a new nanny at her house, and there was also talk of Kate's husband occasionally taking the children overnight. That was confusing. Where did he take them? And why didn't she go too? But Kate was tight-lipped and Stanley incoherent on the topic whenever pressed.

Stanley was out of sorts a lot lately, a recent development. His waking hours now seemed to flit between a normal lucidity and a cloudy dream state, though Mary knew that if his attentions were truly required, he could still rouse a focused response. She'd made the monumental error of underestimating his faculties earlier, the first time she broached the topic of his will.

Stanley had been flat on his back as usual, and she'd sat in a chair by the bed, massaging his feet. His hands tapped gently at his side, and from his throat a weak purring sound occasionally rasped, in pleasure from the sensation.

"Stanley," she said.

"Hmm?" He craned his neck.

His benign expression bolstered her. "Remember when you told me what you were going to do with your will? The seven million, split three ways?"

"Hmm." His fingers continued to tap. Then after a pause: "After we went to Schwab."

"After the Schwab visit, yes! Exactly. And the seven million." She emphasized the last part. "Stanley, where is that money? I know some of it is the house. But the rest, where is it? Where are the accounts?"

He fell still. She thought it was another break, a brief hiatus for air, until a hand rose and pointed at her. "You've been poking through my business," it said.

"No!" She was horrified. "Of course not! Stanley, I just want to understand, so that in case something were to happen, I can help with the details. . . ."

"I don't need your help." His voice was like sandpaper. She rushed to find his water bottle and raised the straw to his lips.

"Of course not, you're so good at these things. I would never think I know more than you. I just wanted to understand for my own information, and of course Fred and Kate have been asking. . . ."

"Stay out of my business," he said with venom.

Mary had wanted to flee then, far away to the relative safety of the other side of the house, but she'd feared stopping the massage. So she remained at the foot of the bed, kneading his legs and feet. After a few minutes his fingers resumed their tapping, and it was only when they once again stopped that she dared cease the activity in her own aching limbs and peer at his face.

He was awake, staring at the ceiling. His eyes were milky, and he wore the death face, the one where his mouth hung ajar and loose skin pooled around his mouth. Mary knew he was alive, though. Heard the breathing, in and out. Steady.

The interaction terrified her. She already knew he had a nasty temper—they'd fought often enough in the past, and there'd even been screaming rows once or twice, which always ended in her tears and his stony silence. But he'd never before spoken to her in that tenor, which his children referenced and she'd previously always dismissed (killing a *bird*? It was too outlandish to be true). It was a voice that stated unequivocally that a conversation was over, not to be discussed further, that hinted at a barely controlled violence. Normally it would have been enough to dissuade Mary from ever approaching the topic again, to definitively demonstrate that her questions had been a one-off, an innocuous mistake to be quickly forgotten. But this was the most money she would ever see in her life, she knew that much, and each move counted. Every mark in her favor meant the potential of yet another comfort to enjoy the rest of her years—a better car, a new dining room set; two yearly holidays, instead of one.

And time was important.

Stanley, she understood now, was going to die, no matter how many herbal concoctions she made. Each meal she had to try harder to find foods he was willing to eat—she'd given up on the green juices and fresh fruit and had returned to his old favorites, cream puffs and chocolate pudding pie. And still he would push the plate delicately aside, shaking his head. He only had bowel movements every few days, and he no longer attempted to shuffle to the guest bathroom, instead opting for the sitting toilet next to his bed. The last time he'd used it, Kate had been over, arranging his medicine. She'd discreetly turned her face away, and then as soon as her father had grunted his satisfaction, she called to Mary to clean him up.

"And I think we should toss out the . . . feces as soon as possible," she said. "For sanitary purposes."

It had taken all of Mary's resolve not to slap her hard across the cheek.

A few days passed before she attempted a second salvo, this time aided by a magenta lace silk robe Stanley had gifted her at the beginning of their courtship. He had told her it reminded him of some movie with a Vegas showgirl, but Mary always felt whorish when she wore it, so once they were married she'd hidden it in the back of the guest closet. When she retrieved it, she'd had to spend a precious hour ironing out wrinkles; as she pressed the fabric, she rehearsed the conversation, testing various lines.

She waited until after dinner, when there was little chance Kate might still stop by with food but not so late that Stanley had ingested his final dose of painkillers and become sedated for the night. Then, she donned the robe and climbed in bed next to him. His form was hot, and she knew he registered her appearance. "Stanley," she whispered. After a few seconds, he took her hand.

"Stanley, I'm so worried about you." She threw her arm over him; she could reach almost all the way around at this point, as if she were the man, spooning the woman. She freed her hand and began to stroke his legs, starting at the knees, going higher.

Eventually he asked, "What are you worried about?"

"I worry that you're going to go away," she said. "And that I'll be alone. And I don't think I can live without you. I don't know what every day will look like." She buried her head into his back and was surprised to feel the sting of real tears. Her hands kept stroking. "I don't want to be without you."

His hand moved back to hers, which had been softly petting what remained soft. He stilled her, and for a moment she froze. Then he turned and faced her. "You'll never be alone," he said slowly. "Even when I'm gone, I'll make sure you're taken care of."

"But what am I going to do? I haven't worked in so many years, I'm afraid of starting over. . . . I won't know what to do with myself."

"You needn't worry." He caressed her hair. "I have worked out a plan that will bring you joy and purpose. I keep meaning to tell you, but each time it slips out of my head. And to think, you were the inspiration." And then he explained about the foundation, which she had vague memories of nodding her support for earlier, even though she didn't know what a foundation was. "It's to aid those less fortunate than us," he said. "To give young people a chance for education."

"You're so thoughtful." She nuzzled his neck, which felt cool compared to the rest of his body. "You care so much about other people. But Stanley . . ." She paused, as if the thought had just materialized. "How much is left after the foundation? After that, and the house. What is left?"

"The house is paid off. I wrote the check yesterday."

Finally, a bright light. Mary offered a mental thanks to Shirley Chang, whom she had never liked due to how brassy and superior she acted but who'd turned out to be her savior nonetheless, bulldozing in the week before and making a big scene about how Stanley had to take care of his poor, poor wife. Mary didn't particularly care for how much she'd said *poor*, but what did it matter when the house no longer had a mortgage?

"That's wonderful. You're so capable. But what about other than the house? The rest of the accounts?"

"Well." He'd begun to lightly knead at her palm with his thumb; in response, she tenderly swept back one of the few remaining loose strands from his forehead. "After paying off the mortgage and a little for the foundation—" His voice dissolved to dry air. He motioned for the water. He drank haltingly, and then continued.

"After that—that's almost all of it."

The words landed with a hallucinatory dullness, and like a bad dream, she first tried to negotiate her way out. "How can that be? It must be the amount you want for the foundation. Are you sure it isn't too much?"

He shook his head. "I'm not even sure there's enough for the foundation. But I want to do it for you. And me. For our names to live on."

"But the seven million?" she whispered.

And he gave a little shake of the shoulders: no. Then he pet her wrist and touched her breasts, fondly, without sexual desire. And she let him, because she had no choice, because her husband was dying, dying but still a liar, a liar who'd promised her an amount beyond her wildest fantasies and made it real, before taking it all away. Such was his power and her powerlessness, where everything she had was itself taken from someone else and for which each crumb she had to be thankful.

That's when Mary finally felt the anger, the resentment she had seen in the eyes of Stanley's ex-wife and children. The impact as it landed, sinking deep in her bones. The mess he was leaving! The promise of the house and money to live out the rest of her life, not to mention what he might have pledged to the rest of his family, all in shambles. And Stanley knew it, had known this entire time yet done nothing, and now still here, quite literally on his deathbed, he chose to be a coward and curl away from her disappointed face and indulge in the elixir of sleep. She understood now that Stanley meant to sap her goodwill little by little until he died, safe in and comforted by her eternal presence by his side. Leaving her to settle and tally up the humiliations only once he was already gone.

Even from their earliest moments together, Mary had known that her love for Stanley would never be pure. The differences between them were too vast, and their collective baggage too heavy, to have the sort of relationship she'd dreamed of as a young woman, the kind she'd hoped for with Ed. Yet there had been a cleanliness to her beliefs, that she would do her best to love Stanley in the manner he desired most, and in turn he would take care of her in the ways he best knew how. She would be his wife, and he her husband, just as he had been a husband before, and a father, and a son. Until now, she hadn't understood that he had no interest in any of those roles—that for Stanley, there was only himself.

At that moment Mary felt closer than she'd ever been to Kate and Linda and Fred, yet she knew at the same time that they were as far away as they ever could be. And that it would stay that way now, because their interests were so opposed.

———————

The next morning, Mary called Jeylin and Grace. She humbled herself with a mea culpa straightaway, divulging the mortifying details of her betrayal so thoroughly that it was quickly clear to all parties there was no more left to tell. As a result, they were almost gracious. They came over that evening after Stanley was asleep, coordinating their arrival without their husbands, and sat on both sides of her on the couch in the living room, the plaid one she'd always secretly hated. It took mere minutes for her to break down and cry.

"What's important now is that you make sure you really have the house," Jeylin said, not bothering to mask the triumph in her voice. "Are you sure it's actually paid off? Because now you know you can't trust what he says. And what about Stanley's children? Maybe they will fight for the house, once they know he has nothing more."

Mary nodded. "I saw the statement. Stanley's friend, Shirley Chang, she said she would make sure it goes to me. She's the one who helped with the mortgage."

"Then we figure out what you do next," Jeylin said. "The house— can you pay for it alone? Do you know about property tax, all those costs? Otherwise you'll have to sell it, move somewhere smaller. An apartment. Many women in your situation do this."

"Remember Fang Wu, our old manager at China Garden?" Grace chimed in. "He is part owner now. I'm sure he would hire you back."

"I don't know. What would I do? Hostess again, or serve food? Stanley used to go there; his friends would see me. . . ."

"Is that so bad?" Jeylin cut in sharply. "Nine years ago you were there. What have you done since that makes you think you are too good?"

Slept each night in a million-dollar house that would soon be hers; gone on six cruises, three trips to China, and two to Europe. Stood next to Stanley as he paid $5,000 for a jade amulet in Beijing, $7,000 for a rug in Istanbul, and another $10,000 for a custom-designed furniture suite in Guangzhou. Gone to dinner with multimillionaires who lived in the most expensive cities in one of the most expensive states of the richest country in the world. Played mah jong with them, laughing with their wives as their husbands secretly eyed her. Had the wealthiest of them all, Shirley Chang, who lived in a vast mansion filled with golden objects, call her a friend.

Her sisters meant well, Mary decided. But they no longer played on the same level; she had evolved past them. She knew now the truth that at first had been so frightening, that success in America was less about what you earned than your particular luck on the day you decided to take it for yourself.

She would manage things on her own.

STANLEY HAD TO HAVE *SOMETHING* LEFT OVER, AFTER THE HOUSE. The documents upstairs seemed to indicate as much—Stanley had been like a squirrel, hoarding morsels of cash and treasure in many different pockets. There had to be accounts left over, safety deposit boxes. Money he had stashed for a rainy day. After he was gone, why shouldn't it all be hers?

The morning Mary launched her charm offensive, Stanley responded to her homemade custard bun by slowly eating two bites and then, a few hours later, defecating his pants. They'd started to use diapers overnight, because she could no longer stand waking up to the sound of his electronic bell—navigating downstairs numb with sleep, helping him squat, all while the *ding ding ding* continued incessantly—but during the day, she had still been assisting him with the toilet. He'd generally been able to hold his bowel movements until she arrived, though he never waited more than a few minutes. Mary didn't like diapers—one of the many benefits of childlessness was never having performed all the degrading tasks, the casual intimacy of changing someone's shit daily over a period of years. So she left Stanley in his regular underwear, except on the days the palliative care nurses were due to visit.

A system that worked until the day he pooped himself.

The smell was overwhelming. The putrid odor assaulted her as soon as she walked into the kitchen, and she'd had to drop the special vegetarian rolls she was preparing to bring to temple later to rush and clean both Stanley and the sheets. She propped an arm under his torso, lifting him slowly from the mattress; even though Stanley was lighter every day, he still weighed more than her, and Mary struggled to keep his rear away from her clothes, as she could see the stain spreading on the back of his soft pajama pants. Eventually she got him upright and motioned for him to grip his walker, a request he refused.

"Stanley," she hissed. "You need to hold on! I can't wipe well enough otherwise." He didn't respond but eventually put his hands on the walker for support while she cleaned up. His pants had been beyond repair—she'd tied them in a plastic grocery bag and thrown them in the garbage—but she'd gone and soaked the sheets in the sink, before returning to soap Stanley and make sure he was clean, moisturizing him in the same manner she imagined you would a little baby. He'd been temperamental during the ordeal, impatiently asking when she'd be finished, but she had tenderly ministered to him as she bit back the urge to cry.

Then, five hours later, it happened again. And twice more the next day.

Stanley was going to die very soon, Mary saw. If not in a week, then several. And now she realized it was too late for him to sign anything else over or fix his past financial mistakes, too late for her to strategize a path to keep the house without working for the next thirty years. That is, if she lived that long, because she was convinced the exhaustion of managing Stanley was aging her exponentially. She had always known that he might deteriorate to this, but she thought the American healthcare system, with its seeming panacea of medications and Medicare, would adjust accordingly. But when she asked the nurses when they would begin daily visits, she was met with frigid silence.

"It's up to his doctors to determine that," Paolo, the one who had complimented her earlier, said eventually. "But usually people in pain like this, they want their spouses involved as much as possible. Someone that they love and trust." And given her a long look, as if reassessing everything he'd previously thought.

So when Deborah, Stanley's sister, called to announce her imminent arrival, Mary was flooded with relief and thankfulness. It was the afternoon, and she'd been running on five hours' sleep from the night before as she ran emergency loads of laundry and attempted to fix the TV (Stanley still wanted his programs on all the time, in the background). Deborah had always been friendly with her and vocal in her opinions on Stanley's children, whom she found to be weak and rude. And so Mary had sobbed upon hearing that familiar sympathetic voice, crying out all her fright and frustrations: Stanley's health and her fatigue; the will; what would happen to her, after it was all over.

"It will be okay." Deborah's voice poured through the phone like a smooth tonic. "I'll talk to Stanley. Believe me, everyone thinks these things. I'm thinking them all the time. About my own husband and definitely his mother. And they aren't even sick!"

And that had made her laugh so much that in a moment of weakness Mary confided to Deborah her deepest, ugliest truth: that she had brought Stanley home so he could die in peace, but that now she wished for nothing more than to move him out, away to a nursing home. Which she knew was a possibility, because she'd studied the hospice materials carefully, painstakingly translating every unfamiliar word, and she also knew that by moving Stanley she might be able to preserve more capital in the house, because she herself wouldn't want to buy a home in which someone had died. Because she might have to sell the house, she said, to make ends meet when Stanley was gone. And Deborah had murmured some more and told her not to feel bad, it was perfectly understandable, she was being so brave. And

Mary had fallen asleep that night for the first time in weeks with calm in her heart.

And then that fucking double-talking witch had gone and called Shirley Chang, and the two had conspired and called Stanley's children, and all the times Mary had sat next to Shirley at dinner, the volumes of Chinese DVD sets she'd searched for and tracked down for her, the massage therapy she'd provided her wrinkly old back on that one cruise to Mexico when she'd had spasms—all of that meant nothing. Because Deborah and Shirley were of one world and Mary another, and she understood then that even if she had it all, everything that had been promised, she would still never be one of them.

Still, she almost succeeded. The hospice care worker had already been at the house, literally handing over the paperwork to begin the move, which they called *transitions*. Cindy Ziegler, a white woman in her fifties with orange lipstick on her teeth, who, unlike Paolo, had been wholly understanding, assuring Mary that a nursing home was the choice many loving but ultimately struggling families opted for.

"We had someone move his wife into one of our properties just this Tuesday," Cindy said. "The doctors said only weeks left, but the husband couldn't take it anymore. Been married for more than forty years, that one."

Mary had bristled when she heard the part about forty years. Cindy had seemingly sussed her out as a second wife as soon as she'd arrived, inquiring if she and Stanley had been married long; when she answered nine years, Cindy had nodded satisfactorily to herself, as if confirming a theory. "Probably married to the first a long time, huh?" she said. "At this age, I'd guess maybe around thirty years? And then he met you and got to have some *real* fun. Sorry if I sound flippant, just like to inject some levity into these situations. Most families appreciate it."

Mary had just laughed, ha-ha, I'm not so good at English and don't understand. Inside, she had fumed. As if her years with Stanley and Linda's had been the same. As if Linda could have ever served nine years of this tenure—cooking, cleaning, massaging, flattering, pleasing without end. Didn't anyone ever think of that? The variable difficulty of time spent in a marriage? But she'd kept silent and smiled, and Cindy dimpled back in understanding response, her expression saying that she sympathized with it all. That she understood that Mary, too, was deserving of relief.

Mary had been that close, dreaming of the respite to come, when Fred heaved open the door with Deborah and her husband and her ancient mother-in-law close behind. And then the shouting had begun.

CHAPTER 18

FRED

M en's feet were almost always ugly, and as they aged, they only grew more hideous. Fred had a thing about feet—not a fetish, because beautiful feet on a woman never served to attract him on their own—but misshapen toes and cracked nail beds and dinged polish were all immediate disqualifiers, no matter how alluring the rest of the package. Fred tried to keep his own neat and hygienic, clipping his nails once a week and moisturizing regularly, with an expensive Aesop balm he slathered on without restraint. Still, there was only so much that could be done.

If Fred's feet were unattractive, however, then his father's were outright disgusting. Fred had been massaging them for nearly an hour so far that morning, working up from the heels. Subtly averting his gaze each time he reached the toes, which were yellow and fungused, with outrageously long nails. Interesting how the body kept chugging along at certain tasks, he thought, long after it had shut down other more arguably crucial functions. Would Mary ever help clip them again? It didn't seem likely.

The massage had been Auntie Deborah's suggestion, an asinine proposal he'd been unable to wriggle out of without seeming like an ass. Fred couldn't remember the last time he'd touched his father—he thought it must have been when he was a toddler, before permanent memories could be formed—and he didn't know why it had to be now, more than forty years later, that he had to once again take up those gnarled claws, kneading them awkwardly between his palms. Deborah, however, was insistent. She was the commanding officer in the war now openly raging in the house between Mary and the rest of the family, and according to her, rubbing Stanley's feet was a nonnegotiable.

"It's what his wife does," she said, barking into Fred's ear. "How else do you think she got where she is? You think it's so easy to go from whatever village she came from in China to marrying a rich man in California? You know how many restaurant waitresses are just dying for the same opportunity? Your father loves massage; he has since he was a little boy. Our mom used to do it for him every night. Maybe it's how he became so spoiled." She turned away, toward the direction of Stanley. "Big brother!" she called. "Your son wants to make sure you are comfortable!" And unceremoniously shoved Fred to the end of the bed.

The hour mark was nearly past, and Fred's hands were numb. His father's limbs felt like the chicken feet he used to love ordering at dim sum, so devoid they were of fat and flesh. Fred thought Stanley had finally fallen asleep, but then he cried out, in a weak moan, "Mary? Where's Mary?"

Deborah rushed over. "She isn't here," she told him. "It's just us, Fred and Deborah. I'm not sure *where* Mary is," she then added, in a sad voice, as if she, too, were bewildered by what task Mary could possibly be engaged in more important than her husband's comfort. Speaking in a hush, however, because both she and Fred knew exactly where Mary was: upstairs, quietly stewing. Ever since the events of the previous afternoon, she'd been on high alert and refused to leave the house.

A confused look crossed Stanley's face, and he stared ahead, eventually closing his eyes. Deborah nodded sharply toward Fred. "Keep going," she whispered. Another five minutes elapsed before Stanley's breath transformed into the deep guttural regularity that had replaced his regular snoring.

"She knows that we know now," Deborah said, after she'd verified Stanley was asleep by violently waving her hands in front of his face. "She knows that we know, that she just wants the money." It was her explanation for why Mary hadn't already fled the house, after they'd caught her in her awful treason—why she continued to stick around like a stubborn virus, even after she'd been so thoroughly shamed. Fred ushering out Cindy the chatty hospice worker with a firm hand, while Deborah dramatically tore the transfer paperwork into pieces; Deborah's mother-in-law flopping over on the couch in histrionics, as she bemoaned the lack of respect within the younger generations. It had been Fred's first experience with the sort of shrieking brawl he'd always heard possible but had never before witnessed between the older female relations of his family; there was a part of him that almost respected Mary for continuing to live in an environment so openly hostile to her, as he wasn't sure he himself could survive under similar circumstances.

"She needs to stay now," Deborah continued, "because she knows she is in trouble. She has to keep near Stanley, to stay in his good graces. She is afraid what he might do otherwise, if we tell him she is only interested in his money."

"Wasn't that always the case?" It wasn't as if they were ever one of *those* families, the sort that clasped their hands in pleasure over dear old Dad finding love in his golden years and giving toasts at the wedding, only to go into spasms when it came time to read the will. Mary's interest in Stanley's money had been a given, a topic openly discussed and remarked upon, like the weather.

"Yes, but she should have followed certain rules. Every relationship has rules, especially this one. What do you think China would look like, if there were no rules? A mess! So many people! White people don't always follow them; that's why they're always losing fortunes in one generation and leaving everything to strippers. Can you imagine a Chinese person doing that? If Uncle Billy even *thought* it, I would murder him, but at least in his sleep, so he wouldn't suffer. And nobody would ever catch me." She paused. "Of course by white, I don't mean Jewish. They're even better at following the rules than the Chinese!"

"Okay, but you and Uncle Billy are still married. And everyone knows you're super successful. Dad's not exactly that. Or even close."

"Yes, that's true." Deborah grimaced. They were both recalling the sob story Mary had relayed, practically shouting at times, after the hospice representative had left and the first wave of hysterics settled. Fred had been surprised to hear that Stanley had revealed to Mary his net worth, all $7 million of it; then somewhat less so when he learned the sum no longer, if ever, existed. He'd suspected for many years that his parents sucked at money. At least Reagan had finally come through with the formal Lion consulting contract; the generous terms would help cushion the blow of a vanished inheritance.

While Fred had sat impassively through Mary's telling, slouched in a wooden chair with his arms crossed, Deborah had been openly contemptuous, heckling loudly as she paced the room. "Seven million?" she'd spat. "How could you ever believe Stanley had that much? Or that you deserved any of it?"

"He promised," Mary cried, loudly whimpering, at one point

collapsing at the foot of the stairs. "He's had the best years of my life. What more can I give?"

"You miss the point," Deborah hurled back. "You don't *have* anything to give. Your currency is worthless. That is your fate. Now get out of my face."

"As if Stanley ever had seven million," Deborah said now with a sniff, recalling the memory. "We always knew he liked to exaggerate, although to be honest, I didn't think he'd become *so* reckless. After paying off the house he has almost nothing left! And then these crazy ideas of his. Is it true what Mary was saying, about the foundation?"

"First I heard of it." Fred had initially thought Mary was lying, before he realized she could never come up with such a bizarre concept on her own. He'd never once heard his father mention anything about a foundation, or for that matter, that particular word that as of late had begun to creep into the vocabulary of his own peers: his *legacy*.

"I wonder where he got the idea. Or why he thought Mary would be the best person to administer it, even if there had been any money. She's an idiot, but I didn't know your dad had become so foolish as well. Of course, it's impossible. Mad!" Her voice began to creep louder, and Fred served a nervous glance in Stanley's direction. "Oh, don't worry, he's asleep. When he's out, he's out. Ever since we were kids. We took that one cruise together a few years back, me and Billy and him and Mary, and they had this emergency drill where they blasted noise into the cabins for twenty minutes, so loud that we had to put in earplugs and cover our heads with pillows. And *still* it was unbearable. I blamed Stanley, you know, because he made us do the cheap deck, where it was even louder. They probably insulated it less, like the *Titanic*. Of course, he slept through the whole thing."

"I forgot you all took that trip together." Fred studied his aunt, whose face was still youthful and unlined—a result, he suspected, of the best plastic surgeon and dermatology artisans in Beverly Hills.

She was eyeing a loose thread on her Marni cardigan; in one ferocious movement, she clipped it off with her nails. "You think Mary's
surprised you're being so hard on her? I thought she really liked you.
Most people do. You're so charming."

"Ha." She waved away the compliment. "You don't need to flatter
an old lady. Mary was okay before, always quiet, knew not to discuss
things she didn't know anything about, not like your father's friend,
that fat-mouthed Shirley Chang. Does she think she has to display
all the diamonds and gold she's ever owned on her body at all times?
There's something called a safety deposit box, you know. And at least
Mary always called me on my birthday and showed up to dim sum
when I came to visit—unlike you or your sister." She gave Fred a
pointed look. "That's why I was so surprised to hear about this, wanting to move your father. What does she have to worry about real estate
values? Too greedy! Someone like her, a free house in the Bay Area,
she should already be happy. Do you know that through your dad's
pension she will have healthcare for the rest of her life? I blame myself
a little, because I was talking to her about housing that one time on
the cruise, although to be fair many people ask for my opinion on the
topic, so I have the habit now, to share. But Mary, she took it too far;
she wants too much. There is a deal between every couple, though it
isn't between husband and wife. It is between who has the money and
who doesn't."

"Does that mean you have all the power and Uncle Billy has to
do whatever you say?"

"Naughty boy!" Deborah swiveled her head. "My God, for a moment I thought they were still in the house. And no, there's a certain
balance. For example, Billy's mother is ninety years old and wears
two listening aids and never responds when I ask what she wants to
eat for lunch, but then she miraculously overhears every word when
I'm whispering about her to my friends. And still I let her live with
us! Of course she's in the in-law wing, and our house is five thousand

square feet, but still, she makes her presence known. Oh yes, she does.
Don't you understand this? You were married before. And I thought
you have that fiancée, that white girl, the one who sells things at Saks.
Hey, you think she can get me a discount? Don't feel pressure to answer now, but if so, just pick up some gift cards. Up to $20,000. So I
can buy whenever I want."

"We're not engaged. She's just my girlfriend. I assume."

"Ah, so you do know the rules. You think that ex of yours, the
rich Korean, *she* would have let you get away with not proposing for
so long? No way José."

Fred smoothed his hair and grinned, before recalling the current
situation with Erika. His aunt observed him with her characteristic
shrewdness.

"You having problems? You want to call, ask her to have lunch
with us tomorrow?"

"No, that's okay." But then Fred reassessed and determined that
it might not be such a bad idea. Erika always loved meeting his relatives. To her they were like bowling pins—each additional one she
managed to win over inched her that much closer to ultimate victory.
Stanley's sister would be a big get, and there was still the present he
had yet to give.

"Let me grab my phone." And then he found it, and his breath
slid to a halt.

————————

From: ErikaV@xmail.com

To: Fred@Lion-Capital.com

CC: serenahchang@xmail.com, ryan828@gmail.com, Kate@XCorp
.com, noravarga@gmail.com, bhorowitz@a16z.com, rohing@draper
carlyle.com, charles@greylock.com, suzanne.goldstein@morgan
stanley.com, jdoerr@kpcb.com, will@tatapacker.com, tom.g@google

ventures.com, 5bot2@goldman.com, Mchang@tencent.com, Shane
.west@xmail.com, fnevins@bloomberg.com
BCC:
Subject: Fred Huang

To whom it may concern,

My name is Erika Varga, and until last week, I was Fred Huang's girlfriend and assumed fiancée. You may be wondering why I've emailed
you. Perhaps we've never even met.

My purpose in writing today is this: to expose one Fred Huang, venture capitalist and liar. I believe that by doing so, I will have cleansed
my soul and done society a useful favor.

Let me first assure you that I am not a foolish woman. I have a degree
in legal studies and have traveled internationally and dated numerous
powerful and high-net-worth men. For years, I believed Fred to be
a man who kept his promises and treated the women in his life with
respect, gratitude, and chivalry. Unfortunately, recent events have
proven me 100% wrong.

Please be warned, ladies and gentlemen: this man is despicable. And
my eyes are now open to his true nature.

The proof? Fred's decision to abandon me, alone and defenseless, in
a third-world Asian country known specifically for its high Triad population. His refusal to propose marriage, after countless delays and
promises (please reference the attached photo of myself and Fred at
the French Laundry on my last birthday, where you can clearly read
the cake as addressed to the "love of his life"). His reprehensible dis-
respect toward my parents, both esteemed professors of the Détente
School of Diplomatic Science, an internationally recognized and accredited university in Budapest. Not to mention the naked photos of
his ex-wife, still stored in a file cabinet in the back of his closet. Surely
none of this indicates the behavior of a gentleman? The woman in

question, though at least a decade older than myself, is now a mother, after all!

Additionally, I personally know of and can provide evidence for several occasions where Fred has returned used clothing to a luxury department store (including one Tom Ford tuxedo, retail value of $5,600, worn to a wedding with tags then reattached, and returned). He has also referred to his superiors and colleagues on many instances as "fucking imbeciles," "retards," and "dumb cunts."

These disturbing facts have left me with no choice but to come forward and share with you all my knowledge of this wolf in sheep's clothing. As I send this email, please know that I feel peace, as my intentions are pure.

God bless.

Yours truly,

Erika Varga
A Concerned Party

PS: Fred also has a deep obsession with pornography which I believe to be of moral and possibly even legal concern. I personally have verified that Fred has several videos on his computer that show instances of potential unwanted train groping in Japan. If any of you are acquainted with the women in these videos (I have attached screenshots), please direct them to this email address.

———————

At first, he was certain he was having a heart attack. All the signs he remembered were there: nausea, shortness of breath. A severe, crushing pain in the chest.

He forced himself to put down his phone and count to twenty.

Then, he read the message again. The second round the pain was even more acute, and he thought he might pass out but for the beating logic of self-preservation. He knew he had to immediately face the worst of it, to begin damage control. Starting with: Who was on the distribution list?

At initial glance, he was largely relieved to see friends and family. Serena Chang, the luxury goods–obsessed wife of one of Fred's few close friends, with whom Erika had hit it off at a dinner party. Kate, though thankfully not Linda. Nora, Erika's sister, whom he didn't care about at all.

He decided to allow himself a moment of respite before turning his attention to the remainder of the list. Closing his eyes, he tried to summon some gratefulness for being alive.

And then there it was, as he knew it would be. Marching one by one, a nightmarish procession of the most prominent names in his industry. Kleiner Perkins. Greylock. Tata Packer. Andreessen Horowitz. The BCC line, its very presence a blank void to fill in with the worst of his imagination.

A deep intake through his nostrils, which were quivering. How had Erika procured all these emails? He didn't even have most of them! It wasn't as if she regularly mingled with the financier crowd. . . . Was there a chance they could be fake? Fred took a closer look, suddenly hopeful. Everything looked to be spelled correctly, the names looked real—

And then in a vicious burst he recalled the pile of business cards she'd amassed over the years, the creams and ecrus and occasional clear vinyls, all stacked in a corner on the dresser. Her persistent diligence in asking whom she should be impressed by, as she skimmed Wikipedia profiles. Collecting and researching and sorting—for *him*, he'd assumed at the time. Jesus! Fuck!

His phone chimed in his hand, flashing a name he knew he couldn't ignore.

"Dirty *dog*. Good morning from Bangkok."

Fred did a quick, desperate scan of the message but didn't see Reagan's name. The fucking BCC line! "The email?" he asked. His voice came out quaking, too high.

"I'm afraid to say it's making the rounds in Asia. It's been a slow morning."

Fred's heart began to beat with extreme violence, as if attempting to untether itself from its doomed accommodations. "How bad? Did you see there's a Bloomberg reporter on copy?"

"And the *Wall Street Journal*. Freelancer."

"OhmyfuckingGod ohmyfuckingGod." He had to sit down. In the bathroom where he'd secluded himself, the toilet lid made a loud slamming sound. The noise attracted Deborah, who poked her head in. Fred made a shooing movement with his hands, mouthing *sorry*. She shot him an annoyed look but closed the door.

"Don't worry, I don't think the *Journal* will pick it up."

"Are you kidding me?" Until the very recent past, the reading and dissemination of such emails like the one he'd just received had been one of Fred's preferred sources of entertainment. Each time another celebrated name was dethroned, felled by a neglected mistress or nosy board member, the schadenfreude was near orgasmic. "If two reporters were on it, my life is over."

"That was before, when Gawker was still operational and there was less concern over libel suits. Top-tier media are more cautious now, especially with what I assume are, ah—unsubstantiated and un-truthful claims." Reagan cleared his throat. "It's actually early morning here; I've got a whole list of things to take care of. So let me get to the point. I'm calling to check on the reaction from your management. Any blowback? I didn't see anyone I recognized from Lion on the email. Any problems at home base?"

Fred scanned the recipients list again. "No, I don't think she sent it to anyone at work. She doesn't have their contact information."

"Good, good. That's the most important thing. Don't worry about anything else."

"But what about the next few days? What if this goes"—nearly choking on the next word, releasing it in a gasp—*"viral?"*

"Oh no." Reagan chuckled. "I don't think so. Don't get me wrong, it's definitely making its way through a certain circuit, but it won't hit the mainstream. You'll be fine. You know Jack and I think the world of you, but you're not exactly a public figure. And Lion isn't nearly as sexy a name as, say, Motley or Goldman Sachs. Without those elements, the email is dead in the water."

Reagan's words were calming, rational. Fred pushed against them, to eke out any last scraps of reassurance. "Maybe not the mainstream, but what about everyone else? You got the email. What about all the other people who were on it, and the people they're going to forward it to?"

"You know, all of us really do sympathize with you. The stuff your ex is accusing you of—and again, I'm not saying you *did* any of it—even if you did, well, it isn't as if a good portion of us aren't guilty of the same, hmm? What was her name? Erika? How would she like for her internet browsing history to be published, I wonder? Right. This will be done and forgotten in a few days."

"I'm going to kill her."

"Take a piece of advice from me." Reagan's voice turned serious. "Do not speak to her again. Someone like that, you end all communication, immediately. Witches feed off attention. Take away the broom, they can't fly. All right?"

WHEN KATE FINALLY ARRIVED, HIS AUNT TOOK HER LEAVE.

"I'll be back tomorrow," Deborah promised. Then, speaking directly to Kate, "You must not let your father out of your sight." She'd already made Fred swear to the same earlier, but now she seemed doubtful of his ability to execute. "This is very important. If he wakes, get him food and water. If he's grouchy, massage his feet and legs. Though if he needs to use the bathroom, have Fred do it. It's better for his self-esteem not to have you see him."

"We promise, Auntie," Kate said, widening her eyes at Fred. As soon as Deborah left, she added, "She's a bit paranoid, isn't she?"

"It worked for her all these years," he said. "Maybe we all need a little more paranoia in our lives." If he'd been more proactive, better at being suspicious, maybe he wouldn't be in this situation now. He used to think Erika collecting those business cards was cute, a compliment of sorts, like a dog laying unburied trash at your feet. He should have remembered his lesson from Charlene, that in a woman's hands, any information could be weaponized.

"So . . . ," Kate said, as she dropped eye contact. "I got the email."

"I know. I figured." This was something else he'd have to do, Fred saw: reassure those Erika's missive had targeted, comfort them as they briefly inhabited the pit of his shame. "We can talk about it, don't worry."

She exhaled. "I only read it once I was in the car heading home from the airport. Sorry it took me so long to get here. I had to stop by the house, see the kids and Mom, and one thing led to another. . . . But how are you doing? Are you miserable? Of course you are. But do you want to talk about it?"

Kate was always best in a crisis; Fred suddenly felt acutely grateful that she was here. He couldn't remember the last time it had been only the two of them, just hanging out. "Maybe later, if Dad still has some alcohol. You think it all got thrown out in the Great Health Purge?"

"I'll go look," Kate said, rising. "I've become very acquainted with the kitchen."

"How are you?" he called after her. "Hearing some bad news from others would cheer me up. Any catastrophes befalling mutual friends? What's the deal now with Denny?"

"What do you mean, what's the deal? It's a disaster. Everything's a disaster."

"You know that Dad's got way less than we thought, right? How are you going to fund Denny's harem?" By the way her shoulders slumped, he knew he'd gone too far. "Whoa." His sister, as far as he knew, wasn't a crier. "I'm sorry. I didn't mean it like that, I'm just a dick. You know I have a bad habit of saying thoughtless shit. What you're going through right now must be scary."

"It's not that," Kate said in a strangled voice. She returned with two glasses of red wine on a black leather tray, along with the rest of the bottle and a bowl of cashews. She sat, not looking at him, while she blew her nose and composed her face, before continuing. "I'm not that scared. Just disappointed. You think you're so special, so exceptional, and then your marriage ends up collapsing for the same stupid generic reasons as everyone else's."

"Hey, I'm divorced, too, remember? Now we can match."

"Mine is way worse. Do you remember how when we were younger we thought people who were divorced with young kids had totally fucked up their lives? Well, now that's going to be me. Of course I love Ethan and Ella, but when I think back to how flippant we were about the decision to have them. . . ." She groaned. "I don't want to talk about it anymore. Yeah, you're a thoughtless dick."

Fred picked up the bottle of Cabernet. "You know, I think this is from when Charlene and I got married."

"I totally forgot! You mean when you had to do that Chinese banquet for all of Mom and Dad's friends who couldn't make it to Hawaii?"

"Exactly. As soon as dessert was served, a bunch of old Asian people started grabbing up all the unopened wine bottles. I guess Dad was one of them. All the flowers got cleaned out too." Including the fairly expensive vases they'd been arranged in, purchased on sale at Pottery Barn, because Charlene had wanted their wedding to be a cut above the normal Chinese banquet. She'd been furious about the missing vases, which she'd meant to save and insisted was evidence of his parents' tacky friends. "Mom made me do the banquet. Charlene and I had this huge fight, because she didn't want to have one, and Mom won because she claimed that since they'd gone to all their friends' kids' weddings, they would lose face if they didn't reciprocate. And now she doesn't even talk to most of those people. Isn't that crazy?"

Instead of responding, Kate knocked back an enormous gulp of wine. She bent forward, elbows on knees, kneading the stem between her hands.

"There's something I'm considering sharing with you," she said. "I've been debating with myself ever since I arrived. I think I want to, but you've got to promise not to overreact. It might freak you out."

"As opposed to everything else going on right now?"

"I'm serious. If I tell you, you have to swear to stay calm."

"Okay, okay."

"Swear!"

"I swear. Jesus. I forgot what a hardass you are."

"And another thing. You have to promise not to ask about how I came across what I'm about to show you. It wasn't something I meant to capture intentionally."

God, she was being dramatic. "I can't take the suspense any longer. My body might give out. It's been through enough in the last few hours."

"Fine." Kate went to her bag and retrieved her laptop. She opened the screen. A clear video feed: Full color, very impressive quality. Fred made a note to ask if she knew the brand of cameras. If it was a hardware start-up, he should keep them in mind for Opus. "Just watch," she said.

To his surprise, Linda appeared. Fred squinted. "Wait. Is that your attic?"

"Yup." Kate skipped forward.

His mother held a tablet in her hands. "Hello? Is this working? *Aiyah*, I always have problems with the internet here." She stretched out her arms so that the device faced her directly. On her screen an app was open; in a bold, modern typeface, Fred read *Tigerlily*. A man's face materialized in its window. He looked to be Chinese, roughly their father's age, though this clearly wasn't Stanley.

"Who is that?" Fred asked, alarmed. "What's going on? Is this *recent?*"

"Shut up and listen."

"I miss you too," Linda was saying. "I wish you were here. I hope your work is better."

"I can't wait until we see each other again," the man replied. "A few days was not enough. The time we spend, I never feel such passion."

"Why would Mom and this guy be talking like this . . . oh my God, *gross!*"

"What did I say about shutting up?" Kate jabbed him. "Focus!" She returned to the video. On the screen Linda was looking about nervously, as if she suspected that at some point in the near future her children would be assessing this very interaction. "I told you before, Winston, I don't like such very romantic talk. If you have to say it, you can write to me."

"Sweetheart, you know sometimes I just can't help myself. Where are you, anyway? I don't recognize this room."

"I'm at my daughter's house. I am helping her babysit for the week. I'm worried, you know her husband is gone, and now there is this blond woman she talks to, she thinks I don't notice—"

"You get the idea," Kate interrupted, quickly shutting the screen. "But if you don't, there are several other segments I can play. I thought that given the day you've had, I would save you the exposure."

"Who is that dude? Where did he come from? Does Mom have a *boyfriend?*"

"From what I've been able to gather—from several painful extended viewings—his name is Winston Chu and he lives somewhere abroad, though I'm not sure where. And yes, if you couldn't already tell, they're in some sort of romantic relationship. I know I said I'd spare details, but I will share that he uses the word *lovers* several times."

"Ew." Fred immediately worked to banish this disturbing knowledge from his consciousness. Though it was plausible that Linda didn't believe sexual relations were even possible without marriage; perhaps she and Winston were just eating consecutive meals together and sitting side by side on the couch while watching black-and-white movies at night. "How long have you known about this?"

"I just found out. I checked the recording, almost on a whim, right after I finished some work emails when I got home. As soon as I saw what it was, I went to my car to watch. Obviously Mom didn't see."

Fred wondered why his sister had a video feed in her attic. What kind of perverted games had she and Denny been into?

"There's more," Kate said. "He asks her for money."

"*What?*"

"Well, not exactly, but he mentions a condo development in San Jose, which he claims would be the perfect investment property. Although from what the proposed arrangement sounds like, it'd be her buying it and him living in it."

"So this guy is some kind of gold digger? We have to do something! Should we confront her?"

"Let's not act impulsively." Kate reached for the Cabernet and looked surprised to find it empty. "I wanted the two of us to discuss this first. That app they were using, Tigerlily? It's a dating site. I looked it up, and it seems like some sort of start-up. I wanted to ask if you'd heard of it."

Fred thought he had, vaguely, but couldn't place the name. Dating was hot—he probably saw ten proposals a month. "I'll look into it. But I still don't understand what you're suggesting. What do you actually want to do about this guy right now?"

Kate was quiet. "I think we should leave it alone." She hesitated. "At least for now. Mom seems happy. Maybe she already understands the trade-offs."

"Are you out of your mind?" Fred didn't understand why his sister was so calm. "From what I'm hearing, our mother is in a romantic relationship with a stranger we know nothing about, who might be trying to exploit her. *Sound familiar?* This guy is a male version of Mary, have you considered that? He could bankrupt her!"

She laughed. "I think the term *bankrupt* is a bit of an exaggeration."

"Really? How is Mom going to afford a condo in San Jose? It's not exactly small change, you know. She's retired! There's no more income coming in. She'll have to sell the house or cash out her retirement savings." Both of his inheritances were slipping down the drain, Fred thought, into the clutches of Asian temptresses, male and female. "And let's not forget, the Palo Alto house is probably already mortgaged to the hilt. Like Dad's was, before this whole Mary fiasco. That's why there's no money left in *that* honeypot."

He felt a vague satisfaction in seeing her flinch. Then she leaned back, cradling her hands behind her head. "You're wrong, Fred. Mom has a lot. More than enough for a condo in San Jose. Probably more than enough for a few. I doubt the Palo Alto house still has a mortgage, and if it does, it's purely for tax purposes. You know she just bought a Porsche?"

"A Porsche?" Fred flashed back to all the times Linda had mentioned her investments over the years, musings he'd dismissed as the ramblings of a casual retail investor. The sort who waded in at market peaks to buy overhyped technology stocks, only to stand helplessly by as they cratered to the floor. "What kind?"

"I don't know. It had four doors."

"Did the model say anything at the end? Turbo, maybe, or S?"

"Maybe a number and a letter, but I don't remember what they were."

"A 4S." That alone was a $40,000 premium. "So *Mom* is the rich one?"

"Well, by Bay Area standards maybe not so much, but compared to Dad, certainly. She's a really good investor, I guess, very level-headed. She keeps her cool when the market is going crazy, doesn't get nervous—that's what that gossipy advisor at Schwab is always yapping, anyway. You know I buy all the stocks she tells me to now? I wanted to sell my vested X shares after that last big dip, which freaked me out, but she convinced me not to. So I held, and now it's all gone back up along with Google and Amazon. She told me once that she has more now alone than she and Dad ever had together. I wonder whether that's why he told Mary he had all that money. Because you know how he liked everyone to think he was the financial genius. And she let him save face on that, with all their friends, even after the divorce. Even though she obviously kind of hates him."

For a while they sat in companionable silence, pondering Linda and her mysteries. "Remember when Dad killed my bird?" Fred said at last.

"The parakeet?" Kate stuck out her lip. "I hate thinking about that. I think I blocked out the memory all these years. The poor thing; that should definitely go down as one of the top five crazy Stanley moments. On par with when he said my jeans were too tight, and he went to my closet and cut all the pants in half with gardening shears." She cocked her head. "What made you bring that up?"

"I don't know. Just thinking about Mom and how much she loathes Dad. Why do you think she didn't leave him earlier? Would you have let Denny get away with even half the stuff Dad pulled when we were growing up?"

"I'd like to say no, but it's probably best for me karma-wise not to armchair quarterback our parents right now. God knows what Ethan and Ella are going to say about me when they get older."

She looked depressed. "You'll be fine," Fred said quickly. "The Huang lunacy gene is limited to the males." When she failed to respond, he tried again. "Didn't you get your own bird at some point?"

Kate nodded slowly. "A green parakeet. I named him Sprite, because yours was Coke."

Fred had forgotten that the birds had names. "Whatever happened to Sprite? I can't remember. Did Dad kill him too?"

She groaned. "Please, let's stick to only attributing animal deaths to our father that can be substantiated."

There was a foreign creaking noise and they looked toward Stanley, who was still in the deep sleep of morphine. Fred craned his neck to survey the room. Mary stood at the foot of the stairs, wearing a gaudy pink robe. She had clearly been expecting to find them gone. "You're not leaving?" she asked. "Deborah, she already go."

"We're staying here tonight," Kate said in a pleasant voice. "Remember how you complained we weren't spending enough time with Dad?"

Fred returned Mary's cold glare. He could hit this woman, he thought. All day he'd been resisting the urge to indulge his anger, the sheer wrath Stanley himself had never held back. He understood for the first time how good it must have felt, each time Stanley fed his weakness. Would his father approve of what he was thinking, if he knew how much his wife had yearned for him to die alone, surrounded by strangers, in an unfamiliar place? But then there was no use in telling Stanley, it was too pointless and cruel; yet another responsibility skirted in his passing.

Mary considered Fred as if she could read his thoughts perfectly. Then she walked over to Stanley—carefully avoiding the items strewn across the ground, the rolled-up sleeping bags and pillows and laptops—and climbed into bed, pulling over the blankets to cover both their bodies. Fred could see her rubbing Stanley's limp shoulders as he snored, his back to them all.

Sometime after midnight, after Kate had crept to the bathroom to take a late shower, Fred fell into a deep sleep. When he woke, it was to Stanley pressing the electronic bell, sounding the alert that he had to urinate. Kate's eyes were closed, and Mary had gone back upstairs, to the comfort and sleep of her own bed. Fred went to his father and slid an arm under his back, slowly moving him upright.

CHAPTER 19

LINDA

In person, Winston looked smaller than he appeared on-screen. And older.

When Linda saw her paramour for the first time in the flesh—framed in the doorway of his hotel, some soulless scummy property in Santa Clara—she'd been surprised to discover missing on her boyfriend's physical person a good chunk of hair and several inches of height. She'd meant to wear her favorite shoes that morning, a pair of patent Ferragamos with a two-inch heel, but she had swapped them out last minute for loafers. It was the right decision, because even in flats she was slightly taller than Winston. Her height allowed just enough of a vantage to see across the entirety of his head, an angle he'd carefully avoided during their video chats, she realized, presumably to hide his overwhelming baldness. The few strands that remained were obviously dyed, and Winston had made the mistake of selecting the jet-black hue of his youth, which created the unfortunate effect of a large spider tenuously clutching the top of a beige spotted egg. He was clad in an austere navy woolen vest and trousers, a nod to her strict advance guidance on wardrobe, though she noticed his shirt had ostentatious buttons, shiny black faux mother of pearl.

She was instantly awash in regret, that she'd pushed so aggressively to meet in person. Over the screen and phone Winston had at least been a blank tapestry, a partially revealed canvas upon which she'd been able to imprint on its hidden remainders her most optimistic of desires. His in-person absence endearing him all the further, as it allowed her to ascribe the noblest of motives, while sweeping aside any lingering disappointments. His problems with financial management were isolated and remote; a tendency to drone easily sustained with an issue of *Forbes* placed discreetly on a stand just behind the tablet. In real life, however, there was no escaping the entirety of the person, this man to whom she had recently begun to refer (given his significant prodding) as her soul mate. Why had she been in such a hurry?

The accommodations, too, were unexpected. Winston's stay at the Diamond Palace had been prompted last minute, after Winston claimed the hotel's owner, a prior acquaintance, would be greatly insulted were he to lodge elsewhere. As soon as Linda saw the property, however, it was obvious its name exaggerated its charms, almost to the point of recklessness. The room was small and drab, the sort with clear plastic cups wrapped for hygiene, which served as an inadvertent reminder as to the relative sterility of the overall space; during her brief interlude inside she'd maintained a firm grip on her handbag, unwilling to set it on any surfaces.

Linda knew she should be thankful for the Diamond Palace, regardless of its squalor. Before its appearance she'd been so stressed by the thought of Winston staying at the house that she'd had to take a sleeping pill nearly every night. Her hands kept twisting nervously at the duvet otherwise, as she lay in the dark pondering various logistics, with the idea repeatedly implanting itself that she had to urgently empty her bladder as soon as slumber crept near. Upon returning to bed, she would then toss back and forth, before giving up and reaching for her tablet for another game of mah jong.

She wouldn't be able to do that if Winston were there, Linda reminded herself—she should train herself to lie peacefully still, so as not to violate the invisible boundary set in the middle of the bed. There were likely a plethora of accumulated habits that would have to be jettisoned—it wouldn't be hospitable to hog the blankets like she usually did or inflict her breath on him in the morning, like some rotting old dragon. And she definitely would have to learn to sleep on her right side, which was her least preferred but the best in terms of snoring.

Was it so wrong to want her own bedroom, her own space? It wasn't as if she'd ever been a *talker*, the sort of wife to sit up in bed with her hair around her shoulders, recounting the petty tribulations and victories of her day. So many of her waking hours were already spent in some physically compromising position or another—shoving her body into hard restaurant chairs, suppressing flatulence in public, crossing her legs whenever she sneezed. Increasingly her only period of real refuge was at night, when she could finally lie down under whichever covers she had chosen for the day. (Linda collected duvets and blankets like other women collected handbags. She only ever bought natural fibers and excellent thread counts, and she had variations suitable for five-degree bands of temperature.)

So when Winston announced he'd be staying at the Diamond Palace, Linda had felt immense relief. She'd made her peace with the idea of his sleeping over by then; after all, it was only a weekend. But given her anxiety, the best outcome would have been for Winston to spend his nights somewhere else, and the fact that events had naturally turned out that way, she thought, was a very good omen.

LATER THAT AFTERNOON, WINSTON ARRIVED AT THE HOUSE. HE'D showered and changed to an acceptable pair of khakis and what looked to be a Ralph Lauren polo, though Linda noted that the horse appeared blotchier than what she thought was normal. They greeted each other with an easier familiarity than earlier in the day, and she felt the tension in her neck dissipate. Upon entering, he presented her with a bottle of wine and a small wrapped box. "Open it!" he exclaimed.

Linda demurred, afraid it might be something extravagant, with all the accompanying expectations of physical affection. Instead, she led him to the garden, where they sat on her favorite bench (purchased at Home Depot and stained by Linda herself on a sunny afternoon). "This is my treasure," she said, pointing to a Japanese maple that currently sported bright red foliage. "Every season the leaves change color."

Winston took the time to carefully admire the tree. "You have a wonderful sense of landscape," he said. "It's in the perfect spot. One day, I'll buy us a big new house with a spacious backyard, like the ones in Kyoto. Even though I hate the Japanese, they have very elegant gardens."

"I don't need a new house." Linda used to dream of a husband who would build her a home, a tranquil retreat nothing like the deafening monstrosity she'd endured for years in Cupertino. Now, she wanted less space, not more. "I'm comfortable here."

Winston took her hand and squeezed it. "Why couldn't I have met you earlier? So much misery would have been saved. I'm beginning to believe my former wife has no other goal in life but to make mine a living torture."

He launched into his latest grievance, the overdue payment of yet another Yale-related bill. Linda listened without input. She'd long graduated from that stage of initial curiosity, when she had prodded Winston to elaborate on his ex's profligate spending and other associated faults; she'd been so active with her questioning, and Winston so eager to play the victim, that she felt she'd already eviscerated the poor woman to near completion. Winston's ex now lived in a small studio in Jersey Village, having lost the five-bedroom in River Oaks he'd left her with when they first divorced. He'd purchased the condo in cash, way outside the legal obligations of their divorce agreement— another reason he was so overstretched financially.

"I couldn't have her homeless," Winston had explained. "My children stay with her." But at least he'd kept the property title in his name, which Linda approved of. Stanley would have never thought of such a clever and responsible gesture, which was why his affairs were in such ruin.

"My ex-husband, he has been trying to contact me," she said. "I'm sick of it."

Just yesterday morning she'd had to suffer through another attempt, when she'd picked up the house phone while stirring her morning oatmeal, wincing when she heard Stanley on the other end. She'd been forced to inquire about his health, setting him off on a garbled tangent about the foundation, a headache she thought she'd fully dispensed with.

"Can you come over?" he asked. "When can you visit?"

"I. Cannot. Hear. You. Stanley!" she'd announced, and added a "Very busy!" and hung up. Hadn't she already wasted enough of her life ministering to his problems, both real and imaginary? She refused to go over anymore unless Fred or Kate accompanied her; she wouldn't want Mary to get the wrong idea. That woman was unpredictable, crazy! She'd come somewhat unhinged after the whole nursing home scare, which had been satisfying initially, but now the situation had become overwrought. The latest update was that she was accusing Fred of stealing some sort of Rolex from Stanley's safety deposit box. Since when had Stanley ever owned a *Rolex*?

Winston didn't respond, and the silence dragged. Maybe she shouldn't have mentioned Stanley, Linda thought. Was he jealous? When she looked over, he was staring off at some undefined point in the distance, eyes glazed. Jet lag, maybe.

"Do you feel like some wine?" he asked. "I think I'll take an afternoon glass."

"I'm fine. But feel free to serve yourself." She kicked up her feet on her wicker stool and enjoyed the simple beauty of the day. Certain things were just better with a partner. When was the last time she'd come out to this bench without a book or newspaper to occupy her?

When the sky grew dark, they went inside and shared a simple dinner of dumplings and spicy cucumbers and beef noodle soup. She asked Winston questions she already knew the answers to about his time in Hong Kong, which was how she preferred to envision him—as a young man who'd endured a series of unfair hardships and who would ultimately persevere. Afterward she opened her present, a diamond Cartier pendant in the shape of a bird that could be removed from its chain and turned into a brooch, far more ostentatious an item than anything she would have chosen for herself. She felt a flush of annoyance that Winston had purchased such an expensive gift.

"Are your finances better?" she asked, and it was soon clear from his evasive explanations what the answer was, and she insisted on writing him a check. The resulting squabble over payment felt entirely transactional by the end, and Linda chastised herself for spoiling the moment. She was never good at receiving gifts; she and Stanley had struggled for too many frugal years to indulge in surprise luxuries. And afterward, when she could finally afford such things for herself, it was better to have the money in her bank account.

In the kitchen after dinner, once she'd put away the clean dishes,

Winston approached from behind and kissed her neck, which she assumed was an awkward introductory push for sex. She hadn't known how to transition—didn't want to come off as frigid, or, even more horrifying, inexperienced or disappointing. So she begged off to pour herself a glass of wine from the bottle he'd opened earlier, extricating herself from his hold, and because Linda almost never drank, the sensation of relaxation it carried arrived as a pleasant surprise, and she quickly downed her glass and poured another.

And finally in the end it was Linda who took Winston by the hand and led him to the bedroom, tired of the frightful agony of waiting. By then the alcohol was coursing through her body in such a way that she completely forgot about the ecru slip, which she'd conveniently hung on the other side of the bathroom door. They'd simply undressed underneath the covers and then, well.

It was over with and better than her worst nightmares and lesser than her greatest fantasies. After an appropriate amount of time, Winston rose and departed for his hotel room, leaving her the privacy of her bed.

———————

The next afternoon they went to visit an acquaintance of Winston's, a former colleague turned property developer in San Jose. "You will love Arman, I'm sure of it," Winston said. "A very high-quality person." As they approached his rented Jaguar he rushed forward to open the passenger-side door, and Linda was temporarily startled. She recovered and descended into the seat delicately, swinging her legs together in one smooth movement. This was something she could get used to, she thought; after a few times it would be like second nature, and she would automatically adjust her stride as she neared the door. That was how relationships were formed.

Arman met them at his latest work site, a mixed-use residential and commercial project a mile off of Guadalupe Parkway. Winston had made several references to the development before his trip, chattering about his fantasy of one day living there. Though Linda had mostly tuned out these musings; she considered the daydreams of others to be the least interesting form of conversation.

The short Armenian greeted them with iced coffee and grappled Winston in a bear hug. "This guy," he announced to Linda. "This *guy*!" He insisted on giving them a tour, boasting about occupancy and making brash claims about build quality. Afterward he and Winston took a short walk, leaving Linda to drink her coffee alone at a table, though she didn't feel excluded. It was gratifying to observe Winston in his natural habitat, among friends—he appeared younger somehow, more dynamic. The jocular patting, hands in pockets, confident posturing—these were all reassuring indicators, to be considered when he lapsed back into sappy extravagance.

At 5:30 p.m., they left for dinner. She wasn't familiar with the part of San Jose the development was in (why would she be? Such bad school districts), and the drive took longer than expected. By the time they arrived at China Garden, everyone else was already seated, and to Linda it felt as if each pair of eyes immediately locked on their entrance. She saw Candy take in Winston's navy blazer with the gold buttons and his ascot tie, which he'd insisted on foppishly tying in the car. She had thought it made him look like an aspiring yachtsman, someone who scrimped to buy a country club membership, but she'd seen no way of informing him of such without hurting his pride.

There was a charged quality to the air: two women were debuting new partners, more gossip than the group usually saw in years. Linda was satisfied to note that Teddy, the alleged future husband of Shirley Chang, was at most the same height if not shorter than Winston and had the same pitch-black pomade hairstyle—it must be a trend with older Asian men, she thought, just like how all the women simultaneously emerged with the same enormous perms after sixty. Teddy

was quiet and self-effacing when badgered about his much-touted-by-
Shirley Princeton teaching credentials, and Winston largely took the
same cue, except for spontaneous moments of ardor: intertwining his
hand with hers, rubbing her shoulders at the table, swiveling her head
to meet his for a lip lock. "I love you," he kept whispering in her ear,
which despite her best efforts she was only able to respond to with a
smiling grimace. Did they look ridiculous?

Soon dinner reverted to a version of their usual gatherings: a smattering of Taiwanese politics mixed with vague plans of an undetermined future group trip to Guangzhou; gossip of the various financial
and moral misdeeds of mutual acquaintances. Flitting through the air
was a certain excitement—the tacit understanding that fortune was
smiling, had selected each of them to participate in pleasures that were
already being denied to many of their contemporaries, sometimes permanently so. The heady atmosphere amplified by the two bottles of
Syrah Winston had insisted on opening, which everyone had taken an
initial sip of to be polite but now was consuming in steady amounts.

No one ever brought alcohol to a Chinese restaurant, Linda had
informed Winston, at least not in California and at the sort of establishment they were going to, but he'd been emphatic, maintaining that
the vineyard was a hidden treasure. The waiter had looked nonplussed
when presented the bottles—at first Linda was afraid he thought it
a gift for the staff—but then he'd consulted with the manager, who
brought over eight water glasses. She made a note to check whether
they dared charge corkage when the bill arrived.

During the course of dinner Linda noticed that Winston was relentless in his hovering over the beverages, zealously refilling teacups
and glasses seconds after they became empty. The habit touched her.
It was obvious he had never been taught proper table manners and
had instead memorized rules by rote. Due to his vigorous attentions,
she soon had to visit the bathroom, an event she'd originally wanted
to delay until they were back home. Leaving Winston alone, she felt,

would be like abandoning a talkative goldfish in the middle of a pond inhabited by hungry piranhas. But eventually her weakened, aged bladder betrayed her, and by the time she returned, Winston was indeed holding conversational court over the table.

"It's a fantastic investment," he was saying. "Very modern. Green is the new trend. Renewable energy, right? And there are so many young people in the area, big companies moving in. I would be putting money in myself, if I had the available capital. I've been telling Linda that at the very least she should buy a condo. Perfect timing! What do you think, my love?"

"What sort of mixed-use development?" Jackson leaned forward and settled his elbows on the table. "Do you know what companies yet? Is this the new Amazon Silicon Valley office?"

"What do you mean, *if I had the available capital*?" Shirley asked.

"Where did you go to college?" Candy Gu interrogated. "And what year did you say you graduated?"

Linda's stomach gave an unpleasant flip. The building again. Despite Winston's vocal enthusiasms, she hadn't found much to like about the development. The location in downtown San Jose was less than ideal—investors had been trying to wring cash out of the area for decades, with paltry success—and the lessees so far were underwhelming: small businesses she'd never heard of, without a single anchor tenant of the sort needed to attract and sustain traffic to a center of its size. And she'd been far from impressed by the model condo, though Arman had repeatedly given his assurances that the cheap carpet and countertops could each be upgraded, that a full selection of flooring options was available. "Of course you'd want something better," he'd crooned. "It's because you have *taste*." But then she'd walked onto the balcony and noticed how flimsy the bearings were, alarming on a two-hundred-unit complex. Eventually a few would give way, and then they'd all have to be redone to code. Didn't these people know anything?

Cut it out, she wanted to scream. She already knew none of her friends would invest. If there existed a single topic local Taiwan University graduates were universally expert on, it was high-quality Bay Area real estate. But she and Winston hadn't yet developed that inner code between couples for when it was time for the other party to shut up, so he prattled on for nearly five minutes, to the point where even Shirley Chang looked bored, having ceased mining the diatribe for interesting morsels of gossip.

Finally, Yvonne intervened. "Winston," she said. "I'm such a dummy with real estate; Jackson takes care of everything. Maybe we can discuss another topic I can actually contribute to. Otherwise, I'm sure to feel bad about myself. Help this dumb old lady out, will you?"

Afterward, when it seemed as though the conversation was deliberately being kept away from Winston and thus her, volleyed between the other parties by unspoken agreement, Linda sat in rigid silence. Waves of humiliation over being the least popular group at the table warred with the relief of no longer having to engage. Despite her agony, Winston, the social butterfly of the two, seemed utterly unaware of their banishment: stroking her hand, whispering tender words; continuing to pepper himself throughout the conversation, the few instances he could. At one point in his excitement he knocked over her wine, spilling its contents into her lap. "Oh no!" he cried, as he clutched for a napkin. "I'm so embarrassed! I'm a clumsy fool!"

Yvonne materialized beside her. "Do you need a stain remover pen?" she asked. "Here's mine; you can take it to the bathroom."

"There's no need," Linda replied calmly. The red blotch continued its merciless progress on her cream Akris skirt—given the delicate fabric, she already knew it was a goner. She had watched Winston for some time as he waved his hands in conversation, observing the path his palm made with each gesture, its narrowing proximity to her glass. Had understood the inevitable conclusion, yet done nothing.

After all, how could you stop an event already fated to happen?

CHAPTER 20

FRED

Just over eight weeks earlier—as he had sat hunched over in his leatherette seat, two rows from the back of the plane on the four-hour connection to Bali from Hong Kong—Fred had opened his Smythson journal and scrawled out his goals for the year:

1. Extract full utility from Founders' Retreat (network with at least five high-potential targets per event, be photographed walking outside—note to wear clearly printed name tag, for ease of Getty Images caption)
2. Promotion to senior managing director (or lateral move to more prestigious firm)
3. Develop Opus opportunity and protect position from encroachment

4. Buy single-family home: Menlo Park, Woodside, possibly Atherton fixer-upper

5. Increase public profile/be top-ranked search result for Fred Huang. Land keynote speech (how??)

After the events of the day, however, certainly one through three and possibly all five were in serious jeopardy, a spectacular domino collapse of everything important in his life.

Erika's letter had taken exactly one week to reach Lion, a period during which—contrary to Reagan's predictions of an ephemeral shelf life—it had first meandered through a smattering of high school and college acquaintances, as well as what Fred assumed to be the near entirety of his nine-hundred-person Harvard Business School class. During that time he'd oscillated between terror and annoyance, batting away inquiries from distant friends who felt compelled to "check in," all while fervently praying for another yet another stay of execution at work, each day bringing him closer to the fantasy that Erika's email might bypass Lion altogether, as new public embarrassments replaced his own. By the end of day six he'd thought this might have actually been achieved; a rare spot of sunny fortune in an otherwise unstoppable run of shitty events.

Until this morning. Day seven.

When Fred walked into the usual conference room for Griffin Keeles's Tuesday Investment Roundtable—five minutes early instead of the usual four minutes late he had deliberately calculated to be of maximum irritation to the time-obsessed Brit—he did a double take at the sight of Leland Wang, who he hadn't known was in town, at the head of the table. By the time he registered that there were only two others in the room—Griffin, and a middle-aged woman bearing a hazy familiarity—the mental fire alarms had begun to clang.

"This is a casual conversation," Griffin began, as he motioned for Fred to sit. "So I don't want anyone to misconstrue the purpose of this meeting. However, to be prudent, I've asked Maria to join us. She's here to represent you and your interests, Fred."

The woman stroked a red folder and allowed a thin smile. "Good morning."

Ah, so that's who she was. Maria Watkins, the fiftysomething-ish so-called head of human resources, who worked remotely most days while drafting the draconian policies that required everyone else to be in the office. No way this battle-axe would be representing anything close to his concerns, Fred knew—more likely that she would leap across the table and stab him deep in the heart, all in the name of corporate interest. "Now, Fred," Griffin continued. "As you know, here at Lion we have a very strict moral code. One that was pioneered, of course, by our founder." He served a respectful nod toward Leland, who remained engrossed in his phone. "Fred, you must be aware that there's a certain communication making its rounds, in which a former . . . acquaintance of yours makes some startling allegations."

"I'm sure *you* can discern by the nature and tenor of those statements that the person is not of sound mind," Fred shot back. He had actual proof corroborating this, in the form of an email György and Anna Varga had sent acknowledging their daughter's "unstable behavior" as of late, a mea culpa prompted by Fred's changing the password on their iPad, since it was still registered to his Apple ID.

"Of course. In situations like these we want to cover every angle. Our aim is to ensure we're conducting our assessments with as much information as possible." Griffin cleared his throat. "When you first started at Lion, you were given a set of corporate guidelines. Do you remember completing this paperwork sometime during that initial week?" He gestured toward Maria, who opened the red folder and removed a stapled set of worksheets.

"No." This wasn't unusual. These days he signed almost everything placed in front of him without reading it. What was the point of wasting time with the fine print when you knew you had to sign anyway?

"Most of it is the standard boilerplate you'd find at any large company. Section 10.3 designates the full contents of your corporate email, as well as any activity on your laptop, as data owned by Lion Corp."

"Understood." Fred had always been exceedingly careful never to download porn on his laptop, so they weren't going to get him on that one; he had a separate MacBook Air at home, specifically reserved for this purpose. Its constant presence on his desk was likely how Erika had become so familiar with its contents in the first place.

"In the course of a normal review, we unfortunately discovered some concerning material. In-depth searches for reviews of massage parlors and their, ah, associated services."

Fuck! Fred cursed Kate, who had brought on this calamity, being the one to inform him of the prevalence of Asian brothels masquerading as massage outlets in the Bay Area to begin with. Her longtime hairstylist operated a few doors down from an especially notorious purveyor; as the stylist owned the salon and in fact the entire building, she was especially privy to the inner workings of its tenants. "The pimps are usually women, called *mama-sans*," Kate told him. "Of course, they don't work; they just manage the operations. And after a while the most successful girl will leave and set up shop somewhere else, sometimes right down the street. And then she becomes her own *mama-san*."

Fred had been immediately fascinated by the ruthless economic efficiency of the business model. "How do they know you're not an undercover cop?"

"Well, they get you in a room and start to massage you and see how far they can go. They'll also wait to see if you ask them for anything directly off the bat; I guess that's entrapment if you do. Then, they assess whether they think you're a narc. If they believe you're clean, they bring up whether you want to tip. Tip being the code word."

"Is this just in recent years? I don't remember seeing so many massage places in our area growing up. Or were we just oblivious?"

"Oh they were around," Kate said. For some reason, she had avoided his eyes. "But maybe in other cities."

The conversation had been merely interesting over lunch, but by the time Fred returned to work, his interest had taken on a more prurient color, and he'd hunted online for further details. A few news features on local busts, primarily in San Jose, led to a website that reviewed brothels in the manner of restaurants, where users shared graphically written overviews of services rendered and received (*High marks for girlfriend experience, except for very beginning—too obvious a show of counting cash inside envelope*). The discovery ate up the rest of the afternoon, though Fred was certain he'd never even enlarged a photograph (that required a premium subscription).

"I visited those websites from links in a *San Francisco Chronicle* article. I did not engage further."

"Unfortunately, given our corporate bylaws, the access of such portals is enough. But then there's also the length of time spent on each of the sites, which appears to be substantial, as well as the numerous subpages visited. And certain search terms that were entered, we assume with the aim of viewing content featuring specific acts. . . ."

That was when Fred knew for certain that they had come for him, had lined up the cannons in advance.

It took an additional forty minutes for them to strip everything away, wipe clean all evidence of his existence at the place he had spent the majority of his waking hours for the past nine years. Termination at the end of the day, with the remainder of his vacation to be cashed out the next pay period; his laptop, which Maria had pointed to as if infected with leprosy, was company property, to be turned in when he left the building.

When it was over Fred called Jack, who didn't answer. Not surprisingly, neither did Reagan. Fred hadn't been able to reach him for several days now. He wondered if Reagan had known what was coming, had watched the journey of Erika's email as it multiplied and spun, concluding that at some point it would inevitably pool at the feet of Leland Wang. Leland, and that idiot Maximilian he was now installing in Fred's place at Opus. Leland, who'd barely uttered a word during the entire ordeal except to parrot a quick phrase he'd no doubt cribbed from some famous person's Wikipedia page: "Personnel is policy."

And what sort of policy was that, Fred thought, when you fired good workers and elevated your own cretinous son?

He could have left the office immediately, but he decided to transfer the remainder of his contacts and important emails from his laptop. He had two meetings left for the day, including an alumni interview for Harvard Business School; Fred figured he might as well show the prospective candidate a living portrait of a less-publicly-touted HBS career. He was informed by the front reception that the applicant had arrived right as he was almost finished with his technology housekeeping. The only item left was Erika's manifesto, which had been sent to his work address. After a moment's hesitation, he forwarded it to his personal account.

Fred would have overlooked the man in the lobby had he not been the only person waiting. He was used to prospective students being in their early twenties, a by-product of the arms race between the business, medical, and law schools to capture future Zuckerbergs in their infancy. "Josh Stern?" he asked.

"Indeed," the man said, and he stood. Fred was taken aback. Stern was maybe five four at most, a stature he was used to among Asians but less so with white men. More so, he was *old*—Fred's own age at least. Was HBS losing its touch? Maybe this guy was from a rich family. He did have a super Jewish last name.

"Should we go into your office?" A rather direct question, for an interviewee. Definitely wealthy. No manners or respect for those in senior positions.

"Of course." Fred directed him to the space, which now appeared embarrassingly spartan. On the desk stood a solitary plastic crate, the contents of which were all he intended to leave with at the end of the day.

Stern didn't appear to notice the barren surroundings. Instead, he leaned back in his chair and smoothly swung shut the door with his hand. "As you may have noticed, I'm a bit outside of the stereotypical profile of a Harvard Business School applicant," he said.

"Well, I had thought, but . . ." Fred let his voice trail. Who the hell was this guy?

The man sat back forward. "Mr. Huang, my name is Josh Stern, though I'm not currently interviewing for any business schools. I work for the Federal Bureau of Investigation, based out of the Manhattan office. I'm here in the Bay Area this week with several of my colleagues from the SEC, conducting a coordinated investigation into wire fraud and money laundering, among a comprehensive list of other items." He paused. "Are you aware of an investment entity recently formed between Lion and an outside party based in Thailand, currently referred to as Opus?"

Fred's knees gave a violent wobble. "Yes." Weren't you supposed to provide the least possible amount of information in these sorts of situations? What did rich people do on TV?

Stern cracked his knuckles and eyed him as if he knew what he was thinking. "This is not an official conversation, Mr. Huang, nor is it one that has particular legal standing, so I would advise, if you're looking after your best interests, to be open and transparent."

"Uh . . . okay." Could Stern be lying? But then Fred thought there must be some rule about entrapment, like with the undercover cops and the brothels. Besides, he didn't even know why the agent had come. "Okay," Fred repeated. "Yes. Understood."

"Are you aware that on January thirtieth, a payment of $20 million was made to the legal pooled holding account of Draper Carlyle by the Opus parent entity in Thailand, followed by another attempted balloon payment of $855 million?"

"No!" He felt a streak of panic. "No, I had no idea. I mean, I knew that they were supposed to be funding an initial tranche of $200 million, and we, I mean Lion, would be putting in our agreed-upon tranche of $20 million, and that it would all be kept in a holding account until the fund was launched. But that was the extent."

"Extent of what?"

"Extent of my knowledge. Listen, have you spoken to Reagan Kwon? Because he knows a great deal more about this than I do."

"That would be very nice, but for the fact that Reagan Kwon has disappeared. If you've had any contact with his person since last week, it would be viewed as very cooperative to inform me of such now, along with the details of your conversation."

Oh, shit. "Has something happened to him?"

"Mr. Kwon is one of the key players we are investigating, along with several other individuals in the Thai finance ministry, in the embezzlement of $1.2 billion from the country's economic development fund. Unfortunately, the actions of one of our sister agencies prematurely shut down an entity we suspect was being used to launder portions of that money in the United States, and in that time Mr. Kwon managed to vanish."

Fred processed this in shock. Even when the agent had announced Reagan's disappearance Fred had never thought Reagan might be the villain in the whole matter; Reagan was already so fantastically rich, it didn't make any sense. "Do you have any proof of what you're claiming?"

Stern looked at him with disapproval. "At the moment, no, which is why this is a friendly conversation. We're in a phase of information-gathering, and the Thais are dragging their feet. But I, along with my superiors, am convinced that significant fraud has occurred."

"This is insane. Reagan Kwon is from one of the wealthiest families in Asia. He has a genuine, bona fide yacht. His sister is a minister in the Thai government!"

"Regina Kwon is no longer employed in any capacity within the official administration, and like her brother, has also disappeared. I can't speculate as to the actual holdings of Mr. Kwon's extended family, but I assume the boat you're referring to is *Killer*, on which Mr. Kwon hosted several events late last year and early this year. The actual name of *Killer* is *La Tulipe*, and it belongs to one Mr. Jacques Spruch, the former chairman of UBS. Mr. Spruch reported the boat as stolen last February; apparently it had undergone an extensive paint job, as well as had several physical modifications performed on its trim, before ultimately making its way into Mr. Kwon's possession. I'm told Mr. Kwon disavows any knowledge about the boat's origin and claims to have purchased it via an anonymous broker. It has since been returned to Mr. Spruch."

Fred's mouth had gone dry. He swiped behind for his fridge, but his hand met only air; the equipment had already been scavenged by office looters. "Excuse me," he said, clearing his throat. A piece of phlegm had become lodged somewhere in the back, forming a sturdy web; he coughed again and tried to swallow.

"I've come to understand," Stern said, ignoring his discomfort, "that you acted as a sort of intermediary for Opus in the United States, facilitating and expediting the introduction of the entity to Draper Carlyle. Is this correct?"

"Well . . ." It didn't take a genius to understand that it would be best to disassociate as much as possible. "I was the person Reagan may have first approached, but there were a lot of steps taken along the way to set this up, many different players. . . ."

"And that you continue to have indirect access to Draper's pooled accounts." The agent said it flatly, like a statement.

"I did, but circumstances have, uh, recently changed. My role has significantly shifted."

"Are you not," Stern said, as he squinted at a printout he'd pulled from his bag, "Fred Huang, Founding and General Partner of Opus Ventures?"

"Yes, but—"

"And as of, let's see—twenty days ago, in fact—did you not provide a quote to TechCode, referring to yourself as the '*lead partner and chief American investor for Opus Ventures, the new face of the global technology revolution*'?"

Fred sighed, throwing his hands up in the air.

"I may not have a Harvard MBA, Mr. Huang, but that sounds like a pretty senior-level position to me."

"It is," Fred blurted, before he could stop himself.

The agent smirked. "Do any of these names sound familiar? Rivermark, Golden Industries, the Warsaw Aluminum Extrusion Corp . . ."

"No. Are these Opus's international portfolio investments?"

"These are all front companies, originally created with the intent of laundering stolen funds for a group of individuals we've determined includes several members of the Kwon family. The consortium, as far as we've been able to determine, has been around for decades. It may have been initially funded in part by money stolen from the Chinese Nationalist government in the mid-1930s. Each of its members has deep connections to government entities; in the Kwons' case with Opus, it was the Thais. Money's skimmed, needs to be made clean, reappears somewhere else—what do you do? Make up a bunch of fake companies to move it through. Which sounds good, but over time and as the amounts get larger, you need the entities to pass increased scrutiny. So you start to add more layers, and structure, and even employees, and eventually the companies become real. Of course, given the nature of the people we're dealing with, most of them are pure trash. Pornography sites, fake pharmaceuticals, knockoff luxury goods. Though to be fair, a few are quite impressive. Viable business models, lean operations, real product development cycles. It appears that even senior management at some were unaware of the true nature of their employment."

Puzzle pieces were reluctantly clicking into place; all the stories regarding Reagan and his very, very rich family; the conjectures about where, exactly, his wealth came from. "So Reagan was stealing money from the Thais? And moving it through these businesses . . ."

"Yes, though the majority was supposed to transit through Opus, and thus Draper Carlyle. It's not easy to launder a billion dollars selling $2 Viagra on the internet. A law firm's pooled account is a far simpler route, if you want to quickly clear a big chunk of cash. And once the money's in, it can be near impossible to trace. Luckily for us, a junior banker at HSBC who didn't know he was supposed to turn a blind eye to these sorts of things noticed something unusual about the transaction when the second Opus request, for $855 million, came through, and he notified his superior." Stern returned to his printout. "Cannabis City, Sino Development Corp, the Parisian Shoe Company, Sugar Enterprises, Tigerlily, Designer-SunGlasses-R-Us . . ."

"Wait. Tigerlily. I've heard of that one."

Stern examined him with interest. "In what capacity? Do you have access to documentation detailing its financial holdings?"

"No, I mean in more of a personal fashion. My mother is . . . she's a client. She met her boyfriend, or whatever he is, on it." Fred still couldn't believe Linda had managed to find love across international waters, while he himself had been publicly dumped and shamed, triggering the worst professional crisis of his career.

"Well, Tigerlily does operate a legitimate business on the side," Stern allowed, "though its main source of revenue appears to stem from far less scrupulous avenues. Has your mother's boyfriend ever asked her for money? Is he by any chance based overseas, in Tunisia or Nigeria? Has she traveled to meet him?"

Tunisia? Linda wouldn't even go to dinner in Berkeley, since it meant she'd have to drive on the 880. "I know he's been pushing for some kind of condo investment. He's overseas, but I'm not clear on the location."

"Where is the real estate based? Has your mother actually transferred funds?"

"I think in the United States. I don't believe any money's been moved yet." Or had it? Goddamn!

"Have they met in person?"

"Yes, but here in California. From what I know he came for a few days."

"I hope this isn't true for your mother's sake, but it sounds like she could be the target of a scam. Tigerlily is a massive entity, very sophisticated. Our best estimate is that its revenues land at about $7 million per day, which would make it one of the key levers in the laundering operation. The company's activities run the gamut—from your basic pop-up ads, *Do You Want to Marry a Millionaire?*, that sort of mild catfishing, all the way up to actual marriages, which last until the victim's been sucked dry. We're currently investigating a case in Florida where the couple was married for six years before the wife died, and the husband subsequently disappeared—we assume back to Egypt. Unfortunately, right now forensic evidence points toward homicide; she owned several lucrative commercial properties in Coral Gables, which have since passed into his name. Your mother must be a fairly significant target for them to have flown out a specific operator. They only do that if they think they can get half a million or more."

"Homicide." Fred felt dizzy. "I know they talk a lot, exchanged some gifts, but I never dreamed . . . I mean, I thought the whole thing sounded shady, but an actual conspiracy . . . my mom, she's normally such a suspicious person. She thinks *Lion Capital* is a scam, for God's sake, because she's never seen it on the *Forbes* 'Midas List'!"

Stern looked sympathetic. "You have no idea how sophisticated these operations are," he said. "No one is immune." He hesitated. "I'm going to tell you a personal story. If that's all right."

"Uh, sure." Fred hoped the agent wasn't about to share some horrific online dating anecdote that he'd later regret revealing. "Only if you're comfortable."

"Just last month I was in Bangkok," Stern said. "For our first family holiday in Asia. Our whole time there, I'm driving my wife crazy. I keep nagging that she shouldn't talk to anyone, to let me manage the interactions, because of all the scammers. But somehow—even though I did my research and scheduled everything in advance—we still end up visiting the Royal Palace on the one day a month it's closed to the public. No can do, the guard says, as soon as we arrive at the front. So we turn around, and right outside the gates we meet this guy who offers us a discounted tuk tuk ride, on account of it being low tourist season. If he'd said it was free, I would have immediately said no, but the idea of a discount, and plus he still haggles. . . .

"The driver takes us to this local temple, and there we see another American, who I notice right away because he's wearing a Chapel Hill baseball hat. And I get excited, you see, because I'm an alum. Honestly, what are the chances? So we chat a little about basketball, really hit it off, and he ends up pulling some strings and finagling us passes to this jewelry showroom where we can buy gems at wholesale. And these are beautiful pieces—no mall crap, I know my stuff, my brother's a GIA gemologist. Real quality rubies.

"And I decide what the hell, we're on holiday, and I buy a ring for my wife and a pair of earrings for my daughter. They're beautiful, the girls love them, I'm a hero, and we're all having a grand time, and it's only when we get back to the hotel and I start talking with the concierge that I find out the whole thing was a scam. Starting from the guard at the palace gates who turned us away. The rubies are technically real, but they've been filled with lead glass. The tuk tuk driver must have eavesdropped on our conversation or looked me up somehow, and the guy at the temple must have hundreds of these hats to change into. I'm still fighting my credit card company a month later to get the charge reversed. And I'm a fucking *FBI agent*. So go talk to your mom after this, tell her you love her and that she needs to be careful. Make sure you keep track of those gifts you say she's received—most likely they were purchased with stolen credit cards."

"Excuse me." Griffin opened the door. "Fred, I was just informed you were still here." His thin, pale neck swiveled through the gap, taking in Stern. "I'm Griffin Keeles," he said, extending his hand. "Fred reports to me. Formerly reported."

"Josh Stern." The agent eyed Fred, looking for some visual cue; Fred subtly lifted an eyebrow meant to communicate the low esteem in which they were to hold the intruder. "So you're Fred's manager? Fred, you moving on? Big promotion?"

Griffin preened. "I am the senior managing director of Lion Capital. And Fred Huang is no longer employed here."

"That's news to me," Stern said. He turned back to Fred. "Is this news to you?"

"Yes, that's what I was trying to tell you earlier. I no longer have access to—"

"Excuse me for being abrupt," Griffin interrupted, "but this is a highly unusual situation. During your meeting today, has Fred Huang represented himself in any official capacity as an officer of either Lion Capital or Opus Ventures?"

"Maybe." The agent crossed his legs. "Should he have?"

"Emphatically not. Fred Huang has been fully relieved of his responsibilities. We thank him, of course, for his years of service."

"Let me make sure I understand," Stern said. "As of today, Fred Huang no longer has any involvement—in any capacity—with Opus, Lion Capital, or any of its associated entities and partners, including Draper Carlyle."

"Correct."

"And Mr. Huang is no longer employed with Lion Capital."

"His employment has been terminated, and he has signed paperwork acknowledging such."

"And all inquiries on Opus should be now directed to . . ."

"Me," Griffin completed.

"Well, fuck." The agent looked at Fred. "I guess you're free to go. But keep your phone near."

Fred left in a daze. Once outside, he realized he'd forgotten his crate, which contained nine years of office swag. He let it go; the most pressing issue now was Tigerlily.

Kate picked up on the first ring. "Where are you?" she asked in an agitated voice. "I've been calling and calling. I even tried your office!"

"Why? What's happened to Mom?" All of a sudden Fred felt a deep panic at the thought of someone hurting Linda, either physically or mentally. Mama! he cried in his head. Ma! I'm so sorry!

"Mom? No, she's fine, why would you ever think otherwise? She would survive the apocalypse. She's meeting me here. I'm on my way to Dad's." Kate's voice broke. "They think his time is very soon."

CHAPTER 21

KATE

She was with Camilla when Deborah called. This time it was
Kate who'd reached out, for the simple reason that she was in a
badly confused state after Vegas. Though the two were interlinked,
she found herself struggling to reconcile the random violence of Lars
Sundstrom and the pride and uncertainty of Sonny's offer; lurking
over both were the continuing tragedies of Denny and Stanley. She
thought of dialing Linda before quickly dismissing the idea as insane;
next she went through a variety of the usual suspects, but each would
require too much backstory. Only then did she admit that Camilla
was the only person with whom she could easily share the most
shameful and sad parts of her life.

When did it become so difficult to say certain truths to old
friends? Like *Denny cheated on me*, or *my marriage is done*, or *I wonder*

about my father's will. Sometime during the journey into adulthood these details had become too burdensome to share; the dread of the stressed silence that usually followed such admissions, the subsequent awkward straining of friends to reveal a secret of their own. So now Kate opted not to see those who'd known her in a better period, in favor of someone who'd started off meeting her at her worst.

"Do it," Camilla said. They were back at Maggie's in Mountain View, this time inside, having lucked into one of the two small tables that allowed the establishment to call itself a café. Kate had intended for the meeting to be a quick coffee and pastry, a verbal unloading and then an efficient call for the check, but Camilla had immediately ordered a series of dishes as soon as they'd been seated, ensuring a multi-course meal. "Do it," she said again. "Do the bras. You have to."

It had been a relief to unburden herself of the memories of CES, after the drama of the last few days at Stanley's. While Kate normally hated to talk excessively, with Camilla she felt none of the polite anxiety that usually came with monopolizing a conversation. "I don't have the bandwidth for any additional responsibility. There isn't the time."

"Time." Camilla's voice held an edge of disgust. "You sound just like Ken. He was always going on about being Mr. Busy, so *pressed for time.* Of course, that only really applied to the things he didn't want to do, anyway."

"I really don't think I rate a comparison to your ex-husband. Last night I had a bed-wetting incident to mop up, and after that I spent three hours on a presentation for Sonny. What would you have me do, get fired and let my children sleep in urine?"

"Don't be flippant." Camilla tapped her fork impatiently. "Get more help. What's the point of being a martyr? You know how much I'd love to have a schedule like yours? Boredom is its own sort of busy, except there's less variety. You think Denny wouldn't immediately go out and blow the money for assistance? He would consider himself above scrubbing wet sheets even if he didn't have a big, important job. Which, I'm just saying—"

"Now you're being cruel," Kate interrupted. She didn't like it when Camilla dug into Denny, which she sensed was done in some way for her approval. "You willingly slept with him." She felt the fact needed to be vocally stated. "Multiple times."

Camilla reddened. "Well. That was then. And you have to admit I make a good point. What's the big deal about hiring some staff? You didn't seem to have any particular scruples about Isabel. Isn't that how men get ahead? They all want to build their little empires. Ken never had a real office job like that here, he was just a bored old guy playing investor, but I remember when Manesh Das would come by, he would always announce how he was *growing his influence*, gobbling up all these partners for his little fiefdom. Hey, why do you care so much about what I say about Denny, anyway? Have you seen him lately?"

"Yes. He is the father of my children, you understand."

"Right," Camilla said. Her face turned sulky. "You're not going to get back together, are you?"

"I don't think so."

"Good. He's an ass and not deserving of your forgiveness."

"Stop it," Kate said, annoyed. "You don't need to make him sound like such a jerk. If I want to bitch, I'll tell you. Otherwise, if you want to be friends, you need to cool it on the nasty monologue."

"Okay," Camilla said. She had brightened after hearing the bit about friends. "Did I tell you I'm dating someone? And he's not even married."

"Rich and boring?"

"No! Retired air force captain. The most annoying thing about him is that he bicycles."

Kate was surprised to discover she felt happy for Camilla. "If that's as bad as it gets, I think it merits further exploration."

"We'll see." Camilla dimpled, then frowned. "Did you ever see that guy from Vegas again?"

"Lars Sundstrom? No way."

"That's his name?" Camilla began to saw at her Croque Madame. "I should write it down. Did you take pictures of your arm? You should if you haven't already. Continue to monitor what he's up to, and if you hear he's having any hint of success, figure out a way to take him down. Wait until he thinks he's in the clear, that he's gotten away with all the nasty things he's done. Then, when the time is exactly right—*boom*!" She violently rang her knife against her fork. "Rise up and smash his world to a bloody pulp."

Kate flinched. "Jesus, you're vicious."

Camilla wagged a finger. "Don't pretend I don't just say out loud what you secretly think."

DEBORAH'S CALL MEANT THAT LUNCH ENDED ABRUPTLY, RIGHT before dessert. Since Camilla had driven, she dropped Kate off in front of Stanley's, pulling up as Fred parked across the street. Her brother was in his work clothes, an ivory collared shirt and slim jeans, which was a relief. When Kate had called the Lion offices earlier, something in the receptionist's careful phrasing made her suspicious he no longer worked there.

"Who's the blonde?" Fred asked.

Camilla idled the car, daintily waving her fingers from the window. "Are you sure you don't want me to come in? Need anything? Just text."

"Is that her car?" Fred asked. "She opted for the turbine wheel upgrade. Expensive."

"Just a friend," Kate said shortly. Then, back toward Camilla, "You can go now. We'll talk later."

"I've never seen her before. All your other friends are mousy. Are you a lesbian now?"

Inside, Kate was distressed by the change in Stanley. Since the last time she'd seen him, his face had begun to sink, collapsing in on itself. She had just been with him, less than twenty-four hours ago, when he'd been relatively alert, if unsettled, murmuring on and off about the foundation, calling for his wife. He seemed to have Linda and Mary confused on a nearly permanent basis now, asking for one when he meant the other, not caring who showed up. Most of the time it was neither.

Three days ago, after noticing some bedsores, Kate had hired a nursing service. That itself had been a battle, with Linda insistent that Stanley pay for the care himself, since it was his own fault he had selected a wife with such miserly fortitude. When they went to look for his checkbook, however, they discovered it had disappeared, along with his wallet. Mary had secreted them away, like an animal desperately hoarding for a hard winter. While Linda had been furious, Kate privately thought it was for the best; she didn't want to quibble with Mary over what constituted an appropriate amount of hours or a decent under-the-table wage. She'd gone and hired the best she knew, round-the-clock coverage, and paid the bill quietly.

One of the Samoans was there now, bent over Stanley's mouth, holding a foam block soaked with water. Neither of the twins ever showed any indication of recognizing her from their stint with Sonny, nor did they seem to mind working alone for the twelve-hour shifts they traded off. Kate had attempted conversation when they first started, asking if she could bring anything to make their visits more comfortable, but they'd pointed to the coolers they held. "We bring our own food. Every day," they responded. And made it clear they preferred a quiet workspace.

When he saw Kate and Fred enter, the nurse gave a quick nod, handed Kate the water block, and left for the kitchen.

"Where's your mother?" Deborah asked. "She coming today? I want to chat."

"Yes, but I thought you didn't like her." After the divorce, Deborah had made very clear her stance toward Linda, who she considered a traitor. She couldn't understand why Linda had all of a sudden decided she could no longer abide living with Stanley, when she had successfully tolerated him for decades.

"What do you mean, don't like? Of course I like. She always has the best stock tips."

"She's on her way. I think she stopped by McDonald's." Linda refused to eat or drink anything from Stanley's kitchen. "How is Dad?"

"The doctor says he can keep going for few more days, but I think he's ready. He won't eat. The last time I told him Mary wasn't here, I think he almost wanted to cry. But he didn't have tears."

"Dad *crying*?" Kate had never seen Stanley cry, not even right after her parents' divorce announcement, which was the closest instance she personally knew of. He had sat across from her at Shanghai Noodle, just the two of them, and forlornly asked if she would still see him once he lived alone. When she herself started to cry, he suddenly became cheered and asked if she had time for a movie that afternoon. "I didn't think it was possible."

"Oh yeah, he used to cry all the time, when we were kids in Taiwan. Whenever he wanted something and didn't get it: Wah! Instant sprinkler! He was pretty sweet, too, always hugging, offering his snacks. His favorite was these pears, a certain kind in Taiwan that are much sweeter than in America, almost too sweet. A nearby farmer grew them, and your dad used to sneak away to pick them off his trees. A lot of people did that, especially during World War II, so the farmer had these big tall fences installed, all around his property. They looked to me at the time like they were a hundred feet, but of course I was just a kid, so maybe they were twenty. And Stanley was almost the same size as me, just a little bigger, but still he would go and climb for those pears. I'd stand there on the ground watching him, biting my nails. Until one day he fell! I was terrified; I thought he'd died and everyone would blame it on me. I wanted to run away but didn't want to leave him alone."

"Wait," Fred said. "He was unconscious? For how long?"

"I don't know. A long time to me, but remember I was just a kid. For sure he had, what do you call it now, a concussion, but we didn't have that idea or term at the time. Afterward, though, that's when the temper started. I don't know if it was from the fall or just growing up."

"You know he could have had CTE." Fred turned to Kate. "Chronic traumatic encephalopathy. That brain thing football players get with too many concussions, that makes them violent."

"But he only fell once," Kate said. "Football players get hit hundreds of times. And they can't control it."

"Dad couldn't control it either."

"Then how come he never went after Mom?"

"I don't know." He ran his hands through his hair. "I'm just thinking."

"It's because he knew he couldn't cross that line, Fred. She would leave him. He had complete control of himself."

"How can you be so sure?" Her brother sounded so defensive, and Kate felt a touch of guilt. She didn't understand why it was suddenly of such critical importance that Stanley not have an easy out. But she also didn't want Fred to inhabit some comforting delusion, while she alone was left in the cold.

"Because after the divorce, once he was lonely and didn't have other options, he immediately became much nicer to me. There would be times when we'd fight, and I'd see him get worked up, but instead of going crazy like he normally would, he'd force himself to calm down. Once we were on our way to lunch, and we were arguing about something to do with politics, and all of a sudden he got pissed and hit the brakes, hard. I already had my bag on my shoulder, I was getting ready to dodge traffic, you know how he used to kick us out of the car. But instead he sat there and swallowed and then we moved on. That's when I realized it. He was always able to control his temper, when it was in his interest. He just didn't care to do so with us."

Fred was silent. "Stanley always loved himself very much," Deborah commented. She seemed to consider this the final word on the subject. "He was very good at preserving himself."

WHEN LINDA ARRIVED, KATE WAS BY STANLEY'S BED, READING aloud. He could no longer focus on the TV; displayed none of the interest in the programs Kate had watched with him only a few days earlier, at his written request. Now he just lay in mute apathy, staring ahead, so Kate had decided to find a book. She did the same with Ethan and Ella when they couldn't sleep at night, sat by their sides and described in vivid detail the pictures.

She'd hunted for some titles she recognized, realizing that most of the ones she remembered were actually Linda's. Nothing on the shelf looked familiar—they were all Chinese, or hardback editions on health and diet—until on the very top, shoved deep in the back, she found a ragged paperback. *The Godfather.* She had read it when she was in high school and seen the evidence of Stanley's highlighter marks on the paper. Opening it, she was filled with pleasure at the softness of the pages, like a small pillow in her hands.

"Mom's here," Fred said. "Let's go talk to her."

"Can't it wait a little? I'm still reading." She'd forgotten how the wedding scene ended.

"No, we've got to grab her. You won't believe what I found out about Tigerlily. It really can't wait. And Dad's sleeping now anyway."

Kate looked back at Stanley. You couldn't tell if he was awake anymore simply by his breathing—it was uneven and jagged, and agonizing seconds would pass between each breath.

"*The Godfather*?" Fred asked. "That was one of his favorites."

"Wasn't it yours too? Look at how much he highlighted it."

"I haven't read it in years. I forget—do Sonny and Fredo get into a fight with the Don's mistress over the will, and then at the end we find out it all goes to some crazy foundation?"

Kate laughed. "You know there's nothing," she said. "At least not for us."

"Yeah."

"I'd pick out something from the house to remember him by, before Mary snatches it all. I took one of the walking sticks."

"I got a fake Rolex," Fred said forlornly.

"Fake? How do you know?"

"Mom told me. She pointed out that it was still keeping perfect time even though I hadn't worn it yet. Which of course means it has a battery, which real Rolexes don't have."

"How does she even know these things? That's kind of amazing."

Fred tilted his chin toward the bed. "You think he thought he was Don Corleone?" he asked. "Every guy thinks they're the Don."

"I don't know. What does it matter now?"

And they left, to find Linda.

WHEN KATE HADN'T LOCATED HER ON THE FIRST FLOOR, SHE thought Linda might have fled the premises, sick of the stale smell and Deborah's aggressive inquiries regarding energy investing. She assumed Linda wouldn't have ventured to the second level, which she regarded as Stanley's private domain and thus filled with undesirable objects and people. Kate went up mostly to eliminate the possibility, and then immediately spotted her mother, who stood in front of a portrait of a naked woman with auburn hair. "Ma?" she called softly. Linda didn't respond. As she neared, Kate saw that the picture was a painting, thick oils on canvas, the colors individually subdued but collectively lurid. Though she'd passed the portrait on multiple occasions, she'd deliberately never stopped to look at it. The woman's nipples, she noticed now, were enormous—drooping chocolate tear-drops to match a downturned smile.

Linda continued her reverie. Kate geared up for another conversational attempt and let out a yelp. Mary was behind them—had appeared without a sound, like an apparition. She never came near Stanley anymore, and as a result Kate hadn't seen her in days. She looked half crazed, as if forcibly kept from sleep; she wore a stained cotton bathrobe, and the skin on her face was red and flaked. Without thinking, Kate took a step, positioning herself in front of her mother.

Mary thrust an arm forward. "Here," she said. She seemed to have eyes only for Linda. "I found it in the back of his desk." She opened her palm, which held a thick gold ring set with a black stone. "He never liked me to go into his office. But I would pass by while he was in there, so I knew where he kept it. He would take it out and play with it sometimes. I always knew it was from your wedding."

When Linda was silent, Mary angrily curled her hand into a fist. She already had begun turning away when Linda spoke. "We spent $50."

Mary stopped. "I don't understand."

"Fifty dollars. We spent $50 on the whole wedding. It was at the Sunnyvale Community Center. I didn't even buy my own dress. I borrowed my friend Yvonne's, and Stanley wore her husband's suit. We bought a cake from Chinatown and served some fruit punch, and then Stanley and I stayed late sweeping and mopping up and throwing everything away to make sure we didn't pay a cleaning fee. There was no money for rings, so we didn't buy them until a few years later. Stanley wanted something different, but onyx was the least expensive. That's how we built everything we had."

Mary stared at her. "Life is very difficult," she said slowly. "I never knew how terrible it could be."

"Life is about solving problems," Linda answered. "If you cannot respect this, then I have nothing more to say to you." She turned to Kate. "Take the ring from Mary," she instructed. "You can give it to your brother. Something for him to remember your father by."

Kate did as she was told. Then she put her arm around Linda's shoulders and led her downstairs.

CHAPTER 22

STANLEY

He was on his back. He'd been on his back forever, it seemed, though it couldn't have been so. His memories from before— when he could stand on his own two feet and walk and sit and drive—all seemed to be from a prior life, the baggage of another person who had lived those events. They weren't him. He was here on his back and it had always been so and this is how it always would be.

His sister was there, in the near distance, as she put into words one of those remote memories, the one with the orchards in Taiwan. He had always thought they were apple trees, and just extraordinarily sweet. The best apples he had ever eaten. How come nobody had told him they were pears? Maybe he wouldn't have climbed the fence for a pear; it was the idea of the apple that had always held him, the perfectly shaped fruit in his hands, the way it tasted even better than he thought it would when he bit into it, each time. If he had known it was a pear he would have never climbed so high, no matter how delicious. There wouldn't have been that moment of gratifying surprise.

His daughter's voice was back now, murmuring lines into his ear from a story that had once been familiar but now was far away. His hand was being held, and maybe that was his sister, or his wife, at the end of his body. He thought whoever she was might be touching his feet, but he couldn't feel sensation there anymore. His mother once had feet, when he was a little boy. The smooth feet and legs of a young woman, and he had placed the soles of his against hers.

His son had arrived. He'd been asking for him, though he couldn't recall his name. What was it? "Fred," he said, remembering now. But did he say it out loud? He grasped the hand that lay in his. The palm felt cold, unmoving. When had Fred become such a dead fish? Why wasn't he more alive? If he had his son's force, if he could still compel his limbs with a mere mental command, he would walk his body outside and stay there. Take a nap, or go for a stroll in the shade. Everything good in his life had happened outside. Why wasn't his son there? Didn't he understand that one day, the knowledge would dawn that the last time he had walked outside would be his very last, in this lifetime; that there would come a point when he would lie on his back and try to summon the warm recollection of a sun never to be felt again? Suddenly he was angry, and then he remembered the real reason Fred was inside; it was because he had asked him here! Of course! He remembered now! He laughed. The deep chuckle emerged from his throat a weak gasp. What was wrong with him?

"Dad? Are you awake?"

Stanley raised his hand to wipe his brow, but it didn't move as he wanted it to. "Take care of your mother," he said instead. She was there, wasn't she? He thought he saw her, off in the corner, a tissue over her face, but then Linda never cried. Maybe it was another woman—his sister, or his wife. Mary. He knew that at the end there had been some disagreements, but she had always taken such good care of him. Had been with him, allowed him to be the real person he was, even when he had let the ugliness out, setting it free because that was the right he had earned in this world. One in which he had lived a better life than his parents', and his children a better life than his own. He opened his mouth to tell his son to take care of Mary—she was a nice woman, and they would need each other after this, when he went—but he couldn't summon the words. He lifted his head; when did speaking become such a struggle?

"She's here, we're all here."

He relaxed.

"We're here. We're here to take care of you, Dad."

That was silly, because if there was one thing he could do, it was take care of himself. He always had, hadn't he? And in the end he'd achieved what he always wanted, become a man of substance, of real means and significance. . . .

What joy life was. He heard his sister's voice again, and then his son's, then his daughter's, and finally his wife's. He wished he'd been born a less clumsy person. He was always falling over things, tripping over his anger. How different might have everything turned out? But then he was here, and his children were here, and all of those who had cared for him so well. How fortunate he was in life, to have always been surrounded by those who loved him. How smart he was, to have chosen them. And how lucky he was, to have always been lucky.

Please, he said. *Please*. And breathed a deep sigh, and died.

NINE MONTHS LATER

FRED

It must have been an impulse born out of pure insanity, Fred thought, that had made him email Don Wilkes. The second after he pressed Send he had wanted to undo the act, but it was already too late, and the message pinged its way through the Motley Capital servers. He tried to calm himself: a gulp of air to consume his anxiety, a few limp sessions at the gym; an ensuing dash for easily consumable content, before his brain could rationalize a path down any number of undesirable scenarios.

The story was just starting to appear in the mainstream, after the *Wall Street Journal* broke the news with a piece titled "An Opus, a Yacht, and $6 Billion: The Ultimate Bangkok Scam." After that the other major outlets had piled on, eager for a fresh new scandal. At least Fred hadn't seen his own name mentioned, though there was another foolish part of him that was almost irritated by this. For from the media coverage alone one could be forgiven for assuming Leland and Maximilian had masterminded Opus from the start, instead of merely arriving at the end, trampling over everything and then getting mired helplessly in shit. In the past year, Fred had learned that

everyone—journalists, government regulators, federal agencies—
gravitated to the most compelling story. And what was more en-
thralling than one billionaire being fooled by another, a tale of greed
and subsequent betrayal between modern-day robber barons? Even
his own dramatic agony appeared tame in comparison—his future
career and romantic prospects gone flaccid, perhaps permanently so,
his so-called generous inheritance existing as it always had, only in
his father's head. The foundation a figment of lunacy, Stanley's house
gone—now being rented to a young Laotian family through a management company, with the proceeds supposedly going each month
to Mary, wherever she was. Fred hadn't seen her since the day his
father passed. No one had. After Stanley's funeral, at the reception at
China Garden, Fred had stood by himself in the back of the banquet
room and stared vacantly at the large gold plaque on the far opposite
wall, which bore the Chinese traditional symbol for *shuangxi,* or double happiness. Right as he'd begun to space out, he felt a tap on his
shoulder and turned to find two Chinese women, both looking about
nervously.

"Do you know where Mary is?" the younger of the duo asked, in
a respectful hush. "Have you heard anything about her or where she
went?"

He'd shaken his head, still numb, and they nodded and slipped
away. Later he recalled what Shirley Chang had whispered to him—
rather sheepishly—at the service, that Mary had skipped out to some
other state, Arizona or Utah maybe, a warm place with a lower cost
of living where she could inhabit a new skin for herself as a leisured
widow. But by then he'd been unable to find the women and didn't
know their names. Later on, Kate told him they'd been her sisters.

Almost immediately after he sent the email, Fred wrote off the
idea of Don Wilkes ever responding. Even if Wilkes did, it'd likely
be months away, long after the incident had been forced from his

mind at the strict behest of his ego. So Fred was surprised to receive a response the same afternoon, and even more so when it appeared to have been penned by the Don himself. Since his earliest attempts to claw out from the swamp of unemployment, Fred had mostly dealt with the assistants of his targets, who efficiently arranged for fifteen-minute slots months away, which were then rescheduled days before, for another six months out. A cycle with no end and no beginning, a reminder of the powerless tenancy he now occupied in the vast landscape of Silicon Valley.

Don, however, asked to meet that week.

The Motley headquarters were less than a mile away from Lion Capital's on Sand Hill Road. Fred drove with his eyes locked toward their destination, sneaking a glance last minute at the nondescript office park he'd commuted to for nearly a decade. The Motley receptionist, a striking brunette wearing showy Christian Louboutin heels, led Fred to a large office where a tasteful arrangement of white orchids sat atop a bronze Diego Giacometti table Charlene had once begged for a replica of. To the right was a private bathroom reported to contain a small Bosch—the idea of a piece of art being reserved exclusively for taking a dump being one of those details irresistible to journalists—and all around, scattered on tables, were various brightly colored Japanese figurines, a clumsy attempt at dabbling youth of what was clearly the den of an elder mogul.

Fred had assumed he'd have ample time to study the office in detail—he would have snuck a photo for future inspection, had the incident with Linda in Kate's attic not implanted in him a profound fear of hidden cameras. So he sat in carefully composed casualness for a brief period until the door opened. And then there, directly in front of him, extending a hand: the vicuña-bedecked Master of the Universe himself. Don Wilkes.

"I saw that email about you," Don said.

Fred silently cursed and suppressed the urge to cry. He'd been hoping Wilkes's interest in meeting had been born out of some other reason—a confusion of identity perhaps, or an act of random charity.

Don descended into his chair. "A colleague of mine who knew of my interest in such stories forwarded the message to me, back when it first came out," he said. "So when I saw your email—it was just lucky circumstance that I did, because usually these things go straight to my assistant—I thought I knew your name from somewhere. Quite a feisty lady, your former girlfriend. And attractive, of course. I saw the picture of the two of you she included with the original email. She obviously attached it for one reason since, no offense, the eye isn't really drawn to you. What's she doing these days? What was she before, a sales gal?"

"Yes, at Saks. She's no longer employed there." There'd been exactly one news piece written about Erika's email, a short article in the *Daily Mail*, run far enough down the site that you had to scroll. "A Woman Scorned! Jilted Hungarian Socialite Blows Up Financier Lover's Career." Erika posed on a stool in a navy Roland Mouret shift dress and pointy black heels, a self-described "luxury stylist." She'd sent him several messages before the piece ran, attempts to have him provide a quote so that they could print his name. He'd ignored them all. Her short period of notoriety had already fizzled, though not before she'd gained several thousand Twitter followers.

"You're lucky this was post–Hulk Hogan and Gawker, otherwise it would have definitely been picked up by the mainstream media. Your ex, she's too good-looking not to be. And you, well. You're one of us."

Did he mean ugly? Or dare Fred believe that the eminent Don Wilkes was actually referring to them as being in the same industry? Lion and Motley Capital, uttered in the same stinking cigar breath?

"Men who've been targeted by women, it's not exactly a catchy cause célèbre," Wilkes went on. "Believe me, no one's out there feeling sorry for you. But it's a real thing. Happened to me, too, though thankfully a few decades back, before everything was online. You ever hear of *Moth Magazine?*" Fred shook his head. "Hmm. I wouldn't have thought you were that young. Regardless, they did a long segment on me, one of my first-ever pieces of publicity. Initially I was thrilled. *Moth!* Before it folded, it was our generation's *Vanity Fair*. I had just started MirrorStream a few years back; the company was finally getting some traction. I figured it was all coming together. Then the article came out, and I thought I would die. It barely touched on MirrorStream. Instead the majority of it covered a personal detail from my past, the fact that I had an ex-wife and three children in Japan. My ex's parents, they were upset because she and the kids had moved in with them into their house in Tokyo, and they gave an interview that I never saw the kids. And the reporter, she was one of those uptight bitches, a real nose-in-the-air type—she really hated me. So you can imagine how the article turned out. And afterward I thought it was all over, nobody was going to want to have anything more to do with MirrorStream, or me, ever again, because I was painted as this bastard who refused to pay child support. The situation, of course, was more complicated than that."

It didn't sound all that convoluted to Fred; even Leland Wang managed to at least foster his own offspring. He adjusted his arm placement on the couch to mimic Wilkes's, a lesson he recalled from a Harvard seminar on building trust. "That sounds far from ideal."

"Once women get past forty, something happens. You ever date someone that age?"

"Close to it."

"Close to forty and over forty is a big difference, my friend. You'll learn that eventually. You think younger women are a lot of work? Try someone who's looking at forty in the rearview mirror, coming up on fifty. You'll find they require validation. A lot of it. A point will come when they'll want to send out a signal to the universe. To test whether the world is still receptive. And if they discover it isn't, then all hell breaks loose. And God save you if they think you're the reason why."

Fred coughed. "I may have some experience with that particular phenomenon."

"Of course." Wilkes barked a laugh. "I'd temporarily forgotten. The whole reason we're here."

A break in their conversation descended, a pause in the natural flow. Fred struggled to recall one of the lines he'd rehearsed at home for precisely this sort of opportunity. "At the Founders' Retreat, you mentioned the concept of data convergence—"

"It's the porn," Wilkes interrupted. "Back when I was growing up, we didn't have all this variety. All I had were old magazines, and I had to wait until my dad left the house to go riffling through his office drawers."

"Um." Jesus. Was Wilkes losing his mind? The abrupt subject change reminded Fred of the old-man stories Griffin Keeles used to launch into at the slightest provocation, droning on about when Britain had been able to colonize all sorts of different Asian countries at will.

"But now," Wilkes continued, "porn, well. There seems to be something for everyone these days! No matter what seemingly unique, deranged act I come up with, it always already exists, and in more detail and variations than even this old twisted mind could ever imagine possible. What do you all call it, Rule 34? If it exists, there's been a porn made of it? Lately I've realized there's a whole religious section, plots set in the Vatican. . . . Well, I'm sure I don't have to tell *you* any of this, your ex's letter made that pretty clear! But what I'm saying is that the sheer availability out there can make one do some crazy things. In fact, there was a half hour—well, if I want to be honest, a few minutes, really—last week where I was willing to dedicate the rest of my life to getting my little wife trim enough to fit into a white crop top and a long rosary bead necklace, just so I could act on some deviance. If someone had come up to me during those moments and placed a contract on my desk, I would have happily signed away my whole partnership in Motley in exchange for that fantasy coming to perfect fruition. And then, of course, as these things always do, it passed. And nobody knows anything about that momentary lapse, except for, well, now . . . you."

Despite an underlying sensation of disgust, Fred felt the thrill of inclusion. "Privacy is the most valuable commodity in our modern age," he said. "It's a luxury that everyone thinks they have but few actually do."

"Precisely what I've been thinking and wanting to put into words." Wilkes glanced at his watch. "Where were you before this? What was that—of course, Lion. An interesting place to be, corporate venture. Any chance you were privy to what went on? Heard Leland's under the gun."

"I worked closely with Leland Wang, though my tenure ended right before the official announcement of Opus." For which Fred owed his sincere thanks to Maximilian, for hurriedly pushing through the launch even after news of the SEC investigation had begun to filter out. Personally approving all purchase orders for the press event himself, driving relentlessly to the original date even when major cracks were beginning to show; a random terrified-looking Thai official trussed up and thrust in front of the cameras to shake Leland's hand. Jack nowhere in sight for any of it, Reagan missing from all official photography but named on the invitations. Rumored to have still been involved at that point, as he worked behind the scenes from an undisclosed location to provide celebrity talent for the after-party, which included a former Disney star and current ensemble actress whose numerous nightclub promotional commitments and inability to reschedule was reportedly what had cemented Maximilian's resolve to needlessly, recklessly, announce Opus to the world.

"Right, Opus. You know I met the mastermind, the one who's

on the lam now, at last year's Founders' Retreat. I was actually on that boat, *Killer*. Awful name, but beautiful decor. Better than the original."

"I was there as well. You gave an excellent talk the closing night."

"So you were." Wilkes studied him for a long moment. "Did I happen to mention there my behind-the-scenes take on the Wiretel acquisition? Quite the interesting saga." He segued into another speech, at which Fred's brain gave a mighty squall of protest, having been fed for the last nine months on binge-watched TV and exciting paperback thrillers, weaned during that period from the prattle of old men long past their prime. He almost stopped Wilkes a few times, told him that he was sorry, he had to go—something had come up, a forgotten appointment—so that he could return to his regular life, the one where he sat at home and researched protein shakes and day-traded his portfolio. It was over for him already. What was a meeting with Don Wilkes going to change? But then the man neared the end of his lecture and once again uttered those words: "You're one of us."

And followed them up with, "What can I do?"

And Fred didn't know exactly what Wilkes was saying, whether he meant that he, Fred, was a capitalist like Wilkes or simply a man who had done something bad to a woman and then been punished for it. Either way, he understood that this was it, that in a year in which many doors had closed, another gilded portal was now being held open. This was going to be his moment, and he would use everything he had learned in the last wretched year to grasp tight the opportunity and not let go until he emerged a man.

KATE

The idea had been Sonny's, which he said arrived to him from a dream. A dream that to Kate had at first seemed closer to a nightmare. To spin off the bra project as an independent entity, separate from the Labs, with X Corp taking a 50 percent stake. Kate to lead as CEO—no longer in charge of a project but an entire company (albeit a start-up).

When Sonny first proposed the concept, she'd been hideously frightened, paranoid that they had given her the title of VP only to claim the statistic for diversity reporting and were now forcing her out. She wasn't an entrepreneur! After the arrival of children Kate had been wholly satisfied with clocking in and out of a well-oiled corporate machine, one where health benefits and company holidays were clearly defined. What Sonny was describing—at the glass conference table in his office, surrounded by sample packs of proposed flavors of the now-terminated Grommix—was never a fate she'd envisioned for herself.

"I don't understand why you'd promote me and then not have me stay on under you," she asked. "Aren't you happy with my performance?"

"Don't be *ridiculous!*" Sonny was annoyed with her resistance, which he viewed as groundless and hysterical; as she'd continued to push, his face had turned to thunder. "Is this how you act, when someone gives you a fabulous gift?"

"This is a gift?"

"Of course! I want you to be successful. Now that you've made vice president, you will want to prove that you didn't get the title just because you're a woman. Although as we both know, that isn't entirely true."

Kate toyed with a container that, when examined, revealed itself to be a biltong variety of Grommix. "Wouldn't we have the best chance at success developing internally?" she asked desperately.

"Of course not. The company, it's gone fat! Too many entrenched interests. If it weren't so, wouldn't Grommix have been a best seller? The perfect product, brought down by jealousy and sabotage. Do you know they wouldn't even let me attend the Costco meeting? Since when are EVPs not allowed at regional sales functions? Fujihara said that the placement of a hundred thousand smartphone units was too important to allow any variables, even when I said I would offer Grommix at cost for a bundle. Costco's all about the bundles. You don't want to be constrained like this. The underwear, it has great potential. Go."

When she finally agreed to exit, Sonny flexed his Friend of Sokolov muscle and negotiated her "pink badge" status, which meant that she was technically still an inactive employee, with vesting stock. Though she lost access to the building and her corporate email, she noticed her photo was still on the Labs site, under executive bios.

As an independent entity, X Fit—she'd have to get a new name, but that could come later—would need manufacturing connections, engineering resources, and advisors in the industry. Each of these components was difficult enough on its own, and the combination even more so, especially outside the plush confines of X Fit's former parent. Which was how she found herself where she was now, at the most odious and dreaded of events. A venture capital function.

The room had a richness of high tables with a corresponding paucity of chairs, which meant she'd already been standing for an hour. The floors were a light glossy wood, and on each creamy wall was a single installation of abstract art. Everything about the space—its size, location, quality of coffee, and jittery exuberance of attendees— spoke to the power of the entity it served. Motley Capital.

Since neither the operations director nor the mechanical engineer Kate had extended offers to had officially started yet, she'd brought along Camilla for moral support. "You're too timid," Camilla said as she sidled up, freshly lubricated from a visit to the bar. She had dressed for the occasion, in cream pants and a loose silk blouse, cut deep at the throat. "You know who you were talking to just now, yes? Don Wilkes! I was standing right behind you guys. You have this weird habit where you stammer and say *ah* a lot. Why do you do that? You're thinking the bitchiest things to yourself. Say them! It would make you appear a hell of a lot more interesting and intelligent than you're currently coming off."

"Jesus," Kate said. She wasn't accustomed to such blunt feedback from a friend. Though it was the kind she always wanted, the sort Linda used to lavish and Denny had provided early on, before the barbed resentment began to show. He was in Mountain View now, in a three-story townhome, the purchase price of which would just be covered by her VP stock grant at X Corp over the next four years. In exchange, he'd signed away any rights to spousal support. The day they completed their divorce papers, she'd told him she was happy for him, with the pleasure of actually meaning it—the kiss-off compliment to a friend you see only once a year and whose developments can be followed from a safe distance on social media. Until she remembered once again that this was Denny, and that he was in her life forever.

"Do more," Camilla urged now. "Be more aggressive. Tell everyone about your brilliant idea."

"It's not really mine. As you know, I kind of stole it."

"Everybody steals. It's the nature of the business. You think there are any original thoughts left in the consumer space?"

"Consumer space? Nature of the business? Who are you?"

Camilla looked pleased. "It's from Manesh Das. Though I didn't pick it up here. He said it at a dinner I was at once, when I was seated directly next to him. Of course it wasn't to me; he barked it right over my head to another man at the table. It's really quite good, isn't it? That fucker is basically constructed out of one-liners. Speaking of Manesh, is he here? I doubt he'd know who I was, anyway; he's not the type to remember wives. Isn't he your brother's boss?"

"Yes, but if you see Fred, don't mention it." He was prickly about that sort of thing, not reporting to the alpha animal in the food chain, even though given his past year, Kate thought his new job should be considered a minor miracle. Who cared if his official title was junior partner? She'd noticed he'd already surreptitiously removed the *junior* part from his LinkedIn, anyway. "Let's cut out of here soon."

"What? We just got here!"

"Yeah, but I'm tired. I can't stand much more of this. Some kid just told me he wouldn't hire anyone that he couldn't see himself doing shots with, and when I heard that, a feeling just crystallized. I don't belong here. I'm too old and have too much hate. I don't want it enough."

"Now you're making me pissed. You know what I really hate?" Camilla pursed her lips and blew, as if expelling smoke from an invisible cigarette. "Liars."

Kate drew back. "What?"

"You know exactly what I'm saying. You want me to cheerlead you? Fine. You want me to pretend you don't already know your idea is a good one? Sure, whatever. But stop with the posturing. No one gets to where you are if they don't want it. Do you know how stupid and demeaning it is, to keep playing that you're just some nice girl who got lucky? You want it. Why not own up to it? You'd make things way easier for yourself."

It'd been that one sentence that did Kate in. *You want it.* Was it true? How much? She went back to all she had done in the past decade that she'd never before said out loud, partially because she had no one to tell it to. Her stubborn insistence on living for five years under continuous renovation, to finally get her dream home. How she'd gone to bed past midnight every weekday for the past three years, to be the first on the team to talk to Europe. Always answering yes to the extra good-night book, because children need their mother; never saying no to putting out, because she didn't want her marriage to be like her mother's. The thousands of extra hours spent with engineering and operations, family dinner on the table each night, the countless personal pleasures set aside, forestalled in some unnamed quest.

Do I want it? Do I?

And she allowed herself to answer and felt the freedom in its release. Yes. Yes. I do.

LINDA

To: Leonard168@apple.com

From: LLiang1945@gmail.com

Subject: Linda Liang's 72nd Birthday Email

Dear classmates,

I hope all of you are doing well and remain in good health. I am still standing, though we all know how quickly events can change at our age. I am thinking of course of our beloved classmate Jackson Ho, who recently passed. My thoughts and well wishes go to my dear friend Yvonne and their children.

As for myself, my biggest news is that I recently moved and now live with my daughter, Kate. She is very busy with her new venture (but remains an employee of X Corp—as a vice president), so I help with the grandchildren. Currently I am living in her top floor, in a converted attic, until the guest home I will move to is finished. It will have a full bath, washer and dryer, and even a kitchen. When I was young, I never dreamed that there could be houses like these in people's backyards. Isn't America wonderful? I hope it is completed soon, because I cannot climb these stairs for much longer.

Of course, I still have my place in Palo Alto. That way, I can take a break from "grandma duties" whenever I want. My garden is doing very well, and I have two new dwarf Japanese maples!

Unfortunately, at my daughter's house, I have discovered many new TV programs. Premium cable is very expensive, and I keep hearing about ways to "download" these shows for free, so that I can watch them at home on my laptop. Can anyone help? Leonard?

In regards to my personal life, I have discovered how much I have become settled in my ways. I am accustomed to peace and quiet and selecting my own meals and bedtime. I think it may be too late for me to change these things about myself. So for now I am still alone, although I have recently become more open to the idea of one day having more friends and relationships. Though I don't think I'll be married again. These days it seems like even young people don't need to get married, and I'm already an old woman.

I have shared more than I have in past years, which was my intention. Lately, few experiences bring me more joy than reading updates from old friends. I wish you all well.

Best regards,

Linda Liang

PS: Many of you may remember my ex-husband, Stanley Huang. I'm sorry to report that he passed earlier this year. Everyone, please re-member to exercise and to eat vegetables (I myself have switched exclusively to organic produce).

She didn't cry when Stanley died. Right before it happened she'd suffered an allergy attack, an inconvenience, really—she was so old and still having *allergies?*—and retrieved some tissues to keep her face neat, and then her children had seen and comforted her and she'd let them, because it had been so long since she'd been touched by either. But she hadn't really been crying. It was how it was always going to end, for all of them, though naturally Stanley had never believed it for himself, and that was his own fault for not taking to heart the ample hints sent from the universe. Stanley, who never denied himself the natural inclinations of the human existence but who refused to believe the biggest and most inevitable truth of it all.

For the longest time she'd hated him. Had loved then hated then pitied then finally in the last moments before his dying come close to loving him again, but in the way you might an errant child, or a teacher a poor student. Though Stanley had taught her things too. Taught her the ways of marriage, at least the only marriage she'd ever known—and afterward, the silence of divorce. Shown her how life could reward the places where you least exerted effort, while denying what you desired and worked so ardently toward most.

And revealed to her the true nature of men.

Men with their grasping ideals, their need to have a *legacy*, still such a stupid word, to be remembered for something larger and more important than themselves. But what could be more important than one's own self? As surely Stanley had considered his own body and desires sacrosanct above all else, and she had loathed him for this disloyalty, but in the end she had reserved the lesson for herself to keep. Moved in with her daughter because she felt safe there at night but kept her own house, continuing to pay for its maintenance so she could have the luxury of privacy. Gone to Stanley's funeral and accepted the condolences accorded to a *wife*, one who spent thirty-four years building the lifestyle he enjoyed so much afterward. And allowed herself the moment of hot humiliation that came when she learned of the true nature of Winston. Kate and Fred coming to her with downcast eyes, both still so timid when sharing the inconvenient or ugly, which had exasperated her until she understood that this time, the truth was about her.

"He's a scam, Ma," Kate said. "Your boyfriend, the one you met online. Winston, right? He's not real."

"Not real?" She'd immediately tensed, as a searing pain ran through her shoulders. She didn't understand what Kate was saying. She had spoken to Winston, seen his face, held him. How could he not be real?

"I mean, he's a fraud. He was part of a bigger scheme, the same one Fred got caught up with."

Linda felt herself relax. A fraud. A man guilty of wrongful deception. That wasn't so terrible. If that was the worst-case scenario, she could certainly manage it.

Of course, she rid herself of him immediately. Performed the shameful calculation of what the experience had cost her, ultimately judging it inexpensive at a few thousand for months of conversation. Next, she took care of the task at hand. No phone call, no video chat, a simple message, as succinct as she always was:

Please do not contact me again.

A month later a package arrived from Van Cleef & Arpels, marked as sent from Raymond Chou. *AKA WINSTON CHU* was printed below, with no return address.

She sent it unopened to the agent Josh Stern, who called to thank her. "You're very responsible, Mrs. Liang. Not everybody would have returned these items."

"I don't want them. I want to be rid of all these things."

"We're very sorry this happened to you. You seem like a nice woman. You didn't deserve to lose that money. Though if it makes you feel better, what you lost is nothing compared to other cases we've seen."

It didn't, because the money had never particularly mattered to her to begin with. She had more than enough, didn't she? Enough wealth, companionship, freedom. The life spark to move and do as she wanted, to enjoy a long nap on her sofa or savor a favorite meal by herself, when the mood struck, in the middle of the afternoon.

The last time she saw Stanley he lay with his eyes closed and mouth open, the way he had looked all those years as he slept next to her, the last time she ever really shared her bed. *Good-bye, Stanley,* she'd said, and closed his palm for him. Thirteen years had gone by since their divorce; nine months since his passing. And in that time, she hadn't missed him. She'd kept the best parts of him, anyway. And that had been her final gift from Stanley—to accept and cherish all that she had managed to create for herself, in her short and precious life.

Linda opened the door to her garden. It was a magnificent day; she would spend it outside.

ACKNOWLEDGMENTS

My agent, Michelle Brower, and my editor, Kate Nintzel.

Ana Giovinazzo, Andrea Molitor, Andrea Monagle, Andrew DiCecco, Alison Law, Carla Parker, Dale Schmidt, Katherine Turro, Lauren Truskowski, Liate Stehlik, Lillie Walsh, Lynn Grady, Mumtaz Mustafa, Nyamekye Waliyaya, Sharyn Rosenblum, Vedika Khanna, and the team at William Morrow/HarperCollins.

The Wang Family, near and far.

Tom, for his enduring encouragement and support, and Daniel and Vivienne, for giving it all meaning.